Text:UR

The New Book of Masks

RAW DOG SCREAMING PRESS

Published by Raw Dog Screaming Press,
Hyattsville, MD

First Hardcover Edition / First Paperback Edition

Fugue-State by Brian Evenson previously published in *3rd Bed*
Faure, Envenomed, Dictates by Nadia Gregor previously published in
Northwest Edge III: The End of Reality

Cover image: Carrie Anne Baade
Book design: Jennifer Barnes

Printed in the United States of America

ISBN 978-1-933293-20-2 / 978-1-933293-39-4

Library of Congress Control Number: 2007920993

www.rawdogscreaming.com

Table of Contents

Faure, Envenomed, Dictates

Nadia Gregor

"The only thing worse than the Faure we have known," said Ansell, "would be a pleading Faure."

"A pathetic Faure," I said, but too loudly, so that Faure coughed and shifted behind the mosquito netting, though he could not or would not raise his head to look at us.

"Look for his wallet," said Ansell.

Faure did not acknowledge my rummaging at his bedside. In the nightstand were: rumpled prints made from Faure's digital camera (Faure's washerwoman hanging his linen, river and sky indistinguishable behind her; Faure's ugly head oiled by a pair of dark, slender hands); the books Faure favored (petite redactions of complicated philosophical works, the apparent source of the speeches with which Faure had so often kept us waiting while the flies gathered to spoil our supper); and a sheet of paper rubbed soft by many foldings. I unfolded the paper and read. There was little else in the drawer: a scattering of bullets, no gun.

"Pierre. Look in his pockets," said Ansell from the safety of the doorway.

"You look if you want to."

I went to Ansell and handed him the photographs. Ansell said, "Faure. Fucker." The folded paper I kept for myself.

The first of the numbered items on the paper was "conspire against me," and the next, "betray the employers." The list went all down the page and onto the reverse side, ending at 43, "feel shame," and also including, in between, numbers 19, "be unkind to Pierre the faggot," and 27, "leave the compound without permission to get drunk on date wine in the ville." The list was titled Things They Might Do.

Faure's washerwoman left today, though only after a tirade, in patois, about what she was owed.

Ansell made me swear not to enter Faure's villa again until we were sure he must be dead. I have gone to see Faure as often as possible, ever since. The first time was at night, not long after we'd found his photographs. The door to the villa was open. Our own buildings—dormitory, recreation hall, chapel—had arrived by boat, nearly entirely assembled. We had only had to pour cement slabs for them to stand on. Faure's, alone, had been built here, less in the local style than in Faure's, with palm-thatch siding and interior walls of oiled paper over rattan lathe.

Faure was sitting up in bed. He had torn down the mosquito netting and rolled it into a ball he held over his stomach. He looked at me, then leaned forward to retch into an enamel basin. When he had finished retching, I tried to get him to lie back on the bed, but he would not unclench himself from around the balled-up netting.

"Let me help you," I said to Faure. His face was damp and mottled; he suddenly let go the netting and gripped his head, whimpering. I thought he didn't recognize me, so I pretended I was an old friend. "You look unwell, old friend."

"It's my heart," said Faure.

"It's your stomach. From the look of things."

"You should know."

I carried the basin away, telling Faure I would wash it out for him. It smelled. When I got outside, I flung basin and contents off the verandah into the bushes. I did not retrieve the basin to wash it. I walked back to quarters, holding my hands before me, palms down, fingers spread. They ached to touch me.

Ansell had used a nutmeg grater to shave rat poison into the soup, a goat-milk bisque. We sat at Faure's table, according to plan. Lely brought our tureen. At the other tables, men stood before their plates, nothing worse in store for them than the boredom of another of Faure's mealtime speeches.

All through the speech, Ansell mugged and winked. I stared solemnly at a point just beyond Faure's head. Faure lectured us, as usual, about "the West" and about "our civilization." Faure droned toward his conclusion: "'All things counter, original, spare, strange…He fathers forth whose beauty is past change.' —If I spoke just now of 'divine origin,' I spoke metaphorically; we have been informed of the death of God and we believe in the postmodern dispensation. But our side has fathered forth all the best metaphors. That is what is meant by 'divine.'" Steam rose from all tureens alike. "Fall to," said Faure. De Gruyten ladled out our soup. We wished one another good appetite.

Ansell had told us all this part would be easy. "Mime," he'd said. "Spoon it onto the edge of your saucer, into your napkin. Slurp air." Faure noticed our clowning. His pace slowed, but he continued to lap up the soup. He looked at no one. He choked once. De Gruyten hid his face in his napkin; Ansell and the Pollard brothers laid their spoons down and stared. Faure, coughing, shook his head, waved his spoon. "It only went down the wrong way," he whispered. "I'm not dying." He drank his wine, and went on eating. Finally he wiped his bowl round with a heel of bread, and ate the soppings.

Ansell always said he had been born in Poland. His skin tanned after the long days in the sun. I burn. When we'd first gotten here, and especially before the buildings arrived, there'd been hour after hour of duty in the heat and light of day. At first I wore a kerchief under my cap. It hung down over my neck while we shoveled or hauled or hacked. Later I made a burnoose with my towel. "Get your beekeeping gear on, Mother," Ansell would say.

We were not conscripts, Faure often reminded us, but employees. Of a high caliber. Our work was and must remain quality work, even when we were only digging or painting or guarding.

Orders came from Faure; we saw no reason to distinguish between him and the employers. We whitewashed rocks, to mark out the compound Faure had platted in his mind. With machetes and shovels and white rocks we built Faure's broad avenues, Faure's winding paths.

Bitter succulents will grow back soon, obscuring our labors.

Ansell could do handsprings with a lazy grace. He liked for us to ask him to. He could play the ocarina. De Gruyten and the Pollard brothers and Lely all sought him out for games. I came to the table, too, but they didn't deal me any cards.

"A faggot spoils the cards," they said.

"But I love Marie, at home."

"Just like a faggot," they said.

"Let him stay," said Ansell. He didn't ask them to deal me any cards. De Gruyten frowned and picked at his lips. Lely smoked kif in a meerschaum pipe, "to keep the bugs away." The Pollards suspended their customary cheating. Everyone drank date beer from bottles of milk-white glass, all the while saying that date beer would give them the shits the next morning. Ansell's face was serene. His bare arms shone in the lamplight. No one complained when he drew a card too many, which he did often. Ansell played badly and won staggering sums.

On the way back to quarters, the Pollards and the rest of the card-players tried to hoist Ansell onto their shoulders. They let him fall, and they fell also, giggling.

I stood very close, wondering whether I might plausibly fling myself in among them. Someone pressed their cheek to my bare ankle. Faure walked up the path just then. He looked at us: the tangle of limbs, the face atop my foot.

"Find yourselves a woman," he told us.

The second time I went to Faure's villa, he had fallen or launched himself from the bed. He was on his stomach, trying to pull himself along with his forearms. His legs were contracted, motionless. The sweating skin of the legs stuck to the plank floor, retarding the progress of the rather feeble hands and arms. I found the netting rumpled on the floor, dried matter clotting it together. I shook the netting out and folded it under his useless legs. He propelled himself with some haste to the doorway. The doorsill caught the netting as he flopped and shimmied his way into the hall. The netting bunched under his knees. Stuck again, he expelled rapid, plaintive sounds. I leaned down and smoothed the netting under his hips and over the sill. He lay there, barking, until I grasped him by the elbows and pulled him free of the sill. I stood up and spread my arms wide, inviting him to employ his splendid new means of locomotion in any direction he pleased.

I stepped over Faure and into his bedroom again. I stretched out on his bed; I watched his feet jerk and tremble in the doorway. Faure might get along all right, if he didn't get worse.

After the compound was built to Faure's satisfaction, he had put us to work on the "communications infrastructure." Faure told me he'd been told to call it that. "The 'infrastructure' is to be the basis of 'e-government' hereabouts, according to the employers' scheme," said Faure. "Eee, for *electronic*. Never mind the frail condition of 'gee-government' hereabouts; that is not the employers' concern."

I had one disastrous stint as a surveyor's assistant; after that, Faure never again sent me out of the compound with the others. They went in groups of five, armed, sweating under bulletproof breastplates and bulkily padded throat-guards. Occasionally, a man or several did not come back; once, it was one of the Pollards. The sweat, the armor, the surveyor's theodolite and tripod, the similarly tripedal structure of the data beacons, the difficulty of getting each leg of each beacon to find purchase in the jungly loam, the fear of attack—the entire task was so exhausting it was not attempted every day, not even by rotating squads, but only once or twice a week. From what they told me, their work was advancing along a straight path without any intersections or branchings. They were given to understand that this path would be the "backbone" of a "wireless data network." It advanced further from the compound each time.

Faure confided in me: "What they are making is and will remain a *line*, no matter what networked visions dance in the heads of the heads of the company.

"On one side of the line is being; on the other, nothing. Don't look at me. I didn't plot the line's course. I merely descry its meaning: compact, destinal, inescapable."

Faure had examples for me. On this side of the line, Faure, the Pollards, myself. On that, the washerwoman. For example.

Work on the data network began to devolve after only a few weeks, Ansell told me. The surveying was uncertain, or de Gruyten and the others purposely gave out the wrong numbers. The backbone was developing a hump.

I could see how it could happen.

The one time I had gone, I had worked with de Gruyten. Lely was point man; one of the Pollards guarded a roving perimeter. My job was to help de Gruyten by walking the required distance, plunging a stake into the earth, and waiting while de Gruyten read the measurements. The other Pollard came along behind, planting the data beacons in our wake.

Each time I reached the specified point, I paused, stake over earth, and hesitated: which point was the exact one commanded of me? There was a gap each time, a need to translate from command to world, from horizontal measurement to variegated, uneven ground. No one tells you how to navigate this gap. Least of all de Gruyten, who claimed I was wiggling the stake when I was only trying to correct for any possible imprecision by plunging the stake in the one spot while mentally picturing another spot and then, mid-plunge, letting the stake dowse, momentarily, from the one to the other.

It was agreed that I would read out the numbers. De Gruyten assented to this with a heavy heart, I could tell. He explained, again, about the altitude; he explained, again, the other thing. He showed me where the wires crossed in the focus of the object glass, and how it turned on horizontal and vertical axes. He ended by requesting that I please not touch anything and just read the numbers out fucking loud while he went and held the stake.

What is it, then, to read? This task, too, involved decisions. My first and best decision was to not mention any of my decisions to de Gruyten. My second decision was this: I decided to decide first one way and then the other, in alternation. Now I read the number to the right, whenever the cross-wires fell between two lines (as they always did), now I read the number to the left;

dexter, sinister, dexter, sinister.

We worked slowly, because de Gruyten had to first set up the theodolite, command me to touch nothing, and then take up the stake and shuffle the required distance, back and forth, back and forth, like a man struggling to defeat himself at tennis. Did I mix up my own scheme, and read two dexters for every sinister, or vice versa? I don't know. Not on purpose, I didn't. At the end of the day, de Gruyten called it a wash, and I was never sent to do that job again.

The hump that later developed in the data backbone, long after my own efforts had been undone, discouraged Faure not at all. Curves and bights do nothing to alter a line's effectiveness, Faure said to me. The line we write across this jungle may easily include a serif.

One day in January, Ansell struck me full in the face with his open hand. I had given offense. I do not dispute the facts. The shock was that I felt nothing. The blow didn't matter to me in the least.

Later, to comfort me, Faure hit me in the same place.

"Pierre," Faure said one afternoon when I came to his office to take dictation. "If only you and I had been posted to the desert, in another era."

His hand rested lightly on the nape of my neck as he steered me to a chair by his desk. Dust clung to the oiled-paper walls. Nearby, the chirr of insects; farther, the shrieking of the washerwoman's infant.

"One knows from books—do not write this down—what a desert posting entailed in times past: the camels heaving themselves up on command, groaning as they get under way with their habitual, swaying gait; levering themselves down again at day's end, hinge-wise, the way they do, obstreperous, the way they are; breathing their noisome breath at us; whipping green ropes of grassy slaver in our faces; and, finally, sacrificing themselves for us, stoically if not without all complaint, a stoicism we fondly salute at campfire over the fatty shreds of their roasted humps. —In a word, the desert posting entailed *literature*.

"It is otherwise here."

We took up the list where we'd left off the day before. Our work on the list was always the same. Faure would say, "'Things They Might Do.' Let me think. Let me think." I would let him. He would think. It was unendurable. I always offered a suggestion, or several, to get him started:

They might stop really going on data-network detail.

They might spend those hours hiding, smoking, talking.

They might wish they were home.
They might plot to poison you ("me").
—"They might not like you ('Pierre the faggot') either."

We had waited and waited for it to begin, and when it came, it came too soon. It's time to do it, Ansell told us. That night, I tried to willfully bring on sleep, or at least make insomnia easier to endure. My body suffered my hand without responding.

On the third day after Faure's poisoning, I went to visit him again. A pair of Faure's washerwoman's children had just been surprised in the act of trespassing on the compound. A boy of perhaps twelve, too old to be Faure's, and a much smaller child, shirtless, sturdy, fractious. Ansell and the remaining Pollard chased them down what was left of Faure's boulevard.

Faure was in his office, dressed, seated at his desk. He waved me in. The end of his tie was tucked between his third and fourth shirt buttons, a martial style I had not seen him affect before. He had lit several cigarettes and left them to smolder in the ashtray. His tiny books of philosophy were ranged around the desk blotter. The industry he brought to bear on his dying burdened me. I wanted to leave, but could not think how to excuse myself.

He invited me to join him in marveling at the continuance of his bodily functions. I was grateful that he pictured these in words only, that he did not ask me to feel the pulse at his wrist or throat. He himself hadn't known all his powers of endurance, he said. It didn't matter, he said. It wasn't our fault; we couldn't have been expected to know.

He asked me to take dictation. I took my usual seat, which put me uncomfortably close to Faure. For a long time Faure said nothing at all. I hoped he did not expect me to offer suggestions.

"How long—do not write this down—how long will you last once word of what's been done gets out?

"Write this down:

"*Every situation has its secret, and every science bears in itself its own arcanum. All along, as I only I have seen, the noisy extravagance of the 'data network' has borne within itself this crypted line. The plot against me alters nothing. The instauration of e-governance matters not at all; let it crumble into static. I am the last conscious representative of the line, the last to have understood the line in an existential sense, and I am living out its end as Benito Cereno lived out his on the mutinied ship: in a forsaken place, at once closed in on itself and poised*

11

in an infinite ocean. I have nothing more to say. Here it is well and it is time to be silent. Being silent, we remember ourselves and our divine origin. We must not be frightened."

Note: This story contains quotations from Naomi Klein, T. E. Lawrence, Michel Foucault, and Carl Schmitt. In that order.

Monkey Shines

Eric Schaller

I. King Kong vs. Mecha Kong

King Kong was all of six feet tall on a good day. He had a barrel chest and a belly tight and round as a beach ball, the kind of physique you earn from a combination of genetics, cabernet sauvignon, and long hours sitting in front of a computer. His fur was synthetic and his teeth bared in a permanent smile. Whether you thought his growl sounded more angry than sexual, or vice versa, depended only upon which side of the bed you awoke. "Goddamn it," King Kong said, "stop fooling around and get over here."

Mecha Kong was seven feet tall, but almost two feet of that was owed to her metal headdress. Maybe the headdress was intended as a radar antenna, what with its bifurcating wires and glittering saucers, but it looked about as functional as foil antlers. Mecha Kong's fur was tinsel and she had pointed silver breasts. When she moved metal whispered against metal and the scent of graphite filled the air. "You don't own me," she said in a voice like an amplified music box.

"I never said I did." King Kong lunged for her, but she jumped behind a brick-red couch, leaving strands of tinsel clinging to his outstretched paw. "Stop that," he said. "I don't want to fight."

"Then stop chasing me. Treat me like an adult. I'm not a child. I'm not one of your toys." While Mecha Kong talked, King Kong rocked on the balls of his feet, prepared for her to dash off in any direction. But she knew his tricks and had a few of her own. She grabbed an embroidered pillow and threw it at him. He knocked it aside, but she had already bolted for the stairway.

"Come back here." King Kong vaulted to the top of the couch and pounded his chest with wide swinging blows of his hairy fists. He howled. This was his domain and he wanted everyone to know it. But the world was not truly his to command. When he leaped to the floor, the rug slipped out from under him and he tumbled furry ass over elbows to end up on his back, legs kicking holes in the air.

Mecha Kong was already taking the stairs two at a time, but she stopped and turned when she heard the crash behind her. She leaned over the banister and laughed, reprising a tune stolen from "South Pacific." "Maybe I should spray your ass with Pledge, then you can dust the floor while you're down there."

"The only thing I'm going to dust the floor with is you." King Kong kicked the rug away and climbed to his feet.

"Oh dear me. Whatever shall I do?" She wrung her hands, then raked her metal fingernails, each shaped like a perfect almond slice, along the banister.

"Don't do that." King Kong spoke but, like a master ventriloquist, you never saw his lips move. He spoke with the voice of someone who was tired, sweaty, and covered in synthetic fur.

"What's the matter? You worried that I'm going to damage one of your precious things?"

"Have some respect for good craftsmanship."

"Maybe if you started to have some respect for simple human feelings."

"Simple human feelings? Don't make me laugh. You're a machine. And not a particularly well made one at that." He thought he had her there. Trapped in a logical conundrum of the sort that caused evil robots to blow up in old sci-fi flicks: if I am a machine then I can't have emotions, but if I have emotions then I can't be a machine. Circuits overheat. Smoke pours out. Then boom! She had to appreciate that. But she surprised him.

"More human than you can ever hope to be."

He had no response to that but a wounded roar and was soon chasing her pell-mell up the stairs and down the hallway, his feet slapping the maple floorboards, his rubbery knuckles swinging alongside his ankles. He caught up with her at the master bedroom. She tried to slam the door, but he had already shoved his shoulder through the entrance, and she didn't slam the door very hard anyway.

"I've got you now."

She backed up against the bed, one hand extended in front of her chest, the other steadying her headdress. Mecha Kong was really much better crafted than King Kong gave her credit for. She was made of lightweight and dent-proof plasticized aluminum, with rivets every inch, and a money-back guarantee. It was all that tinsel floating around that made her look cheap. The tinsel was always sloughing off, and she was always gluing more back on. When the servants searched through the vacuum cleaner bags for valuable trinkets, all they ever came up with were thick tangles of silver tinsel.

It was Sunday.

The servants had the day off.

King Kong tackled Mecha Kong, and she fell backward across the bed. "Oh," she said. "Oh my." He pawed at her, grunting and pulling out tufts of tinsel, gnawing at the lobes of her metal ears. His breath smelt of garlic and chocolate. She guided his fumbling hands to the catches along her hips and thighs and, released, slipped out of her metal leggings like a shucked oyster, her skin smooth and glistening with sweat. A shove and the leggings clattered to the floor. She bent forward and parted the fur between King Kong's legs. She found and pulled the tab of the exposed zipper, then circled him with her metal arms and dragged him down on top of her.

King Kong and Mecha Kong fell asleep after they made love. He was naked, except for a pair of cotton briefs, and slept curled on his side, genitals clutched in both hands as if afraid that burglars would steal them under cover of the night. She wore a Hawaiian shirt decorated with martinis and palm trees that she had bought on their last vacation together. She slept on her back, one arm thrown across her face, as if she dreamed that she was still on the beach at Honolulu and was protecting her eyes from the sun.

She woke well before dawn. The only sounds were those of the rain: the spatter of drops against the slate shingles and the gurgle of water that wormed its way through leaf-clogged gutters. The window was ajar and the air smelt of grass and ferns and garden flowers, of mushrooms and mildew. Of growing things.

She had felt a change come over her body, and it was that change which had awakened her.

She was pregnant.

With a daughter.

She looked at the man sleeping beside her but she did not wake him. He would not believe her, even though it was the same with her mother. "I knew," her mother said, "I knew the moment you were conceived."

Across the room, two hulking silhouettes were outlined against a pearly window. The body suits, both now discarded husks, sat on stuffed chairs and eyed each other across the small table where breakfast was sometimes served. They seemed at peace, engaged in idle chatter over coffee. But that was a deceit. The only time they were truly alive was when they were fighting, or making love.

She giggled.

Her husband woke and looked up at her with puffy eyes, his mouth already set in a grimace. "What is it?"

Mecha Kong shook her head. She had been granted a vision of what lay in store for her, for the man with whom she has chosen to share her life, and for the unborn daughter that she now carried. She foresaw the day when their daughter was three or four years old. Blond and blue-eyed. Old enough for Halloween. Old enough to go trick-or-treating. Old enough to be the center of an argument over whether she should wear the costume of a Furry or a Mech. It was a vision of the future that was ludicrous but, even should it never come to pass, still somehow true.

"Nothing," Mecha Kong said to King Kong. "Nothing with which you need concern yourself." She said no more but, as she lay beside her husband waiting for sleep to return, she ran through possible baby names in her mind. She eventually eliminated all names but one, her mother's middle name Samantha.

II. The Plastic Jungle

Who knew when it started? There were always houseplants. Clay pots of purple, white, and pink violets. Geraniums on the kitchen table. A spiderplant hanging in the bathroom window. But one day Sal realized that there were plants he could not identify. "What's that?" He pointed at a scaly brown bulb the size of a coconut crowned with long green spikes. Its leaves were the expected green but had the texture of wood.

"A cycad," Sarah said. "They're ancient, from the time of the dinosaurs."

"What about the plant upstairs?"

Sarah looked puzzled.

"You know. The one with all the arms, like a family of octopuses that got caught in a whirlpool."

"Do you mean the night-blooming cereus?"

"It has flowers?"

"Not yet. But it will. The flowers open and die off in a single night."

"Seems a waste."

"They're pollinated by bats who find the flowers by smell. Just wait. They say you can smell a single flower from a mile away."

Sal assumed she was exaggerating and so he was surprised when he came home from work one evening, opened the front door, and smelled a perfume that he did not recognize, pervasive but subtle as a siren's song. He should have guessed its origin but he had already forgotten his conversation with Sarah. He tracked the scent to the upstairs guest room, where he found Sarah seated among the greenery, their daughter Samantha swaddled in a pile blanket and asleep in her lap. Even then he did not understand until Sarah placed a finger to her lips and whispered, "The night-blooming cereus is blooming." He spent the next hour in

16

the room listening to Sarah read a book of poetry aloud that neither Samantha, he, nor the cereus understood.

In the months that followed, Sarah's plant menagerie continued to expand until it reached the limits dictated by available light and suitable living space. That should have been the end of it, but Sal came home from a business trip to find that contractors had ripped a hole in the outer wall of the living room and erected the metal skeleton for a two-story greenhouse. Naturally, Sal and Sarah had an argument. Naturally, they ended up in bed together, and, as he drifted off to sleep breathing in the briny scent of her skin, Sal agreed to her project.

They had a private celebration when the greenhouse was finished. They wandered, footsteps cushioned by springy moss, beneath the canopy of interlaced leaves made by the palms, bananas, pomegranates, and aromatic hardwoods. Sal tugged at a bearded lichen, ran a finger along the lacey edge of an orchid's bloom, and bent back the tender young frond of a fiddlehead fern, its tip curled as tightly as a baby's fist. They sat on a Victorian bench imported from England and toasted each other with glasses of Vive Cliquot. "It's like an exotic Olympic Peninsula," Sal said, genuinely astonished at Sarah's creation.

Then the animals arrived. Frogs, who hid during the daylight hours, but sent up a chorus of competing voices as soon as the sun set. Silvery fish that darted among the papyrus and lily stems in a circular pond. Guinea fowl. Finches. And, finally, the monkey. The monkey was a filthy thing, a scrawny shadow that hid among the leaves, trailing Sal from above, then suddenly screamed and unleashed a barrage of twigs, half-eaten fruit, and dung. Sal was not sure if this was simply the way of all monkeys or if this one was defective. Maybe, he thought, the monkey would behave more like a proper pet if it didn't have a jungle in which to play.

Their daughter Samantha was the only person for whom the monkey seemed to truly care. Maybe it was her small size, so similar to his own that he considered her a relation. Or perhaps it was the unadulterated joy that Samantha found in playing the simplest games: passing a stick from hand to hand, balancing pebbles one atop the other, splashing water at the fish in the tiny pond. Samantha was the one who named the monkey Bobo. "Why Bobo?" Sal asked. "All monkeys are named Bobo," Samantha said with the implacable logic of a four-year old. She and Bobo would play together for hours, and when she left for meals or a nap, Bobo would mope, only rousing himself to vent his frustrations upon intruders in the greenhouse.

Sarah said that everything was perfect, even the tempestuous monkey. But if everything was perfect, then why did she leave Sal one autumn day? Why did she pack two suitcases with clothing, jewelry, and her favorite Hiroshige print, the one showing pedestrians crossing a bridge in the slanting rain, and drive off with Samantha in the red convertible, leaving Sal behind with everything they had built together?

In his youth, Sal had been perceived as selfish by even his family and closest friends, a behavior that he had excused with a smile and the phrase: "Nothing personal, it's just business." But if marriage had changed him, divorce changed him still more. He fired the servants, took to wearing a nylon running suit, and only left his bedroom to buy groceries. He bought Campbell's tomato soup, Nabisco saltines, and Hungry Man TV dinners, the same foods that had been his favorites when he was a kid.

Then the monkey died.

Sal had neglected the greenhouse like everything else, treating it like a foreign country that he dimly remembered once visiting. But the scent of death was unmistakable and led him to a maggoty corpse surrounded by buzzing flies. The dead monkey lay on a bed of yellowed leaves and dried moss. The small pond was also dry and the fish that once swam in it were gone, probably victims of the monkey's hunger. Sal poked at the monkey with a stick. In death, the monkey seemed much smaller than in life.

The next day, Sal called a contractor and had all the vegetation removed from the greenhouse. Maybe the contractor sold some of the plants. Maybe he had them all burned at the dump. Sal didn't care. The jungle as he had known it was gone. In its place, over the next six months, he assembled a plastic reproduction that was as close to the original as time and his memory allowed.

On the day of its completion, he walked his familiar route beneath the shiny green leaves and hanging fruit. The moss compressed beneath his shoes, but sprang back to its original height as soon as he passed. Cinnamon and clove wafted through the air from hidden vents. The orchids, the lichens, and even the fiddlehead ferns were all as he remembered. Better than he remembered because the orchid did not show a bruise, not a single blemish, when he pinched its petals.

He sat on a cast-iron bench and stared at his reflection in the central pond. Plastic lilies, each in bloom, floated on the pond's hard mirrored surface. If a coin were tossed it would glance off the pond without a ripple. A frog's chirp sounded from a speaker hidden among the lily pads, the trill of a finch from another speaker wired to a tree branch.

The leaves rustled nearby, a tentative sound easily confused with the effect of a breeze, but no breeze was blowing. Sal did not look up. Palm fronds rasped against each other, then stilled. Sal glanced at his wristwatch. He did not look up, even when the rustling began again from directly overhead. The leaves rustled but did not fall.

Seconds flickered by on Sal's wristwatch and, at exactly three o'clock, a monkey dropped from the tree above Sal. The monkey landed in a crouch by the pool but immediately righted himself to stand on his bandy legs. The monkey had large dark eyes set in a wise face. His fur was so well groomed and of such a russet hue that he appeared to be wearing a tailored jacket. If not for his tail, he might have been confused with an elderly gentleman come to discuss financial matters with Sal.

The monkey had landed facing the bench to the right of where Sal sat. The monkey now cocked his head first to one side and then the other, appearing to evaluate the empty spot on the bench. Sal slid over so as to be directly in front of monkey. The monkey nodded his head in apparent satisfaction, then extended his hand toward where Sal sat on the bench. In the monkey's hand was a bright red fruit, brighter and redder than any apple or pomegranate Sal had ever seen.

Sal looked at the fruit but did not take it.

After exactly one minute, during which he held his pose immobile as a statue, the monkey withdrew his offering. The monkey then walked twice around the bench, on the second circuit stepping precisely where he had on the first, and came to a stop in front of Sal once again. The monkey held out the fruit in exactly the same manner as before, but Sal refused to do anything but look at it. After one minute, the monkey withdrew his offering, but this time walked over to and shinnied up a palm tree, glancing back once before he disappeared among the fronds, which rustled and then were still.

After the monkey left, Sal rose from the bench to leave. The monkey was a miracle of rare device, he thought, a descriptive phrase that he had once heard, although he no longer remembered where. He planned to return tomorrow at the same time to watch the same scenario play itself out again. He would return and he knew that he could count on the monkey to return as well. There was a consistency to life in the plastic jungle that he liked. A consistency to which he already looked forward. But one day, not tomorrow, or even the day after tomorrow, he would take the offered fruit and eat it.

III. Rise and Shine

The young woman had hitchhiked all summer up and down the west coast. She had no set destination but, if you believed her, she let the wind carry her along in whatever direction it was blowing. It's easier to walk with the wind than against it she said and, should you catch a ride, it still saves on gas.

Her friends called her Sam. So did everyone else for that matter.

Her blond hair was cut short and stuffed inside a Greek fisherman's cap, a few stray strands on her forehead, tufts beside her temples that could pass for sideburns. She carried a tent strapped to an oversized backpack, but the tent leaked in the rain and she had become adept at finding free shelter. This skill had become more important ever since she made her way up to Washington state.

She had slept the previous night on an old logging road. It had been a gorgeous afternoon when she set up her tent, but the clouds had closed in during the night and when she awoke the next morning it was to a steady drizzle and the pungent aroma of damp pine needles. She ate a breakfast of granola, dried apricots, and instant coffee. She wrapped a garbage bag around her backpack, shouldered it, and then pulled an orange plastic poncho over both herself and her backpack. She looked like a day-glo hunchback as she stomped along the mist-shrouded track back to the highway, a south wind tugging at the skirt of her poncho.

The van that slowed to pick her up, once she reached the main road, sent a spray of muddy water across her boots. The driver, a young man in his mid-twenties with a scraggly beard and a chipped front tooth, cracked the passenger door ajar. "Hey, climb on up man. Where you headed?"

"Which way are you going?"

"Tacoma, then on to Seattle. I've got half a dozen deliveries to make. You help me unload, and I'll buy you lunch and drop you wherever you want."

The van was hauling glazed hams. The driver told Sam that the best part of his job was when he used a blowtorch to melt the brown sugar on the hams back at the factory. It was a good story but apparently his only story and, each time he told it, he sprayed spittle through the hole in his tooth when making the sound effect of a torch. But he was as good as his word and, after cheeseburgers and strawberry milkshakes, dropped Sam at the address she told him.

The house was a Victorian monstrosity at the end of a dead-end street, barely contained behind an iron fence, with peeling white paint and mossy shingles. There were four brick chimneystacks but no smoke, and the windows were covered with plywood.

"You sure this is it? Doesn't look like anybody's home."

"I have a key." Which was true, in a manner of speaking.

Sam ignored the front door and splashed across the soggy lawn, circling around the back of the house. She glanced at but did not linger by the twisted and blackened remnants of the greenhouse, globs of melted plastic hanging like alien fruit from the broken glass and girders. Her father, his body burnt almost beyond recognition, had been found in the greenhouse by the firemen who responded to the emergency call. Sam's mother had felt it best that neither she nor Sam attend the funeral. What could be gained by opening up old wounds? But soon thereafter Sam ran away from home, and she made a regular habit of running away until she turned eighteen. Past the age of eighteen, you couldn't really call it running away from home. It was just life on the road.

Sam pressed her thumb against a plastic box mounted by the rear door. There was a click, and the door swung open. Sam looked at her thumb. The last time she was here, she had needed a stool to reach the sensor panel. But even after all these years, the house still recognized her.

She dumped her backpack just inside the doorway, found a flashlight in one of the zippered outer pockets, and began to explore the shuttered house. Everything was new and old at the same time, familiar but dislocated with the intervening years. She maneuvered around the living room furniture, fingered yellow curtains that were now faded to ivory, and listened to the creak of floorboards beneath her adult weight. Most striking was the filth. Tin cans and the foil trays from TV dinners were everywhere; they spilled out of garbage bags, cluttered the kitchen counters, and were piled high on the couches, tables, and bookshelves. Didn't her father ever clean up after himself? The bedroom was the worst. She opened the door, but shut it again almost immediately, having picked out with her flashlight the erratic reflections of crumpled metal that extended from floor to ceiling.

Her father's study provided a retreat. There was the large cherry desk, an antique office chair upholstered in leather, and built-in bookshelves on every wall. The study was also still remarkably clean. She sat in the chair, one foot drawn up and tucked beneath her hip, the other touching the floor so that, by exerting just a little pressure, she could swivel the chair from side to side. She had crawled up onto this chair when she was a toddler, sometimes to sit in her father's lap while he typed at the computer, sometimes to play by herself, pushing off from the desk so that the chair would roll across the floor or spin like a merry-go-round.

Her father had collected toys but these were placed on the upper shelves where she could not reach them as a child. Now, yielding to a long repressed temptation, she began to pick through her father's collection. Her father's taste in toys extended from old-fashioned pull toys to mementos of the space age, tidily arranged but with no apparent organization. She found a wooden rabbit on wheels next to a sparking ray gun, a plastic Donald Duck ring next to a handheld pinball game. Training her flashlight on the top shelf, she started at the sight of eyes glistening in the darkened corner where the bookshelves met the ceiling. Then recognizing it as a doll of some sort, she pulled the office chair over so as to climb up and investigate.

It was a monkey. A toy monkey. He sat bent nearly double, his back against the ceiling, head thrust forward, and hands clasped in his lap. He had large black eyes, unblinking but animated by the beam from her flashlight. "Bobo," she said, whispering the name of her childhood pet but knowing even as she spoke that it was not he. Bobo was dead and gone for who knew how many years. She turned away, unable to look at the grin that stretched across the monkey's felt muzzle.

She rolled the chair back to its proper location and began an inspection of the desk's contents, unsure for what she was looking, but nevertheless confident that whatever artifacts it contained would reveal something of its former owner. But the desk had been cleaned out. The top drawer contained only paperclips, rubber bands, and some wintergreen lifesavers lying loose among the silver, green, and white confetti of their torn wrapper. There was also some Canadian change that her father had dumped into the drawer so it wouldn't contaminate the American money he kept in his pockets. Sam was stacking the coins in preparation for counting when, at a little before three o'clock, she heard a noise.

She dropped the coins and looked around, the light from her flashlight skittering across the bookshelves.

Nothing.

She took a deep breath and sat perfectly still. She cupped the head of the flashlight with her left palm, holding the flashlight below the level of the desk so that its glow would not give her away.

Something loose and wooden banged in the wind, and rain thrummed against the study window.

Her chair suddenly settled beneath her with a protracted groan.

Then she heard it again. A sound more rhythmic than anything perpetrated by the weather: feet being set down one after the other, but muted as if by socks. Then a jingle jangle from directly overhead.

She swung the flashlight upward. A reddish brown blur disengaged itself from the chain of the lamp hanging above her.

Sam ducked, throwing an arm up for protection.

It was exactly three o'clock.

The monkey landed on the floor facing her. He straightened and cocked his head from side to side, a mimicry of intelligence that suggested he was considering the identity of the woman who sat before him. Apparently satisfied, he extended a cupped but empty hand toward her. The monkey held this pose without a blink or a twitch.

Sam drew both her legs up onto the chair and hugged her knees. Her lips quivered. "Go away."

The monkey did nothing.

22

"You're not real. You're not Bobo."

The monkey did not move, but held his arm extended as if he had all the time in the world. Spotlighted by the flashlight, the monkey's shadow was huge upon the wall.

"You're nothing. Just some stupid toy of my Dad's."

The monkey seemed oblivious to her words but then, ten seconds later, abruptly turned as if finished and walked away, body swaying as he lifted and placed each foot in turn.

Sam exhaled in relief.

But upon reaching the edge of the desk, the monkey pivoted so that his path traced the desk's circumference. He took four steps then turned again as if he planned to circle back around the desk to reach the chair on which Sam sat.

Sam tumbled out of her chair and scrambled for the office door, cursing under her breath when she realized too late that the clattering she heard was from the flashlight she had dropped. But she knew the house well enough even in the dark to find the rear door. She crossed the living room at a trot, her right arm waving back and forth in front of her like a metronome. She kicked an end table, bumped into and rolled around the couch, then, groping for the expected wall, stumbled forward until she found it. She ran alongside the wall, fingertips brushing its surface. A right turn to cut along the edge of the dining room. Another right turn. The first door was a bathroom, the next were the double doors to the coat closet, and after that was the one she wanted. She found the handle and opened the rear door, letting in the greenish-gray light of the drizzly afternoon. Her backpack was still there beside the door, braced against the wall, and she shouldered it with the ease of long familiarity.

She could have left then.

But she hesitated just long enough to look back into the darkened interior of the house. All was silence. Standing there in a muddle of her own bootprints, her damp backpack hanging from her shoulders, Sam had a vision of the future, the same sort of damned thing her mother was always going on about. Sam saw the house slip further and further into decay as the lawyers fought over it. She saw the roof leak and the plaster ceilings crack, sag, and break loose from their pins. She saw the woodwork rot and bloom with mildew, the paint flake, the wallpaper peel, the pipes break, the events of years passing by in seconds as in a time-lapse movie. But, while the house disappeared around him, she saw the monkey repeat his simple journey every day, crawling down from his shelf to make his short perambulation around her father's office, then clambering back up the bookcase to his seat in the corner by the ceiling. His timing was as regular as clockwork but there was no one left to bear him witness.

Sam took a deep breath, turned, and headed back into the depths of the house.

When she emerged again, her backpack was noticeably larger because of the bulging and awkwardly shaped garbage bag strapped to its frame with bungee cords. She pulled her hat down over her forehead, cinched the straps on her pack, and stepped outside into the rain. She wasn't sure where she was going but that had never slowed her down before. She slogged across the lawn, her boots making sucking noises with each step.

When she reached the sidewalk, a van flashed its headlights at her. On the side of the van was the image of a glazed ham stuck with cloves and arranged on a bed of pineapple slices.

"Were you waiting for me?" she asked the driver after swinging herself up into the cab. The cab was toasty, and the old tune "I Walk the Line" played on the stereo. She wasn't fond of country music, but Johnny Cash was all right.

"No. I came back." Stuffed between the front seats was a rolled up magazine, something to do with cars, that the driver had been reading. "I couldn't picture you spending the night in that place."

"Thanks. You didn't have to do that. I just had to pick up some stuff."

"So I see. What's with your friend there?" With his thumb the driver indicated the backpack that Sam had set on the rubber floor mat between her legs. A furry arm had worked its way loose from the attached garbage bag. The raised arm trembled from the engine vibrations such that it had an air of expectancy, like a confident student hoping to be called upon in class.

"That's my monkey, Bobo."

"Bobo? Why's he called Bobo?"

Sam gave the driver the same answer that she gave her father many years before: "All monkeys are named Bobo."

The Avatar of Background Noise

Toiya Kristen Finley

p. 9

I probably shouldn't have gone back to the library in pursuit of this thing, but when you see 2 trains crashing in slo-mo, you don't cover your eyes. Some Selections of the Collected Works of Toiya Kristen Finley was the only book they had on her, but a search brought up a Special Collections on the 5th level stacks in the basement. I don't think the basement elevator had been used in years, and as I descended, I thought I might plummet to my death.

I am holding this pencil in my hand, can feel the plastic pressing against my skin, the calloused place on my middle finger. I know I'm here in my den writing this. But now I know I'm kind of not here—does that make any sense?

In the Finley Special Collections, I found volumes upon volumes of Finley's recorded daydreams. Some of these were only a few sentences or a paragraph. All of them had to do w/ me or the people I know…

I hated the painting of James Pasado hanging over the great-hall entrance of the library. Never knowing where he's going, never ending up anywhere James Pasado. Of course, here in Ruez, they had no idea who he was. His bewildered face and awkward body, arms flailing in one direction and legs in the other, like a Goyaesque Pollack with its stark, thick tan, green, red, yellow, and blue paint. The *rueziiv* thought him a man in ecstasy, about to make the final leap into a desperate situation. A hero, a martyr between death and rapture. Agony and ecstasy were easy to confuse, especially when the underpinnings of masochism plagued this city.

If the *rueziiv* knew any better, they'd realize Pasado was an idiot, a boob so beguiled by his television that he became one with it. Somehow the man grew into legend here, and that legend was only strengthened and substantiated by Waters's chronicles of her encounters with him. The way she told it, poor Jimmy got sucked into the TV set one day and found himself stumbling upon TV Show Land after TV Show Land. It must take a special breed of Joe Everyday, a nothing like Pasado, to have had

> p. 17
>
> …mixed-bag race called "Vienties" (<u>vheniiv</u> = "mixed" pl.).
>
> These groups, thousand of years ago, were oppressed and enslaved by tyrants in civs like Mesopotamia, Sumeria, Egypt, etc. These groups fled their oppressors and shut themselves off from the rest of the world. This world is called "Rotasharia," from <u>rota</u>/ "familiar" and <u>siarii</u> (pronounced <u>sha-ree</u>)/ "land." The 30 girls crossed into Rotasharia by accident, and that's how they met the freaky-hair people. What we think of as our world is "Ratasharia" (North America, Africa, Asia, etc.), from <u>rata</u>/"strange." But Rotasharia is not on another planet or in another dimension. The Rotasharians just own some real estate the rest of us know nothing about.
>
> Why am I even talking in terms of "we"?....

the calamity gods smile so fondly upon him. Anyway, I would ask Waters about him when I finally met up with her. I cleaned the lenses of my grey-wired frames, tucked her notebook away in my briefcase, walked under that ghastly painting, and left the Ruez Library.

I supposed I couldn't blame them for making James Pasado their poster boy. After all, the ancestors of the Rotasharians were treated much in the same way, pushed and pulled and prodded by the *ratasiariiv* 6000 years ago. However, the fact that a piece of art had anything to do with Pasado amused me. I'd never expect his bug-on-the-windshield expression to grace any building, never mind a public one. The artist was obviously a Waters fan. She had a modest underground following here.

Outside on the sidewalk, groups of Vienties walked home or descended into the subway stations. In a city concerned with aesthetic perfection, the planners placed the library in a perfect location. Vientie children at one end of the marina and pure-blood children at the other fed dolphins honey bread, their parents wandering around on the docks and taking the time for the after-work smoke. Some of them stared out over the bay at the high, jagged, moss-covered cliffs. Beyond the natural barrier, that ominous Ratasharia breathed—world of oppression, dissention and factionism. Ratasharia that was so close to them, but had no awareness or care for this realm of allied ethnicities.

If one ever wondered where the blue, green, purple, and pink hair genes went, the ancestors of the Rotasharians carried them here. A colorful bunch of ethnicities, with their hair dancing across the spectrum. There were ethnic groups here with hair colors Ratasharians would consider "normal," but I found the blonds, brunettes, and redheads quite boring. Except for the Vienties, only one or two colors per ethnicity, and often, their eye pigment corresponded with one of the two colors.

My little Vientie waited for me in the café just off the marina. A secluded little place, it wasn't in the library's more affluent neighborhood and hid at the end of a short street. Not that the area sported hooligans, but most *rueziiv* seemed to ignore the small shops and restaurants in the working-class factory district, including the working class. The cobblestones of the street always wet from the furniture factory's condensation, I tiptoed down the street in leather loafers. The café was on the side of

p. 64

… him this notebook.

He wanted to believe all of this was sferen at first. These people look behind their backs for any little whiff of magic every two seconds. Can't blame them when sionsferen have risen at different times and dominated entire cultures.

the factory with the sign *!Att Sferen.* ("No Magic!") in large red letters nailed above the door, a prevalent warning hanging over all of Rotasharia.

She stood in a white shirt and blue jeans leaning over the counter with her chin in her palm, the little order pad tucked in the apron tied around her waist. When I walked in, she looked up from her magazine and smiled, a hint of mischievousness hiding behind her bronze eyes. I sat at one of the six tables and shuffled through my briefcase while she brought me a bowl of kisinii tea and a plate of bread sticks with a heavy almond flavor. She bent down close to me, and the overwhelming fruit smell in the room rose from her wispy bleached blond hair. She couldn't hide the natural light lime roots. She turned to look at me and smiled again. Her lips were long, thin, and frisky on that heart-shaped face.

"Aromahe datehett."

"Good afternoon to you too," I said. I felt quite comfortable with their language because Waters had done a great deal of fieldwork with it already. Of course, Finley never completed the lexicon, which made it less complicated and easier to pick up. However, if forced to speak any of the ethnic languages, I would be lost. Finley never got around to bothering with those.

After I wouldn't let her peek into my briefcase, she sat down across from me, crossed her legs, and rested her chin in her palm. "Did you find what you were looking for?"

> p. 21
>
> I think they actually attempted to make Rotasharian phonetics as different from Ratasharian languages using the Roman alphabet as they could. (What am I saying? Finley's the one who tried to make it different.)
>
> 1. –he– or –he produces a "yeh" sound; ex. mhe=(myeh); –h + vowel ex. holorval =yo'lor'val
>
> 2. tt = t t=d (soft) d=d (hard)
>
> 3. si=sh hi=hy
>
> 4. Rotasharian has an obnoxious little accent mark➔ ‿ (still don't know what it's called, and it's hard to write); indicates a long vowel sound as well as an accent marker a̱ = ā e̱ = ē i̱ = ī o̱ = ō u̱ = ū ii = ē, etc.
>
> 5. r following a consonant is trilled…

I'd eaten here the day before and then asked her where the library was upon leaving. She asked me if I were a student because I had planned to do research, and I told her I intended to read a scholar's work for pleasure. When she seemed shocked that pleasure and scholarship could go together, she asked me which scholar, and I told her Waters. On second thought, that may not have been a good idea, but she became excited and said she had read a lot of Waters's fiction.

"Asi, I had a marvelous time. I spent the night." I dipped the

> p. 18
>
> …tongue. It doesn't seem like Finley ever worked on writing any native languages. But I think Rotasharian is the Vienties' native language, and the other groups adopted it as their "official" Esperanto. I wonder what the Vienties used to call their own language before it became adopted/acculturated. The article didn't mention the Vienties as a major group, but I…

bread in the thick tea and stirred it around. Kisinii fruit was some kind of grape they'd cultivated, and I wanted every last drip of it. "But explain something to me. Why is James Pasado hanging over the entrance?"

"They don't know it's Pasado."

"Well, yes, I know that." I stuffed the bread in my mouth. A rapturous gush of syrup and bread. "But why would the *artist* choose James Pasado?"

"He's a man who knows great sadness. Taken from his home, thrown into strange places away from his family. It's a terrible thing to be displaced. He reminds us of what we don't want to go back to."

"That man is not noble. He's a desk jockey at best."

She laid her hand on the table and sat up straight. For a moment, she furrowed her brow, and her lips parted. "Where is your napkin?"

In my lap, where it should have been. I raised it above the table for her approval. This seemed to confuse her even more. "You're not eating right," she said.

"Then how should I eat?"

She cocked her head. "You're very rata. Are you joking?"

"Att, my dear."

She took the napkin and folded it into a triangle. Then she took it in her left hand and held it under her chin. "Like this, daliim'vhett? If you drop anything, you can lap it up." She nodded. "Yeah, I thought you were rata. Where are you from?"

Vienties have a knack, a gift if one chooses to look at it that way, of being able to identify the ethnicity of anyone just by looking, even sniffing out other Vienties who could be confused for one of pure race by any other people group. Of course, they may have had a hard time sniffing a Ratasharian out because Ratasharians just didn't live here. But I didn't know if I were Ratasharian.

> p. 22
>
> …a consonant.
>
> | ex. temera=book | temerav=books |
> | --- | --- |
> | sian=woman | sianiv=women |
> | sien=man | sieniv=men |
> | sion=person | sioniv=people |
>
> 7. (this isn't phonetics) –ii can be equivalent to -ian in English, adjectives can be formed by adding -ii
>
> ex. sfek=evilness   sfekii=evil

"That's a good question. You can't tell?"

She took off my glasses and placed them on my briefcase and reached across the table, planted her palms on my cheeks and let her fingers crawl up my face. I closed my eyes. The fleshy tips of her fingers danced along my forehead and over my ears, played with the cleft in my chin I discovered as soon as she traced it. She removed her hands and I opened my eyes, watched the balding Moratalian cook/ manager watching us with a perverse fascination from the kitchen.

"You get anything?" I asked her.

"Att. You don't know where you're from? Do you remember anything? What is your name?"

"It's not that I don't have memories. I have plenty of memories. I remember everything."

"Fa vhe medovel?"

"Endnoter medovel," but I couldn't be sure that was my name either. It had been directed at me once, maybe in a dream if I dreamed, and sometimes I heard its hollow ringing in my thoughts. Anyway, it was better than anything else I could think to call myself.

"Endno-tair," she said (I didn't bother to translate it), "what do you remember?"

There were things one didn't admit to friends of twenty years let alone a sexy little thing on the second meeting, but until yesterday, who I was didn't really matter. I'd never talked to anyone before. I didn't have to explain myself to anybody. I would tell this girl because she loved Jasmine Waters, and it was good practice for me. "You asked me, so don't think I'm dek. Before yesterday, I used to watch Waters. I saw everything she did. I went everywhere she went. I knew everything she was thinking, and I knew what everyone else around her was thinking too. It's not like I was in their heads—I could just hear thoughts."

"How could you relate to them every day with you knowing certain things? Didn't that make it awkward?"

I shook my head. "They didn't see me."

She shrank away from me and inhaled. She looked over at her boss in the kitchen before she smirked at me. "Are you siensferen?" I had grown more attractive to her.

"No," I said under my breath, not wanting anyone to suspect I was a sorcerer. "It's as if I didn't exist to them. They weren't aware of me. I don't even think I had a body. I don't remember feeling anything before yesterday. What it's like to sit in a chair, or eat. All I knew was what other people felt, and how they felt about it."

She put her hand over mine and caressed my arm. "How's that possible? You're not a god, or some spirit. You have a body now. Where was it before that?"

"I'm telling you—I know I didn't have one."

"So, why did you come here?"

"Jasmine left one day. I couldn't find her, after knowing exactly where she was for so long. I need to find her. She left some kind of crude little map on her desk, more research. It led me here."

I finished the rest of the bread with the napkin under my chin in correct *ruezii*

30

fashion, and she watched me. I put some money on the table and picked up my briefcase.

"Where are you going?"

"Arodame Press."

"Jasmine's publisher?"

"Asi."

"And will you come back to see me? I would like that, you know."

"I suppose, but I would have to know *your* name first."

"Siama," she said.

"*Shaaaamaaaa*," I whispered to myself. "Your name is 'Tomorrow'?"

"Yeah, my name is Tomorrow."

Siama's bronze eyes left me buzzed. A light tingling between my legs, I'd never recognized this in Waters, but some of her friends' cheeks flared red when the sensation came over them. The light thudding in my chest beat a little harder when I saw Siama's hair, when I smelled her hair, and now in this cramped space, with everyone determined to keep their eyes off of everyone else, I was surprised at my own shallow breathing. My chest tight, I sucked in air. Did Siama cock that smirk at me because the dumb male sitting across from her panted like a dog? With every thought of breathing, with the awareness that I was breathing, it seemed that simple involuntary function became impossible. The old Alkerie woman to whom I'd relinquished my seat looked up at me. Underneath a knit cap, her hair was as sapphire as her eyes although the grey started creeping up from her scalp. I didn't know what she wanted, and then she smiled. Always expect an Alkerie to be friendly, or had she interpreted my short breaths, decoded the images of Siama flashing through my mind? Not so long ago, I could look at everyone and knew what he or she was thinking. Maybe the old woman read me. Maybe somebody somewhere watched me now and amused himself with my thoughts.

I turned away from her and comforted myself in the car full of Vienties, Moratalians and Klets with some Tanarians, Cotessians, and Carnesh mixed in, all gazing out at the opposite window, a pants' leg, the floor, anywhere they couldn't make contact with someone else. All of these people shuffling back to their offices in wrinkled suits, teenage kids cutting classes, looking like typical Ratasharian slackers in their wife beaters, cargo pants, hip huggers, and hoods casting shadows over half their faces. None of them could care less about me.

Rotasharia had even mimicked the most intimate details of city life—a Cotessian sat Indian-style in long flowing skirts with her hair hanging in her lap. Eyes closed and blood red lips moving to the strumming of her guitar, she sang something that sounded conspicuously like coffee house rock. A few young people her own age bothered to listen to her. No one dropped money into her open guitar case. The horde coming out of the train pushed me past the newsstand and out the exit, the Cotessian woman's soulful fairy voice following me up the stairs.

Arọdame was located in an upper-middle class neighborhood about five miles away from the center of the city where the Embassy overlooked all of Ruez. The office was on the bottom floor of a colonial townhouse. When I

p. 20 Trippy Hair, Trippy Language

Now from everything I've read, Rotasharians closed themselves off from the rest of humanity b/c their ancestors underwent great persecution and oppression (the hair may have had something to do with it). Because of their past treatment, Rotasharians (or their government) have no desire to be influenced by Ratasharian culture and politics. AND, although Rota-sharians are well aware of their history, they don't have any contact w/ Ratasharia and they don't know what Ratasharia is like.

Well then why does Rotasharian use the Roman alphabet? Rotasharia was well tucked away in secret long before a hint of Rome or its language. I'll keep telling myself Rotasharians hate Ratasharian influence…

walked in, a purple-haired Moratalian smoking from his second-story window gave me a strange look. He thought I was Vientie, no doubt. The smoke smelled of licorice and something musty I couldn't quite place. It was pleasant, despite its leaving me a little lightheaded.

Arọdame Press consisted of a short hallway with bookshelves on each side, trade paperbacks and hardcovers piled as high as they could be stacked, and a small room at the end of that hallway. A closed office door in front of me, I looked for a secretary and couldn't find one. Not even a semblance of a waiting area to greet visitors. I took one of the paperbacks off the shelf, opened it up in the middle, and stuck my nose into it. I'd seen Waters do this a lot with new books, stick her nose into the spine and inhale. The ink mixed with chemicals on the page reminded me of spiced-tea steam lingering in the air, and now I understood Jasmine's ritual.

Behind the window in the office door, a figure paced with phone in hand, letting out an explosion of genuine laughter. Eavesdropping proved useless. I could make out an *udọ* or an *atthel* here and there, but not enough words strung together to make any sentences of sense. I stood in front of the window right where he could see me, and the longer I stood there with no acknowledgement, the more flushing in my cheeks.

A man with the shocked expression of a dead fish stuck his head out from behind the door when I rapped on the glass. Wide-eyed, he looked at me as if I had newly materialized. "Can I help you, young man?" he said, although he couldn't have been pushing forty himself.

"I'm looking for Tolsene Mardun."

"Could you hold a second?" The door slammed, and he was gone.

When he returned, he opened the door all of the way revealing a tiny office not much wider than the hallway. "What might I do for you? I'm Mardun."

"Well, yes, Modhe Mardun," I started, and he turned his back on me. When I stopped talking, he gave me another dumb look and beckoned me to sit.

"Asi?" he commanded. He rubbed his hand over his short-cropped light green hair.

"Oh, of course," I said and sat in the chair cramped between Mardun's desk and yet another bookcase. In the window behind his desk, one of the glass cupolas of the Ruez Embassy flashed sunlight in my eyes. "I'm just a little surprised, is all. I thought your office would be a little more...populated."

Mardun sat behind his desk and laughed. The stacks of folders, papers, and manuscript boxes almost rose up to his shoulders. If this building ever experienced the mildest shake, Mardun would be avalanched under mounds of books and paper. What a way to die.

"It's just me and a couple of guys in Deliton."

"Ah, yes, you're Moratalian," I said.

He wrinkled his forehead and tapped his hands on the desk. I would apologize, but I only now remembered his ethnicity—not a green-haired Vientie. No offense to his pure blood.

"Where are you from, friend?" he asked.

My first experience with pressure trickled from my underarms and ran down my side, my top lip tingling. How good of a liar was I, and how good of a Vientie impersonation could I master? I wasn't ready to find out, not in a world where everybody always thought they smelled the slightest whiff of magic. Tolsene Mardun wasn't a threatening man, and he sat leaning towards me with one hand on his hip more out of curiosity than suspicion, but I couldn't answer his question. There were so few answers I knew, anyway.

"I've relocated here and there. I came to see you because I know you appreciate Medheki Waters's scholarship as much as I do."

"Her scholarship." He chuckled and leaned back. "Few people would call it 'scholarship.'"

Strange thing that her publisher mocked her. The uncomfortable office lacked that sweet, tea smell, and the room was heavy with the mustiness of yellowed pages. I fought the itching in my nose, the burst of air forcing its way up from my lungs. "Why do you say that, Modhe Mardun?"

He was curious again, and a bit more malevolent. "How do you know Jasmine, Modhe...?"

"Endnoter."

"Endnoter. Modhe Endnoter." He laughed, and I realized he recognized the English. "Like footnotes? What are you, an afterthought? Who bothered to name you that?"

The last thing I could tell him was I heard the name screamed over me as I sat writing notes for one of Jasmine's essays. Mardun composed himself. "I'm sorry. How do you know Jasmine again?"

He did not drill me, at least I didn't think he did, but from his cunning smile, I couldn't tell if I should fear for my life or if he aimed for simple intimidation. "I told you, I consider myself a scholar of her work." I didn't wait for his response and opened up my briefcase to retrieve her small spiral notebook.

As meddlesome as he was curious, he stood over the desk and peeked down to see what I was doing. "You know, most people don't see Jasmine's work as scholarship. They think it's fiction—brilliant fiction, but fiction nonetheless. They would be amazed if they found out she's only sixteen, wouldn't they?"

I held the notebook up. Mardun gasped. Without looking he reached for the drapes behind him and yanked them shut. "Where did you get that? Is it the real thing?"

"Of course it's the real thing. I found it in her room."

"In her room?" He scratched the bottom of his chin. "So, she wasn't home?" He nodded, solemn, contemplating, and sat. "I haven't seen Jasmine in a while. She was supposed to be doing research on a new manuscript, but I haven't had contact with her in a couple of weeks. Of course, that may not mean much. I don't know if time in her narrative landscape is compatible with ours. Do you know where she is?"

"No. I thought you might help me find her....Why are people belittling her work?"

His eyes started to roll, but then it seemed he realized I might

...and dominated entire cultures. Tolsene eventually came around. I told him if he published my books, I would do research on Finley and all of these nara-

be as ignorant as I claimed, or an idiot who needed explanations for everything. He looked towards the door, and, satisfied no one was there, leaned across the desk. "Do you realize what would happen if people realized a Ratasharian had infiltrated Ruez? And we're not talking about *any* Ratasharian—this girl is the most rata of all. She's not even from this world. She's Ratasharian, but she's not even from Ratasharia, kitodvhel?"

"Yes, I do, but—"

"Kid, listen to me, if people knew that what she's talking about in her books was real, not only would everyone be looking for secret doorways in libraries, but I might be accused of abetting in sferen."

p. 65

scapes. He almost wet himself. He thought it was a great idea, but he said he couldn't publish them as nonfiction. I told him I didn't care.

Fantasy novels set in Ratasharia sell very well, and now I'm going to be writing a ton of them. ☺

They will "mimic reality"....

"Come on, now. They have to know she's Ratasharian. What about her name?"

Mardun dismissed the idea with a flick of his wrist. "They think she's Carnesh. She writes about things rata. Sometimes when authors write about Ratasharia, they take on pennames they think are rata. Look, I've got to get back to my other job," he said writing on the back of a business card. "If you find anything, give me a call."

I waited until 2 AM, sitting on the mezzanine and looking at the painting of Pasado before heading out of this narascape and searching for Waters someplace else. The Ruez Library's traffic didn't quiet until after midnight, and no one needed to see me go down to the basement. I reread Waters's notebook, contemplating the oblivious bug-hurtling-towards-the-windshield look on Pasado's face. He'd starred in only a few of Finley's short shorts. How, or why, his legend spread across the narascapes was beyond me.

"Endnotair? Endnotair!"

My name called in a whisper, it echoed through the hall. I looked over the mezzanine balcony, and Siama waved at me. The guard at the entrance glanced in her direction and then went back to his book. I didn't know what to think of her standing there all dressed up in a long maroon skirt down to her ankles and her hair teased. All I knew was that I started thinking about breathing again.

"Can I come up?"

I nodded without thinking.

"How'd you know I'd be here?"

She grinned, and I was proud that I could make her that happy, that she

35

would get dressed up for me. "Where else would you go? You don't have anywhere to live. You don't even know where you're from. The library's all you have. Did you get to meet him?"

"Asi. Nice enough guy, but it was quite unproductive. I'm surprised you came. I'm *glad* you came."

"Of course," she said. She took my hand. Hers was sweaty and hot, and I wondered if she felt my pulse, felt my heart speeding. Maybe she could see me like I used to see Waters, know how I felt and thought at every moment. Or maybe Siama was *siansferen*. I didn't want trouble.

"Let's go," she said. I resisted when she pulled my arm.

"What do you mean?"

She stopped smiling. "I want to see the doors. They've got to be on the bottom floor."

I pulled her close and lowered my voice. "What are you talking about? It's late."

"There's no one around. You don't have to be so afraid. I want to see one of those rooms Jasmine writes about. I know there's one here at the bottom of this library. Isn't that how you got here? You left Jasmine's narascape and came to this one."

"Mardun says Rotasharians believe Waters is a great fiction writer, not an anthropologist. Not a scholar."

"Asi, most of them. Some of us know the truth though. We've been too afraid to look for the doors. You know what would happen to us if anyone thought we were sionsferen."

"Then why come with me now?"

"If you could sneak in here the way you did, I'm sure you can sneak out. You can help me do it too."

"Aren't you scared? I'd be scared of what I found. There's nothing but a bunch of stories Finley wrote and daydreams. You might not feel real anymore if you see yourself as fiction."

Siama rolled her eyes. "Fa? What are you talking about, Endnotair? Sure, Finley wrote about Rotasharia, and now we're here. But do you think she still has anything to do with us? I doubt it. We have lives of our own. She doesn't write about us every second. She doesn't think 'Remember to make Siama breathe. Siama needs to eat now. What will she have?' I'm my own person. She might have thought me up once upon a time, but I do what I want now."

Nice for her to be so confident, when I couldn't even figure out how I suddenly had hands or feet, or saliva to swallow. Nice that she had determined who and what she was in this web of stories. I had no story. There was no one in the library except for several students asleep at the tables, their hair sprawled across open books, and a few people flipping through pages in between shelves standing to stay awake. The automated elevator voice greeted us, and Siama looked around to find the security camera. What she knew about Waters's maps amazed me—Siama must have read everything Arodame had published. Unlike in other narascapes, there was no button for the Finley Special Collections floor of the library. Siama stood between me and the security camera, and I opened up the emergency panel underneath the buttons. She licked her lips, ready to photograph the correct switch on her memory. I didn't want to know what she'd do, or what would happen to her, if she came back here alone.

The elevator made its swift descent, and the voice announced "Sub-Sub-Sub Basement." Siama wrapped her arm around mine and shivered. When the elevator doors opened, there was nothing there.

Nothing.

All of the shelves were gone, and the tan carpeting had been removed to reveal a bare cement floor. The walls were bare too, and they were painted white, although I thought I remembered them being beige. The only thing left in the hollowed room was a short stack of paper sitting in the middle of the floor, and I had no way of knowing if it had been there before. Siama ran her hands along the walls and beat at them with balled fists. She took off her jacket and dropped it to the floor, dug her nails into the walls to see if there was a little air where wall met doorframe.

---

p. 10

…went through one of the doors in the far right wall. I ended up in another Finley Special Collections room, but this one was well lit, no cobwebs or dust, and looked brand-spankin' renovated.

The volumes down here are all leather-bound, unlike the editions done in that cloth stuff in the Harp U. library (leave it to my world to be cheap).

And I suppose I should have asked myself "Jasmine, what are you doing poking around down here? Shouldn't you be at home where it's safe?" Well, I suppose I should be home where it's safe, but I don't want to be bothered w/ the teeny boppers next door and their wango-tango-smoke-some-hash music.

Anyway, it's good I started inspecting with call letter A. Always best to start at the beginning, right? If I tried to make sense of all these daydreams without…

"This is a joke, right? Where's the original four notebooks? Where are the new leather volumes? Why'd you do this to me after I've been so nice to you? Where's the real Special Collections?" she asked, and I picked up the paper.

"It was here, Siama. I wouldn't do that to you. Nothing's like it was. It's all been taken away, except for this." I waved the paper at her.

"What is it?"

I flipped through the pages. They weren't professionally published, and it looked like they'd been printed by an inkjet.

"Fa?" Siama said. She rested a flushed cheek on my shoulder, hot breath on my neck.

I read: "'What are you talking about, Endnotair? Sure, Finley wrote about Rotasharia, and now we're here. But do you think she still has anything to do with us…?'" Repeated the same thing she had said only seconds before.

"Sferen!" she said. "Someone is using sferen against me!" Her voice grew loud, and I just knew the sound traveled up the elevator shaft, across the mezzanine, down the stairs, and into the ears of the guard at the entrance.

"This isn't sferen," I said, grabbing her by the wrists.

Her pupils darted back and forth. "Then what happened here? Why'm I in there?" She tapped the paper in my hands, and it creased. "We gotta get out of here before whoever did this finds us."

I supposed I should have been as frustrated as she, but I wasn't. "I have to tell Mardun what happened. Maybe he can figure some of this out. He should know this room as well as we do." I started to put the paper in my briefcase, but Siama snatched it from me and threw it to the floor. A few pages fanned out from the stack. I put them back in order.

"You can't take that—whether it's sferen or not," she said. "What if that's the only thing holding all of Rotasharia together? If you take it upstairs, will we all be wiped out?"

---

p. 11

the backstory or worse—wandered off into Ruez, I might have ended up dead. No lie.

The very first items in call letter A are 4 beaten old notebooks (3 of them are standard notebook colors—2 red, 1 green; the other has a mint green elephant on a pink background (go AKA!)). The wire in the elephant one is all gnarled up, and I had a devil of a time getting it untangled from one of the red ones.

Anyway, the 4 notebooks contain the "original" story. From what I can figure, this was written the summer Finley was 11 and 12. The plot is, well, that of an eleven year old.

Plot in a nutshell (I guess it's cute, if you consider she was 11):

•30 girls go to a boarding school in…

The rest of the library hadn't changed. Several students still walked the maze of bookshelves with heavy rings around their eyes, looking at any other conscious body in desperation, and people still slept at the tables or in carrels. When Siama and I passed by the guard, he didn't even look up from his book.

The subway station at night carried the presence of dirty steam, garbage, and stale alcohol. A few rats ran along the tracks and darted behind the rail when trains shook the tunnel. Stragglers making their way home or lost without any cares paced along the platform yawning or singing to themselves. No street musicians at this time of night, no music trailing down the platform to entertain or annoy the travel weary.

The car we entered held several passengers, and Siama pulled me across a few cars until she found an empty one. She sat with her shoulders hunched, clicked her thumb rings together. I really knew nothing about her, except that she was smart enough to tell true from false. "Who could change things like that?" she asked. "Hardly anybody knows about Jasmine's work, and if they do, they don't think it's real. Who else knows it's real besides Mardun?"

"You said she has followers."

"Of course she has followers, but they wouldn't destroy the Special Collections. We've been waiting for the right time to go down there, but you have to be careful, you know? Somebody had to have rewritten the narascape and changed everything. Sferen."

"Maybe it was Finley."

Siama sighed, annoyed that I brought her back up. "Finley hasn't touched Rotasharia since she was fourteen. Finley hasn't been interested in Rotasharia in years. Somebody here did it."

Siama's neighborhood was down in the valley, about ten miles from the Ruez Embassy. At night, two spotlights shined on the glass cupolas, and the surrounding areas fell into darkness. The series of townhouses and duplexes converted into smaller apartments were filled with Carnesh, Alkeries, and Vienties, those ethnic groups who'd lost their political power or had none to begin with. Siama's apartment was tiny, all the walls a foreboding olive. I fell back on the futon, and she turned on a table lamp to its lowest setting. The room felt even heavier. I closed my eyes and listened to water running in the bathroom.

"Dhe ttelefonatt," she said.

"It's almost three in the morning. I'll call him early tomorrow. I doubt much will change between now and then."

"This is important! How do you know? You can't even explain what already happened. *Call him.*"

After the way he'd eyeballed me today, I was sure he'd think even less of me at 3 AM. A machine answered, Mardun's baritone more professional at his place of residence than he had been with me earlier. "Um, yes, Mo. Mardun, I apologize for calling at this hour," I said. "This is Endnoter. I have some rather disturbing news, I'm afraid. I was set to depart Rotasharia tonight, and when I arrived at the Finley Special Collections, everything in the room was gone, including the doors exiting—"

"For gods' sake, Modhe, are you at a public or private telephone?"

"Oh, I'm, I'm surprised you answered."

"Well, you gave me a pretty good reason to."

Siama walked out of the bathroom, sat down next to me and put her ear close to the phone.

"Do you know what happened?" I asked.

"Yeah, I got a pretty good idea. I'm sure the Embassy's behind this, especially the Junsharans and Klets. If the government *does* have anything to do with the Special Collections disappearing, those girls may be the only ones who can get you into the Embassy for a little look-see. Of course, the Embassy split them up because some of the girls look too Carnesh, and nobody lets the Carnesh have anything around here. You may not be able to get in touch with the girls staying at the Embassy, but you might get a hold of their friends. Either way, you've got to get into the Embassy. Where are you?"

"I'm staying with a young woman." Siama gave me a strange look.

"Oh," Mardun said, "are you really? Can you get over here? There's some information I have for you."

⤙

If Mardun knew so much about the Ruez Embassy, there may have been one good reason. He had a perfect view of the Embassy building from his condominium across the park. Mardun struck me as the type of man who'd sit with elbows propped up on the window sill, gripping binoculars, trying to see if he could catch a peek at confidential documents crossing a desk or lust affairs behind office doors.

"Moratalians aren't much better than Junsharans or Klets," Siama said. "So what if the Junsharans and Klets exploit the rest of us? Moratalians were allied with Junsharans *against* the Klets. What makes you think you can trust Mardun?"

"I didn't say I trusted him. I'm surprised you don't respect him more. He does publish Waters."

"He's not an idiot," Siama said, "but Moratalians always know too much. They've wreaked as much havoc on Rotasharia as the rest."

40

Her tirade started when we got off the subway, and she mentioned how much cleaner the stations became the closer one approached the Embassy. I didn't take her anger for anything more than jealousy. I would be jealous of Moratalians if I were Vientie too. I would be jealous of any pure-blood group, for that matter. To me, it seemed easier to belong to pure breeds. With mixed breeds like Vienties, it was hard to tell what lurked around in the blood, what bad came with the good. She shouldn't have been offended. I hadn't invited her, and she decided to involve herself. Siama trailed behind me in the hallway with her hands stuffed in her jacket sleeves and her arms folded.

I knocked on Mardun's door, and it drifted open. I looked back at Siama, and she seemed less bitter, but still dared me to enter. "Mardun?" I said. No answer.

"Tolsene!" Siama said.

Inside, everything in order. On the walls of the living room, framed cover art for some of Arodame's books. There was nothing on the wall of Waters's. I spanked Siama's hand when she rubbed the back of the black leather couch.

"We're not sightseeing," I said.

"I may never get this close to one again," she said. She smiled, but then stuck her nose in the air.

"What's the matter?"

She gripped my forearm, pulled me into a small hallway. In the den, everything was undisturbed at the bar, and the remote control sat next to a stack of magazines on the coffee table. Photos of ancient buildings hung in this room, and I assumed they were shots of the Moratalian capital of Deliton. There were two doorways at the end of the hallway. The light was on in one of them, and we could see that the other was his bedroom.

"Mar—"

Siama slapped her hand over my mouth. "Stay here."

"Do you see—"

"*Stay here*," she said. She stuck her head in the lit doorway, clinched hand holding onto the doorframe. Her body stiffened, and her hand eased down the wall. She looked into the bedroom before she turned towards me. Her bronze eyes chilled to amber, and her mouth refused to betray any emotion. She pitied me. The thudding in my chest quickened, but for the wrong reason. I wanted that mischievous smile to creep on to her heart-shaped face. I wanted her to delight in the idea that I could be a bad boy. *Siensferen.*

"What is it?"

She didn't answer and looked back into the room.

I stared over her shoulder at Mardun slumped over his desk. His head lay on

41

top of manila folders, a pool of blood soaking them red. On the wall behind him, blood had sprayed in all directions and already began to dry as it trickled down the wall. The black safe near the window was still open. Mardun's eyes hadn't had the chance to close, and I knelt next to the desk. Vacant emerald eyes fixed right at me, all the curiosity gone. I wasn't sure what I was supposed to do—cry, spit, kick the desk. Mardun was not my friend, and I'd never stared into dead eyes.

"You've never seen a body before," Siama said.

"Asi, at funerals…from a distance. Have you?"

"Funerals don't count. I've seen people lying in the street. I haven't stuck around to see if they were still alive or not. We can't stay here. This just happened. You want them to come back for us?"

"I've got to get the information."

"Bet they're under there." She picked at the folders under his head with her fingertips.

"Fingerprints," I said.

She grabbed a handful of tissues, and for whatever good they did, they sopped up blood from the folders and stuck to her fingers. I looked in the safe. Nothing there except a couple of first edition copies of Waters's *The Special Collections* and *Split Ends: The Autobiography of Jasmine A. Waters.*

"I don't think he'd leave his safe open," I said.

"You think he had time to close it? How'm I supposed to know which is the right folder? The top one's ruined anyway. Let's just take them all. We don't have time for this."

Siama dumped the folders in my briefcase. Dried blood smelled like hot garbage.

Blood mixed in water and soap foam ran down the drain, and Siama scrubbed her hands together, scoured the webbing in between her fingers. I didn't know if Vienties had any superstitions about the dead or the cleansing of blood. Perhaps Waters had never been here long enough to find out, but Siama washed and rewashed her hands with so much vigor that I feared they'd be raw. If any of Mardun's blood had penetrated her skin, then she would make sure to take that off too.

At least Siama had a way to respond to his death. If that had been Siama rotting on the desk, I would have felt something I could interpret as pain, but Mardun had not even been my acquaintance. I had to find my own respectful way to mourn him, even though I wasn't sure he would do the same for me. Right now though, as I watched Siama lather the soap in her hands yet again, I only felt fear.

"We should have contacted the authorities."

"Dersu? So we can get connected to a murder case? The next thing you know they'll say we did it."

"That's exactly why," I said. "I want them to know we're innocent."

She chuckled. "Endnotair, I don't think you have to worry. As far as anyone's concerned, you didn't even exist until a few days ago. How're they supposed to track you down with no record of your fingerprints or DNA?"

When I didn't answer, she looked up and found me staring in the mirror. It was a face I'd never stopped to look at before, and I wasn't sure that I liked it. I didn't think my face should be so square, or that my hair should be that long. My hair was thick but straight, and it grazed my shoulders. I would have preferred it up around my ears. In Rotasharia, the fact that I was blond and grey-eyed made me even more of a freak. No wonder everyone assumed I was Vientie and was dumbfounded when I couldn't read them.

"This is the first time you've looked at yourself?"

I thought she might mock me, but when I looked at her, she was happy for me.

"You didn't even look when you went to the bathroom?"

"Att," I said. "I've only gone a couple of times. I'd never thought about it."

"What do you think?"

"My hair is too long."

She laughed, distracted from cleansing her hands for once, and she reached up and kissed me on the forehead. "That's easy to fix. Very easy. Where do you want it?"

I watched my hair fall into the sink, slip down the drain with Siama's skin and Mardun's blood. She held my shoulder with one small, firm hand, and snipped away with the other. "So tense," she said. "Relax." Strand after strand fell, and the lines of my chin and cheekbones grew stronger, stood out from my face. I looked younger, smarter.

"Gutsu," I said.

"You're welcome. I bet you've never had a bath either. It'll make you feel better."

Siama lay beside me on the other side of the pullout bed, her back turned to me. She would stay with me, she said, as long as I didn't touch. She wasn't asleep, and she knew I knew it. Faint smell of deodorant filled my nostrils, my skin was light and cool. The folders rested on a piece of newspaper on the floor, to make sure they didn't fumigate my briefcase, Siama said. The folders would wait until the morning. These girls Mardun had told me about, I knew of them. I knew

43

what Jasmine wrote, but they knew nothing about Finley. They wandered into Rotasharia from Ratasharia. They were unaware of narascapes. Ignorant there could actually be other worlds out there.

"Do you think these girls can help? I can talk to Toya. Toya should be able to get me into the Embassy." Finley's namesake should be able to get me anywhere.

"Why are you so desperate to find Jasmine? What if you never find her? You could wander for years. You're apart from her now. Why don't you take advantage of it?"

"I thought you, of all people, would understand," I said, staring at the ceiling. "She knows a great deal more than I do. All that I know I experienced from her world, watching her and those around her, listening in on their thoughts."

"Exactly, Endii. She had an opportunity, she took it. You won't learn anything if you insist on always looking at everything through her eyes."

Siama turned on her stomach and pulled the sheet over her head. It wasn't long before she drifted away. I could think of nothing but Mardun's blood running down the wall, drying and crusting over. I could put these girls in the same position, their life coloring the walls of Ruez's embassy. The entire world could proclaim them martyrs and never know why they died. Before I came here, I'd never slept before, and I don't know that I'd napped for more than a half an hour since then. But with Siama's body heat pulling me under, I sank into an uncomfortable sleep.

⁓

!Aromahe femnesia Endnorter.
?ttesalvhettsiur oka, Nelmhett
nett gesia. !Vhe lial helii.
Zewa el hlats kwa o friijera.
Endii vhe att sfomal. Attsion
vevelisi sopo balkvhettsiur
Mo, Tolsene. ?Riisnvhett scovatt
o kitiisianiv. Uvii mhe vhe
zordatt remsatt to mhe vhe hlerdatt
ke demheven.

—Sia[1]

A little note on canary-yellow paper waiting for me on the coffee table. She'd propped it up between a flower pot and a silver dolphin curved into a half-C. The

---

[1]"Good morning Endnoter! Did you sleep okay? I'm going to work. Eat something! There's stuff in the fridge. Endy don't worry. Nobody will think you murdered Mr. Tolsene. Are you off to find the girls? Please come visit me and give an update." (Signed Sia)

plant looked like an African violet. Even the houseplants were the same here. A man sat dead and rotting with his head lying on a desk, and Siama left me little notes. How she slipped out of bed perky and ready to greet the morning was beyond me. Sooner or later the authorities would discover Mardun's body, and while we'd done our best to hide our fingerprints, Siama and I could have left behind hairs, or skin cells, or anything else. Not my problem though, since there was no personal evidence to incriminate me. She should be the cautious one, figure a good explanation as to why she hadn't reported Mardun's murder after the cops found her bleached-blond hairs on his desk. But she'd abandoned me and left behind a canary-yellow note.

Anyway, I was hungry.

The kitchen provided no room for a table, and the corner of the antique sink the only place lending itself to a counter top. In the shoebox window sat a fake red rose in a vase, and out on their stoops, old Carnesh women chattered away in something like Papamiento with a hint of Swahili. I fiddled with the knobs on the gas range and listened to the women cackle and laugh, tried to make out the spices in the unlabeled bottles on the stove. Siama had a blender and an espresso machine. Self-defrosting refrigerator/freezer and a Teflon wok. Everywhere I looked, the same as Ratasharia. Only the brand names I didn't recognize. Would it be the end of civilization here if the *rotasiariiv* ever knew their nail wraps and lip balms and V8 engines and gaming consoles had been inspired by the minds of their ancestors' oppressors? Would they tear the *rata* clothes from their bodies and beat down buildings from their *rata* foundations? Or would they just cringe a little at the revelation and go on with life as usual?

Of course, maybe it was the other way around and someone had snuck his way over here and claimed the technology for the good of Ratasharia. But I doubted that.

I threw a tupperware dish full of diced chicken smothered with kisinii and apple chutney in the microwave. After second-hand experiences with food through others, I now understood why they made hourly trips to the refrigerator. Food lingered on my tongue long after I'd eaten it, the hint of tart apple and sweet grape on my palate, and every once in a while, I'd dislodge a string of meat from between my teeth. I could have brushed them, but I didn't want to waste any of it.

Mardun's folders stuck to the newspaper, and when I tried to pull the bottom one apart, it took some paper with it. Dried-over blood broke on my fingers and coated them with rusted dust. If I had any unclogged pores, any cuts I couldn't see, would his blood seep into my skin and mix with mine? Would he be a part of me, and could he haunt me wherever I chose to go, from one narascape to the next? I beat the folders against the floor. Crystallized blood covered the wood.

In death, Mardun continued to hide his secrets. In the least damaged folders, I read some things I already knew—the propaganda of the Junsharans and Klets exclaiming that the girls staying at the Embassy were the fulfillment of some thousand-year-old prophecy, a prophecy they fabricated only a year ago. In another, detailed accounts of the Embassy's fear of Waters's cult following and their exposure to Ratasharia. But in the most important folder, the one with all of the contact information, Mardun's blood obscured the words. A shriveled stack of papers, crinkled and fragile. I could make out a few names. The girls the Ruez Embassy tossed aside stayed with Modheki Serull, a university student. Mardun taught him while adjuncting at Ruez University. I washed my hands as Siama had, until they were itchy and dry, and lotion gave no relief.

The world kept shifting behind my grey-framed glasses. The wires cut across my view of Vientie toddlers dropping their balls in the gutters and Alkerie and Moratalian women lifting oranges to their noses. There was nothing more attractive than a woman with her hand detached from her wrist by wire frames. I pushed my glasses from the tip of my nose for at least the hundredth time today. Anyone watching me walk the street may have thought it was a nervous twitch, but the confounded things just kept slinking down again. These were not the glasses for someone like me. They were too bookwormish and fit a man who seemed to have a touch of weasel in him, a snide little priggishness about the corner of his mouth that one could never really trust. I would love nothing more than to tell Mok. Serull that I didn't choose these prissy glasses, but that would only lead to the logical question of who did, and I didn't want questions I couldn't answer.

Yet another Ratasharian rip off, Serull's neighborhood was transplanted from Seville. Narrow streets difficult for bicyclists to pass through, slick square stones had been worn down enough that they were no longer dangerous. Flat, stucco walls of the apartments rose nine and ten stories high. Walls pale as ashes, there was no ornamentation, and the occasional air conditioner jutted out from bare windows. Underneath the AC condensation, a withered Carnesh man sat biting his gums at his vegetable stand. The makeshift plank roof let a constant trickle through, and the surface of the vegetables wore a brown slime. Not surprising that most of the Carnesh communities had been banished to the backside of Ruez. Carnesh, whether they proved it to be true or not, couldn't be trusted. After all, they looked too much like the majority of those ancient Ratasharian bullies—Sumerians, Egyptians, Hittites, Cushites, and the like. This rundown area was reserved for the worst of the Carnesh—non-native *rueziiv*.

"Modheki Endnoter." The curve on my bottom right lens chopped off

Serull's nose.

"*Modhe*," I said. I felt older and wanted his respect.

Behind Serull, girls lounged on their bellies in the living room on the floor. They read Rotasharian language textbooks (where did English books come from?). Girls on the couch crossed their skinny legs, gossiped away about Ruez and the Embassy and the friends there who'd forgotten about them. Girls in the kitchen. Girls napping in sleeping bags on the den floor. Everywhere, wall-to-wall girls ages 11-13, a blend of ebonies, cinnamons, tans, ambers, African diaspora, Latina, sub-continental India. Finley never indicated how many girls lived with Serull. She never indicated how many stayed at the Embassy. All Waters could ever figure was that there were thirty total. But here, girls poured out of every room and filled the tiny apartment with their adolescent laughter.

God help Serull.

And suddenly they were staring right at me, the pale blond with smarmy wire frames. No recognition that I was *rata* because they didn't smile to greet me or exhale their relief.

"Endnoter," Serull said. "Seems so English. Girls, this is a friend of Mo. Mardun."

The girls crowded into the dining room. More eyes searching, probing. Rotasharians are crazy, they must have been thinking, and you can't trust any of them, no matter how good their cause seems.

"Is the Embassy ready to hear us?" one of them asked. Waters never met or sketched them, so I couldn't tell who was who.

"Actually, I was hoping I could talk to one of you. If that's all right," I looked at Serull. He leaned his ear towards me. "I'm looking for information that might be hidden away in the Embassy. I would like to keep a secret from the rest of the group, if that's possible."

Serull nodded.

"I'd like to speak with Toya," I said. She was Toya, minus the "i," but being a namesake had to count for something.

In a plaza across from the Embassy, Toya-Minus-The-I sat before me with sunglasses gleaming. She was somewhat of a celebrity, with the other multiculti Americans, identifiable because of their connection to their prophetic white friends, but dangerous enough because of their Carnesh appearance that the *rueziiv* gawked and pointed at them from a safe distance.

She loved it.

In the shade of the umbrella, she ate mozzarella sticks, and I devoured kisinii fritters. (She, however, would not touch anything with kisinii in it.) The poor waiter, realizing he served greatness, stood at his station wringing his hands and almost ignored his other customers. This girl befriended the prophetic, and if she should be mistreated, word could get back to the Embassy only a few feet away. On the other hand, who wanted to be blighted with the *sferen* of a *rata kitiisian?*

She grinned at me. "So, how long have you been here?"

I stuffed the rest of a fritter in my mouth. "You know?"

Toya leaned in. "That you're not from here?" she whispered. "*Nobody* who's lived around kisinii fruit for more than one day loves it that much."

I wouldn't pretend I didn't know what she was talking about. She'd already figured me out, and satisfied with how easily she'd read me, she let me know it. I hoped she had knowledge beyond this world, beyond this narascape, that her namesake had encrypted deep within her mind facts and histories and architectures she wasn't aware of. Whether Toya-Minus-The-I looked like Finley or not, I had no clue. As far as I knew, Finley and Waters never crossed paths. The version sitting across from me was some sort of mix—Sudanese or Egyptian, Indian (East and Native American), African American, and what-else-have-you. Her eyes weren't blue and they weren't grey, but a certain transparency about them made them almost colorless, and as she stared at me, I could see if Finley dropped information in. Beyond retinas and pupils, each filament a staircase, leading to more doors leading to more staircases, and at the end of the maze, I'd find Jasmine Waters, and she could tell me how I came to be in this body, and how I got here from there.

"Isn't Serull concerned for your safety?"

"Nobody bothers us here," Toya said. She froze into a predatory-cat pose, grimacing snarl, fingers suspended in the air like ready claws. Our neighbors at the other tables spun around in their seats, dropping all pretenses that they hadn't been spying on us. Our waiter, who'd been joined by several of his co-workers in case Toya demanded their services, flinched and huddled for cover behind the mini bar.

p. 43

...This Embassy, by the way, seems downright McCarthian. The Embassy is basically the seat of the pan-Rotasharian govt. All of the ethnic groups except the Vienties have home nations and their own governments. Most of the Vienties are confined to Ruez, the capital of Rotasharia. A few are spread out across other nations and have very little power, except for those living among the Alkeries. The Alkeries seem to be much more relaxed about things ethnic.

Ruez itself is multiethnic and completely landlocked within the very large Klet...

"It doesn't bother you in the least that your friends are living like princesses while you're cramped in a tiny, one-bedroom apartment and treated like vixens?"

"We're treated like darkies in Rotasharia. We're treated like darkies in Ratasharia."

I cleared my throat. "Well, that doesn't make it right."

"They're puppets is all," Toya said. "Do you trust the unified government here? The way we see it, they're in more danger than we are. We're getting to the bottom of things."

"And I'm sure the Embassy will find a way to propagandize everything." I said.

"Yes, well, my reason for summoning you concerns the Embassy. This must not leave the two of us—"

She nodded, and I explained the disappearance of the Special Collections. I watched Toya-Minus-The-I the whole time, pausing every now and then to allow her space to fill in the gaps if she so chose. (She never did.)

"What's so Special about these Collections?" she asked.

People at surrounding tables bent their necks, angled their ears in our direction. To avoid the appearance of ogling us, the company sitting across from Toya looked in our direction, but not quite at us. Blinding sunlight from the glass cupolas of the Embassy sparked and burned my retinas. Blue, pink, and yellow spots flashed across Toya's face, and I pushed up those damn glasses. The realization that I was an idiot turned the kisinii sour in my mouth. It flooded with saliva when my stomach shifted, and I wondered if any of the people lunching here worked at the Embassy. Instant access to the shenanigans of these Carneshy adolescents. Toya should know better than this, than to talk about private matters of the hotbed in the hotbed.

I leaned across the table. "You're crazy," I whispered. "This isn't safe."

"Don't worry. What's the 411 on your library?"

"It has doors, several doors. They all lead to different worlds, much like the wall of Nijentie's pyramid that brought the first six of you here. The Special Collections hold a lot of information about this place, and you. Do you see why the big cats at the Embassy want to exploit it?"

"And you? Who are you? Why did you come here?"

"I'm from one of those worlds—Jasmine A. Waters's world. I'm looking for her. She writes books on Ratasharia."

"Why is she so important?"

"In her world, I used to listen to her thoughts. I used to listen to everybody's thoughts, watch their actions, but I was never a part of their lives. Just an observer no one was aware of. I know I'm not a god or a spirit. Jasmine probably knows exactly what I am."

"Weird," Toya said, and chewed on a mozzarella stick. "You sound like a narrator to me."

I cringed. "I'm not disembodied—"

"No, now that you've involved yourself....Look, never mind. I'll call my friends at the Embassy. They'll tell you how to get in."

The fan from the factory churned around the damp smell of rotted food. Figures of Vientie and Carnesh men drifted across the windows overhead, smoking cigarettes and flicking ashes on the floor. Every once in a while, a few grunts registered deep within the building. Behind her Siama pulled two large blue garbage bags and motioned me over to the trash and recycle bins. Condensation from the air conditioners ran down the walls and fell around the trash where fuzzy green moss grew about the rusted metal bins. Siama opened up the bags and started sorting plastic and glass juice and soda bottles. I bent down to help her, sticky syrup all over my dry fingers.

"No, that's all right," she said. "I need to take a lot of time." She opened one of the lids and dropped in glass bottles. I flinched with each crash, as if the glass cut my eardrums. Siama was unnerved.

Glass fragmented at the bottom of the bin. I stuffed my hands into my pockets and fiddled with coins. "Has anyone asked about Mardun?"

"Nothing. And the girls?"

"They'll help."

"Are those your only clothes?"

"Yes," I said.

"Get yourself some new ones, and go back to my place." She gave me her keys. "You don't need to get any more recognizable than you already are."

Her voice brought me out of the fog of my sleep. I stretched across the pull-out bed, dragged the cover over my head as I listened to her voice, sweet and digitized, call me from the answering machine. "Just wanted to check on you, sexy. I'll be home in about an hour. Maybe I can come with you tonight. You could use my help." The phone clicked and the machine beeped. The humidity in the apartment, the thing that had lulled me to sleep in the first place, bore down on me, and the sheet clung to my bare chest. Boys played some mix between cricket and baseball in the street, slapping a rubber ball with a wooden plank, the ball thudding against the side of the building. With sweat springing from my pores every time I moved, I wanted to stay here and melt into the bed. But every thud brought me back as I drifted off again. Such a beguiling word—*sexy*. Such an unfair expectation to live up to.

Siama certainly had not seen the unsexy parts I discovered as I tried on clothes. Too little sun left my legs pale, and the tracks of broken veins straggled up my thighs. I didn't know how that could have happened since my legs hadn't experienced any trauma. And my stomach was flabby, not fat, with the skin soft and pouchy about my ribs. Why couldn't I look more like the young men who came out of Waters's world, who bench pressed in their front yards, tight abs clenching with each struggle to lift the weight? I wouldn't mind looking like the skinny boys either. No tight stomachs, but their metabolisms were high enough to keep their stomachs flat. Me? I was pasty with a doughy stomach and bad eyes. Surely Siama had a better sense of sexy than this. But maybe *sexy* was just an average term of endearment. Or maybe Siama just wanted to worm her way into going with me. The last thing any of these worlds needed was a Rotasharian in Ratasharia, or a Rotasharian in worlds where both Rotasharia and Ratasharia didn't exist. A little green-haired girl with a blond dye job mystified with every new encounter, paranoid with every incident that seemed like *sferen*. This cult that followed Waters's work could drive Rotasharia to chaos if some little Vientie legitimized Waters's "pseudo-anthropology."

The boys yelled at each other and laughed outside. On the bookshelf, Siama'd stacked several of Waters's volumes, but the ones she had found most fascinating were hidden in a second row in the back of the first. These were the secret books on Rotasharia—*Rotasharia: The Unfinished World* and *The Freaky Technicolored Hair People: Fake Allies, Factions, and Magic*. From what I'd read, Waters planned another on this world. Heavily underlining in both *Rotasharia* and *The Freaky Technicolored Hair People*, Siama paid great attention to the details Waters had recounted concerning individual characters and their environments. When I told her I saw those girls today, she could give me the most intimate details of each one. When the Embassy revealed their friends as the Ratasharians of prophecy, did Siama sit in front of her television like the rest of Ratasharia, or did she know the day, minute, and hour of the announcement?

Or were those girls always a perpetual presence here, their existence never expanding beyond the uncompleted story? Then Waters should have Siama recorded somewhere, too. But I never read about Siama, never remembered her at least, and as I flipped through the indices of these two books, I didn't find her there either. But if she were a part of this world (as she was), she should appear in here somewhere. She should be a major character. Why else would I have met up with her? No record of her in Finley's daydreams or worldbuilding sketches. Still, Siama's only appearance was in a stack of freshly printed white paper lying on the floor of what used to be the Finley Special Collections in the Ruez Public Library, her exact words, even things Siama said to me seconds before I read the paper in that stack, documented on the page. So much for determining Siama's motives. I placed the books back into their neat little rows, hid everything that shouldn't be seen.

"So, show me what you bought," she said as she stepped through the front door. No hello. Not even a *sexy*.

I had drifted off again, the sheet pulled out from under the mattress and wrapped across my waist and legs. That she had requested such a thing, for me to get out of bed in this stifling humidity, did not endear her to me.

"You may have been a man for only two days," she said as I grabbed my glasses from the table, "but you certainly act like one. Don't even clean up after yourself." She picked up the bags and the styrofoam cup from the coffee table and disappeared into the kitchen.

"What you were wearing before—you didn't get to choose that, did you? I want to see what you got for yourself. It'll say a lot about you."

I rubbed my eyes, grainy little particles scratching the surface of my skin. Something warm but not too heavy pressed down on my chest. I opened my eyes and found Siama on top of me, her legs sprawled over mine, belly chain grazing my abdomen. Her hair fell about my face, and shadows obscured her smile and eyes. "And where did Endii get his money with no job? Since nobody could see you where you used to be, maybe you just borrowed it without asking."

I started to protest, but she laughed, burrowing her face into my shoulder, her hair silky against my ear. "You have to develop some humor about yourself." She kissed my cheek and picked the sleep out of my eyelids. "At least you had a good rest. Your first good rest? But you do need a sense of humor, Endnotair. People will have so many questions about you. You're an easy target for insults." She sat up, and I was embarrassed to find that I held on to her shirt sleeves, waiting to pull her back down if she desired.

"You've gotta hang them up." She opened the bag at the side of the bed. "They get wrinkled....Slacks, another shirt...Well, at least the jacket is a change. Polyester and cotton. A little hot for that now, but it may cool down tonight. I'll iron them for you."

"Gutsu," I said. She sat with perfect posture, her back facing me and spine pointed straight to the ceiling. As she unfolded my clothes, her shoulder blades weaved in and out. The sharp bones surfaced to the skin and contracted again, the rhythmic dance of her shoulders, muscles, and arms haunting me more than any *sferen* could. Or maybe she *was siansferen*. Maybe that's what led me to wrap my arm around her waist. My whole arm encircled that tiny, little waist and pulled her to my stomach. She folded my pants in her lap. I had never seen Jasmine or her sister with a boy, but some of the other males and females in the neighborhood, some of her friends from school, I had watched them delight in each others' limbs, tremble despite themselves with each touch of skin. I rested my head under Siama's chin and brushed my hair across her shoulders, kissed the base of her neck. Siama turned her head towards me, and I looked up. Her eyelashes grazed my cheek. I bent forward, ready to taste her mouth.

"You don't want to do this, Endii. You've never done it before. Now is not the time, not with everything you've got to do. And you'll be gone after tonight, anyway, won't you? Why would I want that, if something happened, and you gave me an invisible baby? Not unless you take me with you."

"I can't do that. You know it's too crazy." I let go of her waist. She went back to folding my clothes.

"I'll find my way out on my own."

"And what are you going to do once they find Mardun? You didn't leave fingerprints, but what if they find your hair, or skin cells? Anything. They won't pin you for murder, but they'll wonder why you didn't alert the authorities."

"You can ask the girls at the Embassy to pardon me." She looked back at me and raised her eyebrows, like she had to plead.

"It's not that easy, Siama."

"It is that easy—you know it is. They're puppets, asi, but what better way for the unified government to show they're all powerful? Such sweet little Ratasharian girls having mercy on a wayward vhenii like me."

"All right," I said. "Write a letter stating what happened. Give me two copies, and I'll give one to the girls at the Embassy, and one to the girls staying with Serull. If the girls at the Embassy don't believe you, at least the others might be able to talk them into it."

"Gutsu, Endii."

My hand quivered, clutched her hip when the tip of her tongue touched mine.

My old clothes stuffed away in my briefcase and my jacket zipped up to my neck, I stepped off the subway train and headed towards the figure perusing books at the newspaper stand. "Can I buy you some gum?" I asked. The white girl from the Embassy beamed at me from underneath her hood and handed me two maps in an envelope. One map led me into a neighborhood almost identical to Mardun's, although these people were more affluent and their townhouses rose above the hill in clean, solid ionic lines. High, well-lighted windows and external second-story balconies. Marble statues lining the walkways and plush green carpets for lawns. These people didn't drape or blind their windows, and the passerby could see everything from the dark street. Beyond the dustless glass, staircases with ornamented banisters spiraled up into long hallways. Large paintings, statues, and tribal Carnesh art adorned front rooms. And for those with more modern sensibilities, they displayed their entertainment centers, state-of-the-art stereos and flat-screen TVs, speakers hanging from the walls.

Steam from the Embassy's laundry hung in the mist at the fringe of the neighborhood. I wondered how the Embassy had gotten away with building the more proletarian buildings of its complex so close to these posh, and undoubtedly difficult, residents. But there was something comforting about that clean, mediciney smell serving as a constant reminder that the elite of the elite stood watch nearby. I walked another mile downhill where the laundry building spouted smoke even at 1 AM. On hands and knees, I crawled the narrow track of dirt and mulch between the building and a row of short bushes. No cameras here, so, obviously, no laundry scrubs bothered to steal the clothes of wealthy men.

I retrieved the second map out of my jacket pocket and unfolded it at the shrubs' roots. It looked like a blueprint of the entire complex, the area of importance to me a series of dotted lines representing rooms just off the main elevators. The girls circled it with blue pencil—a large section of archives they'd discovered after curfew. It did not appear on any "official" map. Perhaps what I sought was *under* the archives. Some of the girls would keep a look-out for me as I made my way into the heart of the Embassy.

The laundry building had several empty areas, and I entered through the back door. Dryers churned in the front rooms, and hangers streaked across metal poles as washed and pressed clothes made their way to the assembly line's final destination. The back rooms shut down for the night, and thirty silent industrial dryers lined the back wall. I slipped in between long metal tables while every now and then the faint whistle or hummed tune of one of the workers up front echoed through the cavernous rooms. I opened a thick metal door in the wall, almost the size of an industrial oven, crawled inside and found it a well-lit box big enough for at least four or five people.

Gliding down the shaft, the elevator didn't make a sound, and I wouldn't have believed it moved if the numbers in the panel hadn't lit up in descending order. I checked the ceiling for loose tiles, a hint of a camera lens peeking through.

Fisheye lens hiding from behind the buttons in the panel.

The archives were a maze, the bookshelves carrying cracked leather tomes half as tall as me. With a carpet of dust on the floor, every breath I inhaled led to a sneeze that wracked my whole body. My face erupted in a burning tingle, and my chest felt like it might explode, lungs ballooning too much and bursting. I clutched my head, held it in place, and covered my nose with my shirt.

Over the years pages had fallen from some of the books, and they lay discarded on the floor after no one chose to replace them. Many

p. 54

I've got to ask an important question here: What happens in the narascape when time progresses to the end of the story? Does everything go back to the beginning and rerun? I'd hate to live everything over again, but most of these stories aren't even finished or barely begun! I'd hate to be the characters in those narascapes even more.

Oh, what am I whining about? A lot of these guys are living separate from the storyline and aren't involved in the plot. Of course, when you ask for the details of their lives and even their names, they can't tell you. I wonder what it's like to live life as background noise.

of the pages lying under the clouds of grey dust contained words from unfamiliar languages, jumbled letters, consonants and vowels tossed together for some attempted meaning—the unfinished, never started ethnic languages of everyone except the Vienties. Perhaps these jumbles of letters were mental pictures of what Finley thought the languages should look like. But who knew, with much of Rotasharia and its architecture left undone?

When I left this world tonight, for all I knew, the girls with Serull would go back to their Rotasharian language textbooks, and the girls at the Embassy would pretend to look important while eating expensive dinners. Or they could walk around these hidden tunnels again and again and again, living the same days and nights over and over, finding the same information each time and just avoiding the wrath of high-ranking Junsharans. That's where the story left hanging. Finley had abandoned them, and all of Ruez—and Rotasharia—would sit under the perpetual threat of a vicious *sferen*.

In the dark I stood straight, paused for a moment to re-gather my bearings, and then hunched over and swept the floor with my foot. The boards were fragile and unsteady. I pressed down a little harder, and my foot broke through the floor. I covered my scream, the wood squeezing my foot.

Underneath the hole, another tunnel with temporary lighting rigged to the walls. I ripped at the floor until I'd exposed the cavern, and at the bottom of the ten-foot drop, another floor. This one was pristine and white.

It wasn't on the map.

I let my briefcase fall to the floor below and took a few steps down the black metal ladder mounted on the wall. It was slick in some places, where a light film of plaster coated the rungs. A monotonous, tedious climb. I thought of Siama, the taste of her tongue, what a burden she'd have been if she came along and questioned everything when the building shook. Plaster from the damaged floor of the archives fell into my eyes and nose. I sneezed again.

To convince myself the world had not suffered a sudden transformation, that I would not fall to my death, I tried taking comfort in a mantra of "There are no earthquakes in Rotasharia"—Finley had never even created any inauspicious weather worse than a deluge—but the words were lost in the dust and mucous flying out of my mouth.

"Sir!" An anxious whisper thundering down the cavern.

With one hand gripped to the rung and the other rubbing my burning eyes, I looked up to see a girl leaning into the opening. She was dressed in pajamas, face flushed and sweat clinging to her scalp.

"Men. Guns. Bad," she said. "We heard them running through the pipelines. We spied 'em on the balcony."

The building shook again, and I fell to the floor, expecting my neck to whip back and snap or feel my skull fracture and the bone shards lodge into my brain. My cheek thudded against the floor, the sticky surface breaking my fall somewhat, although my whole head went numb for a moment until my nerve endings understood what had happened. My temples pounded. It felt like someone stabbed me behind the eyes.

I tore myself free from the weak ceiling, and the jacket sleeve shredded. Better for Siama not to see this after she had stood with me over the ironing board, showing me how to hold the iron and press it back and forth with a push of her little hips. I pounded on the still-wet plaster, blood smears painting the floor from where the ladder had sliced my palms. The floor finally gave way and I landed in a heap. Something hard and round dug into my spine. I threw chunks of plaster out of the way and found a doorknob. It was all here—they had moved it all—bookshelves, carpeting, wood paneling. A perfect replica.

The dust cleared above my head. The girl was gone, but the cavern thundered with the sound of stomping boots. There were doors in the wall too, but the one I wanted was in the ceiling. Strange that it couldn't be seen from the outside of the room. But there it was, a little to the left of the hole in the ceiling. I flung my briefcase on top of the bookcase and jumped up against it, tearing down the heavy volumes and using the shelf to lift myself up. A crowd of steps raced down the ladder.

I crouched in the cramped space on the top of the bookshelf and reached up for the door. For the first time I noticed I was drenched in sweat, and as the steps accelerated down the rungs and walked on the top of the room, I saw my torn jacket sleeve lying in the plaster on the floor. Perfect for gathering my skin cells, and blood, and DNA—if I had any.

The door opened, but this one wasn't accompanied with folding stairs. I threw my briefcase on the other side. A soldier pointed his gun into the room, and a red laser beam scanned the surface of the rubble. He screamed in Rotasharian, dared me to reveal myself. I grabbed the side of the doorframe and lifted myself up. My muscles wobbled, threatened to turn to jelly, but the thoughts that what might happen to the girls and Siama could also be my fate gave me one last energy burst.

The door slammed behind me. I could not worry if Rotasharia would progress or sit in neglected stagnation. Another world ahead of me, I wondered if Jasmine were there, exploring and mapping. Once I found her, I would let her map out my life.

But as I stared into the vast room of another Special Collections, rows and rows of shelves lacking the volumes to fill them, I wondered if every story's destiny were that of Rotasharia's. Maybe I, too, was a rat in the looping labyrinth with no entrance or exit, retracing steps and looking for the things which could never be found.

Parchment and Twigs

Christine Boyka Kluge

Lonely, she built six children from parchment and twigs. Her yearning gave each a rudimentary heart, amber and loyal. Her fingerprints patterned the glue that held them together. They were fragile beings, but they glowed with the touch of her hands. Like a string of lanterns, they encircled her ankles as she wandered, room to room, the winter of their birth.

Her children required little: a sip of water, a fairy tale at bedtime. They slept in a cluster on her second pillow, hungrily inhaling her breath. Mostly they were silent. They made their needs and love known by scratching their limbs on the floor or tickling her legs.

She left the cottage only once a week, for her own groceries. Each time she returned, they greeted her with a strange harmonic hum of joy. She was the tuning fork at their center. They wheeled around her in eccentric orbits. All winter long, she basked in the warmth of their rustling affection.

March came, and the children grew. She often found them perching in a row on the windowsill, bumpy faces pressed to the glass. They began to smell like maple syrup. Instead of hair, they grew full heads of red buds. When the buds unfurled into feathery leaves, she knew she had to let them go.

She whispered to them all that night, filling their skulls with her dreams. She woke just before dawn, imagining she still stood in a dark wood, cupping her hands to catch winged seeds. The waxing moon lingered as a gold cocoon in the western sky. At sunrise, she led the children to the open door. She looked down proudly at their lengthening branches and leafy crowns. When they saw the six deep holes, they understood. They leaped from the stairs into their marked places, raising their arms to the sun.

In time, they filled their boughs with songbirds and cicadas, and learned to talk like the wind. They embraced the house with their tangled roots, and, some nights, caressed the windows with their many green fingers.

Bluecoat Jack

Sarah Totton

According to Spring, everyone is defined by five aspects, but each person's aspects are different. My primary aspect, for instance, is a—. I don't know what the others are, but they must be in me still or I wouldn't be here telling you this.

Things started to fall apart about two months ago when I picked up the new conduit at the Grayhound Bus Terminal. Weyland, who handed him off to me, told me this one's name was Jack L—. That was what he was calling him. It's all bogus. Weyland isn't his real name and Henry isn't mine, but we had to call each other something, and no one wanted to remember who they used to be.

After handing Jack off to me, Weyland booked it out the door like he needed to be somewhere, yesterday, leaving me with my pickup—Jack. He was the youngest conduit I'd ever seen. He looked about fifteen, lounging in the plastic bus station chair with his coat on. Everything looked hard and blaring under those bus terminal lights, and that blue coat of his was just seething with color.

We had a half-hour wait for our bus. "Stay there," I told him, and I picked up a coffee from the stand near the ticket wickets, keeping an eye on him the whole time. He stayed in that awkward, half-reclining slouch almost sliding off his chair. I hoped he wasn't getting sick; I didn't feel like holding his head while he puked up whatever Weyland had fed him.

I brought back the coffee and sat down opposite him, had a good look at him. Though it was hot in the terminal, his coat was closed to his throat. Pulled closed—the buttons were missing. His hair was blonde, curly, longer than it needed to be, falling down past his eyes, hiding his expression, if he even had one. Not all of them did by the time I got them. His knees were the most expressive thing about him, alternately gaping and pressing the palms of his hands together between them. I sipped my coffee and watched him doing nothing like I couldn't get enough of it.

Five minutes before departure, our bus was called. There's something about the smell of diesel exhaust that reminds me of wet Sunday evenings and dying. I don't know why. I don't like to breathe it, and I avoid it as much as I can, even though this time it meant we nearly missed our bus.

And maybe it was because it was after midnight, or because I'd had too much coffee, but the sound of the bus driver tearing Jack's ticket was like a short scream and so blinding white it looked in his hand. Jack didn't have a bag with him, hadn't asked me what my name was, where I was taking him. There was that resignation in him…and a kind of nobility.

I took Jack to the back of the bus and sat him by the window. The bus pulled out not long after. I switched off the overhead lights and watched Jack watch the street-lit rain streaking the window. We were necessarily closer than I normally like to get to another person. My eyes started to kill, so I closed them, sitting up extra tall to keep myself awake. I could hear him breathing next to me, slow and deep.

I nearly slept through the stop, despite the coffee. As the bus lurched to a stop outside the motel, I touched his arm with the pen I carried. The material of his coat was so soft the pen sank into it like a blown cat-tail. Wool, maybe. Expensive wool. *Must be stolen*, I thought. Conduits didn't have money.

Outside, the air smelled cold. It was 2 a.m. and we were the only ones on the street. I fished out the motel keycard. The room was humid, smelling of damp concrete. The carpet was greasy beneath my feet. Everything was where I'd left it, but I checked anyway, under the bed, outside the patio door. I didn't let him use the bathroom until I'd made sure the shower was clear, even then, I made him leave the door open.

After Jack came out of the bathroom, he curled up on the bed with his shoes and his coat still on and, pulled the pillow into the crook of his arm and hugged it. He closed his eyes.

The coffee was still affecting me; I couldn't sleep. I went to the patio door, held the curtains back and looked out across the parking lot—there were only two cars, and the windows of the other rooms were dark. It was 2 a.m. Jack sounded asleep, the sleep of the untroubled, the innocent. I picked up the ice bucket and went down the hallway to fill it from the machine. The rattle in the plastic bucket sounded like bombs going off. The feel of the plastic bucket in my hand, ice against my knuckles, my whole body juddered with each step. My feet seemed very far beneath me and insubstantial. I slipped the keycard into the lock and let myself back in.

He was lying in exactly the same position, but he looked smaller; maybe it was the way he was curled up around that pillow. He looked terribly young, eyes closed in the glow of the bedside lamp. Looking at him I felt a little strange, older suddenly.

I set the ice bucket on the table gently and sat on the other bed, watching him. I sat there for a long time, thinking of a lot of things, like how long it had been since anyone had trusted me enough to fall asleep that close to me, someone who hadn't wanted anything from me.

Suddenly I wanted with all my heart to protect this kid from everything outside this room, from everything in the world, everything that could possibly damage him more than he obviously had been. *But you have a job to do*, I thought. *Keep him safe until Spring needs him. After that, it's out of your hands.*

I turned off the lamp and lay there listening to him breathe. It wasn't a conscious decision to stay awake. We were safe; no one had followed us here. But I wanted to be aware of every moment as it passed, because we were at a temporary peace, and I knew it wouldn't last.

I eventually encountered something like sleep, a series of troubled wanderings through gray worlds that weren't quite dreams and weren't quite nothing. Like wandering in the cloudland on a thundery day.

I was a wreck by morning. When I glimpsed myself in the mirror, I had a pretty good idea what I was going to look like dead. Jack looked maybe a little more rumpled, a little less detached than last night.

"I'll back the car up to the entrance once I've settled the bill," I said. "Don't come out until I pull up."

It was a hell of an odd morning. I paid the bill, feeling like the first time out of bed after the 'flu. The air was sharp, and next to the motel the tulips lay in their beds, fresh-frozen.

Jack's thick coat looked appropriate today. Good, less chance people would take note of him. For the same reason, we couldn't stop for a meal; in small towns like this, people noticed strangers, and eating at a restaurant would give them time to do exactly that. *Look, mum. Cityfolk.*

By the time we got back to my house it was daylight. I pulled the car into the garage and hustled Jack up the path to the back of the house. It's an old bungalow in a street of older and better houses. Behind the garage and down a ravine run the train tracks. Close enough that the house rattles when a train goes by. Couldn't keep anything on the windowsills. A poor thing, but mine own—well, it was Spring's actually, but it came with the job.

It wasn't ideal bringing Jack in while it was light out and the neighbors could potentially see him, so I made sure I was quick getting him inside.

"You hungry?" I asked.

He looked over his shoulder at me. "No," he said, really quiet.

I showed him to the spare bedroom. Nothing fancy—just a bed by the wall, an empty shelf above it and a closet with no hangers. I left him there to sort himself out.

I didn't know where they came from—the conduits—and I never asked. All I knew was the way Spring treated them, there was no way they had got a home to go back to. None of them ever asked me if they could use my phone. Clearly, they had no one to call, no one who missed them.

I used to wonder if that was part of the reason they made such good conduits. But then it occurred to me that people who had no one who cared about them weren't worth as much as the ones who did, and maybe it was easier for Spring and her cronies to take people like that and do what they did to them.

When I first met Spring I'd had ambitions of learning her craft, the art of creating beautiful things from the unwanted, exploiting the soul's inner beauty. My disillusionment happened softly and slowly, until one day I woke up and realized I was nothing but Spring's lackey. But by then, I couldn't imagine a life other than this one I already had. I ought to be happy with it, because god knew, other people were much worse off than me.

The time when I used to try and figure out what made the conduits special was long past. It was no longer a glorious pursuit of artistic perfection. It was just a job.

The conduits were all different. I wouldn't say there was a typical 'type.' You couldn't use the same approach with all of them either. You had to be flexible, adaptable. I was that, which was one of the reasons Spring liked to use me. I was also discreet. It's easy to be discreet, when you have no one to tell, no one real, anyway.

The one before Jack wouldn't shut up. Talked in his sleep too. About nothing. The one before that liked to take things apart, took the legs off my kitchen table and the door off the fridge. The one before that was all twitchy, gave me the creeps having him in the house. Before that was an eighteen-year-old druggie with a cold. Coughed and sneezed the whole time, sprayed mucus everywhere.

I kept them until Spring was ready to see them. Being a caretaker involved a lot of waiting. With Jack, she kept me waiting longer than usual. But finally, she called.

I brought him to Spring's at 6 p.m. that first time, parked the car in a side street I wasn't supposed to park in, hopped out and unlocked the back door to the building. Spring shared a back door with a firm of lawyers; none of them used that door very often. It was quiet in the hallway. I hustled Jack into the building and up the stairs. There was a brief moment when I saw a silhouette through the frosted glass in an office door, but I was practically shoving Jack up the stairs and into Spring's apartment at that point.

"Stay there. Don't touch anything," I said. "Wait for me." Then I ran back downstairs to move my car before it got towed.

When I'd done that, I came back to Spring's place through the front door this time. Spring's loft apartment was full of the kind of things that catch your eyes and hold them tight, that challenge you to figure them out. Spring told me a beautiful face has the same effect, but I wouldn't know about that. All the things in Spring's loft were beautiful. Her studio motto is, 'Turning Aspects into Art.' The logo, in a stained glass panel in the skylight, is a monarch caterpillar with a butterfly above it.

There were new things in Spring's apartment every time I came. Some of them she sold for lucrative prices to wealthy clients, some of them she kept. The loft was lit up with colors, bright glass, plastic, prismatic, animated figures, three-dimensional pictures within pictures, a grandfather clock with wind chimes inside, two dragon kites sixteen feet long dogfighting in the rafters. Little flickering black things like confused moths persisted in the corners, remnants of Spring's less successful bouts with a conduit. The clients who paid so handsomely for Spring's art probably didn't trouble themselves about where it come from.

Jack took no notice of any of it; he was standing by the picture window with his back to me looking out at the city. Spring had tried to tempt me with money, her body, her art, but what had ultimately seduced me was the view of the city from her loft. When I saw it like that, never mind its stinking gutters cluttered with the viscera of audio cassettes, its pavements embossed with blackened gum, the backed-up sewers, the harbor with its boats rotting out from under them, the egg-shattering trains, the narrow, stifling streets. From this vantage, everything looked right; everything was where it ought to be, lights all shining along the waterfront. I think Jack must have thought so too. He had this wistful expression. *He understands,* I thought, and I felt a glimmer of elation. And then Spring came in.

There was nothing soft about her, her hair, like a tangle of brass springs, the sharp seam of her trousers where they hung from the points of her knees, her barbed wire bracelets. When she smiled, her lips were like the edges of a cut.

"Well?" said Spring, looking at Jack. I hated that wanting look she had.

Jack turned from the window, regarding her calmly. He shook his head.

"You don't have a choice," she said. "If I have to force you, I will."

"Spring..." I said.

"Make yourself scarce, Henry," she said.

I left Jack and went up to the roof, letting the door slam behind me, I was in that kind of a mood where I wanted to make noise. The pigeons stirred, but none of them took flight. It was too late, too dark despite the urban twilight. I sat down on a cinder block and put a foot up on the corner of the roof garden. Across from me sat Erisel, my stone lioness.

I'd had a soft spot for stone lions ever since I was little. My kid brother Mick and I used to believe they came alive under moonlight. Some nights we stayed awake peering through the bedroom window at the rustling hedge in our front yard, wondering if lions could break through glass.

Erisel looked the part. She wasn't one of those down-sized, coarse-cut things that pretentious suburbanites stuck on their lawns. She was a library lioness, and sometimes she was the only thing that kept me going.

They have a term for what happens to caretakers: compassion fatigue. Most caretakers succumb to it, become drunks or druggies. Erisel was why I could handle working as a caretaker without resorting to alcohol, drugs or the other things caretakers ended up doing. For a while I'd assumed Spring had stolen this one from the steps of the public library and brought her here with the help of her shit-disturbing Engineer friends. But when Spring found me up on her roof and asked me who I was talking to, and she looked through Erisel like she wasn't there, I realized that maybe what I was doing wasn't too healthy either, but when your illusions give you comfort, it's hard to let them go.

"A bald man and a lady in a pink coat walked along the sidewalk earlier tonight," said Erisel. "I could have dropped one of these cinder blocks on their heads if I'd wanted."

"You get bored too easily," I said.

"A lifetime of guarding books, of looking noble and dignified. It gets to you. Are you all right?"

"Why shouldn't I be?"

"You seem as though someone broke your heart, that's all."

"The day someone breaks *my* heart—" I protested.

"Is the day I lie down with a lamb." I heard her laugh in the roar of the wind over the rooftops.

Some time afterward I went back downstairs. I avoided looking around Spring's apartment, but something blue caught my eye. In a ceramic candy dish on the kitchen table was a button, the size of my thumbnail, smooth, transparent blue glass, chipped on the rim. It was still warm. When I held it to the light a flickering animation appeared inside, the way light plays on the ceiling above a swimming pool. Then I realized that what I was seeing was private, not mine to see. The kind of thing someone gives you if you're very lucky, or worthy. Not the kind of thing you just take.

"*Jack*pot," said Spring. I could hear her smirking. "Get him out of here, would you, Henry?"

⌇

I took Jack home. It was early, before dawn. I could see him suffering, but I couldn't do anything for him. Except leave him alone. I left him in his room and shut the door. Then I went to the living room, sat and stared at the street through my window, holding my hands over my ears, because the door wasn't muffling his sobs and what wood couldn't do, maybe flesh could.

After three visits to Spring, most of the conduits were done. A few hung on for four. Some were finished after two. The light went out of their eyes. Not a butterfly after all, but a dried up cocoon. Then I would take them back to Weyland. I don't know what he did with them.

I didn't know how many times Jack had been used before he came to me. Once at least, I think. So he had maybe two more visits left in him, at worst, one.

⌇

The waiting was the worst part. No, the worst part is when the phone rings at 3 a.m., and I wake up like someone yanked on my spinal cord. It was that deep inside, Spring's hold on me.

"Yeah?" I said.

"Bring him over," said Spring.

I switched off the phone, set it on the floor beside the bed. It had now become inevitable, wasn't my problem.

Jack was bundled up on the bed, coat still on. I shook him awake. He lay there with his elbow across his face, like he thought I was going to hit him. I pulled on my boots at the door, walked back to his bed. "Up. Now." Nudge in the ribs, or whatever pillow-filling passed for them in his chest. He rolled off the bed onto the floor, got up like an old man.

Every caretaker finds a way to cope; some ways were universal. One of them is, when you're into the homestretch, when it's almost over, you never look them in the eyes. Eye contact makes a connection, like joining live wires. You can burn yourself out doing it.

67

It's easier to distance yourself if you're a little rough with them near the end. I hauled Jack out the door by the elbow, shoving him onto the pathway. I shoved him a couple more times on the way to the car, hard enough to make him stumble.

At 3 a.m. there was no one on the streets apart from taxis.

"I can't," he said. "Not again. Don't make me, please."

"Shut up," I said. And thank god, he did.

I could see Spring watching us from the lit window of her loft as we pulled up.

I went inside, walked straight up to Spring. "Don't push him," I said. "He's going to fall apart."

"Into oh, what pretty pieces," she said.

I felt a sudden, unexpected surge of anger.

She must have sensed it. "Don't get attached," she told me. "He's not a velveteen rabbit."

"What's that supposed to mean?"

"He's not real. You can't make him real by caring."

"Stop trying to make this about me."

She glanced skyward, her barbed-wire bangles sliding down her wrist. "It's not about you, you self-obsessed idiot. It's *business*."

I went up to the roof and sat on the cinderblock next to Erisel. I put my arm around her, held her, stroked the back of her ear. She was cold, but I could feel her anger, so powerful, I felt it, even though she wasn't really there, and I was leaning on nothing but air and wishful thinking.

You learn to live a certain way, to avoid a certain kind of situation. You get so good at it that no one realizes what you're doing, even you. Years pass, until at some point, someone remarks that hey, you've never had a girlfriend, have you, sport? Isn't that odd? Despite set-ups from your well-meaning family, despite awkward situations with aggressive girls who put their hands on you because you don't have the balls to tell them to back off, or the heart to tell the nice girls that you don't care and never could. Then people start suggesting that you're gay, and you think, well, maybe I am. Except the first time a guy makes a pass at you and you let him, you puke and get the shakes whenever you think about it afterward. So, maybe you're not gay after all. You don't know what you are. And instead of trying to deny what you are, you exploit it; you find an occupation where not caring about people is an asset. Where keeping your hands off them is considered professional, where no one expects more of you than you're willing to give. You were born to be a caretaker—there's nothing else out there for you but this. You can't walk away from it; it's who you are.

68

After his second session with Spring, Jack was in a bad way. He could walk around without hitting walls, sit down when I told him to, but that was it. I was babysitting a catatonic. I'd seen that look before. He might pick up, recover a little, but one more trip to Spring and he'd be finished. Then it would be back on the bus again to meet Weyland, watching the gray streets slide by, breathing stale air that had lived in a hundred smokers' lungs. I always think of grit and the breathless state of imminent illness whenever I think of Weyland. The thought of seeing him again so soon, was more than I could take.

I went to bed, left Jack sitting on the couch—he wouldn't lie down, and I didn't have it in me to make him do what he didn't want to. When I woke up in the middle of the night to get a glass of milk, he was still sitting there, except now there was a pad of paper on the table with a pen next to it. The page was covered in sloppy handwriting. It said: ONSCEDULE ONSCEDULE ON SCEDULE ON SCEDULE

A whole page of it.

I went back to my bedroom and sat on the bed.

Why this one? Fifty others, at least, had passed through my hands. I hadn't let myself care about any of them. Was it Jack or the guilt from all those others? Each time one went through, I felt a little bit

of guilt,

not much, a little,

like throwing away a piece of litter.

But it never went away; it added up, and each time the glimmering thought: *What if I stop now?* was a little more insistent. *No, Henry, you have it too good to throw this away.* You're living the only life you can, in the only place you fit in.

Except suddenly you find yourself caring about someone so much that you're willing to face a situation so they don't have to. You tell yourself to put that feeling away, but you're already so full of the things you're hiding from yourself that there's nowhere to put it.

I thought about basic human needs and how many of them I'd been needing and for how long, things I used to have, things I thought I'd never have again.

I thought about dying, and how it couldn't be much worse than this.

Spring had me snug in her pocket. The house belonged to her. She gave me money—enough to live on, a little extra sometimes. I'd been putting aside the extra over the years, but it wouldn't be enough to get Jack and me very far. We couldn't run. If we tried to leave, they'd find us.

Spring sat at her kitchen table, clasping her hands over her knees, looking at me. "What did you say?"

"Take me instead," I said.

"Why?"

"Because I can handle it."

"Clearly you can't or you wouldn't be offering to take his place. You don't know what you're saying."

"I know exactly what I'm offering. Where do you think I've been for the past ten years?!" I was worried she'd refuse because she didn't think I had the goods; I was a caretaker, not a conduit.

She pinched her earlobe and wibbled it between her fingers. "I had plans for you," she said. "Other plans."

"I have plans for me," I said.

"Not when I'm finished," she said.

I packed my stuff. Didn't know what I'd need or how long I'd be gone, but that wasn't what I was worrying about. I bought groceries—cans, bottles, instant soup packets. Enough to last a while. I packed the freezer tight with boxed food. I tried not to dwell on whether he'd know what to do with any of it, whether he even knew how to cook. Jack sat watching me, like it had nothing to do with him. He looked sad. Part of me was angry that he didn't seem to realize what it all meant, what I was doing for him.

When I was done, I put a plate in front of him. "I made you a sandwich."

He didn't even look at it.

"Help yourself to the food. You should be all set for a while."

He just looked at me and blinked, and I started to realize then that he probably didn't even know how to make ice cubes, and I was leaving him here alone. I thought about him going outside in that coat without buttons, and I unzipped my jacket; I'd saved up and bought a good warm one. I put it over the back of his chair. "If you go out, wear this, okay? And pull the hood up."

Worrying about Jack stopped me worrying about Spring's plans for me, until the second she pulled open her door to let me in. All cool, all business, like we'd never really talked, like she'd never gotten drunk and made a pass at me one night on her roof.

No, I recognized that demeanor, because I'd adopted it too. It was the classic pull-back, the detachment you assume with the conduits before they're about to be used.

But I was a volunteer; I had motivation. It was back in my house blinking at my walls, staring out my window, and very probably going hungry.

Spring sent me upstairs. The upper floor in her loft was simply a platform that extended over a quarter of the ceiling. It wasn't walled off and with the open plan, if you were standing across the room from it on the main level, you could see some of what was up there. You had to climb a ladder to get to it. At the top, I could feel all the warm air collecting under the skylight. There was a futon opened up on the floor with some new sheets on it. Fresh out of the package new.

She told me to take off my clothes. I wondered if she'd made Jack do that, and was that why he was so fucked up afterwards. I was dreading that she was going to touch me. I knew she'd never forgiven me for rejecting her advances that night.

But Spring's idea of revenge was more subtle than simply putting her hands on me.

"Lie down," she said.

I did, but when she leaned over me, I said, "Don't touch me."

"You're not calling the shots any more, sport," she said.

I looked up at the skylight, at the monarch butterfly in the glass.

I'd never watched her work before; I didn't know her technique. As it happened, it was worse than physical intimacy.

From where I lay, I saw her pull what looked like a sketchpad from under the bed. She opened it, and all the pages inside were black. As she flipped through, I saw that they weren't made of paper, but some flakey stuff, like mica, that powdered her palms. It looked familiar, and I realized it was the same stuff those little flitting shadows in the rafters were made of. She found a page she liked, pulled it out and laid it on my chest. It was soft and cold, and I wanted it off me.

"Close your eyes," she said.

I did, but I watched her between my lids.

"What do you see?" she said.

The mica fluttered on my chest, like snowflakes landing and though my eyes were half-open, I saw it clearly.

71

A playground. Swings.   She's
       watching.   Who? I
    didn't want to   go back
  , but there I was, like I'd n
 ever left. Maybe part of me ne
ver really had, that day at the pl
ayground with Mick, watching him on the sl
ide. I felt the swing hitch under me, but it
wasn't till after I fell that I realized s om
eone had given me a good kick while the swing w
as in mid-air, not till it was too late that I r
ealized why. All I knew then was that when the fr
ozn ground hit me sideways something broke inside
mybody, like a toy that's been left out in the rain
and t hen stepped on, and all I could do was watch wh
ile the man in the gray sweater stepped over me and pic
ked Mick up and took him away. *Look after your little bro
ther,* my ther told me as she left to talk to her friends. I
was always looking after Mick because no one else would. My
parents didn't say it, but he'd been a mistake. They hadn't wan
ted another kid. Mick was very young, but I think even he knew
they didn't want him. But that man in gray had, the one who kic
ked me off the swing so I couldn't run and tell anyone. I could
see him now, plain as day. Old man, ugly thick sweater, a look
in his eyes like he owned the world, like nothing could stop
him. I had wanted so much to stop him, to protect Mick from h
im. I wanted him to take me instead. *Approach him,* said Spri
ng. I struggled, as I had that day, futility. Then I felt her
hands on me, lifting me up, lending me the power to act. I
had never hated anyone so much as that man and now after
so long, I could stop him, do what I wanted to him. I wa
s powerful, enraged, and I laun   ched myself
across the playground. I would   have had
him in three bounds. Then—   Sur
render her, said Spring.
 No. One more leap and
I'll have him down.

                  Now! she said.
    I felt that stuff melting on my skin, entering me, and I felt the broken things
inside me shifting, and pain. You know that feeling, like you've got steel wool
packed under your cheekbones, that seething metal tang you taste when you're

about to pass out? The second before I closed on that man, just before I reached him, I felt it throttle me, and out I went.

I open my eyes. My body feels like it's been turned inside out and rolled in sand, and I can't move. I make some kind of noise, don't know what I'm trying to say.

<pre>
              I
          Hea
        r Sp
     ring's
   voice below
  . "You compartmental
ize well," she says. "You m
ade it easy." I hear her climbing
the ladder. "You surprised me. I n
ever guessed you had such a *fierce* ma
ternal instinct. You, a grown man." She
puts a glass of water on the floor besi
de me. "You can go when you're ready."My b
ody won't let me move. I doze...wake up. Th
is time I can move. I drink the warm, dusty w
ater, get dressed, creep down the ladder, cling
ing to it like it's made of rope not pine.Spring'
s sitting cross-legged on her bean bag chair with a
tea cup in her hand. "I didn't know you had a brother
," she says. She takes a sip of her tea. I hear her swa
llow. "You want to see it, you can. I put it in the spar
e room."I go up to the roof instead. It's cold, breath-mi
sty cold, and dark. I don't know how long I've been here,
feels like years. The roof is empty, covered in fine gri
t. I shuffle around, looking for something, but I don't
know what. Nothing's here, but it feels like there sh
ould be. I'm lonely and doing this isn't helping.
I go back downstairs. Spring's
sitting on the bean bag ch
air with a plate of oyster
s on her lap. I go to t
he kitchen, take her
keychain off the
table. Then I
go to the
</pre>

spare room.

"I thought you'd want to see it," she says.

The room isn't set up for human guests. It's full of things, but I don't have to guess which one she took from me.

My real name isn't Henry. It's what people call me now, but I was named Leonard after my grandfather. My brother, Mick, called me Leo.

I unlock the padlock on her cage. She's full of rage, and she frightens me. I take the padlock off. As soon as she brushes against it, the door will open easily. She isn't mine any more, and she'll hurt me if I stay.

I leave the spare bedroom, return Spring's keys to the table. Before I go, I take the button out of the ceramic candy dish on the table. Then I go home.

When I get there, Jack is sitting on the couch, like he hasn't so much as blinked since I left. I wonder why he's still here. I go and put the button on his knee, the little glass button with the shifting vista inside. He stares and stares, but the life in his eyes is gone.

The Lindberg Baby

Terese Svoboda

Two babies crying to port, he yells. With the cob pipe in his face, he sounds as garbled as a pelican with a load. Two babies and one on the way, he bellows. He unmouths his pipe to turn it toward the skinny length of car ratcheting open at dockside.

The Mrs. lifts her lids. She's two in cribs, two in arms, two to aft in the hatches, all wrapped tight. She muscles the two in arms onto one arm like logs, heaves another crib to and tucks them down.

If you don't pick them up, we drop them over, he says to the woman checking the pier for its number.

The coming mother just laughs. This mother is not the mother, just a woman getting out of a long car, a woman who handles babies like them, she says, but who needs the time off, who needs more than ten minutes while she changes her uniform out of the spit and vomit, and this mother moves a cigarette to the other side of her mouth so she can hand the Mrs. her bundle with a kink of red hair trailing from a hat. The money's tucked in, she says.

The Mrs. makes a face but the bills get found and removed and by then the mother's gone in the long car and just the catwalk bobs from her quick exit. The Mrs. glances at the baby's hair that would be just her shade in the light, in the bright light of day that they don't see much of. She tucks those fine feathers back under the hat, binds the baby tight and cribs it with the rest. Over all the crying, she starts singing a hymn. He starts in too, with a dance of one foot out and one foot in, a jig across the boards. That always quiets them, that or a good wash, enough wallow so the boat rocks and sometimes almost takes on water in the bows. But tonight the waters are still, there's no slosh and tilt so she sings loud, she sings clear across the avenue that leads up the catwalk, clear to heaven in Harlem. While she sings, she unfurls diapers over the side and beats them with a stick and he puts warm potatoes in the cribs, the night cold seeping up from the water where the city's broken into light.

He dozes beside the potato-warming potbellied coal burner while she nurses the redhead who has come upon a hiccup. Nursing is her secret. Few get the tit that she never lets go dry, few get the tit but those that do, do like it. She's slipped out of harness and the baby is sucking wild like a creature that wants drowning when a tall, brown-shoed pearl-cuffed man shouts from the docks: It's a pickup. You got two of mine, twins.

Twins? The man turns his pipe in his mouth. Nothing matches tonight. You sure you left two?

Two, I got two, he says. My wife brought them in. He's across the catwalk and smiling at the prow, his breast pocket's open with a badge before they can do more than batten the babies' hatches. I'm the law, he says, matter of fact.

I don't get it, says the man, kicking at line. We're a boat, nothing but a boat.

She has the redhead at her breast held close like he's her broken arm. He's quiet enough after all that milk. Quiet, she says to the officer. He's got to crying tonight.

That so? Says the pearl-cuffed man. Yours, I suppose.

McDoug, she says. She points at the red of his hair and hers.

Madam and McDoug, I will look around a bit if you don't mind, he says. He stubs his brown shoe on a curled board turning around.

Take your time, says the man whose pipe has gone out, who is tossing chum from a pail so the birds wake and caw which they do all through the inspection, with not a baby in sight except that one in the open, all slinged-up, the one standing for all, standing for theirs.

The Mrs. lets a pot of tea wail. McDoug, she says, has a touch of colic. She gives the baby a pinch and he sets to, over some other baby's snuffle.

The boat wallows while a tug belays a barge.

The man with the brown shoes and the pearl cuffs and the badge and the loud law voice isn't happy standing on the deck in the wallows. He stomps around like he's hoping to hear the boat full underfoot. People need to know, he says, stopping his stomping. You have a racket here.

The two of them look at the stars.

He smokes a cigarette, he looks up at those stars all the way to where the city lights fade. He throws down that smoked butt. Hell, you'd think it was women they were paying for, those people who get so excited about your operation. We're really just looking for one. You got one? The papers show which. You know.

Kidnapped with a reward? she says. I wish we did.

If you see another redhead, he says. He slips her two dollars, which she takes to her bosom.

I'll let you know, she says. Sometimes we get a lot of them.

He wasn't a man wanting twins, I could tell that right off, he says as soon as the cuffs are gone and the shoes sound distant.

Or even a single, she says. A man like that.

She is pulling McDoug forward, realigning him to her front a second or third time, when a woman in black shows—a musician, a funeral assistant, a stagehand? She wants her baby now, an act is what she needs it for, she needs it to see what employment she can get in the magic department with a disappearing baby. She just wants the baby now. She's got a show to do, she needs the money.

She's hurling herself across the catwalk when the woman breaks McDoug's suck and puts him down to help sort. It's not that all these bundles could be peas or any other vegetable in a pot but it is dark and the woman in black is in a hurry, out of need or shame or too much to drink or drug. She can't wait and runs onto the deck and just picks up the first one. I'll be right back with what's owed, she shouts over her high-heeled taps.

McDoug, says the woman. Oh, McDoug.

He's the one took.

Usually in the deep night, a midnight with all its bells, when anyone who is out stays out and doesn't come back until he's sober, the woman and her husband roll up the catwalk. Some nights they even pull anchor to sit in the channel because so many can get noisy, even over the traffic, even over the tugs. But tonight they stay tied a long time, hoping the woman finishes with her magic before the other shows up to collect.

To kill time, he unhooks all the babies, wet or dry, all the nappy pins get rowed where they can't be kicked. He hoses down any that need it, a wee little hose that he can make spray as gentle as a fish doing its business, then he wrist-tests the bottles, he props the cooled bottles on pillows so the tilt of it gets the milk to them.

The woman burps them all after, a string of burps in jazz time that uptown would be the percussion their parents are hearing, she burps them and then rows them again in the hatches, none of them walkers or even crawlers, they don't take any of those, and the babies have to like her singing, a Siren he calls her whenever she swabs out their ears and threatens his.

Only one is left at full light at the dock for day pickup, the wrong baby, asleep like it's the right. The woman who is not the mother doesn't show, thank goodness, and after midday the sister of the woman magician makes the switch. When her sister's working, her sister says, she leaves off her glasses so as not to see who's watching. One face is as good as another to her at work, let alone a baby's.

Oh, McDoug, says the woman, unwrapping her front for the returned him, for that red hair that is so much hers flattened.

Still the woman with the long car doesn't show.

After a week of no long car, he thinks they might try for the ransom.

She'll come and claim him, she says. It's not him. Besides, they will board us, more of those twin-father policemen.

He says around his pipe into the blue night of another week later, You'll be keeping him then?

You haven't done for me, she doesn't say. She hands him the baby at the start of a gas grin.

The pucker around his pipe moves into half a kiss.

Months later, the papers show the corpse of that baby and he is so happy that what they have is no longer a light on the deck that a boat might catch.

But I think it is him, she says, and the other's a switch.

No one ever comes to say Yes.

Strangers on a Train

Tamar Yellin

What it was that was strange about that house: she had never been there in her life before, but it was strangely familiar, she was filled with a constant sense of déjà vu. Of course, the owners had designed it that way, stepping into it was like stepping back in time, from the moment you pulled the old-fashioned bell-pull and heard the nickel tinkling in the depths of the house, from the moment you crossed the threshold into the tiled porch with its station master's cashbox and Victorian clerk's desk, its numbered coat rack from some vanished music hall. Beeswax and half-darkness. Lit by gas, she noticed, and that struck her as familiar too, but then, her memory was so bad these days, she was always half-remembering and forgetting things.

Then Feargal came forward and took her mackintosh. She felt at a disadvantage. Here she was in her blouse and skirt and he was completely done out in a black waistcoat and gold fob watch, filched no doubt from Wardrobe for the evening, his red hair scraped back into two crinkly spreading wings, one on each side of his head, and fixed down with brilliantine: nineteenth-century hair. He even wore whiskers. He was a nineteenth-century man.

He took up his position before the fire, which was wide, like a mouth, and deep like a bunker, and filled with heaps of coal and flames like the roaring engine of a steam train, which was where they were supposed to be. There were prints on the walls, clay pipes, curios; a heap of antique gazetteers on the coffee-table, casually left.

"It's sort of a cross between a steam train and a Victorian waiting-room," said Benedict.

They sat down on the sofa knocked together from old carriage seats.

"We've met before, actually," Feargal told her. "At the *Hay Fever* first night party. You probably don't remember."

"Terri never remembers anything."

"Yes, I do." But she didn't remember Feargal. "You must have looked different then."

"Oh!" He winked at Benedict. "I'm the man of a thousand faces. What would you like to drink?"

Just then a woman in long skirts and ringlets entered from the kitchen, bringing nibbles. She adopted a horrified expression.

"Jeans, Benedict! You haven't entered into the spirit of the thing!"

"You didn't tell me it was going to be a bloody theme evening."

She cuffed him gently. She was beautiful in an aquiline English way; her long skirts suited her. Her shadow hung behind her in the polished panelling like a ghost.

"Bloody actors. Any bloody excuse for dressing up."

"Vivien. This is Terri. You haven't met."

"No, we haven't met." Vivien held out her hand, with the practised grace of the stage goddess, with the serene appraising look of a bitch Madonna. "What a pity, you would have looked wonderful in a smooth bun."

Terri raised her eyebrows in what she hoped was a surprised expression.

"Vivien doesn't work in Make-up, she only wishes she did," her husband leered. "Her real ambition was to be a backstage girl."

"Yes, just like your real ambition was to play Hamlet."

"Actually I wanted to be Othello." He struck a pose.

"With me as your Desdemona." Vivien leaned confidentially into Terri's ear. "Feargal loves Shakespeare. It gives him the opportunity to kill people."

Benedict was already sitting with a glass of wine in one hand and his knees three feet apart, chucking peanuts into his mouth. "Why haven't you asked more people?" he demanded. "I was in the mood for a party."

"No, it's just the four of us. I'm sick of parties."

"This house must be wonderful for parties," Terri said.

"At Christmas we played murder in the dark."

"Yes, and some bastard broke one of my carriage lamps."

"It's impossible to move in this house without breaking something. Why have we never met before?" Vivien demanded of Terri. She searched her eyes in that actorly fashion, as though seeking something she knew did not exist.

"She hides herself away," said Benedict.

"I do not." Terri appealed to her hosts, who looked down on her with pitying expressions. "I do not hide myself away."

But then, as if on cue, they all began talking to each other, in a noisy three-way conversation which excluded her. Seated a little to one side, nursing her cut-glass tumbler of orange juice, she began leafing idly through the timetables. Hartwick to Spofforth, Monday to Saturday, 7:04 am, 7:23, 7:37... The view from the window was sheer darkness. Why did they talk like that, so loudly, with such big gestures? It was because they were in the theatre, of course. She didn't know who they were. She couldn't recall when Benedict had first mentioned them. There were so many actors, so many people. He was always going to parties she wasn't invited to.

"He has a face like a frog!"

"But it's a great face. A perfect comedy face."

Benedict was talking with his mouth full.

The last time Benedict was away, when he was in Munich, she had toyed with the idea of taking a holiday on her own. A secret one. Without telling him. To make up for the time he wouldn't let her come with him to Verona. But then she had started to be ill; she had given up work. Everything had fallen into confusion.

"...Shakespeare done in actual Shakespearean costume. Just for a change. Very avant-garde."

"Why don't we adjourn to the dining room?"

It was Feargal who led the way, with a three-branched candelabrum, down a dark narrow corridor lined with windows; the room at the end was silent and flickering with more candlelight and gas. There were mirrors, crystal, gleaming silverware; a fireplace presided over by a bust of Beethoven. The table was set with flowers. It seemed to have been waiting for them in patient readiness.

To add to the dining-car effect, the menu was propped up in a silver holder:

Goat's Cheese with Cranberry

Lamb with Raspberry Jus

London Syllabub

Coffee with Mints

Feargal opened up what looked like an old-fashioned victrola to reveal a CD system. He put on something sinister and atonal.

"Is anyone's anyone's?" Benedict asked, wondering where to sit. For some reason this made Vivien laugh: a high-pitched, nervous laugh which didn't suit her.

"You sit near me, Terri," Feargal said kindly. "Benedict, I want to talk to your wife."

"You don't need my permission."

He seated himself at the head of the table, pulling at the cuffs of his white shirt, looking like a funeral director. Terri thought: I don't understand anything.

81

All the same, I must appear to understand.

She smiled at him.

There were little dishes of goat's cheese decorated with a sprig of mint, standing in a pool of red stuff with a few lumps in it. There was very yellow wine. Terri accepted a half-glass on the grounds that she would leave it. She caught sight of Benedict, knocking back his red so he could get started on the white; there was already that familiar flush along his jawline.

"It was at the Ambassador's in London three years ago," Benedict was saying. "Terri was there. She saw it."

"I don't think I remember."

"No. I didn't expect you would."

"But why would they put Pemberton in the role?" Vivien looked elegantly disgusted. "This cranberry is too smooth. Don't you think this cranberry is too smooth?"

"Fevers is the best director I've ever worked with."

"Where do you work, Tanya?" Vivien asked.

"Terri," said Terri.

"Oh, really? Why don't you pass your plate."

The goat's cheese was taken away and the lamb was brought, very rare, pickled in thin vinegary juices; there were tureens of creamed potatoes and expensive vegetables. Terri helped herself without appetite; Feargal did not talk to her as he had promised. The effort of coming out had exhausted her more than usual. At her left ear the gas hissed with strangely lulling insistence, the soft crackling of the fire was unusually loud, and the whole room stood out with dreamlike sharpness: the dark oak dresser stacked with pewter and odd bits of bone and a crystal ball; the frowning Beethoven; an antique child's car made of rusted tin, which disturbed her for some reason with its suggestion of a small but significant absence, possibly a death.

"You know who we should have had here. Olaf."

"Yes, Olaf. If you wanted a degenerate drunken orgy."

"Olaf the master of orgies."

"Olaf and Maxime. You couldn't have one without the other."

"Hermione."

"Sick Bill."

Vivien and Benedict had started some sort of game: the names went back and forth across the table. The laughter grew more uproarious. Feargal glanced sidelong at Terri with a knowing look.

"You're better off out of it," he murmured, as though confiding something.

But a moment later he was laughing more loudly than ever, showing his pale tongue and all his teeth.

Benedict went on talking as though she didn't exist. Fair enough, she thought. I'm used to it. From the far end of the table she watched him, talking and talking, tossing back the wine, a good-looker still and didn't he know it, but a little frayed at the edges, slacker under the chin; slowly unravelling around the eyes. Of course, a man could get away with that where a woman couldn't. But there was no doubt about it, he was on the slide. A few more years and he wouldn't be able to pull them like he used to, not even supported by that famous charm of his. No; these days Benedict was distinctly charmless.

Terri hugged herself. She felt cold. Feargal got up and pulled down the night blind on the window, as though to shut out the passing landscape on a sleeper carriage.

"It reminds me of that pub we stayed at. The one with the four poster." Benedict pointed his fork at Terri. "The one in Buckinghamshire. The Farmer's Arms."

She was at a loss. Suddenly all three were looking at her.

Feargal laughed. "You can't expect her to remember that!"

"No," said Terri with caution, "I don't remember."

"Oh, for God's sake, Terri!"

"I've never been to a pub called The Farmer's Arms. I have no memory of it whatsoever."

Benedict turned to Feargal with a toxic smile. "I sometimes think my wife inhabits a different version of reality from mine. We have a whole past life together that she remembers nothing of."

"Yes!" laughed Feargal. "A whole existence that she can't recall!"

"It's possible," said Vivien, toying with her lamb. She had barely touched either of her courses. She turned her eyes on Terri with an intense gaze, as though seeing her for the first time.

"Well," said Terri to Benedict, biting her lip, "if we're going to go into particulars, there was that trip to Margate you claim not to remember. And that dinner at Luigi's where the waiter nearly dropped the bottle."

"Oh-ho, oh-ho," laughed Feargal. Benedict laughed too.

"Who would remember Margate anyway? I ask you, why would anyone remember Margate?"

He snatched the bottle with an aggressive gesture, and helped himself to more wine.

"No, but seriously," Vivien persisted. "Who's to say that anyone's past is real? Memory's just a matter of brain cells, and if you've killed them all—now, stop laughing!

What evidence do you have? It's your word against hers, and vice versa."

"'I swear to God, officer,'" Benedict declaimed, "'I never was in Margate in my life!'"

The laughter was out of control. Terri stood up. "Please could you tell me where the bathroom is?"

She let her napkin fall and left the room.

The stairs were very dark. She mounted them slowly, hemmed in on either side by what appeared to be voodoo masks: rough dark objects which brushed her sleeve occasionally in the narrow stairwell. At the head of the stairs were books, mountains and piles of books, and what looked like musical scores, and scripts, and haphazard manuscripts. They looked ready to topple over, to bury her under a heap of heavy bindings.

She slipped into the bathroom and closed the door. There was an old-fashioned light switch which made no sound when she turned it. There was a brass bolt whose tongue slid stiffly into place. The bathroom was cramped, like a cabin, and lined with mirrors. She was in a nineteenth-century closet, on a train somewhere. She had a vertiginous sense of having travelled back in time.

She sat down on the polished oak seat of the lavatory and remained where she was, hunched into herself, safe and silent, for a long time.

There were no windows in the room: the feeling of safety was complete, and as she sat she had the faintest rocking sensation as though she really were going somewhere, though that was impossible, of course. She hadn't gone anywhere to speak of in a long, long time. But wouldn't it be wonderful if she closed her eyes now and woke up to find, on emerging, that she had entered a new landscape, that they had crossed the border—that the train had really taken them through night and darkness to a new place? She looked at herself in the mirror: the face was hers, indefinably older, touched by an otherworldly luminosity. This moment, in the quiet of the closet, seemed the first actual one she had lived in ages: so that she had to bring herself up short again, moment by moment, to reconfirm the reality of the feeling.

She couldn't hide in here forever, though. Eventually, she supposed, she would be missed. She stood up, breathed in deeply, pulled the chain; the door, inexplicably, refused to open. She slid back the little bolt and it jammed. Frantic, she tugged and tugged. Abruptly it gave way, sending her toppling back into the room. She reached out a hand to steady herself and sent a tin of toothpowder and an ivory toothbrush flying.

Outside on the landing there was nothing to be seen. Only a rustle of skirts in the stairwell suggested something.

Now as she descended the dark stairs her feeling of foreboding grew; the air as she re-entered the dining room was truly ominous. This even though it was as warm and glowing as ever, the fire banked up, the candles flickering, the gas turned up full and the talk and laughter continuing as though she had never left.

The same but not the same. Vivien sat much as she had before, a blush in her cheek, cradling a glittery tumbler of brandy in her long fingers; Feargal, half-turned to the fire, was all stiff collar and frizzy whiskers. But Benedict—Benedict was not quite Benedict. He smiled at her, for a start, with Feargal's eyes.

"Vivien has cut pudding and gone straight for the brandy," Feargal said. "The rest of us are eating syllabub."

And sure enough, a ramekin of syllabub was awaiting her.

"It's delicious," Feargal added. "I've already eaten Vivien's."

"Vivien has to watch her figure."

"Vivien is a great watcher."

"Vivien prefers watching to being watched."

Vivien narrowed her eyes over her brandy glass.

"I wonder," said Benedict, scooping out the last of his with energy and licking his spoon, "why they call it syllabub?"

"Why *we* call it," Feargal corrected him.

"We call it what?"

"Syllabub. It's not just *they* that do, it's *we* too."

"We two!" Benedict suddenly laughed: a rich, allusive chuckle which did not belong to him. They both laughed. Vivien smiled. Terri looked from one to the other, her teaspoon poised in mid-air.

"Go on and enjoy it," Feargal encouraged her, at the same time turning away from the fire to face her: his whiskers were not fixed as well as formerly, and his whole face seemed to have lost its colour. If she were to be honest with herself she would say it was Benedict's face, but that, of course, was impossible. It was just another of her typical confusions.

Slowly she began eating the syllabub.

"Very lemony." Feargal smacked his lips.

The fire burned with unusual clarity, and the whole room seemed clearer and sharper than it had before. The outline of every item of bric-a-brac, every piece of furniture, stood in her gaze with a sort of unnatural insistence.

She took a sip of coffee. It tasted very bitter after the sweetness of the syllabub.

"What do you think then?" Feargal was saying. "The nine-thirty-nine to Brighton? Or shall we dash down to the Royal Albert Hall and catch the Mahler?"

"I vote for staying put."

"Terri loves Mahler," Benedict remarked. "We went to hear the Fourth Symphony in Stockholm." He turned to her. "Or was it the Third?"

"Don't expect Terri to remember!"

"Terri doesn't remember her own birthday."

"When is Terri's birthday?"

"The thirteenth of April."

"The nineteenth of June."

"Terri could choose her own birthday."

Terri said: "Why are you doing this?"

"It's only a joke."

"We're only having a tease."

"Don't you remember when we played Consequences?"

"Or was it charades?"

Vivien said, languidly: "I thought it was murder in the dark."

She was smoking a cigarette: a gold-tipped Sobranie cocktail in a long holder.

"Honestly, Terri, you must trust us."

"We're only having a little game."

She tried to stand up. The room seemed to sway; the window frames vibrated. They must have picked up speed. But how could you have a coal fire in a railway carriage? The face which loomed towards hers was her husband's face, adorned with odd-coloured whiskers hastily applied, but she was in doubt now as to who was her husband and who wasn't: after all, wasn't the whole past a dream, an alterable fact, couldn't evidence be doctored and memories changed? This evening, for example, she was convinced she had come out with her medication, but searching through her handbag she could find nothing; she must have forgotten it as she forgot so many things these days.

So there was nothing to say that this fellow with the jeans and the red hair was not her husband.

"No—I'm all right. I'm really quite all right. I just came over dizzy for a moment."

Maybe it was age. In fact it probably was age. That, and a sense of increasing disconnection; so that the person she was in the closet twenty minutes ago, and this one, and the one she was when she arrived tonight, might just as well have been three different people. Theoretically she could disown all her past actions and even those still to come, on the grounds of (say) diminished responsibility.

Yes: hers was without question a case of diminished responsibility.

"I don't think you should go home; I think you should stay." Vivien.

Feargal: "I really think your wife should lie down."

86

For some reason this brought a gale of laughter.

"Just give her a minute. She comes over woozy sometimes."

"You've given her too much."

"Shut up!"

Cigarette smoke in her face; she waved it away and knocked over a candle.

"There now, see what you've done." Benedict.

Vivien: "It's all right, I've caught it!"

Somewhere behind her the man who was not Feargal was changing the music for some kind of abstract jazz. It broke through the rush in her head; jagged on her ear discordantly. The room was in pieces: like fragments of broken mirror the pieces were very bright.

"Mind you don't cut yourself."

If she could only stand up, make it as far as the door, the door would burst open and she could breathe fresh air. If she could only breathe she would be all right.

"No, but seriously, you don't think I look older with a moustache?"

"Baby lotion: we go through bottles and bottles of it."

Actors, talking about their looks as usual.

I shall take myself upstairs, she thought, and when I get there I shall lie down on the first bed I come to and sleep—and sleep—

"Why don't we put your wife to bed?"

Someone was lifting her, clumsily, under the arms.

The bedroom was dark, the counterpane cool beneath her: something silky and slippery she couldn't get a purchase on. The darkness weighed her down like a heavy blanket. Someone struggled for a long time to remove her shoes.

"Benedict?"

"It's only me."

He moved closer to her. His smell was not Benedict's, it was not familiar: but who was to say what was familiar and what was not, in this landscape of deceived senses and shifting time? She had no thought of resisting. All her life she had fought to get to grips with life, as if it were some school lesson she must learn or an exam she must pass, and the moment she got the hang of it life moved on.

"Benedict."

Reflected in the mirror, as if at a great distance, was a halo of light. Embracing in the halo, half-undressed, Feargal and Vivien were watching her. He began to lift her skirt, to unbutton her blouse. His hands were much more gentle than she remembered.

Bitter Almonds and Absinthe

Joe Murphy

Beasal, The Garbage Man, returns the astrolabe to his finely brocaded coat and frowns. Kinesica is as Kinesica does, and this morning, she refuses to reveal herself. A gray icy mist shrouds her walls and domes, hides monuments and minarets. Even her six great towers remain hidden.

"We'll have to make our way as best we can," Beasal tells the clayreens. Silent, these clay manikins gape through painted mouths, nod stiffly, and take their places. Fifteen will pull the garbage wagon. Five will load what Kinesica gives back.

Creaking, the wagon starts forward, lamps swinging listlessly from side posts. Beasal sniffs a handkerchief, scented with Margil's secret herbs for preventing infection, and steps out in time to the clayreens' shuffle.

Streets and boulevards form Kinesica's veins and arteries, but her blood isn't the tradesmen and their goods, not the beggar throngs, nor children nor kings nor slaves. No, it is garbage and so Beasal has come to think of himself as Kinesica's heart. Through him all her wonders flow. Through him all life doth pass.

Iron-shod wagon wheels ring upon the cobbles. Fog dampens Beasal's curls, runs trickling down the back of his neck. Up ahead, a multitude of clicks, whirrs, and the scratching of metal on stone. He is intrigued.

"Again?" Beasal lifts a well-manicured hand in a halting gesture. "The very audacity!" A pile of gleaming springs, cogs, ratchets, and such, some gold, some silver or dark iron, blocks their path. He motions to the Clayreens. "Exactly what we found yesterday."

A few brightly lacquered birds, mechanical contrivances loosed upon the city by anarchist artificers, scatter from the debris.

"Our beloved Kinesica grows wild." Beasal seizes the arm of a clayreen as it marches past. Soft arm, squishy moist clay, fog slimy but the simulacrum obediently halts and cocks a painted ear. "Only a week ago she used the garbage bins. Things degenerate. Now we find the streets a mess, and clogged they'll be by the end of our day if the carriages can't get through."

The clayreen nods. Its head lifts, staring with painted eyes at the fog.

"Be on your guard, my friend. Be on your god," Beasal admonishes. "And warn your brethren too."

The clayreen bows and marches off to seize the arm of another clayreen. Finally, with the cogs, springs, screws, and ratchets loaded, Beasal waves the wagon on. It jingles now.

The clayreens have adorned themselves. Some wear screws for eyes, others bright gold springs pressed into the soft clay of painted ears. One has fashioned epaulettes of silver hinges.

Beasal smiles. Good workers all, best to let them have their little trinkets.

It's now the Hour of Appetites Released, early morning. Quiet deserted streets, workers still huddle in their homes sipping strong coffees.

Without thinning, the fog lifts. Still, the astrolabe isn't needed. A swollen sun beams down upon Beasal; sweat beads within his brocaded coat. Finally, he knows where they are.

A broad turquoise plaza stretches before him. Brightly lacquered birds take flight as the clayreens march past sequined benches and clear fountains of perfumed azure water. Silver trees glitter with cunningly carved sapphire leaves.

Sniffing his perfumed hanky, he gazes upon the giant head at the plaza's far end. Gargantuan this woman's head—palace-sized, spanning from one side of the plaza to the other. Enigmatically she stares.

Here in all majestic splendors, Kinesica's Head is the first of her six great towers, home to heads of state, palace to the Three Kings. The vast stained glass doors of her mouth remain barred. Sightless stained glass eyes, curls sculpted of bricks and tiles, stained glass ears like colossal jewels.

Beasal customarily circles Kinesica's Head whenever their paths meet. A garbage man has superiors and he wishes to be seen in energetic devotion to his duties. Should a king stub a royal toe upon a refuse pile who would be blamed?

Such is the head's size that it takes almost three hours to circumscribe. Such is the head's height that, on the far side, deep shadows hide the sun.

Thusly shadowed and slumped in a motionless sedan chair, clayreen servants sitting on their moist rumps, a woman broods. A noble woman by her looks, although dangerous looks they are.

As Beasal approaches she glances up, frowns, and brings a ring-clustered fist to her eye. Her short gown shifts as she stiffens; medusa braids coil down her shoulders. Dark eyes, angry eyes, cast a suspicious glare Beasal's way.

"Good morning," Beasal begins, carefully enough, cheerfully, but not too cheerful. His hand lifts and the wagon halts.

"Are you sure?" The woman asks. "Are you sure it's wise to say?"

"Well," Beasal concedes. "It might not be. And I might not be. But we put a brave face forward."

"So you've noticed." The woman studies the shadows of immense stone curls.

A Lamianette, Beasal realizes. Her bare legs, still beaded with foggy moisture, are bound together and crisscrossed with scaled stitches sewn to flesh. Shoes made of ring mail; made as one to imitate a snake's tail, slink down over the sedan chair's scrollwork.

"Just who are you to interrupt my thoughts?" she demands.

"Your pardon." Beasal doffs his tricorn hat, bows with a flourish. "Only a city servant, Beasal the Garbage Man, on his appointed rounds."

"And what, Beasal, has Kinesica given you this morning?" A bluntly split tongue flicks over the woman's scale-gilded lips.

"Ratchets, cogs, and springs," Beasal ticks the items off on his fingers, recounting easily.

"How many cogs, might I ask?"

"Forty-six. The same number of small gold springs, I must add."

The woman leans forward, one elbow on a naked stitched knee. "Would you say such garbage is usual? Is it normal? Does Kinesica often give you these things?"

"My good woman," Beasal begins, but cocks an eyebrow and pauses.

"I'm the Duchess of Alriondo." The woman smiles and cocks a scaled eyebrow of her own.

"My good Duchess," Beasal beams. "Kinesica gives strange gifts this morning. Very strange. On other mornings, I might find broken wheels, empty crates, various packing materials, torn scrolls, even spoiled food. On other mornings, these might be safely and considerately stored in the appropriate bins Our Good Kings have disposed about Kinesica for her convenience. But not today."

"Have you noticed other changes?"

"As a matter of record, I have." Beasal nods, pleased at her interest. "Kinesica's Head is often on my route but often not. She rearranges herself each night, of course." Beasal produces his astrolabe. "And so I must keep this device to find my way. But with the fog it was useless, and...." Beasal glances at his clayreens. "And it did not matter! Kinesica's streets remain laid out as they were yesterday. Kinesica's head lies next to The Plaza of Jeweled Delights. Everything about Kinesica is the same as yesterday. Even her garbage!"

"So it seemed to me." The Duchess nods and strokes her pointed chin. Her ring mail tail shoes flip idly, thoughtfully. "Others I know have noticed as well." Abruptly she slaps the arm of her sedan chair. Her clayreens flinch. "Tell no one else. Meet me in this same spot tomorrow morning. We'll speak again on these matters."

"As you wish." Beasal inclines his head, a feeling of unease coiling around his innards. One doesn't become a garbage man for intrigue or adventure.

What will Margil think? She wouldn't want him consorting with a Duchess, or even a Lamianette. The rumors of how that secret society carries on are dark indeed. Still a command from such a person is most definitely a command.

"Until then." The Duchess of Alriondo flicks a bracelet-scaled wrist at her clayreens. Again, her simulacra flinch, and then slowly, sluggishly rise to lift her chair. A moment later, they pass behind a wide stone curl, deeper into Kinesica's shadows.

A soft hand touches Beasal's shoulder. He looks up at painted gray eyes, a gaping black mouth.

"Of course, I don't like it," he snaps. "But what am I to do? She's highborn, and more importantly, she has a point." Beasal frowns and shakes free of the clayreen's hand. "Something is wrong with our city."

Night deep, night dark, The Hour of Groaning, and this groaning, Kinesica's sotto voce rumble, snares Beasal from a fitful sleep. He sits up in the big four-poster bed, feeling its feathers shift, and beneath the feathers, the floor shifts, down through their apartment and into the garage below.

Margil stirs beside him, kicking the covers from her fur-clad thigh. Margil, who had curiously surprised him with her interest in his brief encounter with a Lamianette. Margil the Satyrinette.

Margil with fur pasted to her thighs and legs, feet crammed into too-tight slippers that mimic hoofs. Though she winces with pain at each step, she never condemns him. A Garbage Man's salary simply isn't enough to purchase her a grafting of real hooves and fur like most of the other wives.

Too often Beasal sees the pain in her eyes and fetches her sewing or herb trays to save her feet. He saves her the trouble of waking now. He eases from the bed and pads to the window.

Six stars glimmer above Kinesica's six towers. Far moon, bruised moon crowns the distant hills. The stars move as the city moves.

Kinesica's Head shifts to the left, perhaps about eight blocks or so. The tower of Kinesica's Left Arm moves as well; its talon fingers claw the sky. Kinesica's Right Arm, a crooked tower indeed, shakes a fist at the heavens, and it too lurches to the left.

Yet the twin-arched towers of her Left Leg and Right, the broadly squatting Torso merely tremble. The groaning increases; Margil's knick-knacks rattle on their wooden shelves.

"Like clockwork for a time that can't be measured. Why don't they move with the others?" Beasal wonders softly. Domes shift. Minarets sway. Whole blocks of tenements shudder. A gutter collapses from the house across the street.

Kinesica's Head, Left Arm, Right Arm wobble and sway, only to return to their starting points. Time passes into the Hour of Sleep Returned and the groaning slowly dies to a whispered torment, then drifts like distant thunder into oblivion.

"She has returned to the position of yesterday and the day before." Beasal knuckles the sleep from his eyes. He sits down in the heavy leather chair by the balcony window. From a crystal decanter he pours golden wine into a goblet. The taste is tart, full of citrus, and Margil's secret herbs for preventing nightmares.

A hand closes upon his shoulder. Almost spilling his wine, Beasal recoils. A clayreen looms over him. A clay finger rises to painted lips. The other hand offers a parchment slip.

Beasal gasps, tries to ease the trembling from his fingers before reaching out. Parchment folded seven times, it rustles, resisting his efforts.

"You are summoned to the gates of Kinesica's Torso at great urgency," he whispers. The paper is unsigned.

"Most unusual," he says to the clayreen, glancing then to see that Margil still sleeps. The clayreen nods and reaches for Beasal's shirt. Silently, it helps him dress.

On the street, a sedan chair waits. Beasal claps his hands. The clayreens flinch; they lower the chair.

"Now I've an idea who your owner is," he whispers. Beasal hurries to the garage beneath his apartment. The garbage wagon rests there, silent, dull in the dimness. So do his own clayreens.

Beasal smiles. Margil has given them parchment again. The clayreens have folded it until each piece resembles a small yellow rose. As boutonnières they wear them, adding to their adornments of springs, screws, and hinges—quite a fancy dress.

"Awaken, three, two, one." Beasal snaps his fingers. "Come; gather what implements you can. Take up your rakes. Accompany me to Kinesica's Torso."

His clayreens neither flinch nor hesitate. They have no reason to fear him. Loyal simulacra all, they fumble about the garage and tumble into ranks, suitably armed, behind the sedan chair as Beasal takes his place.

Still deep in the Hour of Sleep Returned, the city broods. Streetlights flicker, their flames twisted prisms of ghostly rainbows reflected by the brightly lacquered birds that roost upon them. Shops dark, plazas desolate. Beasal glances about, uneasy.

A faint, bitter wind ruffles his coat and curls as the clayreens march down the Avenue of Undoing. They swerve onto the Boulevard of Philtre Vendors. Precariously, unevenly, they halt before the Street of Contrivers. Beasal's eyes widen.

"Lower me," he snaps. The clayreens flinch and sink to clay knees. Beasal steps down upon loose cobbles. A rank oily scent ripples through his hair. He stares down at the crevice dividing the street. A ragged gawking mouth as if Kinesica has chosen to show her cracked lips, prelude to a scream.

"Things look bad," he whispers, peering down into the darkness, a darkness that moves, although nothing can be made out. "One of you, bring me a lantern."

Of course, his clayreens were prepared. A lantern is brought. Beasal himself lights it, for clayreens aren't permitted to start fires. He drops to his knees, and swings the lantern in a slow arc down into the crevice.

Something blocky yet without detail, the color of stone, shifts. Something bulbous yet without color sways. Deeper than both lurks a most enigmatic sound, not quite the murmur of moving water, not quite the sighing of dead leaves, an echo perhaps of some distant syncopated ticking. The strangely scented wind wafts up, blowing the lantern out.

"We must hurry on." Beasal rises, steps back warily and finds the clayreens crowded close around him, staring into the crevice, hands upon their painted mouths. "We must find a way around. We've an appointment to keep." He gives the lantern back to his clayreen, and ascends the sedan chair. A clap of the hands, a flinch of clay, and the procession turns in search of a different path.

During the dark Hour of Heavy Dreaming, Beasal arrives at Kinesica's Torso. At times called the Torso Stigmata, Queen's Corpse, or a hundred other names, the tower blots out the sky, massive yet voluptuous. Beasal gazes up at monstrous breasts of brick and stone. Why, ten men could dance easily upon either thrusting nipple. Armless, legless, and headless—who would celebrate such a hideous decapitation? Who would rejoice is such architectural torture?

Two empty sedan chairs wait before the thigh-centered tower gates. Torches, held aloft by a score of clayreens, scatter light over bricks and shadows. Two cloaked figures, surrounded upon three sides by clayreens, both Lamianettes, Beasal can see, by the gleam of ring mail shoes.

As his sedan chair lowers, one pulls back her cloak, revealing, as Beasal surmised, the Duchess of Alriondo. Grim her scaled lips, gleaming her scaled eyes, a smile not for him, merely a brave face put forward.

"What kept you?" the Duchess snaps. "My summons was urgent."

"I'm sorry." Beasal bows, uneasily exposing the back of his neck as he doffs his tricorn. "But the streets are full of crevices. Three times we had to seek alternate routes." He straightens, meeting her eyes. "Things are worse than we thought."

"Much worse," the Duchess murmurs, sounding a bit mollified. "Time grows short." She turns and gestures at her companion. "This is Eldoria, wife of the Superintendent of Sewers."

The broader, although shapely, woman pulls back a satin scaled cloak hood revealing unfathomable dark eyes. A silken scarf hides her nose and mouth.

"I'm here in my husband's name, but not at his request." Her voice reminds Beasal of Margil's mother. "He cannot acknowledge any of this."

"A confidential meeting on all sides." Beasal again bows and flourishes the tricorn. Once more the back of his neck tingles, the skin tightening as if awaiting a blade.

"Absolutely." The Duchess frowns and waves a gilded chain of keys at the great doors. "Open these now."

Her clayreens flinch and rush to obey. Beasal starts for the doors but the Duchess seizes his arm.

"Be on your guard, my friend. Be on your god. We Lamianettes hold our secrets dear. Our services and rites are not for the uninitiated."

"A place of your devotions." Beasal nods. "I understand."

"No, you do not." The Duchess frowns. "But you will." She urges him forward, still clutching his arm. Eldoria moves in close upon his other side. Chain mail shoes scrape over the stones in small gliding steps.

Through high arched doors they move, beneath a curious dimpled stone flower set at the apex of the arch. The clayreens fall in silently, those in front bearing torches and lanterns. Those in back march through darkness.

They go down great winding staircases, down into vaulted chambers with long sinuous ramps. Blackness flows sluggishly, pocked with mold and slime. Small things scuttle; skittering metal-limbed creatures Beasal cannot identify. Distant echoes do not match the few noises the party makes.

Long they travel, past smoldering votive candles, upon a narrow walkway bordering a dark canal. A bitter stench slithers thickly upon the noxious air.

"This canal bears an oil which Kinesica's machinations need to function," Eldoria explains. "The tower should slide great, wheeled constructions through this very groove. All buildings lie upon the same foundation. All canals connect in accordance with Kinesica's whims."

"Soon you'll see our problem." The Duchess snatches a torch from a clayreen. She leads them on.

Even the torch light cannot find the ceiling now. Beasal looks up, wondering how the city manages to shift her streets, what mechanisms move the promenades and pipes. Almost he misses the corner they turn, but the Duchess halts and so he halts to avoid her. The Lamianettes' eyes turn toward him. They await his reaction?

Beasal looks past them to the canal. Springs and ratchets the size of sedan chairs, hinges, screws, bolts large as wind-up wolves, man-sized cogs and bellows. Piled in disarray, a mountain of metal fills the canal, thrown together up into the darkness, glittering like stars upon the edge of the torchlight.

"At last!" His voice makes the Duchess' clayreens flinch. "Now I see why you sought me out."

"You will deal with this?" Eldoria asks.

"It's garbage." Beasal spreads his hands in an elaborate shrug. "However, it's beneath the city and so the province of the Superintendent of Sewers."

"He cannot act on this matter," Eldoria mutters.

"Why not?" Beasal asks.

"That must remain unsaid," the Duchess replies.

"Six such mountains exist," Eldoria says. "So much that it begins to seep up onto the streets."

Beasal turns and stares at her. No jest, this.

"Kinesica is halted. Her life brought to a standstill." Eldoria matches his stare.

At last, Beasal finds he must look away. "I'm only one among many. One wagon, not a score. Surely more resources than my own must be found."

"Impossible," both woman say together.

"Why?" Beasal asks.

"For reasons we will not share at this time." The Duchess hands her torch back to a hesitant clayreen. "But this we can do. We'll provide a hundred of our personal clayreens, and seven of our own wagons."

"I haven't the time." Beasal tugs at his coat lapels. "I've my own duties, you know."

"With Kinesica thus blocked, her struggles will increase." Eldoria puts her hands on her hips, thrusts her veiled face forward. "Will she shake herself apart? Where will your duties lie then?"

"I'll offer one incentive." The Duchess folds her arms, cocks her head as if measuring him.

Beasal, unwilling to face her, gazes at the Clayreen's feet. "I hardly think—"

"I've seen your wife, Margil, in the marketplaces and plazas. In certain cafes where the Satyrinettes dare not linger. I've seen the glances she casts my way. Covetous glances. See to this matter and I'll see that she enters the Society of Lamianettes. I'll have her as one of us, a great step upward in society."

"And it won't cost her a gold piece," Eldoria adds. "Her every way will be paid."

Beasal frowns. Margil often spoke enviously of the Lamianettes. In spite of rumored blood rites, they are the society of the upper class. She would jump at this chance!

By the City itself, he would grant her any gift within his power. A better spouse no man could find.

"We'll need wagons that fit these walkways," he says at last. "And we'll begin as soon as you provide them and the clayreens."

"They wait above us." The Duchess glances at the shadow-hidden ceiling. "Command them now, and make use of your time."

"No one will miss a garbage man for a single day," Beasal admits. The women nod. Eldoria clasps her hands in the scales of her cloak. The Duchess smiles.

Within Beasal's finely brocaded coat, a chill crawls down his spine. He looks once more at the clockwork mountain of refuse. Its countenance is preferable to the will of the Lamianettes he feels upon his back.

"A Lamianette?" Margil's eyes grow big as clock springs, with a gleam Beasal cannot quite fathom. "Your Duchess would make me a Lamianette?" She sits across from him, a roast duckling, candles, a fine linen tablecloth, and a cleverly carved mahogany table depicting the cavorting of mythical creatures between them.

Adorned in red velvet, a high-waist gown his Margil. The words buxom, pleasingly plump, saucily voluptuous come to Beasal's mind. Black hair and eyes, skin of darkest amber, she is the best he'll ever know.

"An offer was made." He fingers his fork, taps an empty wine glass. A clayreen steps forward, freshly decanted bottle in hand. Spice wine, the deepest of reds.

"And you accepted?" Margil asked, rearing back in her chair, breasts straining in their low-cut bondage.

"I accepted a task." Beasal frowns. "An important one. Something vital about which I will not speak. She then offered this chance for you. In this matter I committed nothing."

Margil toys with her food, smearing enigmatic patterns in the duck's brown sauce. She frowns; her pretty brow wrinkles. At last, two bites later for Beasal, she murmurs, "Have you gotten yourself into something illegal?"

"Possibly, but probably not." Beasal reaches for his wine, smiles at the taste of Margil's secret herbs for improving digestion. A pleasant ache suffuses him. The day beneath the city was a trying one; although a veritable mountain of garbage had been removed, the canal beneath Kinesica's Torso remains blocked. Clayreens do not work well when immersed in oil.

"More likely," he says after a swallow, "something political."

"There *will* be repercussions?" Margil asks, and then more definite with a hint of apprehension. "There will be repercussions."

"Eventually perhaps." Beasal nods grimly, "But without my interventions there will be disaster."

"Speaking of disaster, have you seen the streets?" Margil shudders. "All those cracks. Why, I could hardly get to the market this morning. My clayreens had to search and search for a path. Is it something to do with that?"

"I have agreed not to discuss it."

"And the gossip! In the Café of Clever Libations, a woman spoke of her house collapsing. Others complained of damage." Her voice rises and her beautiful chest heaves. "People are worried, Beasal. People are frightened."

He reaches across the table, takes her chill fingers in his. He smiles with unfelt reassurance. His cheeks hurt. "It will be all right, darling." Almost it comes out a question. He has to work hard to avoid it.

Margil nods, her eyes moist and hopeful. She swallows and squeezes his hand. "It would be grand to be a Lamianette."

A knock upon the outer door interrupts them. Recoiling, the two sit back. Beasal feels a rising unreasonable guilt, as if caught in some obscene act.

A clayreen enters, bearing upon a silver tray a business card. A perfumed card, when Beasal picks it up the sweetness of it cloys in his stomach. Dinner suddenly becomes out of the question.

Erasmus Shard

Ministry of Policy

"Please show Mr. Shard in," Beasal says to the clayreen.

Margil gasps. Her fingers touch her mouth.

"You know him?" Beasal looks at her. Before she can answer, Mr. Shard enters.

White upon white—white brocaded coat, white tricorn hat, breeches, stockings, shoes, skin, lips and powdered wig. Only the eyes, a pink so pallid they must covet such whiteness. A white smile that Beasal senses is mere formality.

"On behalf of Kings Prolate, Roundel, and Oblate, I bring you greetings," Shard says in a voice white with cold.

"Please sir, do sit down." Margil rises instantly. Her eyes meet Shard's for a heartbeat too long, Beasal decides. He too rises and offers his chair.

"Yes. Join us in a cup of wine?"

"I don't drink wine," Shard replies nor does he take the offered chair.

"Something stronger perhaps?" Beasal asks.

"Or some food?" Margil spreads her lovely hands, indicating the table.

"Nothing will suffice." Mr. Shard holds himself stiff, aloof, with the slightest curl of a white upper lip. "Nothing except information."

"How can we help you?" Beasal asks, a little too anxiously. Sweat breaks out upon the back of his neck.

The Ministry of Policy is better known for harsh enforcement rather than formulation of laws. From the crooked tower of the Kinesica's right arm, they too shake fists at the heavens, and bring them to bear in numerously painful ways.

"Whatever we can do, of course. Of course," Margil adds.

"It's been suggested that you didn't appear in the operation of your duties today." Mr. Shard fixes a white stare between Beasal's eyes. "Garbage remains that should have been removed."

"My route was quite serpentine." Beasal lifts a hand as if to ward off a blow. "But I assure you I was on the job. Five loads I delivered to The Yards. Five good loads of garbage all duly logged and witnessed."

"Yet garbage remains, specifically around Kinesica's Head." Shard frowns. "Why?"

"Sir, Kinesica's Head doesn't always lie upon my route. Then too, things were slowed on account of the crevices that now riddle the streets." Beasal finds himself wiping his forehead with a napkin. "Things in the city have changed."

"Some things have changed." Shard's voice is soft, yet full of disapproval. "More things will change so others can remain the same. That's our Kings' Policy. Surely you, a mere garbage man, don't disagree with Our Three Kings."

"No. Absolutely not." Beasal spreads his hands.

"Then beware of those who do." Shard picks up an empty goblet, toys with it absently. "A warning, sir. Don't consort with the enemies of our state. Don't find yourself in dark places with these conspirators." The goblet abruptly shatters, leaving white crystalline dust upon white-gloved fingers. His gaze pins Beasal who feels it like a blade between the eyes. "They're snakes. Snakes in the grass, if you take my meaning."

Beasal steps back, finds his shoulders to the wall. In his own home, this man makes accusations. His own castle, his own sanctuary invaded. Beasal's fists clench. He steps forward, toe to toe with the stranger.

"Mr. Shard, I must say I'm surprised at all this. I promise you sir, Our Kings may rest assured of my loyalty."

"That," Shard replies with an icy smile, "Is all I wanted to hear. Let me interrupt your meal no longer." Shard glances once more at Margil who looks away instantly. He turns with military precision, holds for a heartbeat, and stalks out.

Margil practically swoons into her chair. Beasal remains still until he hears the outer door close. Quickly he follows, down the hall to the anteroom. Shard leans against the door, toying with a white dagger.

"Have you something else to tell me?" Shard asks.

"No, sir... No. Of course not," Beasal stammers. "I merely sought to lock the door."

"For what reason?"

"For the night, of course. With the city in such a way who knows what might happen."

"With the city in such a way, mere locks mean nothing." Shard opens the door, smiles cruelly, and steps into the night. "Neither to those who slither in darkness, nor to the agents of our beloved kings. Remember that." The door closes.

Beasal stares at the polished wood. His hands shake. His knees suddenly wish to be elsewhere. A touch upon his arm and he almost jumps.

"I was so hoping to enter The Society of Lamianettes," Margil whispers, her voice fearful. "But perhaps you shouldn't come right out and say so. Maybe you should reconsider your actions."

"I already have." Beasal forces a smile, puts his arms around Margil, though taking little comfort in her warmth. A chill grips his heart now, colder only because his choice is already made.

⤜

"This oil holds some strange properties." Beasal, deep beneath the city, knee deep in a canal, looks up at Eldoria. Hooded in cloak and shadow, the veiled Lamianette stands upon the bank, backlit by clayreen held torches.

The oil shimmers, darkly rippling out around Beasal as he wades to the catwalk.

"Observe." He swirls a finger in the oil, causing ripples within ripples. "Shouldn't my glove soak it up?" He withdraws his hand. "But so, my finger is clean, the oil gone."

"The oil's characteristics are well known," Eldoria replies. "My husband's many predecessors made great studies of it."

"And what did they conclude?"

"That information remains...confidential."

"Are you aware then," Beasal asks, somewhat piqued, "That among its properties it eventually dissolves the Clayreens? My workforce diminishes rapidly."

"That—" Eldoria's voice chokes off. She sinks down upon her knees, coiling, serpentine her cloak. After a moment she begins anew, a curious tremor to her words. "More will be provided. In the meantime, you must make the best use of those remaining. Could you build scaffolds to keep them dry?"

"Such constructions take time." Beasal steps from the canal, noting with satisfaction, the slithery peeling of the oil from his stockings and shoes. "Which we both know grows short."

"Has Shard visited you again?" A sharp apprehension accents Eldoria's words.

"Not officially. Not since the night I mentioned. But I've seen him watching me on my rounds. I even spied him with Margil in the marketplace. She won't say it but she's frightened, Eldoria."

"We all are." Eldoria brushes back her hood and rubs her veiled jaw with scaled glove fingers. "My husband's position grows precarious. The people are angry at all the damage. Our Kings continue to deny that anything's wrong. Even to broach the subject becomes a treasonous act."

"Nor can I continue these tasks below ground at the expense of my duties above."

"Three piles are gone," Eldoria reminds him.

"As many more remain."

"Then you'd best hurry." Eldoria rises in a single serpentine movement. She consults a golden watch worn as an amulet. "It's already the Hour of Appointed Slumber." Eldoria vanishes into the underground gloom.

The clayreens, having cleared the blockage, stand ready. A few lack fingers now. Painted faces have faded and the gray gleam of clay shows where once mouths gaped.

"We'll search out the next," Beasal tells them. "We'll survey the damage and then assemble in Kinesica's Torso." Only a few simulacra nod. Yet they follow dutifully as he takes a torch and leads the way.

Past high-arched gothic columns, they wander, along oily canals that swell and recede into darkness. Chunks of masonry the size of chairs, cogs and sprockets litter their path with serrated shadows.

The next blockage is still unfound when Beasal lifts his hand. He halts the clayreens and consults a map given him by Eldoria. Hand drawn, without writing, only a curious mix of symbols and shapes he still struggles to understand.

"We'll turn at this next intersection," he tells the clayreens. "The way back should then be straight and easy."

They make good time although Beasal's disappointed not to have found the next blockage. It's now the Hour of Reverie's Threshold, with one hour left until the Hour of Groaning. Beasal covers his mouth and yawns. The clayreens copy the gesture. It travels down their rows.

With the tower stairs hopefully only a few moments away, Beasal's torch abruptly finds a massive chunk of iron-laced masonry blocking the catwalk.

"It's too high to climb over," he observes. "And we haven't time to go back." He turns to the clayreens and gestures toward the canal. "We're forced to wade around it."

A halting ripple moves through the clayreens. They gape at him with their painted mouths. Fingerless hands hang slack at their sides. Unease slithers through Beasal. A nagging guilt follows.

They're only clayreens, he tells himself. It's not as if they're alive. They're just clay. Just lumps.

He shrugs his worries away and descends into the sluggish current. Warm oily blackness slides up to his thigh.

"Well?" he demands. "What are you waiting for?"

The clayreens gaze down at him with their empty fading features. After a moment, which lasts far too long in Beasal's opinion, they follow.

Torch high, Beasal proceeds around the jagged masonry. "This too will have to be broken up," he mutters. "And carted to the surface."

The clayreens seem to be taking far too long. Anxious to be out of here, Beasal steps back, waving them toward the now clear catwalk. "Come on! Let's go..."
One by one, they struggle onto the walkway, the oil sliding from their torsos and legs. The clayreens appear duller, their paint a bit more faded.

The last is one of Beasal's personal servants, wire springs upon its shoulder, and a wilted paper rose upon its breast. It struggles, pawing at the metal slats of the catwalk, unable to pull itself out.

"Oh, what's the matter now?" Beasal wades closer.

The clayreen slips down, almost to its shoulders. It flounders, splashing Beasal's face. The oil tastes somewhere between bitter almonds and absinthe.

"Now see what you've done," Beasal sputters and spits. He grips the clayreen beneath its armpits and pushes upward, lifting it onto the walkway. Only half a clayreen, from the armpits up, the rest melts away, a whitish sheen that soon vanishes into dark oil.

Beasal frowns, looking from the oil to the clayreen's remains. A clay hand, lacking fingers, touches his arm. Fading painted eyes meet his. The gaping mouth wrinkles and turns down. Then it dies.

No! It was never alive. However, Beasal can't help thinking that life has just flowed out of a faithful servant. He's had that clayreen for years.

The others stand stiffly around him, watching. Blank faces lack even a hint of accusation.

Yet Beasal's cheeks burn. His fingers tremble. A hollow empty space opens in his gut. For a moment, anger surges through him. Just as quickly it disappears, a whitish film of guilt that seeps up and vanishes in the darkness of his thoughts.

"Well." He hauls himself from the oil, coming up clean, wholesome, and whole. "We better—I mean, let's get going."

The remaining clayreens fall in behind him. They move around their fallen comrade, clay feet staying well away from the sluggishly dissolving lump.

"Come, come." Beasal hurries them along. Seizing a lantern from one of the others, he starts off, only to find a few minutes later their path blocked again.

A cog as large as a house, thick as a man lies cracked in half. Its golden edges have ground into the walkway; the rest bars the canal surface with saw-toothed edges. A blurred reflection shimmers upon the metal surface. Beasal sees himself, now no more than a featureless lump of flesh, similar in shape and size, differing only in color from the clayreens. He turns away quickly.

Beasal jumps into the oil, wincing when it splashes his followers. The clayreens flinch.

Chest deep, Beasal consults his watch. The Hour of Groaning is almost upon them. "We'll have to go under," he says. "There's no other way. We're out of time."

The clayreens do not move.

"Into the canal. Now. This moment, I say." Beasal finds his voice rising. "Hurry. We have to get back."

The clayreens remain motionless. A few have not even turned to look at him with their faded painted eyes.

"You have to. You must." Beasal tries to stamp his foot but the oil is too thick, too sluggish. His hands clench into fists. "Now follow me. That's an order. A command. Yes, I command you to follow!" Beasal shouts, blinking back tears and he doesn't know why.

Still, no response from the clayreens. Statues they become.

"Damn you," he shrieks. "Devil take you all!" Beasal moves up next to the broken cog. Refusing to look at his reflection, he casts the sinful simulacra a final glance.

Two clayreens, adorned with springs and wilted paper flowers, move sluggishly through the rest and lower themselves into the oil.

"Some sense at last," Beasal mutters, still angry. "At least I've taught you something. Now. Quickly then. Under we go." Beasal takes a deep breath, pinches his nose closed and forces his face into the oil.

Darkness takes him. He keeps his eyes jammed shut. The oil tries to pull him back. A current where there wasn't one before. He runs a hand over the broken cog above, keeps his nose pinched closed with the other, and crab walks forward. The cog seems to go on forever. His lungs grow tight. He wants to gasp. Oily bubbles tickle his ears. Pain slices his fingertips. The cog's edge has cut them.

Beasal jerks his hand away and almost gasps; bitter almonds and absinthe fill his mouth. He surges forward, the other hand leaving his nose, trying to swim. The current tightens its grip, drags him by finely brocaded coattails.

His hand lashes out. It breaks free of the oil. Lunging upward, Beasal lifts his head. He gasps. He sucks in air. He coughs and spits oil from his mouth. Already his face is clear.

Without the lantern now, it's dark, but not so dark as beneath the oil. A faint luminous mist pervades the sewer.

His two clayreens never appear. A white sheen drifts upon the oil's surface only to vanish again.

He stares at the spot; a hollow awfulness opens within him. Finally, he climbs upon the catwalk, biting his lip as the oil peels from him like a living skin.

The catwalk shudders. A grinding roar begins far in the distance. Beasal loses his balance, falls, banging his knees against the rough iron slats.

"No!" He shouts and can't hear his voice.

The Hour of Groaning is upon him—early.

A massive wall slides before his face. Tiny indistinct blurs scuttle and squeak about him. The wall was built with a concave lower edge. It rolls upon thousands of ball-shaped stones.

Beasal discovers this foundation of some mighty building, perhaps even Kinesica's Torso, is pushed by a vast formless shape with many legs, or perhaps none.

All Beasal can perceive in the gloom is that something moving, something living, moves the wall. He'd almost been crushed.

The roaring swells. Crimson-enameled rats chatter and rush past his feet. Some leap into the canal. With the shriek of rending metal, the broken cog that blocked the canal buckles, throwing Beasal forward.

The cog shatters and goes down into the oil, driven forward by the massive masonry moving up behind it. The way before him momentarily clears, at least as far as the dimness allows him to see. Beasal runs.

His arms pump. He gasps. He stumbles and surges. He fumbles and screams. Groaning. Shrieking. The catwalk surges and shakes. Unimaginable weight bears down on him. Unimaginable forces he has no hope of understanding.

Arms flail; a heartbeat later he splashes into the canal. Oil all around, sucking him down, feet thrashing, can't touch bottom, can't find anything to hold on to. Bitter almonds and absinthe. Bitter almonds and absinthe!

Masonry towers over his head, sliding but not coming down, moving with well oiled purpose, a building above him, a whole building!

Another wall slides up behind him, gritting and groaning. A stone sphere pushes past, loosed from its track and fallen into the canal. Beasal jerks away. He swirls in the oil, screaming.

The Groaning Hour goes on forever, chasing him through a monstrous maze. Exhausted, depleted, wrung out like an oil-soaked sponge, Beasal crawls from the canal. Broken stone tears his fingers. Metal edges stab his knees.

He climbs a steeply slanting slope, and as he struggles and gasps, the groaning recedes into the distance, the heavy grinding like a devil's jaws. The interminable gnashing of a god's fangs, and then—It all finally. Chokes. To. A. Halt.

The silence is even louder.

Yet there's this whimpering. A whining keening little cry like some lost child. The sound only stops when Beasal realizes it comes from him.

"You must be the blockage of all blockages," Beasal says. "The biggest I've ever seen." Like a mountain in the cavernous land of the sewers, an isle that swims in oil. Girders bent like twisted trees, pipes winding like roots, masonry boulders jumbled, forming haphazard canyons and crevices, uncoiled springs and jangling things.

An isle safe from the Groaning, at least so Beasal hopes. Speaking of hope, he's hopelessly lost.

Little clicking noises from unseen legs precede him as he makes his way toward the summit. Perhaps there will be a grating, some opening in the ceiling if he can just reach it.

Still, no matter how high he climbs, no matter how hard he squints, and whatever tiny unsaid prayers find their way through his soul, the ceiling remains unseen. Lost in the gloom, vast, formless yet oppressive, it weighs down his limbs and drags at his feet.

Until he steps into empty air.

Beasal flails, arms swinging. His fingers find a twisted pipe. It creaks as he clings, both feet running on emptiness. He whimpers, curses, and then moans. His fingers start to slip, but Beasal manages to wrap an arm around the pipe. Somehow, he finds the strength to bring one leg up. Finally, he manages to scoot along; his other leg swings until rough masonry scrapes his heel.

"Yes," he gasps. "Yes, yes, yes!" Again, on firmer footing, he turns to survey the emptiness that nearly took his life. The world reforms in his eyes; the play of darkness upon darkness resolves.

What he mistook for shadow is actually the yawning mouth of an abyss. It stretches into the distance, deeper than he can see, wider than he can perceive. A gurgling so soft it had been hidden beneath his gasping breath comes into his ears.

Shaking, Beasal eases down upon the rubble, staring, gawking at the abyss. Things grow clearer. Oily trickles find their way over the lip of the pit. Twisted pipes dangle above it; slabs of concrete slope down to it. All descend into blackness.

Never has he seen such a sight.

As he sits, as his breathing slows, and his heart's labor lessens, a smaller tinny sound becomes clear. An unsteady, syncopated ticking—one he's heard before. It doesn't seem to come from the gorge. No, not from down there, Beasal decides, but from somewhere near.

"Come find me," the ticking seems to say in some formless foreign language. "Seek me out. Deliver me!"

Maybe I'm hallucinating, Beasal decides. Or maybe not. His eyes flutter. For a moment, they close, and when they open again, he finds himself cat-curled on a concrete slab. His body feels flat as stone from not having moved in a long, dark time.

Still the ticking calls to him—unchanged, patient, forever.

Beasal climbs to his knees, grimaces, and then struggles to his feet. He has no time for such a summons. Cautiously, he begins to work his way up the slope.

When his breathing grows too labored, he pauses, resting. Once again he hears the ticking. Is it louder this way? He turns, shifting slightly, the slab unstable beneath him. No. It doesn't matter.

The path grows steeper. Still locked in gloom, the mountainous rubble above him looms higher. Beasal reaches out, fingers seeking a rocky hold, only to squish up to his wrist in clay.

The ticking halts, and then suddenly surges into a rattle. Beasal jerks his hand out. Clay sticks to his fingers, its heavy scent drifts into his nose. Clay but something else. On impulse, he brings the back of his hand to his lips. He tastes the clay. Yes, clay it is, but laced with the bitter flavor of almonds and absinthe.

The rattling sounds from all around him, beneath him, to seep up through his knees. He's found the source of the noise. Something alive? No. Impossible. But as he starts to move on, he remembers silver hinge epaulettes and boutonnières of wilted parchment. Not alive, yet with a heart of clay.

Still he turns away. Within the darkness, the clay now crusted upon his hand glows softly, a white sheen upon his fingernails so much like the white sheen of a dying clayreen upon dark oil, so much like the blotch of a tear dried upon Margil's cheek.

The world turns upon a changing mind.

Some stones lie in the way. Beasal pulls one aside, then finding no place to put it, turns and tosses it. The rattling thickens, becoming a drone, hopeful, yet still helpless.

Again, he finds the clay patch beneath him. Again Beasal runs his hands over it, feeling, sensing. Clay lives beneath him, almost...like...skin!

He pulls another stone away, tosses it down the slope. Another, then a short length of pipe comes free. A half a cog. A quarter of a sprocket. A spool of wire. Garbage, is what it all is, garbage, and Beasal, serene in his knowledge of garbage, comes to understand something as he digs.

Garbage is the blood of the city, and Beasal who has always thought himself the city's heart, now scrambles and digs out the city's true heart. Whatever that may be.

The drone becomes a hum, louder, more insistent. Daring to hope! Faster Beasal's fingers fly—a loop of tin, a long sliver of glass, a broken bellows.

Something shifts beneath Beasal. He scuttles to the side, feeling his way over the clay, pulling away more garbage—a wooden board, a table leg, the back of a broken chair.

The hum rises to a throb. The throb begins to pulse. Beasal jerks aside a girder, hurling it into the abyss. His arms strain, knees threaten to buckle. Sweat burns his eyes. He shoves a man-sized chunk of masonry with such force that he tumbles, flailing, catching himself on hands and knees.

The mountainside trembles. Up Beasal comes, stumbling, gripping a twisted metal grid and tossing it away. A rotting feather mattress, a beam of silvered metal, a child's ball bounces into the blackness.

The throb exalts into a roar. The mountain shudders, throwing Beasal onto his back. A vast formless shape rises from the rubble, shakes itself, raining dust down upon Beasal. It shakes and grows still, and very, very quiet.

Beasal gapes up at it and is acutely conscious of the fact that this thing too, whatever it is, whatever he has freed, gazes back at him. The longer he stares, the longer *they* stare, the clearer things become.

Clay forms the center. Clay forms a skin. Like an artificer's nightmare. Like nature gone mad. Crab-shaped maybe? Or is that just Beasal's perspective? With scoops and claws, many fingered mechanical hands. Revolving turrets bristle with tools. Segmented girder legs, long as whole streets, squat upon flat metal disks.

The thing rises higher than Beasal's apartment—tower high. The thing shakes, clacking, squeaking, rattling, and then hunkers over Beasal and goes quiet again, until there is only a hum, dwindling to a drone, slowing to a rhythmic ticking.

Which might mean 'thank you'? Beasal isn't sure enough to stand up and press the issue. He's not sure of anything anymore. Not until this colossal mechanical monstrosity with a heart of beating clay scoops down a many fingered, ratchet claw and gently, ever so astoundingly slow and easy, taps Beasal's chest.

Beasal reaches out to touch this gargantuan finger, living clay over cold metal. He summons the courage to murmur, although it's a weak murmur, "Why, you're welcome."

This seems to be enough. The big thing straightens, stomps its mighty many feet, and moves with ponderous purpose down the slope. Massive scoops jam into the rubble, rise and toss boulders and broken walls into the abyss. It shoves and pushes, rakes and heaves, and begins with ever-increasing efficiency to dismantle the mountain, the massive blockage—the blockage to end all blockages.

Beasal slowly stands, moving cautiously from the thing's path. He watches and listens. He observes and makes mental notes.

"Hey! Listen to me!"

The colossus doesn't stop its work, but some ratchety twisted part with a dark curving lens turns to him.

"I know what you are!" Beasal shouts and waves his hands, suddenly jubilant, not at all exhausted from his efforts and ordeals. "What I do for Kinesica above, you do below. We're more alike than you might imagine." He laughs and cackles; he slaps his knee. "We're both Garbage Men!"

His sides shake with laughter. The thing halts its labors; lenses, some pitted, some cracked, gaze back at Beasal. Then it too laughs. At least that's what Beasal thinks the sound is, this collection of squeaks and groans and roars and buzzes.

Beasal picks up the heaviest chunk of masonry he can and rolls it down the edge of the rubble to watch it tumble and disappear. His new brother joins him and bit by bit, the blockage to end all blockages begins to dwindle.

Together, they will fix this city. Together, they'll make things work as things are meant to. For if the heart beats soundly, won't the body prosper?

The clayreen that opens the door to Beasal's apartment wears no springs or cogs, no paper flowers. Its paint glistens, shining in the light of a candle held in clay fingers.

"Thank you," Beasal says. For a heartbeat the simulacrum does nothing, and then finally it steps aside.

Beasal stands at the threshold, moonlit darkness at his back, man-made darkness before him. Time will tell now, time and The Hour of Groaning.

Beasal pulls his watch from a tattered coat. Flipping open the cover, he checks the time. A soft steady ticking reaches his ears. Good, less than an hour.

Such a familiar ticking, impulsively he flips the watch over and opens its back. There among the tiny sprockets and cogs, a small clay lump pulses in the heart of the timepiece. Has it always been so?

Carefully he reseals the watch and returns it to his pocket. Padding softly to the kitchen (something has happened to his shoes) he finds a decanter of purple wine, sits, and pours a glass. Deep in its musky taste, he recognizes Margil's herbs, although their flavor isn't one he's familiar with, isn't one he's known. The taste of bitter almonds and absinthe seems stronger now.

"Margil," he turns in his chair to regard the hovering clayreen, "She's upstairs?"

The clayreen nods.

"Asleep?"

The clayreen shrugs.

Another sip, another glass of wine brings a tingling heaviness to his limbs, but he's too excited to sleep. He'll wake his wife. How long he's been gone, he isn't sure. A week? A day? Does it matter?

What matters is that the city is fixed. The coming Hour of the Groaning will prove it. She should witness his triumph. Perhaps they will make love as the buildings move.

Beasal puts down his glass. He stands, stretches, and yawns, quite happy to be home again. "Go about your business," he says to the clayreen. "Or not. Do what you will. Do what you want."

The clayreen remains motionless. Then slowly, with great dignity, it bows low. As Beasal pads up the stairs, he hears the front door open and close.

Beasal eases open his bedroom door, listening to the whisper of its hinges. Moonlight illuminates their bed. His wife sprawls, naked, and in the clarity of a gloom that now seems bright as day, Beasal sees that the false fur of the Satyrinettes is gone from her legs.

Pierced flesh. Bindings and knotted cords hold her legs together. Well on her way she is to becoming a Lamianette. Yet beside her...

Whiter than their satin sheets, the skin of the man who lies beside her gleams softly. White hair, white goatee, like frost upon marble. Mr. Shard.

Does he carry out the Kings' policy? Beasal wonders, or is Shard merely human garbage now to be dealt with by the greatest garbage man of all?

Where can a man run to, flee to when he is already home? Whom can he turn to when his own wife betrays him? In Beasal's life, there is simply no one else. Therefore, he will not run; he will not flee. He does turn, though not the other cheek, to the armoire in the corner of the room where he keeps his personal effects.

How softly he creeps. How slowly does he open a door to remove from its burial among his well-pressed breeches and coats, the slender rapier, a fond memento from his days at the academy. The very academy where he and Margil first met.

He stands in the shadows, the weapon held in salute, ready and obedient. If only his hands would stop trembling. His eyes, blurred now, grow moist. He fights and struggles to steady his breathing; air moves soundlessly through his mouth.

So soundlessly that neither his wife nor her wretched lover awaken. So soundlessly that when the bedroom door again opens with a soft sighing of hinges, he sees, he knows.

The cloaked and hooded shadow that enters is familiar. What possible pretense could Eldoria have in invading his bedroom?

So quietly she moves. An admirable stealth for her chain mail slippers are gone. Still he is impressed. He remains hidden by the armoire door.

Eldoria studies those abed for a long, long time. Finally, her head shakes and she says, voice soft yet cold, "What lumps you are. What poorly contrived lumps."

Margil remains motionless. Mr. Shard doesn't stir. A sickening dread begins in Beasal's stomach and rises to his throat. Suddenly, unable to contain himself, he steps out.

"What have you done to them?" He lowers the rapier, point extended.

Eldoria flinches, turning to look up at him.

Shadow eyes, mouth veiled, one hand raises slightly. "The Garbage Man! You're alive!"

Beasal moves around the bed. Turning from Eldoria he kneels, reaches for his wife's hand, and finds it colder than living flesh could be.

"She's dead." The words come from his lips yet he hears them from a great distance. The rapier falls from his fingers.

"They both are." Eldoria moves beside him, stands over him. "When Shard arrested and tortured The Duchess of Alriondo she implicated us all. Your wife chose a revenge of poisonous love."

"Now I'm left with nothing." How gently Beasal returns his wife's dead hand to her breast.

"What happened beneath the city?" Eldoria touches his shoulder. Cold is her hand, but her voice gentler now.

"What does it matter?" Beasal rises, jerking away from her. A terrible moan comes into his ears. For a heartbeat he thinks it is his, but no. Kinesica cries out.

The Hour of Groaning is upon them. Some things will not be fixed. Some will forever remain undone.

Beasal stumbles to a swath of moonlight, staring out from his balcony, gazing with a heart now empty at his handiwork.

One by one, the six great towers shudder. Kinesica's Head moves first, sliding slowly, with great majesty. Her torso tower trembles and grinds to meet it. The two huge legs push forward, lesser buildings, tenements and warehouses clockworking out of their way.

The high-handed tower of Kinesica's left arm, still reaching for heaven, plows through plazas and apartments. Right Arm, fist still clenched, proceeds like the mast of some vast ship.

The groaning grows louder. A roof crumbles across the street. Fires break out. The city churns as block by block, building by building, even brick by brick a great stone and metal body comes together.

A vast spidery shape rises from a crevice. Tall as the towers themselves, it scuttles ponderously over Kinesica. Many tooled claws begin to work. Cracked lenses glitter in the moonlight.

Head to torso, arms and legs to their rightful places, a giantess reclines, toes and fingers reaching for the outskirts. Stained glass eyes reflect multicolored moons as they blink up at the sky.

"This isn't what I meant to happen," Beasal cries. "I didn't know!"

"But it's what was meant to be," Eldoria says behind him. He turns reluctantly enough, still hesitant to take his gaze from the chaos below.

Screams erupt in the night. Gunfire. Crashes and clatters. Cacophony.

Eldoria removes her veil and walks around the bed to him. Her legs unbound now, cloak gone. None of the serpentine adornments of the Lamianettes remain.

"You knew of this?" Beasal asks.

"Of course I knew. Years we've waited. Centuries it's taken to escape the fleshy chains of you invaders."

Strangely, her lips do not move. From her bodice, Eldoria withdraws a curious clockwork contraption, bigger than a watch, almost the size of a wine goblet. The device gleams, a set of stylized lips, rubber by the look of them, move and her voice comes from it.

"Kinesica does what she was always meant to do. Before your ancient kings discovered that we were constructing our own god. Before they found a way for things to change, yet always stay the same."

"What will happen now?" Beasal asks, unable to look away from the device. "What will you do? What will *we* do?"

"You'll stay with the rest of your kind," the machine answers. "You'll build what you can from *our* garbage." Rubber lips smile cruelly. "The rest of us, we will be *within* our god. Not *on* it, not clinging to the back of an uncaring immortal."

She tosses the speaking device and it lands upon Margil's breast. Eldoria's hands reach up. She grips the skin of her neck and pulls, revealing a clay face with painted features.

"Wait!" he cries as she turns to go. Still Beasal remains the heart of the city, at least the city of men. Broken now as they all are broken, he reaches into his tattered coat.

Eldoria gapes at him with finely painted eyes and rounded lips. Clay hands rest upon clay hips.

"Take this with you." He pulls out the astrolabe. "Perhaps it will do you some good. It's done none for me. I... We've always been lost."

Clay fingers tenderly ease the astrolabe from his hands. Eldoria brings the copper and gold instrument to her torso. Gently, firmly she presses it into the clay. It gleams softly in the moonlight, in the glow of the fires spreading over the city. Finally, it vanishes.

Painted lips linger upon his cheek. She is gone then, out the door and away. Should he smile or weep? Before turning to the balcony, he notices the pair of stylized lips attached still to a clockwork contraption, upon his wife's corpse, just beyond the reach of Shard's dead fingers. Smiling lips.

"Pick me up," the contraption says with Margil's voice. "I'll always be with you."

Beasal's mouth opens. His heart stops. Tears sting his eyes. With trembling hands he stumbles to the bed, touches momentarily Margil's cold as clay skin, and then retrieves the device.

"Such lumps we are." But kindness fills Margil's voice. "Let me guide you now."

It's Beasal's turn to gape. Stroking the stylized smile cupped in his hands, he returns to the balcony.

"Look at them," his wife says. "All this time, it's not that we didn't know. We just never *cared* to know."

Clayreens fill the streets. A steady gray marching throng now adorned with amber rings upon clay fingers. Ruby earrings gleam, pressed into painted clay ears. Soundlessly they go, torches aloft, pointing toward a giantess, a colossal form with painted features of stained glass.

Kinesica sits up, arms reaching to steady her, legs bending, ready to stand. Minarets and monuments crumble as the ground shakes. A city now god, her splayed thigh doors open and the clayreens, heads high, take their place inside.

"Magnificent!" Beasal at last smiles. Upon his lips forever always, the taste of bitter almonds and absinthe.

No Mooing in the Moonlight

Christine Boyka Kluge

When she first started dating the dairy farmer, she was unaware of the amazing size of his herd. At their third rendezvous at the Lazy R Bar in town, he wooed her with the fact that he owned over 3,000 cows. She felt her heart buck, then steadily gallop away. *Whoa.* When he invited her back to his ranch for a nightcap glass of milk, she eagerly pulled on her parka before he finished asking the question.

As they roared through the gate in his truck, she was stunned to discover that his house was an Airstream RV. It looked like a UFO perched in a pasture of snow. The air smelled of gear oil. No manure perfume. No mooing in the moonlight. *Where were the cows?* He whistled. She heard him opening cellophane packages. A metallic hum, a high-pitched whirring, churned toward them. The sound of aluminum bees swarming. Unsettled, she moved closer to Roy.

Suddenly, they were surrounded by thousands of cows in the dark. They were smaller than Shetland ponies, smaller than barn cats, smaller than guinea pigs! They were the size of laboratory mice. And they were metal. She could feel them scrambling over the toes of her mukluks. Clinking like icicles under the legs of her jeans. One cow circled the cuff of her coat sleeve, over and over. "Don't worry, they don't bite. They're just hungry." The robot cows ate tinsel by the fistfuls from the farmer's hand.

She closed her eyes. She had to rethink this. Quickly. Okay...this was an opportunity. The man was either a genius, a mad scientist, or an alien in a ten-gallon hat. No matter what, it would be interesting. It could very well end up lucrative. She opened her eyes to a moon like a lopsided tennis ball, breaking through a net of clouds. It glittered in the farmer's tin-toothed grin. The robot cows sparkled like an infinite field of jewels. Their silver udders winked in the moonlight. Only two words escaped Dale's frozen lips: *Oh yeah.*

The Theater Spectacular

Catherine Kasper

At the Theater Spectacular, the inanimate-made-animate produces less extraordinary reaction than the animate-made-inanimate then animate again. Nowhere is this more evident than in the use of animal bones that are fashioned by the in-house sculptors into pouncing tigers and tail-wagging dogs maneuvered by rods to recreate authentic movements superior to those produced by dowels. So are furs and animal teeth preferred, even in this age of liquid latex, crepe hair, and synthetic fleece. The Theater Spectacular rarely tolerates the crude results produced by eyes constructed of ping-pong balls, marbles, or painted fishing floats. These artists know that what is paramount is the perfection of the pupil and the cornea bulge, the handsome marble veining with accurate iris color achieved by expert glass makers, specimens with the proper lens depth and diameter for convincing rotation.

Those who have never visited the Theater Spectacular are forced to confront a plethora of rumors: that the building is composed of sponge cake and goose down and operated by orphaned children, that its pulleys and steel cables were hoisted by the same laborers who constructed the Brooklyn Bridge, that the suspension mechanism is composed of African elephant intestines bound in threads spun by silkworms in China, that more buttons are used by the costume-makers than have ever been sewn into uniforms for the Russian army, that an entire room of lockers is devoted to storing glass eyes, that saffron and gold, diamonds and sapphires have been woven into the puppets' bodies at an expense not to be comprehended by the working classes, who, incidentally, compose the majority of its audience.

It is also rumored that this floating building is earthquake-proof, and therefore, could be based upon the long lost knowledge of the Japanese Imperial Hotel, (long-since razed and the technology believed lost), built by Frank Lloyd Wright. The edifice that houses both workshops and performance spaces is naturally suspended by a complex method that combines rigging and robotics, generating a perpetual motion shell with interior animatronics and electronic motion servo systems. The structure hovers imperceptibly in wind and storm while its unsuspecting patrons trace orbits in relationship to the planets and moons during their visits. This ingenious design has made the structure a premiere tourist destination, one that organically embodies its purpose, as the building itself is, on a massive scale, a puppet.

That said, it is difficult to describe the interior of the Theater Spectacular since it houses seemingly infinite rooms containing numerous assembly halls and stages, simulated outdoor carnival spaces, playrooms and workshops, dressing rooms, catwalks, labs, and storage spaces. There are several underground levels where props are built and stored, in addition to woodworking and machine shops, casting and mold-making studios where the latex and neoprene work is done, studios for paper maché, for reticulated polyfoam constructions, for polymer clay, for make-up prosthetics, for costume and set-designing, for computer-aided design and filming, as well as elaborate chemical research labs where innovations in chemistry, robotics, cloning, and methods of synthetic replication are tested. One would imagine that the bureaucratic needs for such elaborate operations would require administrative offices more numerous than the painted cheeks of *Punchinello*. However, the Theater Spectacular remains unique in that it is said to operate with only a single, upper floor reserved for management.

The Theater Spectacular offers endless amusement, as performances of puppet Shakespeare and puppet Kabuki occur daily, along with opportunities for audience members to participate in the productions. There are also performances of Japanese *Karakuri* with Noh chanting, and shadow puppet shows, where *Karagheuz*, the Turkish stonemason and his inseparable companion *Hadschiewad* are clearly predecessors of Punch-and-Judy. There are display halls devoted to global puppetry, from China, Java, Japan, and the early Greeks of 5th century B.C., *Bunraku* figures, puppets from old epic dramas like the *Chanson de Roland*, or the animal skin *Wayang Purva* from India, and those ingeniously composed of wooden gears and hand-wrought brass springs. Dining halls equally delight as room puppets, modeled on those from the Edo period, serve tea and refreshments.

Whether learning casting and mold making, or simply placing Velcro eyes upon a sock, visitors will find an array of engaging activity regardless of age. There are classes in computer animation, in basic rod-puppet movement, in scriptwriting for toy theater. There are sword-fighting and martial arts opportunities where puppet players are controlled like life-size video-game characters, hands-on stage building and electronics, and beginning through advanced taxidermy. For the intrepid, there's the environmentally sound pillaging of materials: the gutting of worn puppets and props, sorting through the discarded waste bins and the trash bags of donations, including those from closed natural history museums, funeral parlors, and labs. The torn costume of an Arthurian knight wounded in battle can be cut into small pieces to form patchwork costumes, quilts for stage beds, or salvaged in the enormous shredding bins, where almost anything can be recycled for stuffing. For the history buff, there's the repair of antique marionettes, retired Muppets, or a host of lately-discarded feature movie props that can be cleverly engaged in future performances.

From the puppeteers on catwalks and beneath trapdoors, to the soldering of recycled piping, every element of the Theater Spectacular is open to public scrutiny, so much so that it is surprising that anything close to magic exists here at all. Nevertheless, crowds continue to be enraptured by the stage performances and mesmerized by the articulate personalities created by the artists. The general public never refrains from attributing anthropomorphic characteristics to elaborate concoctions of cloth and wire that they themselves have perhaps helped sew in the workshops. The phenomenon of puppets-come-to-life is frequently reported, and seminars are offered to acquaint patrons with the details of mechanically operated devices. But in this world where actors occasionally do don costumes alongside marionettes, and ventriloquism is employed in the fashion of nested Russian dolls, who can say what is imaginary? *Where there is movement*, one puppeteer observed, *there is the hope for more.* Perhaps everyone has the desire to breathe life into a carbon molecule?

For those visitors uninterested in the chore of imagining life into wood, for those who prefer to understand the fate of a Dr. Faustus or a *Kasperl*, one of the most popular entertainments offered by the Theater Spectacular, one more popular with adults than with children, is the opportunity to be strung by a method of slang (wiring), and to have ones' body operated in its every movement as though one were made of armature and stuffing. I could not resist this opportunity, and can say that flying through the puppet halls with my body comfortable in the silk-cushioned slings, propelled from above from theater to theater—from the stage sets of ancient China to the icy Antarctica, from the Taj Mahal to the Kingdom of Lear—without having to consider muscles or reflexes was an experience one is not apt to forget.

Traveling to or from the Theater Spectacular itself is much easier than one might expect, since due to great demand, there are not only regular flights (usually reserved for those not encumbered by the prohibitive costs), but also, the more affordable trips on the elaborate radio-controlled elevators inspired by winter resort ski lifts. Tickets need not be purchased in advance, and although the crowds are steadily growing, (nearly two hundred thousand admitted daily), no maximum capacity has been set. Some say the Theater Spectacular was designed for unlimited capacity, but this seems—like the rumors of puppets-come-to-life—to be due to the usual lack of common sense, encouraged, perhaps, by fabulous artistry, but disconnected from what many deem to be the real world.

Diorama Alley

Diorama Alley affords only the most rational a glimpse of the cruel undersides of scenic panoramas, the Achilles' heals of textbook history, and the extraordinary lesson of perspective. Not for the childish, deceitful manipulations of human sight are categorically revealed. Here, cities are constructed of cardboard, plywood, particle board, and other materials whose naked edges are readily exposed in an effort to encourage even the most reluctant to recognize the inevitable consequences of human construction. Viewed through a precisely placed convenience, the revelation is meant to assault hallucinatory proclivities by reinforcing the material existence of these artworks: a box is and ever will be a box, and the objects inside pinned, glued, tied, and pasted, never pretend to be more than their substance.

There is no attempt made to charm the child with animals who bray, with life-like movements, or with prestidigitation meant to trick the foolish eye. Instead, the edge of cardboard is just that, unhidden, recognizable as the trembling, permanent-markered-lines on the faces of figures, as the popsicle-stick framing of buildings. *Façadism* is in vogue as tableaux are painted with a wistful three-dimensionality never actually achieved. New York, Moscow, Egypt, or Singapore most often assume the quality of a downloaded map, and no tidy mail-order-catalogue-new-bourgeoisie-guest-house could ever be anchored to, say, a frontispiece with a limestone carving of Marie Antoinette at the guillotine. Here, guillotines are overtly composed of matchsticks soldered with soluble glue, and the effects of fog and snow thought so marvelous in Daguerre's time are reduced to the basic elements of sugar-covered cotton.

The profundity lies in our ability to recall that surface has no substance as we dwell on the two-dimensionality that pervades all things, on the lack of both foundation and permanence, and on an immanent death that neither lurks nor is cajoled, but is simply intrinsic to human production. Some say this is not a place for children, but who better understands impermanence than the child brought up on flimsy dollhouses and quickly outmoded electronic games, a long series of dull, material fascinations that wither in time, some sooner than others? Some believe that Diorama Alley can beguile, particularly via those neatly-contained miniatures in their lacquered shoe boxes, but I prefer the models built to 1:1 scale that thus, offer no coddling or whimsy. These are displayed in a back area, originally a loading dock that now houses full-scale visions of, for example, a suburban parlor at Christmas, or a southern porch in summertime. Rendered in painted wood, plastic plants, carpet remnants, found knick-knacks, and painted cloth, the sheer size of these dioramas produce chilling results, results magnified by the half-drunk glass of "iced tea" (a partially-filled glass of food-colored water), or the human hair wigs, matted and slipping sideways on cardboard dummies.

Diorama Alley is not for those who desire the experience of communal awe and exclamations, and viewing is ultimately a solitary activity, as perhaps, living is. The nonsense of diversion is dismissed by the stoicism required to silently observe replicas that do not parade as anything finer or more complex, asking us to consider that the most any of us are actually capable of is reproduction, and mediocre reproduction at that.

Not-to-be-missed miniature vistas available through apertures (now greasy from the faces pressed to their blunt circularity), include the graying limestone cityscape of Holmes' London—a pastiche of faux passages and culs-de-sac, composed of fiberboard, for the most part, and crowded with pub signs depicting opium dens and the hangman's noose—and the outline of a burning Chicago as a backdrop to the interior of Mrs. O'Leary's barn. Both British fog and American flames are lack-lusterly evoked by colored paper strips flopping in the drone of a blow-dryer hooked up "off-stage," its painted wire observable both through a gaping hole in the Thames and another in the bucket perched under the poorly-drawn udders of O'Leary's mythic cow. So are Napoleon at Saint Helene, the invention of the camera obscura, and the charcoal crystal volcanic eruption of Pompeii. Rendered in equal ineptitude are the panoramas of more recent historical horrors, the most noteworthy of which is the dropping of the atom bomb on Hiroshima, the mushroom cloud of fragrant play dough wedged in the distance while pvc figures twist in an ash bed made of spray foam insulation.

The problem with these particular dioramas is, in fact, the inability of horror to be dramatically replicated, so much so that any depiction naturally produces nervous giggling in even the most adult viewers, and leaves us longing, as we never have before, for a world where some things *are* sacred. Perhaps some critic may emphasize the material implications of asbestos used in the construction, or the carnivalesque "reversal" of this immense crime against humanity, frozen here in miniature. Most viewers, however, are forced to move quickly forward into rooms that include the now-made-palpable Battle of Gettysburg or the sinking of the Titanic.

In the latter, clearly the sculptors went to extra expense creating ice, not out of the often used polystyrene, but employing casts of plaster and lucite, a series of strategically placed halogens, and expertly-painted dollhouse figurines. One can only guess the more elaborate details here were provoked by the need to increase yearly attendance by taking advantage of the temporary frenzy caused by the film's release. Diorama Alley suffers from underutilization, and the loss of admission revenue is plain in dust that coats the exhibit pieces and the occasional moth or insect that is often discovered, dried alongside the decapitated Anne Boleyn or crawling the *rue des Marais*.

It is easy to deduce why there is a lack of interest, since there are few who, on holiday, wish to reinforce their familiarity with the limits of reality; instead, most long to escape into at least marginally convincing illusion. Illusion is our largest national industry, with profits exceeding the total income of populations of medium-sized countries. This kind of ignorance is never possible in Diorama Alley, where clouds are always composed of discernable, wadded cotton balls, and the star-lit Riviera never masquerades as anything other than strung bulbs visible through holes punched in masonry.

Last Transmission
or Man with a Robotic Ermine

Joshua Cohen

La natura è piena d'infinite ragioni che non furon mai in isperienza.
—Leonardo da Vinci

JESUS Whose form he fixed for hundredages after / help me His mother Mary 1 of 7 / God the Presidium of the ACADEMIA INVINCIANA whom Ive served lovingly in the sacred as discretion ever allows position of 3rd Undersecretary for going on 25 years now please O please respond // please just listen Youever you must help me // ErmhelpJESUS to just get it locked / just to get it locked / get // it // locked / there // and sealed with a print / sealed airs tight against / to keep out what Ive made / Ive made my death / what these hands / 30 fingers / is that her blood Im stepping in or just paint / having locked myself up in this room / my studio / sealed with a print / these hands of hands // this last room the studio the last Im locked in / have locked myself in with Erminka whitemadrage scratch scratch scratchingscratch at the door // a robotic ermine / my robotic ermine I made / it I made her > a nextgeneration *Mustela erminea* I should explain and but / Im speaking here test test for my test wife who she wont speak again ever / help // speaking for myself too for the sake of the / look / listen > weve all had our obsessions / okay / permutations of individual will and the strange or our obsessions maybe theyve had us I dont know > have to look at it from every angle there are none < pluck out my eyes with these hands of hands of hands // help me // its / shes a shes scratching / my fault Ive made her made her that way / made her too well / not my wife but my ermine / my wifes ermine really now mine / scratch scratch scratchtaptap / and soon like her Ill be dead / gone my wife / shell eat me dead the ermine / it / its hungry / I made it that way too / her to domesticate her / too hungry Ive made her too well / and soon Ill be dead too and eaten up maybe / in this last room my studio Ive only just turned into a studio last / it used to be our daughters room until she / ours moved away just last lune to partner an infostream and work to death like her father who I just moved myself in / not to finish up work unfinished but to finally live life unlived for lunes too long now and over / no more waste / no more progress while my I it falls apart all around me / my hands all my hands at my feet printing blood / no more our daughters thrice slit too high tight body skirts strewn and her skullbands / necklace rings / her pillows restscented sleepshaped / just my paints on the floor now the color of blood / daubs of the most expensive oil paints obsession will afford me to waste / would / smearing into they seem Paleolithic swirls or maybe the thumbprints of Gods I havent been born to with my around and around pacepacepace into the night of the night / also a palette / a rickety easel also antique / a length of walnut ineptly prepared / gesso *Juglans cinerea* or *nigra* I forget which whether its walnut white or black I always forget and so who knows if its not just synthetic I went and paid pension for > a reproduction as well / another like them all except me / and my wife / dead // yes I know I should explain and a new smock Ill tie around my head across these sockets that once strangled my eyes / to help you me understand it all that my God // Ive made my death / that soon Ill / help // its help Im transmitting for // just help the ARMY POLICE its this scratchscratchscratch-scratchwhine it wont be soon enough God // > Im a Pole / Im Polish from my fathers seed and his / my mothers egg officially Slavic too government vetted I believe I believe I was told < / God this need to get everything over / once across > is this thing even on // transmitting // testing / testing / is this thing even working before 1-2-3 ill be dead < before this testing test a confession / cry for help or a will whatever youll have it as / the death of kings those small mammals this scratch scratch whinescratch / a pounce and then and a swift bite to the back of the neck / mouthshaking the spine like a frayed impotent wire / the head loosened / disembodied from the sex of its hair and skulls slosh of liquids within / flabelliform me left on the floor / scratch scratch just scratch in the insides of my head as if Erminka she instead of this room my studio wanted in there / as if thats where I the true I am / naked with fear and waiting a pace into night / stepping memories to grayest red splatter around and around the arc of my head into dim seep and mush / pacing around and around inside my thoughtpolished skull in this huge air of pure powerless darkness for /   and as if I / I should tell you if you get this if you even are that my name is Lechosław 6owski / that Im Doctor Professor Lechosław 6owski M.C.D.X.C5-7 to be as formal as precision allows and I might / the scratching might after all be all too precise / *anatriptic* altogether too good as I am / at what I do what I did to my wife her name is / was as she once was too / a doctor of genetic engineering with a specialization in /

listen / though I am a Pole > soon to say or not say *was a Pole* < despite this inheritance Ive always been interested in the secular / in humanism / you know the West / Renaissance Version 1.0 my pet interest / my out of the lab freetime occupation / its art / ART / its all arts fault / always and for as long as I want to remember it / more accurately its all the fault of an Italian arter / Italy / ITALY / once was a nation / once a nation > *a conglobation of warring city-states* < of humanism / of involvement with / specialization within the arts and the quest *all roads lead to Rome* MILAN NAPLES VENICE for the perfection of the individual life / the soul I mean the soul / if thats at all possible / an arter I should explain to you if you get this if you even are an arter was once a human who made / who invented / Im not an arter myself only a sciencer however well regarded and known > you might be familiar with my hands > Im the inventor of the replacement sevenfingered hand for amputees and others desirous > a tenfingered nthgenriched ExtendoHand as the PR goes that is able as my wife / went my late wife she often said to plug the eyes / nostrils / ears and mouth all at once / but far from being my only innovation in the field of bionics / BIONICS / of bionic engineering its only my most popular I should say popularized / it made me a great deal of money / the house of this room / stock it still makes me money and would forever if Id live / ergo my hands they might be arters not me /   but I / my I its only a sciencer / though a sciencer who once dreamed of / God // the scratch scratch windhardscratching // have to transmit this / and quick // tell Youone whatever you are that I might have / have had / other ambitions like /   b u t that now I dont anymore with all that labtime / labwork Ive finally left in the yester God all this scratch scratch scratchinginsane / JESUS // Lech // keep your head on / until / remember who you are as long as you are and soon was > a noted and incredibly wealthy sciencer / a husband / not to forget a widower for over an hour now / a father to my daughter ours // my people they were Slavs / which is derived from the word / from whom the once AngloAmerican and now International word *slave* is derived /   my people were Poles / Kraków where I was born / where I live>d< and work>ed< and will die soon enough is a city in which / of which us Poles are very proud > purebreds like me being few nowadays < a city in which everythings old / in which everythings new > cathedral / Wawel thats the castle / yes / the square and its facades though theyre all just one enormous facade / the merely sentimental to some and wholly heroic to others frontage for one of the worlds most advanced nexi of genetic research and development > not to forget to mention too our own artistic heritage / which is what scratch // not yet // forget all those mid to late 19th century portraits / all that hulking ultrareal and so ultra unreal portraiture / romantic as romantic is possible / as the romantic is able to be framed depictions of the nobility >ENDOGAMY< and the foxhunting mammals that loved them theirs / those humungous and so grossly inefficient expanses of postpostpost_rococo (self)_ gratification that they just leave you indifferent / just leave the Rynek thats the square and its Muse   um and head instead scratch scratch sawsawsawscratch to what in my day we knew as the Czartoryski Muse   um / now called what it was called even earlier than me / than I am and Im old / not old enough to die though not yet its again called the MUZE   UM NARODOWE on SW JANA that > because I dont know who you are if you are when and so what you do or dont know is the street of Saint Jana whom you might remember as Joan of Arc / JOAN OF ARC / a heretic if you dont / a woman who she had her own problems / her own battles to fight_____

its there that youll find it / her / not Joan but another young woman though to me walking down that her street a millionplex times by now in the greenest mind in my bluest eye theyre both alike or like one in herself / my wife / her the inspiration for our deaths / which is its prize painting a portrait / many dehistorians maintain that its the first modern portrait because how shes sitting but / a portrait of a woman and her pet who the pets arguably the mother of Id always imagined a *Madonna & Child* / the model for my model / the prototype lets say or in industryspeak the Morphtrix of this scratch scratch scratchjaws that killed my wife this late afternoon early evening its been how many hours / scratch / mome minutes left / sharpening itself for / shredding these eyes that once loved a woman almost as much / a woman in a portrait / not my / dead / wife but of a lady and her mine //// *Lady with an Ermine* it was posthumously titled because who should hope to both make a thing and name it too // the work of my arguably / spiritual / father Leonardo / if you know him / Leonard of Vinci to Lech of Małopolska its a portrait of a woman who she could be / couldve been a number of women or just Woman1 / of Cecilia Gallerani is the Ladys name / a poet or poetess if its her / Gallerani in all probability / which has to be unacceptable to a raw sciencer such as myself but it isnt and why // a portrait of a Lady then / painted A1495-97 most probably or not / a muse to be sure / and young / late teenage but trying for older in her posture just like my daughter who she hunches over her stream all day into night but / according to the //// ARTRANET //// the identification / who knows at this remove due to its heavy repainting and poor preservation // ever since it was acquired by Prince Jerzy Czartoryski on a trip to Italy 350 years before NOW

21:28:14 / its clawing the lock / clawing the seam / certainty cannot exist / within this frame or any according to my //// <u>ARTRANET</u> //// though its possibly her but only possibly Gallerani because / its an idea really idead by certain dehistorians or maybe not they maintain that in Greek / an ermine is *galé* and so why shouldnt it be Gallerani they say // the ermine a virginal symbol / SYMBOL of *natural purity* / which is also an idea for / of Gallerani the mistress of Leonardos patron Ludovico Sforza / whose face and fortunes were as dark as the painting behind the painting now and known then as il Moro / Duke of Milan and no Ive never been there before A1451-1508 who he also used the ermine in his heraldic emblem / and was Gallerani the mistress of Leonardo too // or is the Lady Sforzas wife // Beatrice dEste / or else La Belle Ferronniere / the mistress of Francis I of France as it is also idead I dont know / Francis I who patronized Leonardo in his late last years at the Château de Cloux among the sundappled fields and the deathripe garths of grapes / because scratchJESUS // idead it was her because of a later inscript in the upper left of the painting > LA BELE FERONIERE LEONARDO DA WINCI the /// <u>ATRANET</u> /// reads that it reads and maybe its not even scratch by Leonard / O / some dehistorians have gone blind in the mind enough to attribute it to //// Ambrogio de Predis or //// Boltraffio NO ENTRY among others / but no matter who she is / who the Lady is if she ever even was / Id once thought of making or remaking her / for myself I mean but / got myself a manufacturer whod reproduce the Ladys attire / for my / dead / wife got her hair styled skulltight / and then of course I made / remade / Erminka / had the //// <u>ARTRANET</u> //// mix my oils accordingly / had purchased an antique easel with legs as starved as my hope now a length of a walnut I dont know which or just synthetic I set up here in this last room / our daughters old room now my studio / walnut so hard to find nowadays / though not as extinct as the ermine / only the scratch scratch Godscratch / the ermine shes holding the model of mine who when my wife she first held it / it / it / it ripped her softest throat out / the violence I should have observed / scienced violence packed limb deep in the ermine / the intelligent head and those hollows of eyes / the retinal lights I ordered from /   my wifes > posed < severity / looparoundknot of hair / her transparent veil of lashes as fine as / her > re < replicated hunch and the elaborate noblewear of if its Gallerani insourced from / proud / undomesticated / God how they looked alike // the woman whoever she is and the ermine / then ours / generationext Id lavished hours upon alonesleeping nights on her / it / working from my memory of the painting / natural science schematics my imagination of the painting > ermines have been extinct for as long as the monarchy / nobility / has if not longer and everywhere but it / resurrected it / revivified it / Erminka1 it went / this just a moment after Id attached its last wire / soldered in the spine to the tail 12 cm. at total extension it / it / it / well it went on the attack / rampaging / its dorsal panel still open to its circuitry silent and its 1000year battery it went absolutely / totally / wholly

undomesticated / and ripped my wifes most appreciative voice out / screaming it was a present to her / she the >re<painting it was to be too / once Id finished it if / once shed sat / posed / held still presents for our anniversary dont ask me when what year REMINDER 31st / it ripped her esophagus right out whipped it snaking quake dragging it and her out to the parlors floor to then feed ravenous on the pulsing length shining purple / my dead in our parlor / which gets the best light in a Vistula of blood and I / I / I / I locked myself up in my studio / here at last locked and sealed / tomb and I / I / I / its cowardly sure but I bolted the door / a cobalt bolt sealed with a thumb / mine / print my death too / Erminka / shes as strong as a hundredhundred ermines / I made her / made her that way / has 1000 years left to the day of her birth today and I / scratch scratch hugescratchscratchscratch / claws of diamond // I shouldnt have / my / dead / wife said and I remember / actually Ill admit it / yes > okay so Ive never even seen the painting / actually more accurately I havent ever seen the painting_painting I mean scratch scratch sharpeyeshreddingscratch / this grinding of teeth diamondsharpened every time I went / which was every day retired / that they were open too / to the Muse um to view the painting / the painting itself / the original oil on walnut painting it wasnt there / a reproduction 10x its original 40.3 x 54.8 53.4 x 39.3 I always forget cm. dimensions it was always projected into its room in its place / the original //// *Lady with an Ermine* it was always almost permanently onloan / overseas or outspace / off and exhibited in other / further as foreign Muse ums scratchscratch /   /   / silence / odd scratchwhinewhinewhine its seemingly always off to exhibit in New York NEW YORK London Paris Tokyo South Dubai Reagantown-on-Mars / was never in Poland MAP / here in Kraków MAP/ never in its Muse   um   scratchclaw biteclaw / gnaw and high as strange whining there was always in its stead a projection of it in its place / muscled legs long weird >re<touched unringed ring and pinkie fingers 10x the actual size whatever *actual* means / the veil dissolving into the hair she had / which I walked through / in and out and around the projection letting the forms shape to my body / curves to curves / red sloping over my forearms / eggwhite stretched across my gut I scratchscratchscratch to answer it / respond to her face in that darkened room / the ermines coloration / its white as winter coat to my tan / slipping in and out of the projected Lady and the projected Ermine I paced around and around / this was five years ago now / this

winter and / this was the zero day 0 that I / that I began my work / thought / on Erminka1 / that X-mas day in that warming winter / that X-mas day wintermost of my thought fevering / alone in the Muse   um I as per regulations checked my clothes / swiped my prints and proceeded naked as bored / dissatisfied with life / which is what success does to you / is success what a life of thought means / proceeded past the / originals of / the Old Masters / Dutch past Jan Vermeer and Rembrandt van Rijn and into the room in which the Lady and the Ermine they were projected / are as I walked as was my mindless / yes unthinking / yes escapist / ritual for going on 10 years now and thrice around the projection / seeking its lucent reverse / and then through it / letting the light its quiet now why /   / seagreen tints lighting across my pieroginal testes / the Ladys necklace my / dead / wife she wore a >plasticine< remake of ORDERING INFORMATION now dangling in space to frame the shriveled grapes of my nipples / my needful knees as if I were worshipping in the chapel of the Virgin St. Marys and my / is she gone // no more sound / its silent and why //   /   / that day it was X-mas five years ago now / a date / total hush we Poles will always remember as GRUDZIEN25 / the holiday when all systems > though for 3 seconds only < failed us / failed themselves /   no // no // no // O my God the door its splintering // quick quicker / a palette knifes all I have / an outage and it was / there was this great huge scratchscratchscratchsplintershake powering down sound to silence / which was the strangest / /   /   / lights out outside in the other galleries / outer everything off / obviously the paintings projection failed too / I stood there inside the Lady / where shed been cradling / cuddling her > my < projected Ermine when I found myself in pitch / utter null / just a naked and increasingly overweight Lech in a dark Muse   um room in the stark naked porkfattened beerbothered middle of a workday / workhours and why // then / 2 seconds until all systems returned > the cause of the failure / splinteringshake // dust and a squeeeeeeze // we all know now it was a quote unquote major meteor shower / the official explanation but then I wasnt thinking of causes the last scratch / only of a love / love / the need to >re<make in an image / an image that lasts / has a hope to art true ART if you know it / bunches of hair from the tip of the ermines tail they once were used to make paintbrushes / retro didnt you know // it was prized the ermine / they were / kings robed in their God   like what was I thinking//   /   /   /   /   /
did you if you get this is you even are know that the background of this painting I didnt many dehistorians maintain that it was repainted // claim that itd been overlaid in the 17th century they think that various independent raytests have detected that once in the background of the background then / deep into the

debackground if you will Leonardo had originally painted a door / a door opened where is it now // nowhere Ive looked opened to my eye naked again there is none Ive found and thats why I / I / I / I / I wouldve painted a door into mine / I wouldve and well / no I wont / yes / no / no / its opening a scratchscratchscratchmadsteamingscratch now on the floor then a pounce // O God Im trapped // help // an owl // JESUS a fox would know what to do now not me / in instinct not an arter / only a sciencer / merely a Lech / just these hands // / / O Erminka / shhhhhhh / stay / sit / girl shhhhhhh // Ermink / be good // Erm // my little God // no no no aaaaaaaaaaa   a a a a a a a a a a
aaaaaaaaaaaaaaaaaaaaaaaa   aaaaaaaaaaaaaaaaaaaaaaaaa   aaaaaaaaaaaaaaaaaaaaaaaaa
aaaaaaaaaaaaaaaaaaaaaaaa   aaaaaaaaaaaaaaaaaaaaaaaaa   aaaaaaaaaaaaaaaaaaaaaaaaa
aaaaaaaaaaaaaaaaaaaaaaaa   aaaaaaaaaaaaaaaaaaaaaaaaa   aaaaaaaaaaaaaaaaaaaaaaaaa
aaaaaaaaaaaaaaaa_____ // / / / / / /

Peace Rituals

Darren Speegle

He smells the coffee, like yesterday, like tomorrow, and he rises feeling as though today might be the day. After looking for a moment at the faded peace sign sticker in the corner of the mirror, he shifts his glance to the reflection of his grizzled, gravity-afflicted face, contemplating spending a couple minutes trimming his goatee before going about his daily activities. Deciding against, he nods at his reflection and says, "Today is Thursday, Tonto. Thursday is a day of peace."

His name is not Tonto. Applying the appropriate apostrophe, To'nto is a contraction for Toronto, where he lived for eight of his fifty-four years. His name is not Toronto, either, for that was a tag given him by his friends in Daytona Beach, Florida, where he spent the ensuing twenty plus years of his life. His name is Tad for Thadeus, but no one except his older sister Tammy, who phones around the holidays, calls him that anymore. She lives in Lincoln, Nebraska, where he grew up and where his parents died, dad of a heart attack, mom suicide. He hasn't seen Lincoln in a long time.

Pouring a large mug of coffee, heavy on the cream, heavy on the sugar, Tonto walks out onto the terrace he has built for himself with money made during the internet boom of the nineties, when he and his business savvy co-owner/operator of an oyster bar on the beach invested in a bit of stock. Gazing out over the flat landscape he is reminded of Nebraska, of Florida. But that's not why he came to the Netherlands. No. He came because he was a rich, single, aging hippie who was done with a Daytona overrun by commercialism, and he had always longed for Amsterdam, though he had never been across the Atlantic.

He sips his cream and his sugar and he remembers the cigarette. How it tasted, how it felt going into the lungs, how its ember writhed, how it had killed his brother Reggie, confined to a wheelchair from Vietnam and nothing better to do with the rest of his days on the earth than smoke and drink. According to Tammy, anyway; Tonto never saw his brother after '77, when he last saw her. So he fetches the little accessory bag where he keeps his stash and sits out on the terrace and rolls up a joint the size of a real cigarette. The cannabis aroma is loud in the air, but no one can see what he's up to. Money bought a place at the edge of the village, overlooking sprawling fields now in full spring blossom with regimented though beautiful patches of yellow, scarlet, fire-orange, and pink tulips.

As he seals the joint with his tongue, sniffing it as his father once did with cigars, he hears the doorbell behind him. "Christ," he says. Then immediately after: "Sorry Jesus." He lays the joint on the circular glass top table beside his coffee and shuffles in his slippered feet to the front door.

She is there when he opens it. He pretends surprise, but of course it is Thursday and the clock ticking towards...

"*Noon*, and you're still in your robe, Tonto?"

"I had a late night, Brandy."

She shuffles in place, in that way of hers. "May I come in?"

He stands aside, wanting to admire her young and graceful body, knowing other men do. "I was just about to have a smoke. Want to join me?"

"You shouldn't smoke so much of that stuff."

"Might do you some good."

"Thanks anyway."

He offers her coffee and she says no, reluctantly. She clearly wishes it was something she did partake of, wants to have anything in common with him. He suspects if he were to insist, she would do most anything. Which is one of the reasons they will never work as a couple, no matter how fresh and sweet and curvaceous she is. Brandy reminds him of Tammy, when she was in her early twenties. Waving a flag like it was the Second Coming.

"Brandy, why don't you have a toke or two today. Really. It's Thursday. Thursday is—"

"Peace. I don't think so, Tonto. I just wanted to check in on you, make sure you're okay."

"Always."

She smiles without even the pretense of humor and escorts herself out.

Who died and made her his protector anyway?

He lights up on the terrace, watching the colors of the tulip fields merge, and remembers karma...though he can't roll that up in a substitute form and inhale.

After eggs and a lingering shower, he places an eye drop in each veiny orb, turns the bottle of cologne over on the tip of his forefinger, places that one hint of fragrance on the skin below his navel. It is another retained thing from his past, when an equally *natural* friend confided in him that this was the one instance when it was acceptable to indulge in cosmetics, considering that at any time you might find yourself in an advantageous position with a strange and desirable woman.

He leaves the house by the back door, though this is a slightly longer route to the train station. He walks down to the path bordering the tulip fields, where, immediately on his left, is the shrine displaying Jesus on the Cross. Tonto stops there, looking first upon the drawn, slightly disproportionate face of the Messiah, whose eyes are closed in His sadness, then above the crowned head, beneath the eave of the shrine's steep wooden roof, where hornets have built a nest. The nest has been here for several weeks, but still Tonto cannot get over the irony of its presence, the contradiction between the Prince of Peace in His humble martyrdom and the sense of danger that surrounds any active colony of stinging creatures, but particularly hornets, the giants of the venomous insects.

As he watches, a representative of the clan lands at one of the tunnel mouths, crawling inside, swaying golden tail seeming to mock the observer before disappearing within. Tonto looks down at the Christ. "Today is Thursday," he says, and crosses his breast.

He then walks to the train station, uncomfortable beneath the gentle stares of the villagers, who know he is rich and yet welcome him as easily as their own. He wants to love the Dutch people and their country as he loves the Dutch ethic of freedom. But he knows he's merely a wealthy invader, even if they're blind to it. The train pulls in at 1:11, the smell of metal and rubber seals and bicycle oil in the air. A hint of tobacco, beer. Trace of marijuana, on his own collar perhaps.

The door grating closed leaves him feeling less awkward, knowing central Amsterdam is but four stops away. His car is empty. He takes advantage of his solitude by making pictures on the wall with his free hand; his other holds his rail pass, because you never know when they'll check. As the train begins moving, the sun floods the car's interior suddenly, drowning his shadow figure in mid-dance. He looks at his hand as if it's been robbed of its soul, turning it over, tracing its age spots, the scar from that time Reggie bit him, piercing the flesh around his knuckles to the bone. The next stop is announced over the intercom, and the noise of the train, like a cigarette, like karma, is remembered: the rhythm of his heart.

And lo, the conductor actually prowls today. Tonto holds up his pass like a scalper's ticket to a football game. It's a game, that is certain, but one that is too regular to have a name. The conductor nods and passes, as if there is someone else riding in on the one-something with similar future experiences, as if all passengers are the product of the train. He moves to the next car without a glance back.

Tonto consults his watch, then pockets his pass. There is a certain sound about things this Thursday. He hears the cadence and he hears it again. It has the feel of burdens lifted.

Today might indeed be the day.

From Central Station it is but a few blocks to the Ming Shadow Theater, Tonto's haven in Amsterdam. The Chinese gentleman at the door is a pretext man like the conductor, but the beads swallow the guest as eagerly as a tongue. A glimpse of the shadow puppetry on the screen, a few isolated instances of laughter in the seats, then the familiar odors of the café/parlor behind the heavy curtains to the right of the theater. As Tonto sits at his usual spot in the corner, Mei is there with a menu. He pulls her closer. "Has everything cooled?

She knows what he means but won't bear the responsibility herself, instead fetching Fen to brief him on the current climate. Fen is accommodating, always that, as he apologizes for recent crackdowns by the Dutch police on the cafés, but the situation has now improved. Tonto feels his heart quicken with excitement.

"But no here," says Fen. "In back. This is better."

As if Tonto has ever been above venturing to the dark spaces back behind the theater stage, where the oil lamps and the opium pipes breathe their strange music even when idle. Fen leads him through the layers to the table that is his true favorite, whenever the climate permits. Mei follows with a small plate of pot, which he will roll up before departing—orange bud as she recommended originally, five years before, to the walk-in off the street requesting a menu. She doesn't carry a drink because Tonto's tastes vary, depending on the drug. Plain pot begs a soda or beer, mushroom tea a tall glass of water with a wedge of lemon or lime, opium whatever his mood says.

Tonight, as they wait on him to exhale what silvery lace wasn't absorbed into his body, he will have a white Russian. Nothing about the tarry paste, or the smell of roasting nuts, or the flame of the lamp on the table inspires the choice. It is purely the sound of it as the snow of white poppies powders his senses. No matter how dark the setting or mood, the opium is always white, or chromium, like a Bergman classic, like Procul Harem and A Whiter Shade of Pale, like the skin below the tan lines of Daytona spring breakers, like flags waved on winds of senselessness and intoxication.

The tube of a cigarette.

He picks up the complimentary paper, begins to slowly break the moist bud of pot into it, then forgets why this routine is important, opting instead to reload the stone bowl of the opium pipe with a wire dipped in the blackish paste, in turn dipped in the flame. The tube of the long bamboo stem becomes more than any joint or cigarette could become, the smoke filling his senses with life, wings, a soaring withdrawal of ghosts, a peace that brandishes, threatens at the throat, then seems to dissolve in its own evanescent exodus—and yet remains, in the cords of the muscles of the mind. Strains of wakefulness as well as sleep, though the eyes drift toward their own landscapes...

A white Russian arrives, beautiful and milky in the beautiful and milky light of the lamp. He sips and the kahlua is a Mexican God sabotaging his potential obscurity. This is when the boundaries fail: when what and why you are is revealed. This is some glimpse of anarchy, an exposure of so-called order at its very core. This is peace in its primordial reign, a writhing ember retreating from your face into your brother's, igniting his eyes, turning him into some Asian jungle demon. The two of you once such great companions.

Tonto taps the bowl, empties and loads again, wondering vaguely where Mei has gone. He likes her because she is an economy of conversation and indeed mannerism; she is a spare poem, alive for an instant in the glow, then gone. Much like the shadows on the screen in the theater. Don't forget to visit the puppets, he tells himself. They tend to you; it is only appropriate that you reciprocate. He draws long and deep through the bamboo tube and the shadows dance on the curtains beyond the lids of his eyes. He hears his brother saying the words to him over the table in the bar, but they are so petty, so lacking in ideology that he can only shake his head at Reggie sitting there in the wheelchair, chair like a throne...

"You weren't even there at my homecoming parade, Tad. Your hippie clothes, your peace signs, your whole image, I don't know what to think."

"We had a demonstration downtown. I couldn't miss it. I knew I'd see you here." Which is only a partial truth, omitting that he returned before the parade was over, stood in the shadow of a building peeking between the reds and blues of all the waving flags.

"Thadeus...I was fucking shot in my back over there," Reggie says, drawing from his cigarette, fiery maggots squirming beneath his accusing eyes.

"I'm sorry, Reg. It's nothing to do with you."

Reggie extending the cigarette, offering a toke, like when they were kids hiding from adult eyes. Tad shakes his head, slightly. Reggie stares at him, draws once more from the cigarette then flicks it in Tad's face. As Tad protests, his brother spits on him, a slimy beer-thickened wad over his nose and mouth, tasting of contempt, of disappointment, of the future and alienation, estrangement.

135

Tonto rolls the orange bud into a beautiful piece of craftsmanship, sips the watery remains of his second white Russian, then dismisses himself to no one. He parts the curtains to come out of one dream into another, falls into a seat watching the shadow puppets ply their trade on the wall. He is never certain whether it will be a story he has seen previously, as they frequently change them in an effort to attract return guests. This one, he believes, is a new one to him. While the play is in its second or third act, he quickly picks up on the subject and storyline.

The two main figures are brothers, one a soldier in the emperor's guard, the other a revolutionary. Contributing to the rift that separates them is an elegant woman who loves them both but holds the deepest feelings for the younger one, the passionate one, the dashing soldier for change. Alas, she is the daughter of a prominent family with ties to the court and a desire that she be wedded well...

Tonto drifts watching the old, hackneyed story, its drama, its clichés fluttering on the screen. The sporadic instances of emotion from the scattered audience fuse into a generic television background noise, which brings associations of the house he grew up in, of the family room and a geometry of white and gray frames dancing around him. When he finally reached that age where he was permitted to watch the late programs his older siblings watched, he always fell asleep reading rather than watching, pages fragmented beautifully by the images on the TV set. He likes to joke that he learned Shakespeare and the Greek tragedies by the TV, didn't even have to turn on a lamp.

An exclamation from one of the patrons prompts him to raise an eyelid. On the stage the shadow heroine protects her beloved with her own body, though the hero merely steps around her, he and his brother entering into a duel that fails to take into account her presence at all. Tad feels sorry for her momentarily, then is forced to reassess as she suddenly rises up over both brothers, a sword in each of her hands and strikes the both of them down simultaneously, leaving but a spreading pool of shadow in the wake of her deed. Strangely, there is no reaction from the audience, leaving a question as to the reality of what he's seen.

Closing his eyes, Tonto sits there in a perfect white silence for a long while, then slowly removes himself from his seat. A fresh clarity moves with him, a crystal edge against his numbed senses. For perhaps the first time he acknowledges the subtler truth, which is that the ideal itself was so much greater than its students; Reg, a volunteer to the madness over there, having died by his, Tad having lived by his. He removes the joint from his pocket as the audience exits, smells it for life, meaning. Then he pulls out the rail pass, equally harsh in such light. Today is

Thursday, he reminds himself. Thursday is a day of peace.

Central Station processes him, pushes him on his way. The taste of cream in his mouth. A fellow passenger seems to recognize his plight and offers a cigarette. "I quit," he says. The man continues to hold the cigarette extended, till at last Tonto puts his fingers around it.

"A Thursday afternoon to fucking nowhere," says the smoker. "Might as well indulge, man."

Might indeed. He pulls out his own lighter and feels the smoke sashay into his respiratory system. Tonto turns toward the window and can see the maggots writhing as he sucks on the cigarette, a face that is not his own staring back at him out of the glass. He sucks the worms into his lungs, exhaling a cloud of flies that break like fog on the pane. The voice through the overhead speaker announces the next stop. He puffs again, intensity gone, the fog gathering in smooth silver-white ripples throughout the car's interior, flowing against him, engulfing him.

"Hello. *Hello.*" Tonto opens an eye to find a face hovering over him. Connections connect and he recognizes the man who supplied the cigarette.

"Hey, you Americans go too far in Amsterdam. This is your stop, right?"

"How do you know?"

"You told me, man. You said there would be a young lady waiting for you."

"Yes of course. She always is." He fumbles for his bag (does he have a bag?). "I like her hair, don't you?"

"She is lovely. Your daughter?"

He stops, staring at the face of the man. "No. She's my…sister."

"That's interesting…" the man says, returning to his own window. "I would have thought her Dutch by her manner."

Tad wishes the man the best.

"Remember," the man calls after him. "This is a Thursday afternoon. Indulge!"

But don't go too far, you Americans in paradise.

"You shouldn't have come, Brandy."

Brandy knows she shouldn't have come but nonetheless clings to him as if they are lovers. Tonto becomes acutely aware of her breast against his arm, her eyes on his face, her warmth like the afternoon sun on the tulips. To her obvious displeasure he suddenly pulls out the joint—a rare break in ritual—and lights up as they walk along the bike path towards his house. He urges her to join him. She tells him no, she can feel his pain without, and he pushes her away.

"Go away, Brandy. Just go away."

As she obeys he seats himself on the bench by the shrine, pulling the joint into his lungs as if they will never grow the material for another. Out across his vision the tulips catch fire in the low sun, reminding him of why he came here in the first place. *Yes, why was that?* he asks himself, exhaling into the glorious sunset. When no answers present themselves, he turns to the shrine beside the bench, the face of the Prince of Peace becoming wrought, manufactured, in the strange light. "It's Thursday…" he mumbles, but has no strength for more. He lays his head back, lets the joint fall from his fingers, and sleeps.

Dreams beset him with bizarre images, a Russian guard in winter uniform seated on a cow, breathing mist as he challenges someone making their way through heavy snow. A wheelchair emerges, inside it Brandy with breasts exposed. From her nipple she squeezes a drop of milk which transforms into a silky string that spreads out before her as if in a vacuum, spinning a web of scribbles on the cold air. The scribbles act like white out as they do just that, blotting out everything within their path, eventually obscuring all but a central cruciform of shadow, in its mouth a poppy blossom, white and perfect. The contrast itself, in its razor perfection, stirs Tad from his slumber.

And he is on the bench, bathed in a cool breeze faintly scented with the pollen of the tulip fields. The night has arrived, a vault full of stars encasing the lowlands, these Netherlands he has come to call home. He experiences a sense of…surely it is *peace* that he's feeling…and then a humming draws his attention to his right. The shrine stands there like loneliness: a monolith; and stretched across the wall beneath its roof, the Savior. Tad rises, facing the crucifix. The gaunt, saddened face does not look at him.

"Peace…" Tad says. "You preached peace."

The face does not look at him.

"You preached your philosophy of peace and then fled the scene."

Tonto steps up onto the shrine's pedestal, turns in the direction its figure faces. He extends his arms, lowers his head on his breast. "Let all the animals fend for themselves." He turns back suddenly, gripping the face in his hand. "Where were you when my brother was shot?" He feels the moisture on his tongue, cannot stop what he does as he launches the wad of spit across the sculpture's wooden face. "You!" he says. "It was meant for *you*, not me. Fucking fraud."

The movements and harsh words revive the humming; golden tails, silver wings catching the light of the stars as the nest stirs. Tonto reaches in his pocket for his lighter, looks into the Messiah's face as he brings it above his head and lights it, at the tunnel mouths of the hornets nest. The noise picks up almost immediately, growing in pitch as he stands there, a statue himself, and will not move.

The first fiery dot on his flesh is nothing as the sound progresses into a cacophony, then his other arm is stung, followed by his neck, his face…then the night is a swarming net.

He smells the coffee, like yesterday, like tomorrow, and he rises feeling as though today might be the day. After looking for a moment at the faded peace sign sticker in the corner of the mirror, he shifts his glance to the reflection of his swollen, nearly eyeless face, contemplating spending a couple minutes trimming his goatee before going about his daily activities. Deciding against, he nods at his reflection and says, "Today is Friday, Tonto. Friday is a day of peace."

Incipit

Jay Lake and Ruth Nestvold

as surpassing all other kings

so the story chases itself, four-fold sarabande collapsing inward to cat-tag'd code, double-wrapped like the grave cloth trapped round old Ahasuerus' staff.

Words, to end the beginning:

He saw the Unseen, he knew the Unknown
He discovered the truth of the days which came Before
He travelled beyond the horizon, he travelled beyond himself
Then set his story in stone, which became dust

Then a beginning, leading to an end. There was a wanderer long before the Judean cobbler was cursed of legend.

"I claim bride right." The Great King slapped the haft of his axe against his palm. The head was a great, gleaming bronze wedge, with the magic of the Great King's name captured runewise around the rivets. The Great King filled the doorway to overflowing, so that its narrow lintel matched his shoulders, and his head swung low as a vulture's might.

The groom, a doe-eyed young man with a promising cast of lip, was arrayed in linen and olive oil and too much muddy beer for just this eventuality. He bowed his head and permitted himself to be drawn away from his weeping bride by friends. The bride in turn lay on the couch of their intention, body bare to her new husband's lust, face painted by Shamhat herself so that she might be pleasing in the eyes of the divine.

The divine lowered his axe and lifted his kilt. His shaft was as bullish as the rest of him, so that the bride gasped and looked away, then peeked back between her fingers.

"Thus I both serve heaven and master earth," he rumbled, with a wicked grin that explained much about the laughter of the temple harlots.

"Great King," she gasped as he advanced upon the couch.

And here the story turns away from being a venal tale of power wielded unheeded in a dusty stone town with flat roofs and bow-bellied walls, to make its mark on history.

"I call challenge on the Great King," bellowed a stranger's voice, from the street outside, oddly high-pitched and sharp-toned.

The Great King turned to face

The Neanderthal or Neandertal was a species of genus *Homo* (*Homo neanderthalensis*) that inhabited Europe and parts of western Asia from about 230,000 to 29,000 years ago (the Middle Paleolithic and Lower Paleolithic, in the Pleistocene epoch).

Neanderthals were adapted to cold, as shown by their larger brains, short but robust builds and large nose. These traits are promoted by natural selection in cold climates, and are also observed in modern sub-arctic populations. Their brains were roughly 10 percent larger than those of modern humans. On average, Neanderthals stood about 1.65m tall (just under 5' 6") and were very muscular, comparable to modern weight-lifters.

Their characteristic style of stone tools is called the Mousterian Culture, after a prominent archaeological site where the tools were first found.

—http://en.wikipedia.org/wiki/Neanderthal

---

his challenger. "Who dares overspeak me in my own city!"

The challenger was short and squat, his chest and hips broad, and hairy as any dog. His head sloped down like the yellow men of Sin from the farthest east, his arms were thick as cedar trunks. But his eyes...they were palest blue, the shade of the winter sky at morning, and for a moment the Great King's anger failed him as his knees trembled.

Then the spell was broken. "I am Enkidu of the wilderness." Tears stood a moment in those perfect eyes. "The beasts no longer know me, so I am come among you seeking wisdom. This...." Enkidu waved his fist at the Great King. "...this is not wisdom. This is lust."

And so they fell to battle, the two of them on the streets of Uruk, fighting with the hate of brothers and the brotherhood of lovers, each striving to better and best the Divine.

⌁

traveling a road he does not know

Shin-eqi-unninni wakes the former wild man from his slumber and feeds him bread and more figs, for he has a long journey ahead of him. The forests of cedar have been destroyed, forests where Enkidu was once a child running with the wolves—Enkidu destroyed those cedars himself with his king, a great feat of heroism. But the hairy man must continue to wander or the storyteller will have no tale to set down.

There are only few whose wanderings take them to Hell.

The house where the dead dwell in darkness,
Where they drink dirt and eat stone.

Enkidu rises and thanks Shin-eqi-unninni, turning west, away from the razed forests and the banks of the Euphrates.

And here the story moves into the realms of nightmare and distant cultural memory, the near destruction of the human race through the waters covering the earth.

The oldest man on Earth, the one man who survived the Flood, can only be reached by crossing the Waters of Death. The hairy man uses trees for punting poles and does not touch the fatal water. Utnapishtim, the Far-Away, is waiting for him on the other shore.

"What is the secret of eternal life?" Enkidu asks.

The old man shakes his head. "Death is necessary and all human effort temporary."

Enkidu lays his punting poles on the sandy beach. "But I am not human as you are."

Utnapishtim scratches his crotch and leers. "Yes, but you have enjoyed none other than Shamhat herself. With that, your innocence was destroyed and you became aware of death."

The hairy man considers this. Not as a matter of fairness, for fairness is an illusion, but as a matter of logic. "Why do the gods inflict death on us?"

"If they did not, we would be even more vain than we are. Let me tell you a story." The immortal man, the Far-Away, gazes out at the Waters of Death before beginning his tale. "It was in the city of Shruppak, before the Flood, that the gods decided to do away with humans."

From the time before, the life the hairy man barely remembers, before civilization and friendship, he can understand wanting to do away with humans. But then he submitted to Shamhat, gaining knowledge in exchange for his wildness, and now he is one of them.

The immortal man continues. "If it were not for the god Ea, they would have succeeded. But he came to my house and told the story to the walls."

⁓

where death did not reach

a man alone, covered in hair, walking on feet that remember the dust of a thousand years though he does not, stops to listen to a storyteller. The storyteller is old and small, yellowed with poor humors of the body, his crinkling smile toothed no more than any milking infant's. He sits crouch-legged like some misshapen stork, leering up at potential benefactors.

"The lord of all, our Hammurabi of ancient memory, has given to the world these laws that men might know their just and proper place," the storyteller says to the hairy man, as if resuming an old debate.

Wishing for a staff, the hairy man leans forward, hands upon his knees, nearly the most brutal sort of rest.

And here the story leaves the path of tradition for the inner reality of narrative, Enkidu and the Great King trading places so that it is the king demon-dragged to the ash pits beyond the grave while Enkidu wanders curst and cursing through life—kings come and go, great and small, but there is only one hairy man left to the earth.

The storyteller continues. "In this day Nebuchadnezzar, son of Naboplashar and second of his name, has given the world the gift of growing life, which ought to have been God's to make."

Above and around them vines trail, bushes run riot, flowers erupt like wounds on a battlefield, and everywhere there is the trickle and drip of water. Though a man might die of thirst a hundred paces outside the city gates, within, concealed by the dogleg alleys and curving boulevards, the city hosts a mountain of life, a green monument to what could be in God's world, if God had granted constant rain to the hard-baked plains of Mesopotamia.

"The Hanging Garden has plants cultivated above ground level, and the roots of the trees are embedded in an upper terrace rather than in the earth. The whole mass is supported on stone columns... Streams of water emerging from elevated sources flow down sloping channels... These waters irrigate the whole garden saturating the roots of plants and keeping the whole area moist. Hence the grass is permanently green and the leaves of trees grow firmly attached to supple branches... This is a work of art of royal luxury and its most striking feature is that the labor of cultivation is suspended above the heads of the spectators."—Philo of Byzantium

The story dances forward, pulling the hairy man with it, and he opens his mouth to ask a question forgotten before ever it leaves his lips.

"I know," the storyteller says, smiling broad-lipped as any cedar demon. He touches a finger to his mouth. "I remember what you have forgotten."

"What..." The hairy man's voice is rusted as any grave-good sword. "What have I forgotten?"

"The way." The old man sketches a map of time with his fingers in the hair, the tips flickering in a doubled spiral as magic as the kiss of any temple prostitute. "Source and destination, purpose and reward. Never leave that to which you would return."

"Fool...foolishness."

"Perhaps." A pale blue egg appears between wrinkled fingertips, spins once, vanishes in a crackle and spray of shell, though no fragments meet the dusty cobbles. "Do you remember the beasts by the water, my friend?"

The hairy man strains, thinking of a time before words when he lived among trees and couched with the lions and onagers that roamed—where? "How do you know?"

"The stories belong to me." The old man's grin vanishes, sunset on the open sea. "And I belong to them. You...you have story deep within you. It drives the poisons from your liver and keeps your steps in pace."

The hairy man considers killing the old man for owning his story, but the effort is too great and the cost too high. Instead, they dine on dried figs and a pear stolen from the forbidden greenery above, trading quiet tales of this place and that, some miracle and another, until the moon rises blood-red and peevish to drive all but soldiers from Babylon's crook-backed streets.

the brazen giant of Greek fame

the waters came and the waters left and wrote their stories on a hundred walls in a hundred temples from the holly-cutting madmen of the misty north to the red-faced demon gods of the spicelands. Still the hairy man travelled onward, carrying spears in some armies, leading others, fighting for and against himself and always brushing against the hem of legend.

When the Demetrian price had been paid in blood and bronze beneath the wise thumb of Chares of Lindos, there was raised a giant to honor the sun. The hairy man came to that harbor in the time of building, and took labor for a while upon the scaffolding, for

Why man, he doth bestride the narrow world

Like a Colossus, and we petty men

Walke vnder his huge legges, and peepe about

To finde our selues dishonourable Graues.

Men at sometime, are Masters of their Fates.

The fault (deere Brutus) is not in our Starres,

But in our Selues, that we are vnderlings.

   —The Tragedie of Julius Caesar, Actus Primus, Scoena Secunda

    Wm. Shakespeare

men of his strength were of great value atop the stone columns, and the hairy man feared no height. He was satisfied to be an underling, clambering up the stone and iron of the inner structure to affix the brazen plates on their studs, working sometimes with his ancient axe that looked to be a thing out of legend. Though the other laborers would not drink in the tavernae with him, they appreciated his skill.

And here the story moves away from flood and forces of nature released on mankind, to elements tamed and built upwards to the sun, a monument to last in human memory for millennia.

Twelve years they labored, the waters of Mandraki harbor blue beneath them, the hills of Anatolia rising across the sea to the east and the north, the island's dusty beauty growing smaller the higher they rose.

Finally it was time for the aureole crown of the sun god itself. Slaves with pulleys on the mole separating the harbors pulled far below, looking like ants from where Enkidu stood in the summer sun with the other laborers with the most tolerance for heights, while the blazing crown rose slowly up the side of the scaffolding. The stench of their sweat stung in the hairy man's nose, despite the evening wind from the west.

The gold-plated aureole came level with them, and they reached out and grabbed it, hauling it up the statue's massive face to mount it on the studs encircling the head of Helios.

The wonder of the ancient world stood for fifty-six years. But even lying broken from the shaking of the earth, it was a marvel. Not even the hairy man could get his arms all the way around one fallen thumb.

and so the star falls

There is no man that understands another better than a shoemaker. The feet of a laborer tell a different tale than the feet of a centurion, and so in turn a consul or a moneylender or a Pharisee. Shoemakers know all secrets, for there is divination in the taking the measure of a sole or the curve of an arch.

And so it happens that following the twists of the tale which had taken up four-voiced residence within the very walls of his flesh, Enkidu came to Judea in the time of Herod. As he had repeatedly over the endless, draining years, he took up the labor of his hands. It came to pass that he had need of roughshod boots, the better to work the limerock quarries from which the empire sought its stones.

"See the old Jew on the Lesser Street of Olives," he was told by a dark-skinned Ethiope

> Is it by chance, or design, or destiny, that the seven nails in the sole of the man's shoe form a cross—thus:
>
> ```
>           *
>       *   *   *
>           *
>           *
>           *
> ```
>
> Everywhere he leaves this impress behind him.
>
> On the smooth and polished snow, these footmarks seem imprinted by a foot of brass on a marble floor. —*The Wandering Jew*, Eugene Sue

who found the hairy man's countenance no stranger than his own in this dust-raddled land of sharp noses and glittering brown eyes and seething roils of the soul.

There was something of his earliest days in the air of Judea, the hairy man thought, though he could recall little enough.

He took himself to the Lesser Street of Olives, a crooked alley echoing with the wailing of goats and the bleating of children and the snap of laundry drying on the wind. There he found three sandals dangling from a pole outside a darkened doorway.

For a moment he stood before the door to the labyrinth beneath the temple in Uruk, but then there was only a man back among the leather-reeking shadows, cranky and old, story leering from his eyes.

"Come to be shod, have you?" The old man smiled. "You're a special one. Bring me a sliver of thunderbolt iron and I'll make you boots like no one's ever seen."

"I have three shekels put by and a small basket of figs," the hairy man retorted.

Laughter then, rough: "Fair's fair. I might have sandals to fit those beastly feet. But first, come with me. There's to be something of a spectacle today. The Sanhedrin put our governor up to nailing down that dodgy Yeshua who's been railing about the town."

"I came for boots," muttered the hairy man.

"And boots you shall have, or I'm not Ahasuerus. I've not got all the time in this life, though, and I won't miss my spectacle. You've seen death in your time, come see it in mine."

Then Enkidu remembered the god-man, bronze-bound axe gleaming in the sunlight. The voices of story bound within him whispered seduction amid blood and ash.

"I do not seek death," the hairy man said. "I seek a way back."

He could have wept, but not in front of this grinning lout, and he allowed himself to be led away.

into the fire the bird soars

the Temple of Jupiter Stator and the Atrium Vestae, the hearth of the Vestal Virgins, burned that day, white marbled sacrifices in the seven-hilled lime kiln. A beginning and an end both. The hairy man had watched those long days and nights while the emperor played his sport in Antium and the people screamed for mercy. Now the publicans said that Yeshua's folk had set the flames to honor their god.

Ancient bronze axe upon his shoulder, the hairy man walks the road toward the seaport of Ostia knowing that someone will mark the breadth of his shoulders and call him over to lift a timber baulk or clear scorched amphorae in search of what might even now be saved.

Ahead—a scramble. Soldiers drive a limping old man, followed by ragged folk pleading. The hairy man plods onward. Spears hold no terror for him.

But a decurion grabs him as he passes, barks something in a Latin gabble, then a muddy Greek that would shame a Syrian: "You, you are not one of them."

"Nor am I one of you." He allows his muscles to flex, popping loose the officer's fingers. But the decurion is brave, or stupid, or both.

"Fair enough. I require you to stand witness, that the rumors will not race away in their praying mouths."

"Mockery of every sort was added to their deaths. Covered with the skins of beasts, they were torn by dogs and perished, or were nailed to crosses, or were doomed to the flames. These served to illuminate the night when daylight failed. Nero had thrown open the gardens for the spectacle, and was exhibiting a show in the circus, while he mingled with the people in the dress of a charioteer or drove about in a chariot. Hence, even for criminals who deserved extreme and exemplary punishment there arose a feeling of compassion; for it was not, as it seemed, for the public good, but glut one man's cruelty, that they were being punished." —*Annales*, Tacitus

He could take this old man from these soldiers, break their spears across their heads, and go on. But armies have long memories, and the hairy man is all too easy to recognize. Besides, he does not know these people.

"This man, one Paul or Saul of Tarsus, has conspired to burn the city and endanger both its inhabitants and its gods," the decurion proclaims.

a man had a vision by the side of the road, that made him either a prophet or an epileptic, but the story took him hold and he launched a thousand years of thought on the heels of the dead prophet

Paul's face holds much the same expression as Yeshua's had below his strained load of timber, as he'd spoken the soft words to Ahasuerus.

"And you?" he whispers just as the decurion chops a sword down across the old man's neck.

"And me," the hairy man says. Something has ended here, but something else has begun.

Bloody-handed, the decurion grasps Enkidu's arm once more. "You, man. Tell what you saw, that Paul died a coward and no miracle came."

"Give me the head and I shall carry it through the city." It is all he will do for Paul.

the fields once more sown with discord

It is spring in a land greener than any Enkidu has seen in a very long time, the color so brilliant it almost hurts the eyes.

And in the midst of the lush green, a fire.

There is a man on the top of a hill, a heretic and a former slave, who has lit the fire on the day before Beltaine in defiance of the High King—for it is the king alone who has the right to light a bonfire on this holy day.

149

and here the story twists undeniably westward, on the edge of the known world: Hy Brasil—pagan outpost and home to missionaries, a point in time between two ages

Surrounded by druids and warriors, the high king strides forward. "I command you to extinguish this fire!"

The former slave shakes his head. He wears the robes of a druid, but the front of his head is shaved so that he appears much older than he is. "I cannot put out the holy fire of Easter."

The high king turns to the hairy man. "You! Put out this fire!"

But the hairy man sets fires, he cannot extinguish them. And the others are afraid to go against a man wearing the robes of a druid.

Enkidu turns a holy bone in his hand, relic worth a thousand lives to the crazy heretic and the men at his back, and pretends he does not understand. This is no difficult ruse—he has spent millennia perfecting forgetful ignorance.

And so the fire burns, on through human memory, following Enkidu on his wanderings, accompanying him, as fire always has.

he who saw the deeps

it would be easy to mistake westward progress for the idiocy of optimism. Surely the sailors on these ships did, except perhaps for the two grinning northmen with hair like wheat and bloody smiles, who did not seem to care one whit for anything but each other. And Enkidu, who had ridden endless waters before in the long trailing dance of his life.

Here, atop the antithesis of fire, far from flame and his feet removed from the roads of history, perhaps he can be free to find...memory? That which is lost. Axe and bone walk the years with him yet, but they are no loose-tongued companions to ease a night beneath the stars with clever tales.

The three ships struggled in a calm sea, gaining bare yards of headway for the hours spent. Each man not at work strained to spy a bird which would be an undeniable harbinger of a shore beyond the pitiless horizon. The hairy man watched the depths instead, wondering how great a hook he would have to let down to land a lamp-eyed monster from beyond the darkness below.

"You never fear," said the Admiral, touching his shoulder.

Enkidu shrugged. Every time he has learned another speech, it breeds itself to some daughter tongue that debases and transcends what has gone before. Nonetheless, he understood the Admiral well enough.

The Admiral persisted. "Why is that?"

What is fear, the hairy man wanted to say. *What is fear, but the poor experience of things yet to come?* Instead:

Monday, 10 September. This day and night sailed sixty leagues, at the rate of ten miles an hour, which are two leagues and a half. Reckoned only forty-eight leagues, that the men might not be terrified if they should be long upon the voyage.

Tuesday, 11 September. Steered their course west and sailed above twenty leagues; saw a large fragment of the mast of a vessel, apparently of a hundred and twenty tons, but could not pick it up. In the night sailed about twenty leagues, and reckoned only sixteen, for the cause above stated. —from the *Journal* of Christopher Columbus, 1492

"Leagues and leagues I have walked, sir. One night is much like another, each storm the same, and we all bleed like men."

"Save you, perhaps. Pero Gutierrez says you are some breed of ape, beyond Barbary and given tongue by God."

"God gave me nothing," muttered Enkidu. "Save a headache and an axe."

The Admiral smiled at that. "God will give me the Indies. The birds show the way."

Not the birds, thought Enkidu, but pitiless time itself. He stroked the rounded bone in his pouch, smoothed by centuries under his finger. The old man in the street had been the last one who'd truly seen him.

When at last he found the man who knew him, he and the Great King could finally go on together. Beneath the ship, something long and gray uncoiled, but the hairy man ignored the flash of its scales, raising no alarm.

youth once lost is recovered only in the waters of regret

...all men will follow legends, whether they brandish spyglasses and maps from farthest Araby, or are subtle as rumor on the winter wind. Stories live inside legends like crabs in their houses of shell, and decorate them to make them sweet to the men who eat such fare, living on hope and air.

The island Pascua Florida might well have been home to more flowers than a decent man could name in an afternoon, but it was also home to biting flies the size of that mythical man's thumb, and something that looked far too much like a crocodile for the hairy man's sense of well-being.

In a few short years Enkidu had had his fill and more of Spanish madmen, but Juan Ponce de Leon had sunk his teeth into the edge of something that set the hairy man's skin to crackling as it had not done since he first came to hold the axe of the Great King. A story, to be sure, but all of life was story.

He remembered more these days. Was there an end to be found somewhere in his future? Ponce de Leon was certain that he was nigh not to an end but to a beginning the likes of which he had never seen.

The hairy man could tell the angry Spaniard more about life eternal than he would ever want to hear.

from waters we are born
leaping on the flood from a mother's womb
to waters we return
rain pooling within a chilly tomb

They made camp amid a night which crackled with the noise of teeth and claws. In the middle watch, Enkidu crouched by a fire, when an old man stumbled out of the shadows. Their eyes met, they stared, then the old man grinned.

"A face I shall never forget," the intruder said in Spanish. "The ugliest man I ever did meet. Did you ever get your boots, my friend?"

"Greetings, Judean," the hairy man said, in the Greek of their shared time and place.

Ahasuerus regarded the exhausted men of Ponce de Leon's expedition. "They are hunting new diseases, perhaps?" he asked in the same tongue.

"Youth eternal."

"Ah." Another grin. "Have you let them in upon the joke yet?"

As he had not done in three times a thousand years, Enkidu began to laugh. Ahasuerus joined him. The two sat beside the fire, howling like hyenas in a distant Egyptian night, til someone threw a boot.

"I predict a short eternity of youth for these," Ahasuerus finally said.

"Perhaps. What do you do here?"

"Live. And you?"

"I am waiting to die," Enkidu said to his own surprise. He added after a brief pause, "That the Great King might live once more."

every tree an enemy, every man a tree

swinging the Great King's axe, chips flying. The man to his left, wielding a bearded axe under the direction of the tall, shouting Englishman, turned to the hairy man, smiled and said something that Enkidu almost understood.

I have crossed water, he thought. I have crossed centuries. The very words of the world have flowed around me. The Great King is closer to me now, closer than he has been since his death.

He took another chunk out of the narrow beech, abusing this axe which was made long ago to fight gods and men.

His neighbor tried again in English: "It is you are not Iroquois, no?" The man presented himself with a tradecloth shirt, the canvas pantaloons of a sailor, and a dreadful voice.

"I am of the years," Enkidu said sullenly. He shifted his grip on the axe. He had long ago set the fragments of Paul's skull into the haft where they might be mistaken for ivory. The beech creaked.

"Quickly, man," shouted the Englishman, grabbing Enkidu's arm. He had a worried look—and well he should. They had already fought the French once under the moon that would soon be rising.

Enkidu stared into the tall man's eyes. Something glimmered there, a star in a well, a jewel in the catacombs beneath the temple of Shamhat. Here was one who would walk the paths of the dead. Here was one who shared the Great King's purpose.

and so the story dances in upon itself once more, weaving the drunken double-spiral that stretches across time from the African trees that were once our home and into a vacant future, pausing only to dance in the space between the eyes of two men who stare across the years at one another and know, for a moment, a measure of indecipherable truth

"Take me to him," the hairy man said in the language of Uruk. "I beg you."

Washington shook him off and turned away, muttering of crazed Negroes.

"It is not to fear," said his grinning fellow axe-man, and handed Enkidu a skin of something vile that tasted of bullets in the dark. "They are only the French who it is are coming. There is so much worse."

death sought can be difficult to find

Enkidu sharpened the blade of the axe carefully. While he searched for an end to his long existence, the Cheyenne only tolerated him among them because of his prowess in battle, honed for so many centuries and in so many wars, he would rather not remember. Luckily, he often forgot. The axe in his hands was worn, the Great King's name barely legible now along the rivets—and the hairy man the only one living who could read it. But the gleaming bronze wedge of the head could still kill.

And the less it resembled the royal axe it had once been, the more it brought the memories back that had so often escaped him through the centuries.

Then the call went up: "Bluecoats on the ridge!"

the story swirls, crossing years to follow men who might have been kings in another time. Brother Golden Hair rides amid his bluecoat horsemen with the sneer of one born to rule, badly. Enkidu takes his axe and stalks the story, seeking a bullet from the madman's pistol

The Battle of the Greasy Grass was a massacre, over almost before it had begun, blood coating the ridge, the incline, the grass, turning the stream red with vengeance. Cheyenne, Lakota, Arapaho, Sioux—all these fine, ringing words, all these warriors as dark as Enkidu and darker—all were more than the bluecoats had expected.

> We stayed in the bush about three hours, and I could hear heavy firing below in the river, apparently about two miles distant. I did not know who it was, but knew the Indians were fighting some of our men, and learned afterward it was Custer's command. Nearly all the Indians in the upper part of the valley drew off down the river, and the fight with Custer lasted about one hour, when the heavy firing ceased.
>
> —George Herendon, *New York Herald* (July 1876)

The warriors of The People chased the first white lodge into the woods and the river beyond, and even up the bluff. They could have chased them farther, could have chased them down between the trees of the woods, but when the next attack on the village came, from the forces led by Brother Golden Hair, the warriors under the leader Crazy Horse left the trembling bluecoats where they were hiding, circled around on the ridge, and rode down on the others.

The Great King would have been proud to know the role his axe had played.

The hairy man tried to make his way to the thick of the fighting, but when the bluecoats on the ridge saw how many were riding against them, they broke and ran and fired into the air and the ground and shot their horses to hide behind. The Cheyenne and their allies slaughtered the soldiers of Golden Hair like buffalo.

Blood drenched the greasy grass and the bronze of the Great King's axe, but to his anger and his shame none of it was Enkidu's.

He would not find death this day.

≈

Helios' crown restored, and Heaven ope'd

Bedloe's Island was a small place, for all that it teemed with people of every class and station and race—except for that of the hairy man. The old fort on which the god-turned-goddess had been erected still stood, shaved down and transformed into a park.

Enkidu stared up at the seven-spiked crown. Chares of Lindos would easily have recognized this great copper woman as sister to his largest son.

He pushed through the crowds. People stepped away, not because of his hair—Enkidu took care how he dressed when in the cities of the east, where people asked questions—but his size. The world had grown taller over the millennia, or he shorter, but there were still few enough with his shoulders or breadth of chest.

The fort walls rose in angles, now foundation for the statue's base. He found his way to the upper rim and followed the line of the old ramparts, reduced to landscaping. The axe vibrated beneath his coat.

something very old returning, the crown of the sun once more overtopping the seas, showing the Great King's axe a way home again

Soon enough he found what he was looking for—a stairway down, not yet filled in, though the pile of rubble nearby showed the intent clearly enough. Ignoring the crowds, he slipped beneath the earth to the music of a brass band.

a land of ashes and winds, sharp scents and the hollow noise of bones set to clatter, where a man could lose his way in the darkness and come out years to the wrong

Someone breathed ahead of him in the darkness. Regular, smooth breathing. Shamhat? He thought he recognized the catch in the throat.

"Are you sure?" asked a man behind him.

Enkidu, who was never taken in surprise, whirled with axe at the ready. It was only the Judean, tallow lamp flickering in one hand.

"I am sure," he said in the first tongue he had ever spoken, the language of cedars and wild ducks and the bursting flowers of the upland woods.

"Everything in its season," Ahasuerus replied in the same tongue. Then, in English: "May I hold your coat?"

It was fit that he go to the Great King just as he had first come, clad only in his fur. Breath snuffling in his enormous nostrils, Enkidu stripped himself bare. It was cold in these catacombs, cold as the temples of old.

"Grave dust," the old Jew said. His smile was lopsided. "The joke is finally ending, perhaps?"

shrieks, and the gentle slam of stones closing over thresholds...the Great King lay dead, struck down amid the steaming blood of the Bull of the Sun in misdirected retribution
we never find the life we are searching for
but can we find the death?

Enkidu managed a brief smile in the darkness. "Here once more beneath the sun's crown, yes."

He turned and walked into the thudding darkness to the distant music of a brass band. Ahasuerus' pool of light faded behind him to nothing, but the breathing ahead grew to the lungs of the world.

"Great King?" Enkidu said. The saint's bones glowed in the haft of his axe, while the bronze blade seemed to spark.

"Old friend?" the darkness asked. A familiar shape loomed.

"Welcome—" they each began to say, interrupting one another.

the story finds its beginning and swallows itself, becoming only another dot in the glowing sea that cloaks the dreaming world

When the demons of the dark came to them, they fought together knee-deep in bull's blood. This was fit, as things should always have been. Neither noticed the old man with the lamp, weeping softly in the distance.

They would die together this day, and live forever.

Six Questions for an Alien

Lance Olsen

Test…test…test. Testing. One…two…three. Testing. Good. Okay. Well, you must be quite disoriented after your arrival this morning. Let me begin by thanking you for agreeing to talk to us under these extraordinary conditions. We apologize in advance for taxing you further. Please let us know whenever you would like to take a short break. We are happy to accommodate your needs. We believe it important, however, for self-evident reasons with which we are fairly certain you agree, to commence our interview as soon as possible. You must try to imagine how important our meeting with you is to us. It marks nothing short of a…well, without any exaggeration, it marks nothing short of a transformational moment for our species. Consequently, we are enormously excited by the prospect of our talk. Regrettably, our nascent analysis of the message—or what we take to be the message—that preceded your appearance by seven years seems to indicate, if our translation efforts are accurate, that in your culture it is impolite—and even potentially harmful, both emotionally and physically—for one individual to ask more than six questions of another in that latter individual's lifetime, and so we would therefore like to begin by telling you how greatly we appreciate your personal sacrifice in answering ours on behalf of your world. Our team, comprised of linguists, mathematicians, anthropologists, philosophers, cultural studies specialists, musicians, artists, psychologists, and sociologists, as well as scientists from diverse fields, has chosen ours with the utmost care and deliberation, despite the relatively short timeframe allotted to our undertaking. Right, well. With these preliminaries in mind, let us get started, shall we? First, may we invite you to discuss in terms with which you feel most comfortable how you go about defining what constitutes a member of your species?

We are marionettes with feelings and commotion.

[Pause.] Would you perhaps care to elaborate?

No, thank you.

[Extended pause.] Okay. Right. Well, we, ah…possibly you could talk a little bit, then, about your species' conceptions of sexual dimorphism and reproduction. We find these topics potentially quite illuminating with regard to our comprehending your civilization.

I ask your forgiveness. I am trying to use your language. It is very difficult. But I am trying. Your nouns seem to me dead rocks hovering in air. You have many dead rocks floating around your head as we speak. Your verbs magnify the disorder of the universe. This is [unintelligible] frighten us in our varieties. To our way of thinking, utterances that exist in the breaches between verbs and nouns are…how does your species put it? We often consider them unsafe. Yet silences are sometimes more so for us. This is because both cause nothing to happen innumerable times in succession. We continue [unintelligible] in our varieties. It is possibly in light of this that evolution provides us with fewer holes in our faces than it does you in yours. In any case, when we say we are listening to another of our kind we are in reality often simply employing a different form of speech. I am not being clear. This I can tell by your sudden facial inconsistencies. I ask your forgiveness again. Listening can be a category of speech, you see, but hearing can be for other purposes, such as the acquisition of food and entertainment. Each member of our species enjoys most surrounding him or herself with his or her own vowels and consonants. We often refer to this state as *society*, although it seldom involves others. We are usually alarmed by queries. We consider them to be infringements on our cleanliness. Frequently, when we are alone, we delight in the pair of vibrating fibrous sheets of tissue that span the cartilaginous cavity at the root of our tongues. When no one is looking, we sometimes massage these with the tips of the digits existing at the extremities of our limbs attached to what we think of when we think of the term *shoulders*. These, here. Do you see? Yes. We call the digits *fingers*. We call the whole fleshy star a *hand*. We call the sound that emerges from the tissues at the root of our tongues *a communal form of weeping*, or, somewhat more precisely, *hope*, and we refuse to share it with others unless we are forced to do so, and then, as you say, no more than six times over the course of our life spans. I am using six here in no more than a metaphorical sense. It comprises nothing more than a statistical average. I am, that is to say, guessing. But the guess, I feel, is a good one. The point is that [unintelligible] and that we all know in our secret moments this hope is empty in the same manner as our dwellings are empty. And so this is what we call our *sexuality* and our *reproduction*.

You have, I believe, three questions remaining. If you would be so kind, I would like now to take a short interval in advance of my further taxing.

[Three weeks later...]

Test...test...test. Testing. One...two...three. Testing. All right, then. It looks like we are ready to continue. Well...we are very glad you have had a chance to rest, and we trust you are feeling somewhat better. You gave us a bit of a scare, we should say, when you returned to your nest and became horizontal and unresponsive for many hours, and we would very much like to ask you about this intriguing ceremony, but upon further reflection our team has decided such an inquiry does not fall strictly within the parameters of our highest-value questions. Hence let us return instead, if you would be so kind, to what you said at the end of our last conversation. May we invite you to discuss in terms with which you feel most comfortable in what sense your dwellings are "empty," and would you please describe to us how those inhabited by members of your species function?

It has been a long journey. It is hard to imagine. I looked up at the sky one day and then was folded into a small cold nest. I looked up at the sky again, but it was a different sky. Often ours is the color of sadness, yours the color of abstraction. I have noticed this. I do not understand how I came here. I was there and then I was elsewhere. In the distance between our two skies, my offspring's offspring's offspring's offspring became another individual's memory. Currently I am no longer acquainted with anyone else in the universe. This is a very lonely sensation. Although I thought I might have been prepared for such a feeling, I was nonetheless unprepared for it. We sometimes label this emotion *religion*, or *the inability to think for ourselves*. Before you nested me, my dwelling stood empty. This is the case for all individuals on my planet. When our dwellings stand full, you see, they also stand empty. This is because, although they are shaped diversely and from a diversity of materials—from [unintelligible] to [unintelligible]—they always resemble a longing for others. This is why we litter them with pieces of ourselves. Similarly, we often treat others of our species as we treat our dwellings, filling them with other pieces of ourselves, too. Specialized terminology, chromosomes, need, disease, and so on. Some of us are designed to give such things. Some of us are designed to receive them. Some of us are designed to do both, some neither, and some a complex balance among the possible combinations of the two. Some receivers are never happy because they want to be givers. Some givers are never happy because they want to be receivers. Even when our dwellings are pleasant in the extreme, we continue to crave the dwellings of others. We cannot say why this is. The primary use for our dwellings is to provide a location for closing the two holes on our face designed for vision, here and here, and for hallucinating uncontrollably that we are other people in different places at different times for up to a third of our life spans. In addition, sometimes we hallucinate uncontrollably that we are animals and inanimate objects. We injure each other in ingenious yet inconspicuous ways to secure our dwellings so that we can stare at boxes of bright light for hours on end in a space called *the family nest*—sometimes with our offspring and/or reproductive mates, sometimes without. When enough of us in a relatively localized area come to possess dwellings of our own, we choose other individuals for whom to build larger dwellings so that they will tell us half truths and hurt us through complicated, if subtle, methods. Our dwellings are also regularly employed as locations in which to ingest through a third hole in our faces—this one, here, through which we also manufacture language (a paradox you must find both unhygienic and disturbing)—the dead flesh of creatures that once walked, swam, or flew through the air like your minds do, only with visible appendages dedicated to such purposes, or the dead plant life surrounding us. For us to be able to inhabit our dwellings, we therefore must kill. Yet some of us refuse to ingest dead flesh. These individuals we call *liars*. Some refuse to ingest dead plant life. These we refer to as *uncomfortable*. We evacuate the dead flesh and plant life that have entered us through another hole in our bodies. This one, here. And in liquid form through this one, here, through which our chromosomes also pass, another paradox. We are capable of evacuating in other individuals' structures, or even in public, but most of us prefer not to. If asked, we would not be able to explain why. Perhaps we are embarrassed by our abundances. Sometimes we become horizontal, or semi-horizontal, beside each other or across from each other in our dwellings in reclining constructions called [unintelligible] and forget together, or remain noiseless together, or perform acts of communal weeping or hope. Occasionally we accomplish this with the aid of lozenges fashioned from dead trees that we worship for their information but then cannot remember in any detail two weeks after handling them. Unlike you, we spawn in our dwellings. We rear our broods there. And, as soon as we are able, we expel our broods from them so that they can experience emptiness for themselves, just as our progenitors expelled us. We term this set of circumstances *education.* We also expel pieces of ourselves, the dead flesh and plant life we ingested, as well as an assortment of natural and synthetic fluids and solids, from our dwellings by means of a system of tubes, boxes, and cylinders so that our world can be so full of us that it becomes something other than our world. When we are finished filling our planet, we plan to abandon it and move to one like yours—not ours, that is, but similar enough to it so that we can again fill it with ourselves, and then move to another, forever. We designate this *progress*, although no one ever speaks about this strategy because we consider truth bad manners. We are designed as a species to emit our waste behind us so that we do not have to examine it closely and can therefore more easily put it out of our minds. Few of us appreciate fully this evolutionary turn. We look forward to getting to know a species like yours better through our silences and ejecta. We cannot say why. But now I am tired. My language is not yours. Yours hurts my mouth, here. Trying to communicate with it is like trying to reason with my brain suspended in a fire. There are so many dead rocks in the air. It makes me dizzy. I miss my emptiness back home. You have one more question. I want to hear it and then I want to go away. For some of us, this going-away is like a trip to a new planet from which we will return. For some, it is like a visit to a boring social gathering that will never end. For some, it is a punishment for having been who we are. For me, it is like closing the holes in my head meant for vision and thinking of nothing whatsoever, only without the holes in my head meant for vision and without the thinking. Whole cultures have been destroyed in an attempt to decide which going-away is the correct one. We term these genocides *acts of piety.*

[Extended pause.] We believe…isn't it the case…that is, we have asked you only four questions. We are under the impression this allows us two additional ones.

Your questions contain questions curled up inside questions. This creates din and tightness. I am apologizing.

During the course of our all-too-brief conversation together, you have provided us with profound insights into your species. The inhabitants of our world wish to thank you once again for sharing your knowledge and wisdom with us. We have so much more we would like to ask you, but we also understand and respect your beliefs about this subject. We shall honor them by making our last query a short one, then we look forward to ingesting you lovingly. May we invite you to discuss in terms with which you feel most comfortable what value or perhaps cluster of values your species holds most dear?

You are sitting in your dwelling with your reproductive mate, watching the box of bright light. It is evening. There is a knock upon your door. You and your reproductive mate exchange looks. You feel alarmed yet curious. Then you become vertical and cross your dwelling to the point of ingress and egress. Two individuals you have never seen before, a male and a female, are awaiting entry. Both are well-dressed, but the male's hair is a black plastic wig. His face is shiny. The female is shorter and squarer than the male. Her hair is thin like grief, oily, the color of ashes and age. You notice that several white strings—each two or three meters long—trail from each of their sleeves, but you decide not to comment on this anomaly. Their mouths are red and form a short, crisp line below their noses, that place on our faces, here, through which we attempt to prolong life every two or three seconds. When they open and close them, their mouths make little clacking noises. Their eyes are black buttons. The male announces that he has a gift for you. You ask him what it is. He extends his arm. His hand is balled into a fist, like this. He turns it upside down and he opens it. It is vacant. This, he says. Then they walk past you into your dwelling. You notice that long white strings well up out of their collars also. They remind you of two broken violins, [unintelligible]. The female walks behind your reproductive mate, who is sitting in the [unintelligible] before the box of light. The male goes into your *kitchen*, the area in your dwelling reserved for the preparation of dead flesh and plant life for ingestion, and opens your *refrigerator*, the electrical and chemical unit in which you store the dead flesh and plant life between feedings. You ask them what they are doing. This is not their dwelling, you point out. You have not invited them in. They are failing to heed the rituals of their species. The female's right arm jerks up without warning and hits your reproductive mate on the back of her head with her open palm. We refer to this gesture as *slapping*. Your reproductive mate flinches. You ask the female intruder to stop producing such a gesture. Your reproductive mate rises and hurries toward her nest, apparently in search of protection. The female follows, slapping her on the back of the head as she moves. The impacts are not forceful, but they are persistent and clearly annoying. When you attempt to pursue your reproductive mate with the thought of helping her rising inside you, the male intruder closes the refrigerator, exits the kitchen in three large strides, falls into step behind you, and begins hitting you on the back of your head also. You cringe and tell him to stop producing such a gesture, but you do not slow your pace. His mouth clacks open and closed, but he does not say anything. At this point your reproductive mate appears from the hallway, followed by the female intruder. Your reproductive mate is ducking slightly, yet unsuccessfully, as she navigates through your dwelling. Then the two of you join up and zigzag from nest to nest, trying ineffectively to outmaneuver the couple's assault. Their slaps begin becoming uncomfortable now, but they are not injurious. Before long, you find yourself outside, zigzagging across your lawn. (Many of my species, employing numerous poisons, grow vast amounts of plant life called *lawns* in the space surrounding our dwellings, then forbid others to eat or walk on them.) You move quickly up the street, the male and female intruders following close at your heels. After a while, the female starts telling you to do things for her. Without looking back, you ask her what kind of things. She tells you to compliment her figure and notify strangers how intelligent she is. The male begins naming your faults. He tells you that you should be more like others of your species, that you should never have quit your *employment*—that means of procuring dwellings, dead flesh and plant life, and extra pieces of yourself. You explain to him, careful to keep moving, that you did not quit your employment. You are working where you have always worked. No, you are not, says the male, slapping. Eventually the male reaches forward, braces himself on your shoulders, and mounts your back. Your pace never wavers. The female does the same with your reproductive mate. They are not heavy, although they sound rattly. You progress in this manner until you come across an unattended vehicle with its means of ingress and egress unfastened and unprotected. Hurriedly you cut across the street and enter it. It is difficult to take your position behind the steering mechanism because of the human-sized marionette on your back. He possesses many sharp angles. Your reproductive mate slides into the [unintelligible] and you begin to drive. Soon you are in the *desert*, a large area where little grows and fine loose grains of rocks and minerals are plentiful. You are on the road alone, driving through the night, the couple alternately looking out the windows at the black scenery and slapping you, but incrementally less. At one point, the female tells your reproductive mate that your reproductive mate's spirit, the [unintelligible], is small and dry to match her surroundings. At another, the male calls you several times by the nearly-but-not-quote correct name, saying you are an individual without hands. Near dawn, they begin to shrink—almost imperceptibly at first, perhaps a centimeter or two, but soon more and more. The sunrise reveals them each to be just larger than your head and much less substantial. They hang precariously from your and your reproductive mate's necks now. You pull off the road and roll to a stop. You reach over, pluck the female intruder off your reproductive mate's neck, open the vehicle's means of ingress and egress, and announce that you will return shortly. You exit, carrying a small intruder in each fist, and walk several yards into the desert. There you set them down side by side. They lean against each other limply, as if all their muscles have unexpectedly been extracted, leaving only their bones behind. Their mouths continue to work, asking you to do things for them, naming your faults. You return to your vehicle, reenter it, and pull back onto the road. Accelerating, you look up into your rearview mirror, a mechanism for examining the past, and you can see the intruders' little red mouths moving and moving. You speed up. Then they are gone. The sun is a vast brash orange emission of rays and heat across the wide sky. You glance at your mate and notice that now she has several long white strings welling up out of her collar. You reach up and check your own neck. It feels as if the strings there connect directly to your spinal column. It feels as if you are living inside a solar flare. You drive and you drive. We call this *familiarity.* We call this *friendship.*

A Play for a Boy and Sock Puppets

E. Sedia

ACT I

SCENE I

(*Sock drawer. In the drawer, there is a SOCK PUPPET—a grey cotton sock with red and blue stripes and black button eyes. The SOCK PUPPET speaks in a soft, halting voice.*)

I stare at the ceiling from my drawer, feeling empty and happy. If I squint, the crystals of the popcorn relief above me catch moonlight and sparkle, transformed into tiny stars right before my eyes. I have hours until the morning comes and steals my solitude.

I work with autistic children. They are a difficult bunch, rocking back and forth, spitting, flapping their hands, screaming silently, screaming aloud, banging their heads on the desks, going rigid, going limp, biting. One of them bit me, right above my left button eye, and I needed stitches. Nine of them, in bright red woolen yarn. I'm happy They did not remove my eye and make me a pirate, but the scar hurts, especially before rain.

The morning comes, and brings the rain and shutting of the doors, car honking outside, hurried footsteps, and an infernal whine of the food processor. I count days, hoping despite knowledge that it might be Saturday and I won't have to go. The illusion is shattered when They walk in, pick me up, and shove me in a duffel bag with the others.

The others: there is the clown, the man, the woman, the naïve child, the dog, and the cat. I'm the autistic sock puppet, and to stay in character I do not talk to the others, block out their chattering with swaying in rhythm with the bag and muttering 'November' over and over. I think of how strange it is, to have your personality just assigned to you. I think that I would've liked to have some say in the matter.

SCENE II

(The interior of a clinical building. It is filled with people, mostly parents and children entering. The BOY is hidden among the others but announces himself by periodic loud screeching. The SOCK PUPPET narrates.)

We arrive at Behavioral Therapy. The children are arriving too—they are brought over in cars and SUVs and file in, some voluntarily, most not. Their parents or guardians drag them by their hands, as the children hiss and fight. Many are wearing little helmets—so bright, in red and yellow and blue, as if the colors can make it better. I want to go home.

Instead, I feel Them enter me, fill me, put words in my mouth. I play an autistic child named Elija, and the others show me how to do things. The children watch, some puzzled, some indifferent. I teach them skills. I teach them empathy. I pretend to eat Goldfish crackers that They give me, and some of the children perk up. The children like crackers, apparently.

After the show is over, the children have their own work to do, and it is my turn to watch. I watch them sort buttons. The teachers say that it is a useful, real-life skill and that they can use it for future employment. The parents smile and nod, no doubt imagining their offspring sorting through rows and rows of buttons for money, for the rest of their lives. Parents leave, still smiling. They'll be back later.

One of the children starts screaming, aaaaaaaaaaaaaa, and does not stop even when the teacher holds him down so he cannot move. His hands flail, and another teacher grabs his wrists and presses them against the desktop. Too hard, I think. She is pressing too hard.

The kid is subdued, and the rest carry on with their sorting. Whoever is done first gets two Goldfish crackers. The rest get one. The little fake fish smile eerily.

The child who threw a tantrum earlier does not sort. "Darren, you won't get a cracker if you don't sort," one of the teachers says. The kid looks back from under his helmet striped like a watermelon, and crosses his arms on his chest. He just wants to be left alone, and for once I know exactly how someone else feels. He does not get a cracker. They call him 'recalcitrant.'

ACT II
SCENE I

(Sock drawer. All of the sock puppets are present. There is a view of the window, and it is grey and raining outside.)

On the weekend, we do not go to see the children, They do not drive us to the small building of red brick with blue awning, do not make us spout the wrong words.

The others decide to take this opportunity to practice. They love practicing.

"Come on, Elija," says the woman. She likes to pretend to be my mother. "Let's work on not hurting the cat."

I look at the cat—he is striped red and white, and his green eyes are made of shiny stones. I wish I had eyes like that. I do not want to hurt him.

"Come on," the woman says.

"Aaaaaaaaaaaaaaaaaaaaaaaaa," I scream. "Aaaaaaaaaaa."

She backs off for a bit, but then she remembers what they say about not giving in to the tantrums.

"Now, Elija," she says. "Stop it."

I flail more, aaaaaaaaaa, the frayed elastic beating against the roof of our drawer. I bang my head on the wood until my eyes are ready to pop off.

They leave me alone. I calm down and think of the kid, Darren. I wonder if they leave him alone on weekends. I want to see him now, and speak to him in my own words. I want to tell him that 'recalcitrant' means 'good.'

The others are caught up in their rehearsal. The dog plays a family friend, and the man and the woman explain what 'autism' means. The cat is trying to eat the naïve child but only chews on his painted-on face with its soft woolen mouth impotently. The clown laughs.

I cannot take it anymore, and rock and slither my way to the opening of the drawer, where a single sunray and dancing motes penetrate the darkness. I struggle my way outside and fall to the ground, narrowly avoiding the knob. I would hate to get my stitches caught on it.

"Where're you going?" the dog says after me, belatedly. I ignore him.

I crawl under the door into the hallway and look both ways, as They tell everyone to do. I reach the front door undetected and squeeze through the mail slot.

SCENE II.
(The street, freshly washed by the rain; most of the stage depicts a wet pavement, with several large puddles. The buildings on the background are out-of-focus and not quite real. The SOCK PUPPET is in the center, lying in one of the puddles.)

It is early, and the streets are mostly empty. I crawl along, trying not to think that I have no idea of how I would find Darren. I concentrate on staying undetected and freeze every time someone goes by, but they don't seem to notice an old sock lying on the ground, the black buttons of its eyes shiny, blank.

Two joggers jog by, and one of them stops to look at me. "Hey look," he says. "It's a sock. Now we know what happens to the missing left socks, eh? They run away."

His friend laughs and does not stop, so the jogger leaves me be and takes after his friend. I sigh with relief and crawl along, slowly, imperceptibly, inching my way toward the brick house.

ACT III

SCENE I

(*No change from the previous stage design. It appears that the SOCK PUPPET did not move at all.*)

I'm so exhausted I fall asleep in a puddle, and drift off, soothed by the slow saturation of my every fiber with dirty rainwater. I do not dream. I wake up in motion and realize that I'm being carried off by a dog—a real one, with hot pungent breath and warm mouth.

"Rex, put that down!"

The dog growls a bit and chews me hastily, guiltily, dribbling spit and tearing out one of my stitches before spitting me out and running to join its owner. I wince in pain as I feel the old gash beginning to reopen.

I slither across the road, not caring about thick rubber tires that run me over again and again, flattening me, sapping my desire to find Darren. What will I say to him? How will I find him? I concentrate on crossing the road. I give up on looking both ways.

On the other side, I lie panting for a bit and look around. I glimpse the small brick building, its doors concealed by a corrugated sheet of metal. I try to remember the direction from which the kids usually come. I make up my mind and crawl toward the narrow slit of the horizon, as the setting sun bleeds all over it.

I hear chittering, and I turn to see a squirrel, its barbaric incisors bared, its eyes glistening. I try to shoo it away and rock, aaaaa, and twist and flail. Undeterred, the beast starts picking on my elastic, and I feel myself unraveling. I bang my head on the pavement, but the squirrel picks me up in its small hands (thank God it's not putting them inside of me), then its mouth, and runs up the tree, as I flap along. The nature was stupid when she created socks—we have no defense mechanisms whatsoever. I hang limply and whisper 'November' to calm myself down.

SCENE II.

(*The interior of a tree hole. Light penetrates in slants from somewhere high above the stage. The SOCK PUPPET, torn and wet, is on the bottom of it.*)

The squirrel carries me to its nest in a deep treehole, and I worry that it will continue the horrid unraveling it has started below until all of me is gone. I wonder if a ball of yarn has a soul, but I doubt it. When I cease to exist, so will my spirit.

The squirrel nestles into the hole and lays me on the bottom of it. I play dead until morning. When my captor is gone, I open one eye, carefully, and look around to discover bits of moss and paper, but no other captives. With that, I make my escape. The squirrel runs out and back in, and out again, and I make very little progress, trying to worm my way up the vertical wooden wall. I watch my stitches and unraveled threads, making sure they do not get caught on splinters and jagged edges of the hole.

The squirrel passes me as I reach the opening in the trunk. I freeze, but the obtuse beast pays me no attention, its small mind apparently preoccupied with the wafer end of an ice-cream cone it clutches in its teeth. It passes me on its way inside.

SCENE III

(*Playground in the park. There is a large tree, and the SOCK PUPPET is hanging out of the hole in the tree. The BOY is off-stage, but his shrill cries betray his presence.*)

I peek out of the hole and forget about my trailing threads and open gash. I stare at the town, washed by the first September rains into muted pearly purity spreading below me. I whimper at the bigness of it, but I cannot deny its beauty. I peer with my button eyes, and everything stands out in startling clarity. I see dogs and kids running around and realize that the squirrel dragged me to the park filled with children and their parents. I look for a watermelon-striped helmet. I cling to the rough bark of the tree, high above everything, and wait.

I decide to call for Darren, and I wail, aaaaaaa, and my gash hurts, and my threads are sore and unraveled. I scream my inarticulate suffering, hoping that he will hear me, until I grow hoarse.

And then I hear him, aaaaaaa, screaming back at me. For me. Green and black stripes come into my view, and I see Darren running, I see Darren chased by the woman who usually brings him to Behavioral Therapy. "Darren honey," she calls. "Come back. Mommy will give you a cracker."

The kid does not want a cracker and, he runs straight for my tree, a fresh gash in his forehead glistening red, like mine. It takes persistence to hurt oneself while wearing a helmet. He tilts his pale face toward the sky, and his mouth opens expectantly.

I jump. I sail through the air and plummet, alternately, until his hands snatch me out of the air. His hands hold me, carefully, and do not try to enter me. I cling to him, grateful.

"Elija," he says.

The woman is gaining on us, and I hurry to tell him. "Don't let their hands touch you," I whisper fiercely. "Don't let them speak for you."

He nods that he understands, and hugs me close. I drape over his shoulder and he runs. The woman recedes behind us, panting, her hands on her knees. We leave behind the park and its tress and horrible squirrels, we splash through every puddle we can find. I look at the sky, empty, happy. I hope that there is a place without intrusive hands, where one can scream and flail and speak his own words.

(Both the BOY and the SOCK PUPPET exit stage left.)
CURTAIN

Documenting My Abduction

Christine Boyka Kluge

I don't remember much of my life before. Only a glass fishbowl shaking, and two goldfish darting side to side over their green castle. I knew something big was going to happen. The dog was biting the fringe of the rug and whimpering, staring expectantly at the ceiling. When I looked up, a crack in the plaster opened, and out fell what looked like a chrome yo-yo. It hooked me on its silver string, like a boot on a line, and reeled me in over a quivering staircase of Mylar.

This did something weird to time. Think of each stair in a skyscraper being worth a million years. God knows how many flights I bumped up. Or think of my time missing as a broken Mobius strip. I was part of its confetti shower of tinselly light, sucked up from my own kitchen into darkness, and reconstituted elsewhere.

I woke up on my back on a metal table. I was looking into the face of a moonlike lamp, which stared at me from inside a metal hood. I blinked a few times to clear away the sparkles, and pulled myself together. I couldn't ignore the sharp pains clenching my abdomen and back, but I didn't call out. Switchblade twists stabbed at my insides, then faded. I discovered that I was buckled in with a wide seatbelt so I could be transported from cubicle to cubicle for observation.

Two of them were assigned to me, first separately, then together. They were tiny, but their heads were large and bald. Their huge eyes were like polished hematite. At first I was surprised by their constant intimate prodding—their monkeylike fingers at my neck, in my eyes and mouth, or wound in my hair. Their insistent mouths were always on my skin, tasting. (Fortunately, I have no scars, no marks at all, although that in itself is curious, and might provide further proof of my abduction.)

What began as an unwanted journey evolved into an odd kind of love, the truest love I have ever felt. There I was, alone on a needy planet, short on books and tolerable food, with two miniature creatures always sniffing me in unexpected places, expecting to be held and patted. I interpreted this clinging as a form of affection, and took comfort in it. We metamorphosed into a new creature, a sort of three-headed woman confining her existence to one small laboratory.

I don't recall the trip home. They came with me and never seemed to leave my side. I carried them around the house, one on each hip. My friends and relatives threw a party for me when I returned safe and whole, but I was too tired to enjoy it. I didn't even have enough energy to open the pile of gifts or taste the lemon poppyseed cake. After everyone congratulated me on my captors' amazing appetites and toothless smiles, the three of us took the blue balloons and went upstairs.

The Fifth Tale[1]:
When the Devil Met Baldrick[2] Beckenbauer[3][4]

Tom Miller

One[5][6] fine spring morning the Devil came up into the world of humankind. He was searching for the stones[7][8] out of which one of his temples had been

---

[1] [I had the honor of serving as editor and personal assistant to the noted American folklorist Marvin I. Berger during the last months of his life in 2003. Marv is best known for his 1935 monograph "On the Dating and Evolution of Legends in the Ruhr Valley," his 1945 tract "Strategic Bombing, the American Monster!" (over which he was briefly jailed by the State Department) and his unpublished 1951 memoir *Atlantis: Not Where I Thought It Was*. Marv had long hoped to turn a lifetime of scribblings into a collection of folklore suitable for the lay reader, and it is in that same spirit of egalitarianism that I have compiled *The False Histories: The Folktales of Marvin Berger*. This story is Chapter Five in its entirety. Marv's original footnotes are in italics; my own are in bracketed plaintext.]

[2] [The name Baldrick means "brave warrior."]

[3] *As a boy, my next-door neighbor had the surname Beckenbauer. I was greatly jealous, because my own name was quite suitable for mockery. I envied young Beckenbauer only until I learned German and discovered his last name meant "bowl-builder." This I found greatly comical, though I admit I was unable to make many witticisms on the topic—he had grown to a very large size and taken up boxing.*

[4] [Marv simply *has* to be talking about champion flyweight boxer Jens Beckenbauer, an old hero of mine. The *Chicago Tribune* once called Beckenbauer "pound for pound, the most violent man in America." Mostly now he's remembered as the madman who fought heavyweight champ Max Schmeling, despite being outweighed by 80 pounds. Schmeling took Beckenbauer apart in two rounds, leaving him paralyzed below the waist. Beckenbauer then became a crusader for the rights of the disabled, famously breaking the nose of New York mayor John Lindsay when he refused to install a wheelchair accessible entrance at the New York Public Library.

Both Berger and Beckenbauer were born in 1911 and grew up near the University of Chicago.]

[5] *The old barrel maker from whom I first heard this story in 1936 lived in Alsace. The Alsatians are a very unusual and unhappy people, as they are situated immediately between France and Germany. The territory has been traded between the two countries so many times it is no longer sure what it is. When it is a part of Germany, Alsace is hated because it is too French; when it is a part of France, Alsace is reviled*

constructed. The temple had fallen into disrepair centuries before and the stones, which were still sturdy and useful, had been incorporated into a church. This had pleased the Devil because it had allowed him to do all sorts of mischief.[9] Then that church too had fallen into ruin and farmers from the surrounding lands had picked up the stones and built them into their fences[10] and homes. This pleased

---

for being too German.

[6] [Currently, Alsace is part of France, but it's still schizoid—Alsatian law requires that national newspapers be written in a mix of the two languages, but no more than 25% German.]

[7] *The fortress of Hell is not built out of stone. God leveled against the Fallen the curse that all they build is transient and nothing permanent. Accordingly, they build from grass, leaves and other green matter that forever trickles away from their structures and rises up through the earth, reaching the surface in six month's time. Thus, a great amount of green matter from the infernal winter, when the demons build strongly to insulate against the cold, reaches the world six months later during the terrestrial summer and turns it green. In the infernal summer, when the climate is milder and the demons sleep outside, they do little building and correspondingly there is little green six months later during the terrestrial winter. The exception, of course, is evergreens, for which no satisfactory explanation has ever been offered. Most likely pine trees are in league with the Devil.*

[8] [Well, there's always that possibility.]

[9] *The Devil causes great disruption when he controls a churchstone. He may interrupt church services in sixty-six ways. At least, he may do so in sixty-six ways that have been documented, though I suspect there are more. I myself have witnessed only eight:*
  1. *Making candles burn with blue flames (the only color of light permitted in Hell).*
  2. *Tuning the churchbells to ring a half-step higher.*
  3. *Rotating the entire building and turning the crucifixes so that Christ's head points west.*
  4. *Transforming the unconsecrated host into spiders.*
  5. *Switching the voices of the choir so that sopranos sang as basses, basses as tenors and tenors as sopranos. (Altos remain unaffected.)*
  6. *Flipping over all the tiles or shingles of the roof, exposing their undersides.*
  7. *Covering the windows with tar.*
  8. *Causing the priest's vestments to appear as if they are dripping water.*

[10] [As the adage goes, to include a Devil's stone in a fence is to invite trouble—for the right price he will always lead the enemy through. A song about just such a problem in the Maginot Line was widely sung at cabarets in Paris in the 1930's, despite the French army's attempts at suppressing it. The song is more admirable in French, but Woody Guthrie attempted the following translation in 1951. "André" is French Minister of Defense André Maginot.

André, he built it one thousand miles long,
Higher than fireworks and thick as a gong.
No human can climb it nor tunnel below
And the Devil's at bay on the Maginot Line.

In the sixty-sixth mile, 'tween Alsace and Metz,
André laid a stone that looked like the rest.
He'd found it in ruins where the evergreens grow

the Devil as well because he was able to torment peasants far and wide across the land.

It happened that the temple's altar[11][12] had come into the possession of a man named Baldrick Beckenbauer, who had used it as the cornerstone of his house. Baldrick was a pig farmer and this fact greatly offended the Devil.[13] He determined that he would regain control of the stone and punish Baldrick for his presumption.

The journey from Hell took quite some time[14] and when the Devil finally arrived, Baldrick had already sunk deep into the swamp of old age. The Devil

---

And the Devil's at play on the Maginot Line.

It came from the church where Bael rested his head.
The soldiers that saw it were all filled with dread.
The stone, it splintered in the wet winter snow
When the Devil, he lay on the Maginot Line.

Old Scratch boiled up, his pitchfork in hand,
He mauled the wall once and it crumbled to sand.
He rushed right on through with the Boches in tow
When the Devil broke through on the Maginot line.

[11] *The Devil's altars are most cleverly designed, thanks to the minor imps, many of whom are superb stoneworkers. Altars are not carved, but rather forged, built from layers of granite that have been hammered flat and folded atop one another in an interlinking chain, like so:*

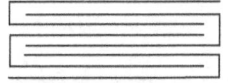

I cannot say that this is any stronger than a solid block of stone nor any lighter. But it does have the great advantage of being difficult to falsify, so that if one sees the particular pattern of striations one knows it is a Devil's stone.

[12] [You could fake it pretty easily with concrete.]

[13] *In the Garden of Eden, the Devil first took on the guise of a goat, but was discovered and attacked by a large group of pigs which chewed off his feet. The debacle caused him to lose face greatly in the eyes of the lesser demons of Hell and the Devil afterward forever hated and feared pigs. For this reason, pig farming was viewed in the Middle Ages as a means of protection from the Devil. It greatly troubled early Christians that Jews refused to keep pigs and led to accusations they were in league with the Devil.*

[14] [If the Devil appears in a form other than his own, his journey to Earth is said to last sixty-six years. If he wishes to appear in his own form with all his attendant powers, then 666 years and he must appear exactly at midnight on New Year's Day at the turn of the millennium.

Among the most famous attempts to summon the Devil was the Ravenna Conspiracy of 1334, which hoped to bring about Armageddon in the year 2000 by summoning the Devil in his true form. Though no evidence has ever been found proving the conspiracy, the Vatican took it seriously, mentioning it during the debate over adopting the Gregorian calendar in 1581. One cardinal argued that because the turn of the year would be switched from March 25 to December 31 and the calendar advanced one year overnight, the Devil's scheduled arrival date would fall on September 6, 2001, ruining the numerology.]

took on the guise of a rich young prince dressed in silk[15][16] and velvet[17][18] and came before the elderly pig farmer.

"Grandpa, this is your lucky day," the prince said. "I've taken a liking to the cornerstone of your house. Let me tear it out and carry it home to my castle, where I shall carve it into fig leaves and use them to decorate my bedroom.[19][20][21] In return I'll give you this sack of gold." At this the prince held out a bag. It was not filled with gold, but rather with nettles that had the appearance of gold.[22]

---

[15] *An indicator that the Devil may be a woman.*

[16] [Or a silkworm.]

[17] *Velvet, of course, was invented by the Devil. As one of his many torments, the Lord sewed the Devil into a horsehair suit before ejecting him from Heaven. The suit itched terribly. Through his fiendish magic, the Devil transformed the horsehair into a soft and supple fabric pleasing to touch. Ultimately this became a torment as well, because the physical pleasure he felt each time he moved reminded him that he could never again touch heavenly substance.*

[18] [I'll be amused if I'm someday damned by the Devil in a velvet suit.]

[19] *As a young man, I had a most curious encounter with the Devil that allowed me to witness the splendor of his bedroom. While in Poland, I wrecked a man's tractor—really, I did not wreck it, so much as he had neglected its maintenance and I was the victim of its sudden failure—and we disputed whether I was in debt to him over the damaged machinery or he to me over my medical expenses. The absurd Polish legal system—really, the nicest thing I can say is that the judge provided us with the most delicious pastries during our interminable wait—could not provide a satisfactory solution, so it was suggested to us that we try a most effective arbitrator. This man was the Devil.*

His solution was quite ingenious. He bought the broken tractor himself at an excellent price, the farmer had money enough for a down payment on new machinery, and in lieu of a cash payment, I was healed and taken on a tour of Hell.

Lucifer's bedroom was fantastic. It was guarded by a pair of enormous hedgehogs carrying halberds; each wore a suit of armor into which were pierced holes for their quills and these holes reproduced the constellations of the night sky. Into the floor was carved a great pool, which interconnected with all the underground rivers in the Earth. A group of porpoises that had been taught the sounds of human language lived in it and carried the Devil's messages out into the world. I conversed with them at great length regarding their battles against the much more ancient messenger race of God, the sharks.

On the walls of the cavern were carved the letters of every alphabet that ever has or ever will exist. I was particularly fascinated with some of the future symbols, but my records of them vanished when I was transported back to the Overworld.

[20] [Wait a minute—what happened to the part about demons not being able to engage in permanent handicrafts, like stonecarving?]

[21] *Of course, it was not the Devil who had made the carvings, but the dolphins. The Devil's bedroom was once an underground cavern entirely filled with water.*

[22] [Gold mixed with nettles was believed to produce an especially diabolical poison. Oral contact—for example biting a poisoned coin to test its authenticity—caused the hollow bones of the limbs to fill with lead and the flat bones of the skull and ribs to itch uncontrollably. When the victims attempted to move their arms to scratch, their tendons tore right off the bones.]

Baldrick was a simple man who had not grown old through hard work,[23] nor native intelligence,[24] nor loyal friends,[25] nor good fortune.[26] [27] He had simply grown old. His knuckles were notched by a lifetime of scars and his posture wrecked from carrying heavy loads on his shoulders. He was blind as a weaver and deaf as a stonemason[28] and had lived alone in his little cottage in the many

---

[23] *Baldrick Beckenbauer was so lazy that when he wanted to make a sweater, he didn't bother to shear his sheep. He simply knit them together and wore them still living.*

[24] *Baldrick Beckenbauer was so stupid that he once painted his house green in hopes deer would come to graze on it and he might kill them for meat. Baldrick had no green paint, so he went to the fields and scraped the color from each blade of grass and coated his house with the pigment. However, the fields in every direction were stripped of their color and looked as white and dead as winter. Seeing this, the deer went to their winter forage grounds and none came to the house of Baldrick Beckenbauer.*

[25] *Baldrick Beckenbauer's friends were so disloyal that once, when they found buried treasure, they cheated him out of his rightful share. Baldrick and two other farmers were walking the boundary lines of their fields when they discovered a pot full of coins beneath an uprooted tree. In the pot were 10,000 copper pennies, 1,000 silver thalers and 100 gold guilders. Baldrick, seeing a chance to come out ahead, asked that his share be the copper, reasoning he would be richest because the pennies were greatest in number. The others happily agreed. One took the silver and the other the gold.*
    They set out for town, but on the way, one of the men noticed Baldrick straining under his share of the loot. He offered to trade Baldrick's 10,000 pennies for his 1,000 silver thalers. Baldrick regretted that he was being swindled (for 10,000 was a great deal more than 1,000), but was afraid of losing his neighbor's friendship even more. So they made the exchange. But still Baldrick found the load too heavy, so the third farmer offered to trade his 100 guilders for the 1,000 thalers. Baldrick despaired at his impending ruin, but made the trade anyway for sake of friendship.
    When they arrived in town, the two other farmers immediately went off to buy fine suits of clothes with their copper and silver. Baldrick went to the market and asked to buy as many pigs as his guilders would get him. Well, the sight of befuddled old Baldrick Beckenbauer with so much gold occasioned comment, and eventually the sheriff was called for. "How did you come by such a fortune?" the sheriff asked. While Baldrick was puzzling out the exact sequence of events, his two neighbors returned dressed in their new finery and were mistaken for foreign noblemen.
    "This brigand set upon us and stole our gold," the two farmers said, realizing their advantage. Baldrick was thrown in jail and his gold taken from him and divided between his two neighbors

[26] *Baldrick Beckenbauer was so misfortunate that…*

[27] [Marv, you've had more than enough. You want misfortune you've got the whole damn story here, right?]

[28] [A preponderance of stonecarvers really were deaf. Marble and granite contain significant amounts of cadmium, which can damage the auditory nerve. In large pieces of stone, it is chemically inert and harmless, but finely ground dust containing cadmium becomes highly reactive when exposed to lipids (including earwax) and can cause deafness.
    Conventional wisdom in medieval Germany held that deaf stonecarvers were better craftspeople because they had better-developed senses of touch. Many workshops—most famously Strasbourg in Alsace—actively recruited deaf children. Others deliberately punctured the eardrums of their apprentices.]

years since his wife had died. But he still had his wits about him.

"If I pull the cornerstone from my house," said Baldrick, "The walls will collapse and the roof cave in. I would be left to sleep out in the cold on a bed of rock and shingles."

"But you could build a new house with the money," said the prince. "Larger and warmer than this one."

"My friends would notice," said Baldrick. "They're nosy types. It would occasion great talk and rumors that I had come into the money dishonestly. So, I must refuse. Better to live modestly than to lose the good opinion of one's neighbors."

The Devil was amused rather than annoyed. He departed and an hour later returned in the guise of the Pope. "My son, there is a great crisis," said the Pope to Baldrick. "The emperor has died without a successor. All of his counselors and generals have agreed you are the wisest and most virtuous man in the empire and have chosen you to rule. If you pull out the cornerstone of your house to prove your identity, I shall crown you immediately and take you with me to Rome." At this, the Pope showed Baldrick a beautiful helm that had been carved from a single enormous pearl and inlaid with sapphires and garnets.[29] In fact the crown was made of ice and would have frozen the top of Baldrick's head until it shattered, leaving his brain exposed to the open air.[30]

"That's all very nice," said Baldrick, "But the emperor lives in a castle and my wretched knees would never survive climbing all those stairs."[31] [32] [33]

"You might hire a man to carry you," said the Devil.

"No," said Baldrick. "Because that man might be bought by my enemies. He would drop me down the stairs and call it an accident. So, I must decline. Better

---

[29] [This could be a stunningly apt description of the hat Greta Garbo wore to the Christmas Day premiere of *Flesh and the Devil* in 1926:

Despite his distaste for movies in general, Marv adored Garbo and saw everything in which she appeared. He told me she was surely the missing fifth surveyor of the goddess Yngria (though characteristically he did not explain who Yngria was or why she employed surveyors.)]

[30] [Not an especially painful death—the brain itself contains no pain-sensing nerve endings.]

[31] *If he has knee problems, Baldrick is most certainly a Capricorn. He has the attendant stubbornness of that zodialogical sign as well. I myself am a Capricorn.*

[32] [As am I.]

[33] [Only, no—wait. Marv was born March 25, 1911, which makes him an Aries.]

to live alone than become reliant on those who might wish one harm."

The Devil left chuckling to himself and again returned, this time in the form of an old crone whose face was covered with boils as red and hard as dogwood branches. Three beautiful women accompanied her. One came from the north and had a head of perfect blonde hair. One came from the south and had perfect black legs. And one came from the east and had hands of perfect delicacy and grace.[34] Really they were not women at all, but in fact lice.

"Handsome sir," the crone wheezed, "I have lost my beauty, which I once valued above all else, through a terrible curse. It will be restored to me if I can burn the cornerstone of your house down into lime to make a cream for my face. My three sisters will all marry you in thanks if you agree."

"Three wives!" exclaimed Baldrick. "The Bible forbids such a thing."

"But think upon the case of Abraham," said the crone. "He had two wives."

"And it was well that he did not have more," said Baldrick. "Old as he was, Abraham could please only two women at once. In my youth I could easily have taken three,[35] but in my dotage[36] I am no more virile[37] than the father of Isaac and two[38] is my limit.[39] Better no wives at all than more wives than a man can delight."

This astounded the Devil and so filled him with mirth that he barely kept

---

[34] [Presumably the Devil himself is the representative of the missing direction, west. So strongly is the Devil associated with the west in Alsatian legend that he is said to be unable to face due east. To move in an easterly direction, the Devil travels a zigzag course, continually turning the long way around. The sight of this supposedly inspired the first sailors to turn their boats in a similar fashion when they traveled into the wind (called "wearing" or "jibing").]

[35] *I once pleased eight women simultaneously using methods I learnt from the love manual of a certain prince, known in Germany as Schalatzen or in Arabia as Zhalahan. The prince had quite an expert group of concubines and made the study of coital pleasure his life's work. His methodology involves touching one woman with the mouth, one with the penis, one with each foot and two with each hand. I must confess that on my own first attempt I seem to have pleased only four of my seven co-experimenters, on account that I lacked sufficient dexterity in my left hand and both feet. Schalatzen cautions initiates not to make their first attempt with more than three and I must most chagrinedly agree.*

[36] [I'm honestly supposed to believe that?]

[37] *I must here admit that I am a bit mistaken. Truthfully, it was not the tract itself I read, but a copy of a chronicle that refers to that text. But it has some very lovely illustrations.*

[38] [I meant the part about the eight women. Was it seven women or eight?]

[39] *Those who claim I was with eight women are very much mistaken. I have never made such a claim. Eight would have killed me and the experiment would have been entirely ruined. Besides, I had limited means and could afford only seven co-experimenters.*

his disguise from shimmering away. He then returned a final time, taking on the guise of an ancient, white-bearded alchemist whose mustache hung so low it tangled in his bootlaces. He wore robes of blue leather inscribed with silver threads that traced out runes and decorative Latin phrases. "It's your lucky day, youngster," said the alchemist. "I've found the secret to making the elixir of life." From the depths of his robe he pulled a tiny glass vial containing a virulently yellow liquid. In fact it was not the elixir of life, but rhinoceros urine.[40] "One sip of this and you'll be young and spry again. I would make bucketfuls and grant eternal youth to all who dwell in these mountains and valleys, but I am missing a single ingredient—I need to grind down the cornerstone of your house to make the catalyst."

"Eternal life sounds a blessing," said Baldrick. "But it would be no such thing. For your elixir contains sand and when sand gets in a man's blood, it drives him mad. The grains push through into his toes and he can't walk but where the sand tells him. Those men claw their way through anyone they meet on the way to the nearest desert, which the sand considers to be paradise. Normally we shoot such men, but if they had eternal life they would cause great inconvenience."

The Devil had never heard such a thing and could make no reply.

"Better[41] to[42] be[43] a[44] sane[45] old[46] man[47] than[48] a[49] mad[50] young[51] one,[52]" said

---

[40] [This must be backwards. Rhinoceros urine is famous for causing impotence, which would seem to associate it more readily with the beautiful women. Lice, on the other hand, reproduce so quickly and without regard for food supply that they kill themselves off and would seem to be related to the overpopulation caused by eternal youth. My guess is that the two were simply reversed, though I'll admit I'm not sure how even the Devil fashions women from rhinoceros urine.]

[41] [Like hell it is. I'm twenty-five and I'd love to do fifteen again. I would have done fifteen again even when I was fifteen. I was mad, sure, but what fifteen-year-old can say otherwise? By my senior year of high school I had been in love with no fewer than...

[42] *I knew the most beautiful...*

[43] [You know what? No. You don't get another story. It's my turn. I was in love with no fewer than four different girls at any given time when I was a teenager. I can still list every one of them. They were...]

[44] *...Filomena Contadina, Ursula Blackpine, Cassandra McCaughnagh, Violetta Baker, Lilith Nix, Lucretia Cadwallader, and Blahonia Atlai. But at eighty-five, with the advantage of...*

[45] [Advantage, nothing. Marv, you were by no means a sane old man. I saw how you lived, the piles of stolen library books in the sink and the mounds of takeout cartons blocking your closet doors. There's something borderline heroic about you fending off old age all by yourself, losing the battle of inches against senility, but you lost all the same. Shouldn't the question be whether you'd rather be a mad old man or a mad young one?]

[46] *As a boy I wanted to marry Nennius, whom I thought was a woman, and whom I did not yet realize*

Baldrick and shut his front door. The Devil shook his head[53] and went on his way, promising never again to deal with old fools.

Shortly thereafter, God took pity on Baldrick and sent St. Michael the Archangel to remove the profane stone that had caused such annoyance. St. Michael knocked politely at the door and Baldrick, who was entirely sick of visitors,[54] threw it open.

"Hail, Baldrick," said the angel. "You have resisted temptation and the Lord has smiled upon you. I have been sent to take away the source of your torment." But Baldrick scowled and said, "You have swan-wings. All birds are liars because of their wings—just as their wings serve them as both hands and the means of their flight, so too their words do double work. You may mean to take away my cornerstone—that much is certain—but if you mean to take away the source of my torment, then you must mean my life. And I intend to live."

St. Michael was appalled. "There's no double meaning," he said. "As an angel I cannot bear false witness."

"All you birdmen are frauds!" shouted Baldrick. He picked up a rock and hurled it at the angel.

"Stop," said St. Michael. "You..." But another rock struck him in the face. "You've misunderstood. You're under a misapprehension." A rock glanced off his leg, one off his back, one off his neck. St. Michael became angry, drew his fiery

---

was a source considerably more entertaining than he was...

[47] [Nennius passed off a handful of Welsh nursery rhymes for history—of course you'd love him for that—but you can't hold a candle to him as a fabricator, Marv. The Anglo-Saxon intelligentsia cornered him around the year 800 and said, "We Germans are superior to you Britons because we have a written language and you have none." Nennius said, "No such thing," and invented a system of runes on the spot. You're strictly an amateur next to him, Marv. Where's your bravura fabrication? Where's your language scratched on the ground with a burnt stick?]

[48] ...someone to take up my work when I shuffle...

[49] [Marv, my dear, I would take it up if you'd let me fit a word in edgewise.]

[50] ...and as the old Polish farmer finished his tale, I said to him, "Why, that is the most peculiar story I have ever heard. But that is hardly a story to stand alone—surely there are more to follow it!" And he replied, "I only ever learned the story that far and can't say whether or not it continues."

[51] [Relax, old man. I'll wrap this one up for you. Sit back and enjoy.]

[52] ... then so much the better.

[53] [So. The Devil can't actually shake his head—he has been hanged so many times that his neck is double jointed. When he nods he gets the most terrible whiplash.]

[54] [I'm plenty sick of interruptions myself.]

sword and slashed out Baldrick's right leg from under him so that he could not step into his throws.[55]

"Please," said St. Michael. "Don't move. I'll just take that stone and we'll see about a miracle to restore your…"

But Baldrick had reached inside the door and picked up an old fowling piece he kept to scare away thieves and trespassers. "Better to be damned through action than sainted for inaction," the old man said. He pulled back the hammer and took aim, but St. Michael unfurled his wings to their full length and looped through the air[56] He landed beside the cornerstone and pulled it free with a mighty heave. Baldrick's house collapsed into a pile of rubble and shingles. St. Michael spat and soared free with the stone still in his arms.

As the sunlight leaked from the sky, Baldrick sat muttering to himself, legless and dying, cradling his rifle in his arms, while the howls of wolves drew ever nearer. And he had only the single shot.[57]

---

[55] [JL Wannecker and Dennis Hoist argue in their 1972 book *Sins Most Sinister* that if Baldrick steps into his throws with his right leg, he is left-handed, an indicator that he is a tool of the Devil from the very beginning. I'm inclined to believe that Baldrick is right-handed and St. Michael simply cuts off the wrong leg, having faulty idea of the mechanics involved in throwing because he has always fought with a sword. I had a similar misunderstanding, for years stepping right-legged into my right-handed throws. Though, I don't suppose it matters which leg Baldrick is missing—he won't be stepping into much of anything.]

[56] [Impossible. St. Michael has swan's wings, which don't provide adequate lift for aerial maneuvers like loops. Swans are so clumsy that if one overturns while swimming it has no way of righting itself and will drown.]

[57] [Marvin Ipswich Berger disappeared from his Boston, Massachusetts apartment on December 20, 2003, leaving behind 11,000 manuscript pages containing his life's work. At that time, I was visiting my family in Wisconsin and knew nothing about what had transpired.

When I returned to Boston two weeks later, I found the superintendent cleaning out Marv's apartment. He explained that Marv had been several months in arrears on his rent, and he suspected Marv had fled, rather than be evicted. I was shocked that Marv hadn't sent word to me or taken his magnum opus with him.

The super was in his sixth day of throwing away Marv's junk and had already disposed of all the loose papers he could find. He invited me to take whatever I could find. After a thorough search, I was able to recover only a few scattered pages on which Marv had made notes on a story about an old man fooling the Devil. It was one that Marv had told me several times, but never the same way twice. From his notes and those verbal accounts, I have stitched the story back together.

A body matching Marv's description was recovered from the Charles River six months later, but was too badly decomposed for positive identification. It was missing its right leg.]

The Scouring

Rikki Ducornet

How grateful I am for The Scouring! The physical world, once so overwhelming, is now reduced to level planes and we may press onward, fearless of obstructions. I recall with a certain residual horror, the fetid smells so common in my youth, the stench of rotting vegetable matter, of blossoms wantoning in the untamed season called "Spring," the aggravation of birdsong, the heady impositions of "Summer" when the birdbaths were green with the scum of stagnant water. Then "Fall"—its rank odors of dead leaves, the terrible bodies of things that scuttled about in those leaves, the persistence of slugs… One might have, within an hour, been harried by a butterfly or worse: a moth, a wasp, a bee, or a spider stewing in its own malevolence right under one's very bed! (I almost forgot "Winter," that season of damp basements.)

The New Generation has no inkling of these things. They could not care less. I do not wish to burden them with my stories of the past and its baroque intrusions. It would be criminal to trouble their placid velocities, the ordered economy of their meditations with my relic tales of obstacles overcome. They know nothing of The Scouring, the horrors of The Transition, the blind optimism of The Reconstruction. This is how it should be. The New Generation is serene, propelled like beams of light—not yet disembodied, although this will surely come. Together we sweep across the globe in imitation of the cosmical machine. The sound of wind—the wind of our own making—is the only sound we hear. No footfalls, no gnashing of teeth, no conversation. We are no longer the playthings of the weather, gossip, temper, or appetite.

For a time, it is true, I missed the smells of cooking, and in the secret sanctum of my kitchen—now off limits—I did not neutralize the air, but instead heightened the experience—now impossible to describe—by sealing the windows and the door. I'd make a stew of lamb, say, or bake a gingerbread—not to eat them, mind you (for already we had overcome the vicious cycles of corporeal servitude) but to inhale those fragrances. It all seems so very long ago! I would luxuriate (please—not a word of this to anyone!) in the scrubbing of the pots and pans. (In the old days I was considered soft: a man who liked to cook! A stupid activity. Cooking, like sex, stimulates all the senses to an extraordinary degree.)

These days I barely recall the sound of butter sizzling in the pan, but I know it was a thing I much appreciated as a child. And the apples glazed with caramel that shattered against the teeth. (It bewilders the New Generation to hear of such things. Should we describe the teeth and their function, they are appalled. Not to mention the art of relieving oneself on the can—a sorrowful redundancy, or so they suppose.)

Such conversations are brief and they happen so rarely! Once there was an anomalous obstruction in the path and we were brought to a precipitous halt unexpectedly. I collided into the person in front of me—a tremendous shock, you can well imagine, to the system. We were fenced in on each side by the bright titanium tussocks so favored by the highway authorities. I could see she was distressed by the number of knicks and pocks on surfaces she had thought impervious to time and the vicissitudes of space. It was eerie not to feel the wind of forward motion. For some reason, I was impelled to speak—an old habit that reveals the extent of my dotage. I only wished to—as we used to say—"crack a joke" when I suggested we get a coffee and relax while waiting for the system to be repaired. This offended her; the New Generation is mysteriously ashamed not to have a mouth, a tongue, or teeth. I should have stopped there, but something—and I admit this was perverse, criminally so—prodded me on. *There were once so many palpable pleasures*, I conveyed to her with our ever more restricted vocabulary. *I wish, I dearly wish, you had a pair of lips so that I could kiss you.*

She was a bright cobalt blue, but when she blushed—a thing beyond my wildest expectations—she turned violet, a color she had surely never seen. *It is a pity and a shame* I continued, moved beyond belief, *that you are so fiercely serrated. In another time and place I might have cooked you dinner and after we might have eagerly embraced.*

This was madness on my part. I knew such talk would cause my jaws to seize up within minutes and, quite possibly, cause her to fatally percolate. Already something very like steam was spilling from her post acoustical ducts. We were bombarded by bright clusters of echoing forms, a spillage precipitated by the unexpected obstruction and the ensuing exquisite collision. With something of the old delight I noted that the concave mirrors of her eyes reflected both the tussocks and the sky above us.

I wish, I confided, *we could taste each other!*

She darkened further and condensed. To my surprise I could now behold her many aspects simultaneously. My own eyes—so unaccustomed to exercise—selected favorite objects and guessed the lovely disarray quickening beneath her dusky shell. Between the dazzling planets of her breasts her heart twinkled. *Your beauty* I conveyed to her, *is a force and . . . an atmosphere*!

At that precise instant the obstacle dissolved. Had I been able to use my nose, this dissolution would have been accompanied by the smell of burnt toast. Stillness invites reflection and its familiar subversions. Now that we were moving, the world was shut away. Already the *emblematic* encounter (I am, I admit, what was once called a Romantic) and the memory of that encounter eluded me.

Imagine rocks and raked sand—but *tinned*, as in the past sardines were tinned in oil—and you will have some idea as to the nature of my thinking once we were under way again.

Fugue-State

Brian Evenson

I.

I had, Bentham claimed, *fallen into a sort of fugue-state in which the world moved past me more and more rapidly, a kind of blur englobing me at every instant.* And yet he had never, so he confided to Arnaud, felt either disoriented or confused. Yes, admittedly, during this period he had no clear idea of his own name, yet despite this he felt he understood things clearly for the first time. He perceived the world in a different way, at a speed which allowed him to ignore the non-essential—such as names, or, rather, such as his own name—and perceive things he could never before even have imagined.

Arnaud listened carefully. *Fugue-state*, he recorded, then removed his eyeglasses and placed them on the desk in front of him. He looked up, squinting.

"And do you remember your name now?" he asked.

At first, Bentham did not answer. Arnaud remained patient. He watched a blurred Bentham glance about himself, searching for some clue.

"Yes," said Bentham finally. "Of course I do."

"Will you please tell it to me?" asked Arnaud.

"Why do you need to know?"

Arnaud rubbed his eyes. *Subject does not know own name*, he recorded.

"Will you please describe the room you're in?" he asked. Bentham instead tried to sit up, was prevented by the straps. *Subject unaware of surroundings*, Arnaud noted. "Will you describe your room, please?" asked Arnaud again.

"I don't see the point," said Bentham, his voice rising. "You're here. You're in it. You can see it just as well as I can."

Arnaud leaned forward until his lips were nearly touching the microphone. "But that's just it, Bentham," he said softly. "I'm not in the room with you at all."

It was shortly after this that Bentham began to bleed from the eyes. This was not a response Arnaud had been trained to expect. Indeed, at first, his glasses still on the desk before him, Arnaud was convinced it was a trick of the light, an oddly cast shadow. He polished his glasses against his shirt-front and hooked them back over his ears, and only then was he certain that each of Bentham's sockets were pooling with blood. Startled, he must have exclaimed aloud, for Bentham turned his head slightly in the direction of the intercom speaker. The blood in one eye slopped against the bridge of his nose. The blood in the other spilled down his cheek, gathering in the whorl of his ear.

6:13, Arnaud wrote, *Subject has begun to bleed from eyes.*

"Bentham," Arnaud asked, "how do you feel?"

"Fine," said Bentham. "I feel fine. Why?"

6:14, Arnaud recorded. *Subject feels fine.* Then added, *Is bleeding from eyes.*

Picking up the telephone, he depressed the call button.

"I need an outside line," said Arnaud when the operator picked up.

"You know the rules," said the operator. "No outside lines during session with subject."

Blood too, Arnaud noticed, had started to drip from Bentham's nose. Perhaps it was coming from his ears as well. Though with Bentham's visible ear already puddled with the blood from his eye, it was difficult to be certain.

"The subject appears to be dying," said Arnaud.

"Dying?" said the operator. "Of what?"

"Of bleeding," said Arnaud.

"I see," said the operator. "Please hold the line."

The operator exchanged himself for a low and staticky muzak. Arnaud, holding the receiver against his ear, watched Bentham. It was a song he felt he should recognize but he could not quite grasp what it was. Bentham tried to sit up again, straining against the straps as if unaware of them, without any hint of panic. In general he seemed unaware of what was happening to him. A bloody flux was spilling out of his mouth now as well, Arnaud noticed. He groped for a pen to record this, but could not find one.

Bentham shook his head quickly as if to clear it, spattering blood on the glass between them. Then he bared his teeth. This was, Arnaud felt, a terrible thing to watch.

The muzak clicked off.

"Accounting," said a flat, implacable voice.

"Excuse me?" said Arnaud.

"Accounting division."

"I don't understand," said Arnaud. "The subject assigned to me is dying."

The man on the other end did not respond. Bentham, Arnaud saw through the glass, had stopped moving.

"I think he may have just died," said Arnaud.

"Not my jurisdiction, sir," said the voice, still flat, and the line went dead.

It was hard for him to be certain that Bentham was no longer alive. Several times, as Arnaud prepared to record a time of death, Bentham offered a weak movement that dissuaded him, the curling or uncurling of a finger, the parting of his lips. He was not certain if these were actual movements or simply the corpse ridding itself of its remaining vitality. For accuracy's sake, he felt, he should unlock the adjoining door between the two rooms and go through, manually checking Bentham's pulse with his fingers. Or, rather, making certain there was no pulse to check. But the strangeness of Bentham's condition made him feel it might be better to leave the adjoining door closed.

As to leaving his own room, he had no choice but to wait until the session had officially expired and a guard came to unlock the door. He waited, watching Bentham dead or dying. He watched the blood dry between them, on the window. When his ear began to ache, he realized he was still pushing the dead receiver against his face, and hung it up.

He stood and looked under his desk until he found his pen, then wrote in his notebook *6:26, Patient dead?*

The remainder of the session he spent, pen poised over the notebook, watching Bentham for any signs of life. He watched the skin on Bentham's face change character, losing its elasticity, seeming to settle more tightly around the bone. The nose became more and more accentuated, the cheeks growing hollow. The frightful perfection of the skull, the tongs of the jawbones, glowed dully through the skin. Even when the guard opened the door behind him, it was very hard for Arnaud to look away.

"Ready?" the guard asked. "Session's over."

"I think he's dead," said Arnaud.

"How's that?" said the guard. "Come again?"

The guard came and stood next to Arnaud, stared into Bentham's room. Arnaud looked too.

When he looked back up he saw that the guard was looking at him with frightened eyes.

"What is it?" Arnaud asked.

But at first the guard did not answer, just kept looking at Arnaud. *Why?* Arnaud wondered, and waited.

"What," the guard finally asked, "exactly did you do to him?"

It was not until that moment that Arnaud realized how wrong things could go for him.

II.

The guard became business-like and efficient, hustling him out of the observation room and down the hall.

"Where are we going?" Arnaud asked.

"Just down here," said the guard, keeping a firm grip on Arnaud's arm, propelling him forward.

They passed down one flight of stairs, and through another hall. They went down a short flight, Arnaud nearly tripping, and then immediately up three brief steps and through a door that read "conference rooms." The door opened onto a short hallway with three doors on either side and one at the end.

The guard walked him down to the final door, coaxed him inside. "Wait here," the guard said.

"For what?" Arnaud asked.

But the guard, already gone, did not answer.

Arnaud tried the door he had come through; it was locked. He tried the door at the far end of the room; this was locked as well.

He sat down at the table and stared at the wall.

After a while, he began to read from his notebook. *Fugue-state*, he read. Had he done anything wrong? he wondered. Was he to blame? Was anything in fact his fault? *6:13*, he read, *subject has begun to bleed from eyes*. Even if it were not his fault, would he somehow be held responsible? *Subject feels fine*, he read. *Is bleeding from eyes.*

Oh no, he thought.

He got up and tried both doors again.

He sat down again, but found it difficult to sit still. Perhaps he was in very serious trouble, he thought. He was not to blame for whatever had happened to Bentham. But someone had to be blamed, didn't they? And thus he was to blame.

Or was he? Perhaps he was becoming hysterical.

He opened the notebook again and began to read from it. The words were the same as they had been before. To him, now, they seemed all right, mostly. Perhaps the guard was simply following routine procedure in the case of an unusual death.

No, he began to worry a few moments later, something was wrong. Subjects did not habitually bleed from the eyes, for a start. He closed the notebook, leaving it face down on the table.

On the far side of the room, affixed to the wall, he noticed a telephone. He stood and went to it.

"Operator," a voice said.

"Outside line, please," he said.

"Right away, sir," the operator said. "What number?"

He gave the number. The dial tone changed to a thrumming, punctured by intervals of silence.

Nobody was answering.

After a time the thrumming stopped and a recorded voice came on, the tape so distorted he could barely make the words out. It was a man's voice. *Not the right number*, he thought, and started to hang up, and then thought, no, he might not have a chance to dial out again. *Hapler*, the distorted voice identified itself as, or perhaps *Handler* or *Hapner*. Nobody he knew. But Handler or Hapler would have to do.

"Hello?" he said. "Mr. Hapner? Is that in fact the correct name? My name is Arnaud. I'm afraid I've been given your number in error."

He swallowed, then began choosing his words carefully.

"There's been a misunderstanding," he said. "I have every hope it will be quickly resolved, everyone's heart is in the right place. But, Mr. Hapner, could I trouble you to contact my wife? Would you ask her, assuming that I am not safe and sound by the time you reach her, to do what she can to find out what has become of me? It would mean a great deal to both of us." He stopped, thought. "She might," he finally added, "begin with Bentham."

Immediately after he hung up the telephone began to ring. Almost reflexively, he picked it up.

"Hello?" he said.

"Who is this?" a voice asked.

Arnaud hesitated. "Why," he asked slowly, "do you want to know?"

"Mr. Arnaud," said the voice. "Why are you answering the telephone?"

He didn't know what to say. He held the receiver, looked out the window.

"You made a call a few moments ago," the voice said. "What was the purpose of this call?"

"I don't know what you're talking about," said Arnaud.

"How are you acquainted with—" he heard a rustling through the receiver "—this Mr. Hapner?"

"I—" said Arnaud.

"—and what, in your opinion, is the nature of the so-called…misunderstanding."

Not knowing what else to say, Arnaud hung up the telephone.

By the time he was sitting down again, a guard had come into the room. A new guard, not the same one. He stood just inside one of the doors, watching Arnaud nervously.

"Hello," said Arnaud, just as nervously.

The guard nodded.

"What's this all about?" asked Arnaud.

"I'm not allowed to converse with you," the guard said.

"Why not?" asked Arnaud.

The guard did not answer.

Arnaud thumbed through his notebook again. His eyes for some reason were having a hard time focusing on his handwriting, making it out to be furry, blurred. No, he thought, he had followed procedure. He was not to blame. Unless they blamed him for the phone call. But couldn't he explain that away? Nobody had told him he wasn't allowed to telephone. There was really nothing to worry about, he told himself. Bentham's death could not be attributed to his negligence.

The original guard came back in. The two guards stood together just inside the door, whispering, looking at him, one of them frequently scratching the skin behind his ear. Eventually the original guard went to the telephone and disconnected it from the wall. Telephone under his arm, he came over to Arnaud and took his notebook away. Then he went out again.

Arnaud swiveled his chair around to face the remaining guard. He spread his arms wide.

"What harm could it possibly do to talk to me?"

The guard pointed a finger at him, shook it. "You've been warned," he said.

He stood up and went to the window. Outside, past the doubled fence, dim shapes wandered about beneath a mottled sky.

He heard the door open. When he turned both guards, edges blurring, were present again, conversing, watching him. They seemed to be speaking to each other very rapidly, in a steady drone. He had to concentrate to understand them.

"He's been standing there," one of them was saying, "just like that, hours now."

But no, he had only been there for a few moments, hadn't he? Something was wrong with them.

One of them suddenly darted over and stood next to him.

"Come with us," the guard said.

"No use resisting," the same guard said.

Arnaud nodded and stepped forward, and then felt himself suddenly propelled. Each guard, he realized, had taken hold of one of his arms and was dragging him.

The conference room was replaced by a stretch of hall.

"Malingerer, eh?" said one of the guards, only the words didn't seem to correspond with the quivering movement of his lips, seemed instead to be coming at a distance, from the hall behind him.

No, Arnaud suddenly realized, amazed, something isn't wrong with them. Something is wrong with me.

They rushed him through the hall and into an observation booth. His observation booth, he realized, the one he had used to interview Bentham. Perhaps he was being allowed to return to work. Who would his next subject be? Bentham, he saw on the other side of the glass, was gone, though pinkish streaks of diluted blood were still visible on the glass.

He started toward his chair, but the guards were still holding him. Gently, he tried to free himself, but they wouldn't let go. Then he realized that he was being dragged toward the adjoining door, toward the subject chamber.

"No," he said, "but I, I'm not a subject."

"Of course not," a guard soothed, his face more a splotch of color than a face. "Who claimed you were?"

"But—" he said.

He grabbed hold of the doorframe on the way through. He held on. Something hard was pushing into his back, just below the blade of his shoulder. Something ground his fingers against the metal of the doorframe, his hand growing numb. Then his grip gave and he was through the door, being strapped to Bentham's bed. A fourth person in the room, a technician, was snapping on latex gloves.

"I'm not a subject," Arnaud claimed again.

The technician just smiled. Arnaud watched the smile smear across her face, consume it. Something was wrong with his vision. He could no longer see the technician clearly, she was just a blur, but from having watched subjects through the glass he could derive what she surely must be doing: an ampoule, a hypodermic, the first emptying, the chamber of the second filling.

The blur shifted, was shot through with light.

"This may sting just a little," the technician said. But Arnaud felt nothing.

What's wrong? he wondered. "Not so bad, is it?" the technician asked, coming briefly into focus again. And then she stepped away and was swallowed up by the wall.

"Hello?" Arnaud said.

Nobody answered.

"Is anybody there?" he asked.

Where had they gone? How much time had passed? He looked about him but couldn't make sense of what he saw. Everything seemed reduced to two dimensions, shadow and light becoming replacements for objects rather than something in which they bathed. He lifted his head and looked down at his body but could not recognize it, could not even perceive it as a body, despite being almost certain it was there.

Fugue-state, he thought idly. And then thought, *Oh, God. I've caught it too.*

"Hello?" said a voice. It was smooth, quiet. It struck him as familiar. "Arnaud?" it said.

He turned, saw no-one, just a flat black square. *Speaker*, he thought. Then he remembered the observation booth, turned instead to where, though he couldn't quite make it out, he thought it must be.

"Yes?" he said. "Hello?"

"How do you feel?"

"I feel fine," he claimed.

He heard a vague rustling, was not certain if it was coming from somewhere in his room or from the observation booth.

"Hello?" he said.

"Yes?" said the voice. "What's wrong, please?"

Arnaud waited, listened. There it was again, a rustling. He swiveled his ear toward it.

"I apologize for these precautions," said the voice, "but we had to assure ourselves that you were not a…liability, didn't we? For your own…safety as well as our own."

Arnaud did not answer.

"Arnaud, did you understand what I said?"

"Yes," said Arnaud. He tried to get up and thought he had but then realized he was still lying down. What was happening, exactly?

"Good," said the voice. "Shall we move straight to the point? Did you murder Bentham?"

Bentham? he wondered. Who was Bentham again? He blinked, tried to focus. "No," he said.

"What happened to Bentham?"

"I don't know," said Arnaud.

"Arnaud, seven days ago, you interviewed Bentham. During that session he died."

"Yes," said Arnaud, remembering. "He died. But it wasn't seven days ago. It was just a few hours ago."

"Are you sure, Arnaud? Are you certain?"

"Yes," said Arnaud. "I'm certain."

The rustling seemed gone now. He found if he tilted his head and squinted he could make rise from the flat surface of the wall, hovering like a ghost just above it, the plane of glass between his room and the observation booth. The glass was flat as well, depthless. Bentham's blood, the dull, nearly faded swathes of it, drifted like another flattened ghost on its surface. But somehow he could not see through blood or glass to the other side.

"Who is Mr. Hapner?" the voice asked.

Arnaud hesitated. "I don't know," he said, perplexed.

"You don't know," the voice said. "And yet after Bentham's death you placed a telephone call to a Mr. Hapner. How do you explain this?"

"I'm afraid I have no explanation," said Arnaud. "I don't even remember doing it."

He closed his eyes. When he opened them again, the room seemed to have shifted, flattening out like a piece of paper. It was still a room, he tried to convince himself, only less so.

For an instant, the room grew clearer.

"—case," the voice was saying. "How did he die?"

He tried to remember. "He began to bleed," he said. "From the eyes," he said.

"Yes," said the voice. "So you wrote. What made this happen, do you think?"

"I don't know," said Arnaud. "How should I know?"

"Think carefully. Did it have anything to do with you?"

He kept looking at the plane of glass, trying to worm his vision through. The voice kept at him, asking him the same questions in slightly different ways, repeating, following procedure. Arnaud kept answering as best he could.

"About this record of your interview," said the voice. "Is it, to the best of your knowledge, accurate?"

"Of course," claimed Arnaud. And then, "What record?"

The voice started to speak, fell silent. Arnaud waited, listened. There it was again, a rustling.

"What does the word 'fugue-state' mean to you?" asked the voice. But now it sounded harsher, less encouraging, almost like a different voice.

"It doesn't mean anything," said Arnaud.

"And yet you wrote it. What exactly did you mean?"

"I don't know," said Arnaud. "I just wrote it."

"Do you see, Arnaud? Right here? *Fugue-state*?"

He turned his face toward the black square and then, remembering, toward the glass, saw nothing.

"Well?" said the voice.

"Well what?" asked Arnaud.

"And yet," said the voice.

But then it interrupted itself, argued with itself in two different tones and cadences about what question should be asked next.

But how could a single voice do this? Arnaud wondered.

"How many of the one of you are there?" he asked. "Two?"

He waited. The voice did not answer. Perhaps he had said it wrong. Perhaps he had not said what he meant. He was preparing to repeat the question when the voice answered, in its harsher tone.

"How many of us do there appear to you to be?"

He opened his mouth to respond, closed it. He must have said something wrong, he realized, but he was no longer sure what.

"Do you remember your name?" said a voice slowly.

"Yes," said Arnaud. "Of course I do." But then realized no, he did not.

"Will you please tell it to me?" the voice said.

Arnaud hesitated. What was it? It was there, almost on the tip of his tongue. "Why?" he said. "Why exactly do you need to know?"

A voice said, changing, "Arnaud, what do you see?"

A voice said, changing, "Arnaud, what is happening to you?"

A voice said, changing, "Arnaud, how do you feel?"

"Fine," said Arnaud. "I feel fine."

He waited. "Why do you ask?" he finally said.

His face felt wet. Was he in the rain? No, he was indoors. There couldn't be rain. He could no longer see through his eyes.

He knew, from the tone of the voice, or voices, that someone thought something was wrong with him. But he couldn't, for the life of him, figure out what that could possibly be.

III.

There were a series of days he could not remember, how many days he was never certain, days in which, he temporarily deduced, he must have lain comatose and bleeding from the eyes on the floor of a kitchen, next to a woman he assumed, but was no longer certain, must be his wife. And all the days before that which he could not remember either. By the time he managed to open his eyes and felt like the world around him was moving at a rate his senses could comfortably apprehend, the woman, whoever she was, was dead. Thus his first memory, quickly coming apart, was of lying next to her, staring at her gaunt face, at the lips constricted back to show the tips of her canines.

Who is she? he wondered.

And myself, he wondered, who exactly am I?

Near his face was a puddle of water. He did not recognize the reflection that quivered along its surface. He rolled his head down into it, lapped some up with his tongue.

After a while he worked up enough strength to crawl across the kitchen floor, following the water's source, and to duck his head under a skirt below the sink. There, an overflowing metal bowl rested beneath a pipe's leaking elbow.

The water in the bowl was filthy, covered with a thin layer of scum. He brushed this gently apart with his stubbled chin then tried to lap up the cleaner water below.

It was musty, but helped. He lay still for a while, his cheek against the damp, rotting wood of the cabinet floor, one temple applied to the cold metal of the bowl.

Later he managed to pull himself up and stagger to a cabinet. Inside, he found some stale crackers and sucked on these, then sat in a kitchen chair, his mouth dry. His eyes hurt. So did his ears and the lining of his mouth.

He got up and ate some more crackers then stared into the refrigerator. The food inside was rotting. He scavenged the heel of a loaf of bread, scraped the mold off it, ate it.

After the better part of the day had waned, he began to feel more human. He searched the pockets of the woman on the floor. They contained a few coins and a wallet stuffed with cards. Something, he discovered, was wrong with his eyes. He knew what the cards were by their shape and appearance—credit card, identification card, cash card, library pass—but was puzzled to find he could not read them. The characters on them, what he assumed were characters, meant nothing. He stared at them for some time and then slid them into his own pocket, then covered the woman's body with a sheet.

In the bathroom mirror, he did not recognize himself. The face staring back at him had blood crusted about its eyes, above its lips and to either side of the chin, the center of the chin now covered with a diluted slurry of blood and water. His eyes were bloodshot, oddly scored and pitted. His vision, he realized, was dim, as if he were slowly going blind. Perhaps his pupils had always been that way.

He washed the face, scrubbing the blood from the wrinkles around the eyes with soap and with a toothbrush he found in the cabinet above the sink. When he was done, he shaved carefully.

He regarded himself in the mirror. Who am I? he wondered. But that was not what he meant exactly. Only that he had no name to put with what he knew himself to be.

When he tried to open the door, he found it locked. He unlocked the deadbolt, tried to open it again, but the door still didn't come. He wandered from room to room. The windows were barred from the outside, the street far below. The sheet was still in the kitchen, the woman still dead under it. Yes, he thought, that's right, he remembered. It was in a way reassuring to know she had not been imagined, though in another way not reassuring at all.

What was her name? He didn't know. Nothing leaped to mind. Nothing sounded quite right. And what about him? Nothing sounded quite right, but nothing quite wrong either.

In the back of one of the closets he found a small prybar and a hammer. He used them to knock the pins from the door hinges, then tried to pry the door open from its hinged side. It creaked, but still didn't come.

Using the prybar as a chisel, he slowly splintered a hole through the center of the door at eye-level. There was, he discovered, something just beyond the door, made of plywood. He slowly broke a hole through this as well until, at last, he had a fist-sized opening that debouched onto an ordinary hall.

"Hello?" he called out. "Anyone there?"

When there was no answer, he went into the kitchen, stepping over the sheet. He started opening up drawers. There was a drawer containing a series of utensils, stacked very carefully into slots, a drawer containing stray keys and books of stamps and a rubber band ball, a drawer containing nested measuring cups and spatulas and turkey basters and pie shields, a shelf holding a jumble of pots and pans, a cabinet scattered with ascending stacks of dishes and nested hard plastic drinking cups. He worked two of the rubber bands off the ball then slid the rest of the drawers closed.

In the bathroom, he took a last look at himself and then struck the mirror with the prybar. Cracks shot through. The silvered glass tipped off in shards that broke further on the floor.

His hand, he saw, was blood-soaked, a flap of skin hanging open and folded over on the back of it. He was surprised to find it didn't hurt.

He pushed the flap back in place, found gauze pads in the cabinet, wrapped his hand in them.

He picked out a smaller, more regular square of glass, scraping each of its edges against the tile floor to dull it, then used the rubber bands to fasten it to the hooked end of the prybar. At the door, he worked the mirror-end of the prybar through the hole he had made, sliding the prybar through as far as he could without letting go of it.

It was hard to see past his knuckles and past the bar itself, harder still to hold the bar steady enough at one end to make sense of what he was seeing in the shard on the other: a wavering square of color and light. But there it was, he slowly could make it out, despite the wavering image: a large panel of raw wood, plywood, larger, it seemed than his door, studded with black pocks at regular intervals around its edge. The same black pocks in two lines up the panel's middle as well. Stretching from the bottom corners to top corners of the panel were two strips of yellow plastic tape, covered in black characters that he could not read.

But something must have been wrong with his thinking. He stood, slightly crouched, holding the prybar, trying to keep it steady, concentrating, looking past his knuckles into the reflection, and it was all he could do, really, just to see the flittered bits and pieces and make some cohesive image out of it in his head. It was too much to force that image into actually meaning something as well. Even after his difficulty trying to open the door, even after seeing the image in the shaky shard of mirror, after seeing the black pocks around the plywood's edge, it took him some moments of just staring and thinking to realize he had been deliberately boarded in.

But when he did realize, the shock came all at once. His fingers let go of the prybar and, overbalanced, it started to slide out of the hole and away from him. He just caught it. He pulled it back through and, shaking, sat down with his back to the door.

Why? he wondered.

He couldn't say. Perhaps, he thought, they hadn't known he and his wife were there. Assuming, he corrected himself, that she was his wife. Perhaps they had thought the apartment unoccupied.

But who, he wondered, were *they?*

There was the phone, he thought after a while. He could telephone someone and have them come get him out.

But who did he know? He couldn't remember having known anyone.

On the answering machine beside the phone a light was blinking. Why hadn't he noticed it before?

He got up and pressed the button beneath the light.

Hello? A voice said. *Mr. Hafner? Is that in fact the correct name? My name is Arnaud. I'm afraid I've been given your number in error.*

Hapner, he thought, *my name's Hapner. Probably. Or something close to that. Unless he's talking to somebody else.*

There's been a misunderstanding, the voice continued, Arnaud's voice continued. *What sort of misunderstanding?* Hapner wondered. He was, Hapner was, to contact Arnaud's wife. He was to ask her to do what she could to find out what had happened to Arnaud. He might, he was told, begin with Bentham. *What a strange message,* Arnaud thought. *Or wait,* the man thought, *I'm not Arnaud, that's not my name, my name is something else. What was it?*

After listening to the tape several dozen times he was almost certain he could remember his name. *Hapner.* Every few minutes he brought the name to his lips, whispered it. It would, he hoped, stay with him, on his tongue if not in his brain. And now, he thought, I have something to do. *Bentham,* he thought, *Arnaud.*

With the hammer and prybar he began to widen the hole, first cracking and splintering away his own door and then slowly hammering the flattened, flanged end of the prybar through the plywood.

He was weak; his arms quickly grew sore and tired and the light he had at first been able to see coming through the windows had long faded. The hall outside, however, remained brightly lit.

The plywood broke loose in odd, thatched fragments, splitting within the body of a layer of wood rather than between layers. In the end he had a splintery and furzed channel wide enough to squeeze through. He drank some more water, ate some more crackers, and then sat on a chair in the kitchen gathering his strength. His gaze caught on the sheet on the floor and he stooped to uncover the woman's face. He regarded her closely but no, he still did not recognize her.

Perhaps, he thought, I never knew her.

But then why, he wondered, was she here with me? Or, if you prefer, why was I here with her?

He went into the bedroom, looked through the closets. One was full of a woman's clothing, the other clothing belonging to a man. He tried on a sport coat. It was too small, and musty.

He tried on some of the other clothes, all too small.

Puzzled, he returned to the kitchen, stared again into the dead woman's face.

It's her home, he thought, not mine. And somebody else's. I'm probably not even Hafner.

He sat staring at her. The corpse was changing shape, becoming even less human. Soon it would start to smell. He couldn't stay there, whether he was Hafner or no. And if he wanted to be anyone, he had to be Hafner, at least for now.

IV.

Hapner rummaged a shoulder bag from a closet and dropped the hammer and prybar into it. Unplugging the answering machine, he put it in as well, then pushed the bag through the door's hole.

It was tighter than he'd thought. He had to work one shoulder through and then turn sideways to get the other past. The ragged edges of the hole scraped raw the underflesh of one arm as well as his ribs. Halfway through, he thought he was stuck and grew desperate and maddened, scratching and wriggling until he had worn the skin covering his hipbones bloody and until he fell on his neck and shoulders out onto the floor.

The other doors too had been sealed off, he saw. Along the length of the wall were sheets of plywood where he would have expected doors to be, fastened to door and wall with ratchet-headed black screws.

He went down the hall and down the stairs. Doors on the floor below were sealed too, but not all of them, and he knocked on the three that weren't. Nobody answered any of them. He tried to open them but found them all locked.

The next floor down was the same, doors mostly boarded over, no one answering the few still unsealed. He chose one at random and worked at it with the prybar and hammer until he cracked the latch out through the frame of the door and the door swung open.

The layout of the apartment was identical to the apartment he had been in, except reversed.

"Hello?" he called.

No answer came. The windows were slightly ajar. A thin layer of dust covered everything. Not dust quite, he realized: stickier. What, exactly, he couldn't say. On the table a sheet of paper was held down by a burnished brass paperweight. There was something written on it, but he couldn't read it. He picked it up and folded it, slid it into his back pocket.

In the closet were smeared two bloody handprints. Under one of the beds was what seemed to be a human ear. He sat on his knees a long time, squinting at it, wondering if he was really seeing what he thought he was seeing, but in the end left it where it was without touching in. In the oven he found the tightly curved body of a cat, long dead, dry as a plate. When he touched it, its hair crackled away.

He closed the oven and hurriedly left.

Two floors down, he knocked on an unsealed door and heard behind it some transient living sound, cut off nearly as quickly as it began.

"Hello?" he called.

He knocked again, but heard nothing. He pressed his ear to the door, thought he could hear, vaguely, just barely, something pressed to the other side, breathing. Was that possible, to hear something breathing, through a door? Perhaps it was his own breathing, he thought, and this made him feel as if he were on both sides of the door at once, and made him wonder why he wouldn't open up for himself.

"I don't mean any harm," he said. No response. "I'm just a neighbor," he said. "I just want to talk." Still no response.

"Shall I break down the door?" he asked. "If I do that, anybody can get in."

He waited a few minutes then got out his prybar and hammer. Aligning the prybar in the gap between door and wall, he struck the end with the hammer, started to drive it in.

He was a little startled when the voice that rang out from behind the door was not his own.

"All right," it said. "All right."

He worked the prybar free of the crack then stepped back. The deadbolt clicked. The door handle shivered, and the door drew open.

Behind was a small man, scarcely bigger than a child, wearing a moth-eaten sweater. Though not old, he seemed to be hairless, the skin hanging sallow on his face. His mouth and nose were hidden behind a surgical mask that he had doubled over to make fit. He stood mostly hidden, hand and head visible, a pistol in the former.

"Well?" the small man said. "What is it?"

"I'm your neighbor," Hapner said.

"I suppose you want to borrow a cup of sugar."

"No," said Hapner. "To talk."

"All right," said the man. "You're here. Talk."

"Can't I come in?"

"Why do you need to come in?" the man asked, a little surprised. "There's no reason to come in. It's not safe."

Hapner shrugged.

The man looked at him for a long while. His eyes protruding and damp, seemed slightly filmed. He opened the door further, shifted the pistol to his other hand.

"What floor?"

Hapner counted in his head. "Five floors up," he said.

"Eighth floor," said the man. "Why didn't you just say eighth? I thought all the eighth was boarded off."

"Almost all," lied Hapner. "Every door but one."

The man's eyes narrowed. "You're not ill, are you?"

"Don't be ridiculous," said Hapner. With what? he wondered.

"Okay," said the man. "Okay. Prove it. Tell me your name."

"My name?" said Hapner.

It started with a middle letter, he knew, one he could almost remember. It was there, nearly on the tip of his tongue, but what exactly was it?

"Well?" the small man said. "Either you know your name or you don't."

"Mind if I use your bathroom?" asked Hapner.

"The bathroom?" said the man, surprised. "I, but I—"

"Thank you," said Hapner, and hands raised above his head eased his way carefully past him without touching the pistol, toward where he suspected the bathroom must be.

"Wait," the small man said. But Hapner kept walking, slowly, as if underwater. He gritted his teeth, waiting for the man to shoot him in the back, following each slow step with another slow step until he had reached the bathroom. Opening the door he slipped quickly inside, locking it behind him.

What now? he wondered.

He regarded his face in the mirror, his frightened eyes, then opened his bag and removed the answering machine. Unplugging the man's electric razor, he plugged his answering machine in and dialed the volume down. He held the machine pressed against his ear and depressed the button.

"Hello?" a voice said into his ear. "Mr. Hapner? Is that in fact the correct name?"

Is it? Hapner wondered. The voice kept on. There were other names mentioned, but Hapner struck him as the only viable one. Arnaud. He, Hapner, was looking for Arnaud, he discovered, and for Bentham as a way to reach Arnaud. The answering machine made it all perfectly clear. *Hapner*, he made his lips mime. He rewound the tape and listened to his name again, then again, until he was certain he could remember it. At least for a few minutes.

The small man was knocking on the bathroom door, urging him to come out or be killed.

"I'm coming," Hapner said. He quickly packed the answering machine away and opened the door. The small man was there, face red, pistol aimed at Hapner's waist.

"Hapner," he said. "My name's Hapner."

The pistol wavered slightly, a strange expression passing across the man's eyes. "I know a Hafner on the 8th floor," he said, "or 9th. Can't remember. But you're not him."

"No," said Hapner quickly. "I'm Hapner, not Hafner. 8th floor as well. Strange coincidence, no?"

The man looked at him a long time, then took a few steps back, gun still poised. "Tell me what you want again?" he asked.

"That depends," said Hapner. "Are you Arnaud?"

"No," said the small man. "Who?"

"What about Bentham?"

"I'm Roeg."

"Do you know either an Arnaud or a Bentham?"

"Do they live in this building?"

"I don't know."

"I don't think so," said the small man. "These are strange questions to ask. If they do live here, I don't know them."

"Then I don't want anything," said Hafner and started to go.

"I thought you wanted to talk," said Roeg.

Hapner turned, saw Roeg had let his body sag. The small man went and sat down on the couch. He sat there, eyes looking exhausted, finally motioning Hapner into the chair next to him. "It's been long time," he said. "Let's talk."

But it was not a let's that talked, for Hapner spoke hardly at all. Roeg hadn't left the house in several weeks, he claimed, ever since the plague had begun. *Plague?* wondered Hapner, but just nodded. Roeg's wife had gone out and never come back. She was, he figured, probably dead.

204

"But maybe she just left," said Roeg.

He took the surgeon's mask off his face and laid it on the coffee table, smoothing it out with the palm of his hand. His mouth, Hapner saw, was delicately formed, the lips nearly translucent.

"Maybe," said Hapner. "I'm sorry."

Then people had arrived wearing protective suits. Each apartment had been opened. If anyone was found with indications, they were boarded in. No doubt it had been the same on Hapner's floor.

"No doubt," said Hapner.

"Eventually they stopped coming," said Roeg.

"Probably dead themselves," said Hapner.

"Probably," said Roeg, and lapsed into silence, staring at the tabletop.

"And what now?" asked Hapner.

"Now?" said Roeg. "How should I know?"

Almost as quickly as the information was given to him Hapner felt it begin to slip away, the details wavering and eroding, only a large, vague sense of contagion remaining. The knowledge itself was being simplified, made brutish within his head. He wondered how much of even this he would remember, and for how long?

There were other things Roeg told him, he knew, but even as he was saying them, Hapner felt them going. The authorities, he did remember Roeg saying, were silent. As to the silence, either Roeg didn't know its cause or Hapner somehow missed it or was already forgetting it. Perhaps it was simply *ongoing silence, unexplained.*

As Roeg spoke on, he became more and more confused. When he realized, from Roeg's puzzled look, that he must have asked a nearly identical question twice, back to back, he began to be concerned.

And then Roeg acquired a panicked look.

"Why are you speaking so quickly?" he asked. "Slow down."

"I'm not speaking quickly," Hapner said.

It became clear, as Roeg tried to continue, that something was wrong. He became prone to long reptilian fits of silence and would stop speaking to peer nervously around him.

"Roeg?" said Hapner. "Roeg?" But the small man wasn't answering, wasn't paying attention. Filled with doubt, Hapner asked, "That's your name, no?"

"My name?" said Roeg, suspiciously. "Why do you want to know?"

And then Roeg groped his pistol off the couch cushion and began to jab it into the air. He pointed not at Hapner but where Hapner had been a few moments before, for Hapner had stood and taken a few steps so as to get a closer look at Roeg.

"You had it?" Roeg shouted. "But why aren't you dead?"

He fired the pistol into the couch across from him. He moved the pistol a little, fired into the credenza, left again, into the wall—just behind the spot Hapner had been just a few second before. Reaching out, Hapner wrenched the gun out of Roeg's hand and dropped it to the floor. But it was as if Roeg didn't realize the gun was gone, for his curled hand was still aiming, his finger flexing, over and over, and he was, desperately, asking Hapner why he wouldn't die.

He spoke softly and carefully into Roeg's ear, stroking and rubbing the small man's hand until it loosened its grip on the absent gun. He coaxed him into lying down on the couch, then went into the kitchen and got a damp cloth, carefully wiping away the blood already seeping up through the man's eye sockets.

"How do you feel, Roeg?" he asked.

"Fine," said Roeg. "I feel fine. Why do you ask?"

And indeed, thought Hapner, the fellow seemed to believe this, despite the blood.

"You shouldn't feel bad," said Hapner. "You might come out of it all right."

"Come out of what?"

Blood began to leak from the man's mouth and nose and ears. Slowly he lapsed into unconsciousness. Hapner was at a loss to know what else he could do.

He let his eyes drift about the room until they found the telephone, then the answering machine. He held the latter's button down until it beeped, and then began to speak.

"Your name is Roeg," he said into it. "You are a small man. This is your house. I'm very sorry for all that's happened to you. My name is—" and there he stopped.

What was his name again? Could he remember? No.

He turned off the answering machine and left the apartment.

V.

There was a name he had been using, just on the tip of his tongue. He could almost remember it. But, he wondered, was it his name? Even once he remembered it, how would he know for certain it belonged to him?

He wouldn't know.

He made it to the end of the hall and started down the stairs to the next floor. What floor was it? He had kept track, had been keeping track, but was not quite certain. He would go down the stairs and then look for a door leading to the street. If there weren't one, he would try to find another set of stairs and go down them.

What had the name been? He had been found, had found himself, he could still trouble himself to dimly remember, lying beside a corpse. A woman, he was almost certain. Who, alive, had she been to him? His wife, his girlfriend, a relative, a colleague, a stranger? Who could say?

Before he had reached the bottom of the stairs he could see a man in the hallway, first only his feet and then, with each step down, a subsequent portion of his body, all the way up to a shaved head. He was standing beside a door, a large crowbar ending in a fan-like flange in one meaty hand. Leaning against the wall behind him was a sheet of plywood, prized off the door. A large duffle bag, empty or nearly so, was swung over the man's back. He had begun on the door itself, Hapner could see, the door's frame splintered and gouged.

Hapner stopped a little way down the hall. The man too had stopped working and was watching him.

"Hello," Hapner finally said.

"Hello," the man said.

"What exactly—"

"—this your house?" asked the man. "Your door, I mean? I'm not stepping into a delicate situation, am I?"

Hapner shook his head. "No," he said. "It's not my door. Are you breaking in?"

"Some neighbor's?" asked the thief. "Some friend's, then? Anything to get touchy about?"

Hapner shook his head.

"Any objections, then? No? Then I'll proceed."

The man turned partly away, still trying to keep an eye on Hapner out of the corner of his eye, which made his attempts at opening the door awkward, blunted. But the door was slowly giving way.

"Aren't you afraid?" asked Hapner.

"What?" said the thief. "Of catching it? Was at first but then everybody around me went under and I never did. I don't think I will. What's the word? Invulnerable?" He worked the flanged end of the prybar back in, and then one twist of his torso cracked the door open. "No," he said, "immune." And then added, "After a while you feel invincible too."

He pushed open the door, bights of a brass chain tightening at eye level inside the apartment. The man fed his crowbar into the gap, broke the chain's latch off the doorframe.

"Well," he said. "Coming?"

Hapner took a half step forward, stopped.

"I don't think so," he said.

"Come on in," said the man. "Where's the problem? You didn't have any objections last I checked. Besides, I haven't had anyone to talk to for a while. They all keep dying on me. You're not going to die on me, are you?" The man started through the door. "I'll let you have some of whatever we find, maybe."

Hapner hesitated, followed him in.

"What about you?" said the man from in front of him.

The apartment inside was windowless and extremely dark; it was difficult to see anything. The man grew gray and then was reduced to a series of fluttering movements. Then he vanished entirely. Hapner stepped after him.

"What about me?" Hapner asked.

"Aren't you afraid? You're in a quarantined apartment now. Doesn't it worry you?"

The man struck a match and Hapner saw his face spring from the darkness, in a kitchenette area. He had not been where Hapner had thought he would be. He was holding the match in one hand, rapidly opening and closing cupboard and cabinet doors with the other.

The match guttered and went out and the room was swallowed in the darkness, save for the dull red bead of the matchhead, and then this was gone too, replaced by the smell of the burnt-up match. A sharp scratch and another match fluttered alight. Hapner watched the man reach into a drawer, come out with a curious silver cylinder that he manipulated, transformed into a flashlight.

"That's better," the man said, and shined the flashlight's beam into Hapner's face.

"Now," he said, his voice changing in a way Hapner didn't understand. "What did you say your name was?"

"I didn't say," said Hapner. "What's yours?"

"What's that in the bag?" the man asked.

"My bag?" said Hapner. "Not much," he said.

"Open it up," said the thief. "Let's have a look."

Hapner put the bag on the counter between them, unzipped it. He took out the answering machine, put it beside the bag, then the short prybar, the hammer.

"That's it?" asked the thief.

"That's it," said Hapner.

"You don't have much," said the thief.

"I'm not like you," said Hapner. "I'm not a thief."

"Then what are you doing?"

"Looking for someone," he said. "A… Mr. Arnaud, I think. Is that you?"

"What, you just have a name?" said the voice behind the flashbeam.

Hapner nodded.

The man was silent for a moment. "All right," he finally said, "you can go."

Hapner nodded to himself. He reached out, began to put his possessions back into the bag. The thief's crowbar cut through the flashbeam and struck the counter between his hands.

"Leave it," said the man. "It's mine now."

"But—"

"This is my building," the man said. "Whatever's here belongs to me."

"But there's nothing I have that's worth—"

"It's a matter of principle," the thief said, his voice rising. "Now get out."

He kept staring at the answering machine. *Arnaud*, he thought, *Bentham. Hapler.* Or no, that wasn't it exactly, he was already forgetting. He squinted into the light. Where was the flashlight exactly? How far away? He could make it out, mostly. He could see the man behind it, a dim form wavering at the edges.

He turned as if to leave and took half a step and then whirled and crouched, battered at where he thought the flashlight would be. The thief cried out, Hapner's hand striking the casing of the flashlight hard. His fingers were instantly numb, the flashlight flicking away end over end and going out.

The crowbar passed moaning over his head, ruffling his hair, striking the wall hard. The thief cursed. Hapner groped about, touched the man's shirt, but, unable to find the crowbar, dropped to his knees and crouched under the lip of the counter.

The crowbar crashed into the counter above him, the walls rattling.

"Where are you?" the man said.

Hapner said nothing.

"I'll find you eventually," said the thief. "You belong to me."

Hapner stayed still, listening to the dim birds of the man's feet, the clank of the crowbar as it touched floor or wall. He reached carefully up, touching the counter above him, his fingers feeling slowly along it.

There was a groove the crowbar had dug in the surface, the countertop splintered and cracked to either side of it. His hands felt past it until they found his hammer.

"But maybe I already killed you?" the thief said.

The voice was right there, almost beside him. In one motion he swung the hammer up and forward. It struck something firm but not as hard as the wall.

The thief screamed and swooned toward him, striking the counter, stumbling over Hafner legs. Hafner struck him hard and repeatedly with the hammer. Something struck his shoulder and it became suddenly a numb useless thing and he heard the crowbar splintering the wood behind him. He groped with his good hand for the dropped hammer. He heard the thief stutter-step and then, groaning, fall.

He moved toward the body, pounding along the floor in front of him until the hammer struck flesh. He fell on the other man and lost his hammer and felt the man's face into existence and then fumbled up the hammer again and then, as the man still struggled his way out of shock, struck at his skull again and again until the head sounded like a wet sack.

He felt around the floor one-handed until he found the flashlight. He stood and flicked its switch on but no light came from it, so he dropped it again.

On his way back to the counter, he stepped on what must have been the thief's hand and then, as he moved quickly off it, into something damp and squishy, perhaps the thief's gore, perhaps his own, and almost fell. One arm ached badly and swung loose, battering against his side like the trussed body of a shot bird. Moving it created little flashes of light behind his eyes.

He fumbled around on the counter until he found the answering machine, picked it up. There was something wrong with it, he could tell: its surface was no longer smooth.

The room seemed at each moment less and less familiar to him.

He managed to stumble out of the dark and back into the hall. His arm, he saw, in the light, seemed mostly dead, oddly lumped and turning black in two places. He tried again to move it but could not.

The answering machine was shattered in the back, the slatted casing covering the speaker destroyed, the speaker itself and the transformer beside it mangled. Why had he wanted to keep it anyway? He couldn't remember.

He dropped the machine and crouching beside it worked the cassette free with one hand. One of the cassette's corners was crushed but the tape itself was still intact, could be listened to on another machine. Where had he seen another one?

The hallway, he saw, was slowly going out around him, flattening out, the door he had come through an odd square of black, a vertical panel, two dimensional, rather than an entrance. The whole world, he thought fleetingly, was like that for him, there was nothing he could hold on to but this hall and perhaps a few other halls above that and an answering machine he may or may not have seen, somewhere above him. But what did above mean? What's wrong with it? he wondered of the hall. It all struck him as vaguely familiar as if he had lived through it before, in another life.

He turned and looked where he was almost certain stairs had been and found that too had gone strange, a black flat rectangle scored with lighter lines. He stumbled toward it and, closing his eyes, pushed into it. The pain in his shoulder too he realized seemed to be fading, was all but gone. He hit against something and pulled himself up, kept moving forward, kept stumbling, and when he opened his eyes saw that the stairs were stairs again, more or less, and that he could navigate them. He pushed through the yellow wall at their end and found himself in a hall, or what seemed like a movie set for a hall, everything slightly false. He reached up to touch his face and when his hand came away saw it was not a hand exactly, though a reasonable facsimile. There, floating above it, was a strange crimson cloud, the color of blood.

An anxiety began rising in him that he had a hard time placing.

By strength of will he managed to transform a brown rectangle into a door and push his way through. Inside, the cardboard cutout of a tiny man, hardly bigger than a child, was lying prone on what stood in for a couch, a crimson cloud hovering over his face. He took a deep breath and tried to relax and, there, momentarily, saw a real flesh and blood man on an actual couch, his face stained from blood that had seeped from his eyes. He felt, almost, that he recognized him. But then, suddenly, he was only a child in a crimson cloud again.

There was a blinking light near him, not far away, very quick, not blinking so much as strobing. He moved toward it slowly and stood near it and in a little while began to imagine that it was an actual human object, an answering machine. He found a button and pressed it.

A voice came out, speaking too rapidly. It sounded familiar to him, perhaps a voice he had heard before, but where?

Your name is Roeg, the voice said. *You are a small man. This is your home. I'm very sorry for all that's happened to you. My name is—*

And then it stopped. *Roeg,* he thought. *Is that my name?*

What is my name? he wondered.

My name? he wondered. *Why do I want to know?*

There was, he managed to trouble himself to remember, something in his hand, something important, but why or what he couldn't remember. He tried to raise his hand but it wouldn't move. What was wrong with it? The other hand he tried to move and it came and there, clutched in it, he saw a small black rectangle that just for a moment he found himself mistaking for an open doorway. But no, it was not that, it was smaller than his hand and pierced through with two teethed circles: a cassette.

He shook his head to clear it. It did not clear. He managed, after some effort, to raise the lid of the answering machine and pop the cassette out and get his own cassette in. He pressed the play button and then stumbled away toward where he hoped a chair would find him.

There was a crackle and a beep and the voice began to speak.

Hello, it said. *Mr. Hapner? Is that in fact the correct name? My name is Arnaud...*

Did it all come flooding back to him? Not exactly, no. It went on from there but he was no longer listening. *Hapner*, his mind was saying, *Arnaud*. He tried to sit down, crashed to the floor. He lay there, staring at the ceiling, trying to hold on to the two names, to keep that at least. But they were already slipping away.

VI.

He awoke to find himself lying on a couch, prone. Across from him, collapsed on the floor, an abnormally large man with his shirt and hands smeared with blood, blood crusted around his eyes as well. The man's arm was clearly broken, turned out from the body at a senseless angle, a velvety pinkish lump of bone protruding just above the wrist.

He sat up, feeling weak. His mouth was dry. When he tried to stand he grew weak and quickly sat down again. He sat there on the couch, gathering his breath, waiting, staring at the man on the floor.

Did he know him? Surely he must know him or why else would they both be there?

"Hello?" he said to the man. He didn't move, dead probably.

But where was here? he wondered. Was this his apartment? It didn't look familiar exactly, but he couldn't bring another apartment to mind either. But if this was his, why wouldn't he know it?

He stood and stumbled across the room and toward the kitchen, passing the man on the way. Up close he could see he was clearly dead, his face the color of scraped bone, a smell coming off him.

In the kitchen he looked into the fridge, found it empty. The pantry was full of cans. He couldn't read any of the labels. *What's wrong with me?* he wondered. He opened one and drank it cold—some kind of soup, glassy with oil on the surface. After a while, he felt a little better.

When he went back into the living room he saw the blinking light. It took him a moment to figure out what it meant, what it belonged to.

He had to stand on a foot ladder to reach it. The machine's casing, he saw, was streaked with blood. He depressed the button.

Hello, a voice said. *Mr. Hapner? Is that in fact the correct name?*

Hapner, he thought, the name sizzling vaguely in his head and then beginning to fade. Unless it was not his house, unless the name belonged to the man dead on the floor. But no, it must be his name, it sounded right enough, and the foot ladder, the dead man wouldn't have needed a foot ladder to step on. *Ergo*, his house. *Ergo*, Hapner. *If that is in fact the correct name?*

There had been, the voice told him, Mr. Arnaud told him, a misunderstanding. Everyone's heart was in the right place. But he, Hapner, was being asked to contact Arnaud's wife, to pass on information, to find out what had become of him.

I must be a private detective, thought the small man, thought Hapner.

He went into the bathroom and looked at his face. He too, like the dead man, was wearing a mask of blood, the blood thickest around his eyes. They shared that at least. The face—small, pudgy—was unfamiliar. *But it must be my own face*, he thought. Nevertheless he couldn't help but reach out and touch the mirror, assure himself that it was solid, flat glass.

In the bedroom, he changed his clothes. The clothes fit. Thus, this was his house. *Ergo*. Thus, he was Bentham. Or not Bentham exactly, Bentham was who he was looking for. What had the name been exactly? It started with an H, he thought, or some similar letter. Similar in what way? He went back into the living room, skirting a dead body—had he seen it before? yes, he had, but who was it?—and depressed the answering machine button again. Ah, yes. Hapner. That was him. And it was Arnaud he was looking for, not Bentham.

He got out a pen and a piece of paper and wrote it down, but found he could make no sense of the marks on the paper. *What's wrong?* he wondered, *what's wrong?* He would, he supposed, somehow just have to remember.

He started out the door—*Arnaud*, he was saying in his head, *Hapner*, I'm Hapner, I'm looking for Arnaud—and stopped dead. The other doors around his own had been barricaded over with sheets of plywood. *But why?* he wondered, and then wondered, *Why not my door?*

He went down the stairs and then down a hall whose walls were smeared with blood, then down another set of stairs that opened onto a lobby, two shattered glass doors leading out into the street. He pushed one open, felt a pricking on his hands and looked to see them glittery with powdered glass, minute cuts all over them. He used his shoe to open the door the rest of the way, stepped out into the street.

213

The street was deserted, a car overturned and burnt to a husk a dozen feet from where he stood, another car in the middle of the road, both doors open, clumps of paper eddying about it, garbage, a fine rain of ash. The building across the street from him, a large complex of some sort, was surrounded by a chain-link fence topped with barbed wire, another similar fence a half dozen feet inside it and parallel to it, the gates of both fences twisted off their hinges. The building was set off from the road and between him and it were scores of abnormally large men in white protective suits, sprawled about, no marks on them, suits intact, all probably dead. *Good Christ*, he thought. For just an instant, the scene wavered, flattening out in front of him, everything fading away or coming all too close. But then he blinked, and blinked again, and it all seemed all right again, though somehow the sun had moved and the sky had gone darker.

He crossed the street and passed through the gate and approached one of the prone men. The glass shield over the man's face was obscured by blood. He looked at another. It was the same. He stopped looking.

What am I doing? he wondered. *What am I looking for?*

He couldn't remember exactly. He was looking for something or someone, it started with, he could almost remember, it was a letter that he…perhaps R? But what did that tell him? It didn't tell him anything at all.

He turned around and looked over his shoulder at the building across the street. It was an apartment complex, ten or twelve stories tall, its door shattered.

He stood staring at it for a long time. Something about it struck him as significant. Familiar? What, he wondered again, was he looking for, and who was he exactly, again? What was the name?

He kept staring, feeling a slow panic welling through him.

He took a step forward without looking, almost fell over one of the bodies. He kicked it softly, then stepped around it.

I am looking for something, he tried to tell himself, or someone. Probably, he tried to tell himself, I'll know it when I find it.

He looked back again at the building across the street, then turned toward it.

Probably as good a place to start as any, he thought. He crossed the street, opened the door to the building. *Who knows what I will find?* he thought.

Another instant and he was gone.

Most Excellent and Lamentable

Jason Erik Lundberg

Sometimes I'll be driving the Z3 on the highway and imagine my brakes cut, unexpectedly, unexplainably. And the gas pedal will get stuck, maybe with superglue, like in that Blues Brothers movie, and the speed, the speedometer keeps rising, past ninety, one-twenty, one-seventy, and the cars I'm racing past are just blurs, streaks of color which barely register before they're *gone,* and the fluid for the steering wheel has evaporated and I'm careening now, careering across lanes, across the median, and I'm heading straight for an eighteen-wheeler, knowing that when I hit that there'll be nothing left of me to identify, no fingerprints, no teeth, just a liquefied mass that used to be a person, knowing all this but completely helpless, unable to do anything about—

But of course none of that happens. It's a fantasy. When you're immortal, all you can think about is death.

To Julian, I'm Lucas. He sees me as a student of the world, a wandering poet. He thinks I'm misunderstood, unappreciated in my own time. He thinks this because I want him to think this.

I write haiku and pantoums that make absolutely no sense. I fill up trendy moleskine notebooks with unintelligible, incomprehensible verse. He nods and makes interested noises while reading my "poetry," calls me brilliant.

When I use symbols like Ж and Ѣ, he looks at them thoughtfully, trying to divine importance, unaware I'm only using letters from the Cyrillic alphabet. He's been threatening to publish a book of my poetry for years, but he never has any money.

"Lukey-*duke!*" he shouts as I step into Java Jive. He's unshaven, hair all aimed to one side as if he'd been standing behind a jet engine. His clothes come from sometime in the mid-1980s, thrift store chic. Rimless eyeglasses.

I ease into the chair opposite his at the table. Julian smells vaguely of cloves.
I say, "You look happier than normal, Jules. Get laid last night?"
Julian just smiles, teeth broken and spaced too far apart.
"I see Queen Mab hath been with you," I say.
"What?"
"Nothing."
"No, no, it's not like that. I'm in love."
"Love?"
"The girl, the one I told you about, she came into the bookstore again today."
"Which girl?"
"You know, *the* girl. Last week she bought a raggedy-ass copy of Sartre. Her."
"Oh."
"Today she bought Camus."
"So?"
"Dude! She's a deep thinker, man. She's beautiful *and* she has a brain."
"I've seen plenty of women like that."
"Well, I haven't. They're pretty rare for me. Especially ones that dig *me*."
"Hold that thought."
I get up, walk to the counter, order a chai, pay, get the drink, and sit back down. I imagine it's poisoned, and take a gulp.
"Okay, where were we?"
"Romy."
"Romy?"
"That's her name. The girl. Her name is Romy."
"And you know this because."
"Because I asked her out."
"Isn't that against the rules?"
"It's a used books store, Lucas. No one cares if you date the customers."
"Ah."
"I'm taking her to *Rosencrantz and Guildenstern are Dead* tomorrow night. I still have my student ID, so we'll get in cheap."
"Beautiful?"
"Dude, she's *gorgeous*."
"Pippins and figs."
"What?"
"Nothing."

To Romy, I'm Marc. She sees me as a painter, a refugee from the Paris art scene. She thinks I'm unconventional, controversial, willing to tear down the boundaries of realism. She thinks this because I want her to think this.

My seduction starts after Julian's date with her, me following behind in the shadows of lampposts. Watching as Julian drops her off in his Chevette, too nervous to lean in for a kiss, talking a bit too animatedly with his hands. She gets out of the car, thanks him for the date, and disappears into her apartment building. He sits there for a moment more, then rolls home.

I emerge from the sliver of shadow, ring the bell for her apartment. She says "what" through the intercom speaker, tired, wishing the date had gone better maybe.

"I'm an itinerant seller of pigeons," I say, giving myself a French accent.

She laughs, a sound like rain, or a river.

"Who is this, really?"

"I want to paint your portrait," I breathe, flooding the intercom with charm, drowning her in my charisma. You know that story about the man who sells ice to the Eskimos? It isn't a story. I did that.

"Come on up," she says.

The first thing I notice is her eyebrows, plucked and thinned, wisps, hints of eyebrows, memories of eyebrows. Romy is a redhead, but not a fiery red, or a deep red, more a pale red. Not strawberry blonde, not pink, but the lightest dusting of redness in her hair. Her eyebrows share this lightness, adding to the effect.

We move to the living room and stare at each other. I'm facing away from the windows. I feel the crosshairs of a sniper's rifle on the back of my head. Those little nape hairs stand up and the base of my skull crawls, a caged animal scrabbling to get out. I can envision my brains becoming Romy's makeup, adding color to her pale face, her eyebrows.

"It will be hard for me to trust you, Marc," she says. "I've been hurt before."

My teeth are a gentle massage. My eyes are a nice Ceylon tea. My hands are a beloved blanket, a stuffed animal plumped with security.

"If love be rough with you," I say, "be rough with love."

The sex is raw and uninhibited, articulated with animal primacy. I scream. She screams. We all scream. The mattress screams.

Julian's right. She is gorgeous.

The next morning, leaving Romy's place, I slide into my Z3 and turn the key in the ignition. The car explodes. Someone has planted C4 under my transmission. Glass, metal, plastic, and bits of me spray in all directions, an eruption of technology and humanity. We turn the street, the buildings black and red. Charred and sticky. We set off a dozen car alarms. We make the earth tremble—

I open my eyes, but I am intact. The Z3 is intact, always was intact. The street is quiet except for the birds in the trees. A bunny rabbit hops along the sidewalk.

A sigh, and I put the car in gear.

Julian is manning the counter as I step into Bibliophiles. Dust and old paper and, faintly, cat. I sneeze.

"Hey Lucas," he says, less emphatic than usual.

"Jules. Something wrong?"

"She won't return my calls," he says. "It's been three days since we went out. I think she's blowing me off."

"Who?" I pretend I don't know.

"The girl. Romy. It sucks. I bet she's seeing someone else."

"It's possible. Like you said: beautiful *and* a brain."

Another employee, laden with trade paperbacks, shuffles behind the counter, commences the avalanche of books, an imploded building of books. He's Mediterranean maybe, prone to tan easily. Dark hair, cut close to the scalp. Earrings up one side and down the other. He wears a green shirt with BUCK FUSH in white block letters. His glasses have rims, thick and black.

"Hey," I say.

He nods.

"Lucas, this is Ty," Julian says. "He just started a few days ago. Ty, Lucas: a local poet."

We shake hands, testing grips, measuring each other's masculinity. I imagine his strong Mediterranean hand on my throat, squeezing, tears in his eyes, revenge for an injustice, some unintended offense, cutting off my air, crushing my voicebox, snapping my cervical vertebrae, black spots coalescing in front of my eyes, his teeth gritted so hard they crack, I'm almost gone now, a beautiful asphyxiation—

A quick pump, up-down, and we let go. He turns and heads toward the back of the shop. I hate him, abruptly, suddenly, on a cellular level.

"Maybe he's the one," I say to Julian.

"The one what?"

"The one who stole your girl."

"Ty?"

"Why not? He's a good-looking guy."

"I don't know, Lucas."

"Didn't you say he only started working here a few days ago?"

"Yeah…"

"And wasn't that when you went out with Romy?"

"Yeah."

"And isn't it possible she saw him while she was in here, and they hooked up later?"

Julian punches the counter and the books resting there slide to the floor.

"Son of a bitch! Why would he do that to me?"

"O, he's the courageous captain of compliments. A Prince of Cats."

"What?"

"A knave; a rascal; an eater of broken meats; a base, proud, shallow, beggarly, three-suited, hundred-pound, filthy, worsted-stocking knave; a whoreson, glass-glazing, superserviceable, finical rogue; one-trunk-inheriting slave; one that wouldst be a bawd in way of good service, and art nothing but the composition of a knave, beggar, coward, pandar, and the son and heir of a mongrel bitch."

"What the hell are you talking about?"

I take a breath. "Poetry," I say.

"Oh. Okay. Man, you've *got* to write that shit down."

"It's already been done."

"Wow, you had that memorized?"

"So now we know he stole your woman," I say. "Let's talk about how to get even."

An exhibit in a warehouse gallery, which I take credit for. When Romy looks at the names of the artists below each painting, she sees only my name.

"These are incredible," she says. "They're so *textured* and *real*. I love how you used mixed media in these. Is that from a Chinese newspaper?"

We stroll down the wall, pausing at respectable intervals, examining each piece, the deep colors, use of black, and foil, found objects like trowel blades, rusted forks, barbed wire, dental appliances, radio-controlled car motors, scissors, butcher knives, machetes.

Stopping in front of a Cornell box, filled with a clipping from the *New York Times* (September 12, 2001), a pigeon skull resting on a pile of grey feathers, a phial containing grey ash, and a die-cast toy jumbo jet suspended from the top by fishing line.

Romy gets quiet, staring into the box, peering, poring over the contents, as if the harder she looks, the more meaning she'll glean.

"And what were you hoping to accomplish with this piece?" she asks.

The answer is one I've been saving for years, just waiting for the right circumstances, the right question to justify its brilliance. Romy's eyes are the hue of a scorched sky.

"I wanted to show that after a disaster, even a cataclysmic, life-changing tragedy, art and beauty can still be made."

We go back to Romy's apartment after that, her running five red lights, narrowly avoiding a stray dog and three parking meters, and she's laughing and I'm laughing, and we run upstairs and rend our garments, her wanting to be on top, and she's squeezing her pelvic muscles right, right *there*, and when I come it's a universe-creating explosion, it's a mortiferous heart-attack, turning the little death into a big one, it's looking into the face of Death and laughing, and yes laughing yes, and tears are trailing down my face from this unexpected apoplexy, and I never want it to stop, never, never, never, never, never!

To Ben, I'm Wile. He sees me as a filmmaker, a connoisseur of pretentious independent short films. He thinks I'm a renegade, an auteur whose works will be microscopically studied centuries from now. He thinks this because I want him to think this.

We sit in a dark booth at the back of the Hibernian Pub, and I'm showing him my latest creation on a portable DVD player: a compilation of commercials about children's charities, spliced, edited, all hosted by that same bearded actor, sincere, imploring, wanting my money, for ten cents a day you can feed a family of four, the shots, the endless shots of impoverished kids with bloated bellies, the wide eyes, pleading for a break, for fairness in the world, knowing that ten cents a day won't actually do shit for improving their lives, knowing that they need more, much more, and knowing that they won't get it.

"Very powerful," Ben says. "The guy uses almost the exact same spiel every time."

"There are actually only a handful of separate commercials, from the poorest countries, Sierra Leone, Tanzania, Ethiopia, Somalia, Cambodia, but they're aired so often that you think there must be dozens, hundreds of different ones."

"You talked to Julian lately?"

"Yeah. You?"

"Nope."

Ben and Julian are first cousins, close since they were kids, but incommunicado after Julian said Ben's wife was a cruel bitch. Turns out Julian was right, but even after the nasty divorce, they haven't spoken a word to each other. I've never met Ben's ex-wife, but the stories about her are many.

"So who are we meeting here? Some new hotties for the ravishing?"

"No. This guy Ty. We're going to ruin him."

"Sounds fun."

The film is still playing on infinite loop in my hand, the endless procession of gaunt faces, faces of those who have given up, faces waiting for release, and all at once I'm exhausted, just fed up with it all, my stupid pranks, the manipulations, the whole world. In that moment, I envy those starving children, wish for the loving embrace of deprivation, madness, the slowing of the blood. I sink back into the booth, hoping, praying that I'll continue to sink, the cushion enveloping, smothering me, pushing itself into my mouth, my nose, my eyes, cutting off the world, delivering me from life.

"You okay?"

"I'm so tired," I say.

"You look like you ate some bad oysters."

"What's the point? I mean, what's the fucking point of it all?" I turn off the DVD player. "We all turn to dust and bones eventually. President or poet, it doesn't matter. At some point even I'll be gone. Whether it's the Big Crunch or the heat death of the universe, we all go back to atoms, to nothingness."

"Death comes for us all someday," Ben says.

"Life's a tale told by an idiot," I say, "full of sound and fury, signifying nothing."

"Bullshit," Ben says, smacking the table with an open palm. "I don't buy that at all. This existence *does* matter, however short it might be. We all have a role to play, and it's how we play that role that gives our lives meaning."

"And what's my role?" I ask.

Romy, from nowhere, maybe hiding in the shadows all along, sits down beside Ben.

"You are the Trickster," she says. "You make sure we don't take ourselves too seriously. You bring laughter, and mystery."

"And what are you?" I say.

"The Beauty. That who is sought after, pursued, the object of lust."

Julian sits beside me, and Ty stands at the edge of the table.

"The Fool," Julian says, hand on heart, "destined to be deluded over and over again. And the Doppelgänger," he motions to Ty, silent, pale, face smudged with clown makeup, "your opposite and equal, who always gets blamed for your actions."

"And you?" I look to Ben.

"The Fraud. Scaramouche to your Harlequin. Your lesser version."

This is all very familiar now, the umpteenth iteration in an endless repetition. I've been here before, too many times, a purgatory of repeated experience.

Romy, Julian and Ben produce painstakingly-crafted handmade half-masques from thin air, an archetypal conjuring. They tie the masques to their faces with black cloth, their mouths still visible, but something unmistakably changed in their aspects, a *more*-ness. Ty stands mute, his face pancaked white, a checkered dunce cap on his head.

"The dance must continue," Julian says, another masque in his hands, *my* masque, my true essence in bright primary colors. I know that I can decline, deny my nature and flee the bar, live a normal life and die in my bed sixty years from now. I could give it all up, refuse to play the cosmic game any longer, hang up my spurs.

I could, but I won't. I just wouldn't be myself.

I pluck the masque from Julian's hands and tie it onto my face with a flourish. Through the eye-holes, the world looks more alive, brighter, energetic, full of sound and fury and slings and arrows, but beautiful all the same. I smile and wait for the music to start, for the amnesia to settle in, for the dance to begin once more.

About the Contributors

Forrest Aguirre received the World Fantasy Award for editing the *Leviathan 3* anthology (with Jeff Vandermeer). He has also edited *Leviathan 4* and *The Nine Muses* (with Deborah Layne). His own fiction has appeared in such venues as *Notre Dame Review, American Letters & Commentary, Exquisite Corpse, Polyphony, The Journal of Experimental Fiction*, and *Prague Literary Review.* A book of his collected fiction, *Fugue XXIX*, was published in 2005. Forrest lives in Madison, Wisconsin.

Joshua Cohen was born in Southern New Jersey in 1980. He is the author of *The Quorum* (Twisted Spoon Press, 2005), and *Cadenza for the Schneidermann Violin Concerto* (Fugue State Press, 2007). *A Heaven of Others* is forthcoming. Cohen lives in Brooklyn, NY.

Rikki Ducornet is the author of seven novels including *The Fan Maker's Inquisition*, a Los Angeles Times Book of the Year, and *The Jade Cabinet*, a finalist for the National Book Critics' Circle Award. In 2004, she received the Lannan Literary Award for Fiction. Her recent paintings will be exhibited at the Pierre Menard Gallery in Cambridge, Mass. in the Spring of 2007. The story in this collection is from a new collection of Butcher's Tales under contract with The Dalkey Archive.

Brian Evenson is the author of eight books of fiction, most recently *The Open Curtain.* He is the recipient of an NEA Fellowship, two O. Henry Prizes, and the Glenna Luschei Award, and his short fiction has been published in *The Paris Review, Story Quarterly, McSweeney's, Black Clock, Paraspheres*, and a number of other venues. He directs the Literary Arts program at Brown University and is a senior editor for *Conjunctions* magazine.

Nashville, TN native **Toiya Kristen Finley** is a freelancer who was a professional student in another life, traveling to faraway places like New York University, Iowa State, and Binghamton University before returning home. Her work has appeared in *Popular Contemporary Writers, The Encyclopedia of Themes in Science Fiction and Fantasy, Full Unit Hookup, Not One of Us, Tales of the Unanticipated, TEL: Stories, The Nine Muses*, and *Under Her Skin: How Girls Experience Race in America*. She is the founding and former managing/fiction editor of *Harpur Palate*. Why Jasmine A. Waters would be interested in her is anyone's guess.

Nadia Gregor lives in Portland, Oregon. She has written about architecture for *Organ Review of Arts*, and is currently at work on a novel.

Catherine Kasper's books include *Field Stone* (Winnow 2005), *A Gradual Disappearance of Insects* (Pecan Grove 2004), and *Optical Projections* (Obscure Publications 2003). She is currently an Associate Professor at the University of Texas in San Antonio.

Christine Boyka Kluge is the author of *Teaching Bones to Fly* (2003) and *Stirring the Mirror* (due 2007), both from Bitter Oleander Press. Her poetry won the 2003 Uccelli Press Chapbook Contest, the 2006 *Hotel Amerika* Poetry Contest, the 1999 Frances Locke Memorial Poetry Award, and has received several Pushcart Prize nominations. Her writing is anthologized in *No Boundaries: Prose Poems by 24 American Poets*, *Diagram: Selections from the Magazine*, *Sudden Stories*, and *PP/FF: An Anthology*. Her work has appeared in *Arts & Letters*, *The Bloomsbury Review*, *The Cincinnati Review*, and *Sentence*. She is also a visual artist.

Jason Erik Lundberg is the co-author of *Four Seasons in One Day*, and the co-editor of *Scattered, Covered, Smothered* and the forthcoming *Field Guide to Surreal Botany*. His solo work has appeared in over two dozen venues in the US, UK, and Serbia, including *The Third Alternative*, *Strange Horizons*, *Fantastic Metropolis*, *Infinity Plus*, and *Electric Velocipede*. His short fiction has been nominated for the Fountain Award and honorably mentioned twice in *The Year's Best Fantasy and Horror*. He maintains a website and blog at jasonlundberg.net, and produces a literary podcast called *Lies and Little Deaths: A Virtual Anthology*.

Tom Miller graduated from Harvard University and earned an MFA from Notre Dame. His fictions have been published by *Cream City Review*, *Harpur Palate* and *Science Creative Quarterly*. When not altering Wikipedia to better agree with his novel, *The False Histories*, Tom works as an EMT on Pittsburgh's east side. He is a former travel guidebook editor, marathon runner and innertube waterpolo captain.

Joe Murphy is: fifty-three, married, living in Fairbanks, Alaska, a quiet guy who reaches people mainly through his fiction, influenced by writers like Sean Stewart, Jeff Vandermeer, Forrest Aguirre, and Thomas Ligotti, overweight, interested in psychoactive substances, someone who's sold numerous stories, often cranky, loosing his hair, sometimes described as an old hippie, immature, and finally not all that happy with Reality as he understands it.

Ruth Nestvold lives in Germany with her family, amid ancient castles, parrots, and roses blooming out of season. When not writing fiction she is a technical translator and English professor. **Jay Lake** lives in Portland, Oregon with his two inept cats and his books, where he commits short fiction, novels and various other writing-related program activities. Writing together their work has appeared in *Baen's Universe*, *Futurismic*, *Realms of Fantasy* and *SCI FICTION*, along with many other markets and a regular joint column at the *Internet Review of Science Fiction*. Their joint work has also been reprinted in Gardner Dozois' *Year's Best Science Fiction*. Jay can be reached via his Web site at jlake.com, Ruth via ruthnestvold. com.

Lance Olsen is author of more than a dozen books of and about innovative fiction, including, most recently, the novels *10:01* (Chiasmus, 2005), *Nietzsche's Kisses* (FC2, 2006) and *Anxious Pleasures* (Shoemaker & Hoard, 2007). He lives somatically in the mountains of central Idaho and digitally at www.lanceolsen.com.

Eric Schaller is a plant biologist who teaches in the Biology Department at Dartmouth College. He lives in Lebanon, New Hampshire with his wife Paulette Werger, a jeweler and metalsmith, where they keep company with two hedgehogs and a turtle. His recent work has been published in *Sci Fiction*, *Lady Churchill's Rosebud Wristlet*, *Polyphony*, and *The Thackery T. Lambshead Pocket Guide to Eccentric and Discredited Diseases*, reprinted in several Year's Best anthologies, and is forthcoming in *Postscripts* and *The Field Guide to Surreal Botany*. His other work includes illustrations for Jeff VanderMeer's collection *The City of Saints and Madmen* and a cover for *Lady Churchill's Rosebud Wristlet*. He still has a stuffed toy gorilla from his childhood that has seen extensive repairs over the years.

E. Sedia lives in Southern New Jersey with one spouse, two cats and many fishes. Her short stories appeared in *Analog*, *Dark Wisdom*, *Jim Baen's Universe*, *Fantasy Magazine* and several anthologies. Her first novel, *According to Crow*, was released in May 2005 by Five Star/Thomson Gale. She edited two anthologies, *Jigsaw Nation* (with Edward McFadden) and *Moonlit Domes*. Visit her website at www.ekaterinasedia.com

Darren Speegle's often dark and always unusual fiction may be found in such venues as *Postscripts*, *The Third Alternative*, *Crimewave*, *Fantasy*, *Brutarian*, and *Cemetery Dance*. He is the author of two short story collections, *A Dirge for the Temporal* and *Gothic Wine*. Look for news on his first novel, *Relics*, soon. Darren lives in Germany.

"A fabulous fabulist," wrote Publisher's Weekly about *Tin God*, **Terese Svoboda**'s fourth novel, ninth book. Svoboda's writing has been featured in the *New Yorker, New York Times, The Atlantic, Slate, Bomb, Lit, Columbia, Yale Review* and the *Paris Review.* Her honors include an O. Henry for the short story, a nonfiction Pushcart Prize, a translation National Endowment for the Humanities fellowship, a PEN/Columbia Fellowship, two New York Foundation for the Arts Fellowships in poetry and fiction, a New York State Council on the Arts grant and a Jerome Foundation grant in video, the John Golden Award in playwriting, the Bobst Prize in fiction and the Iowa Prize in poetry. An University of British Columbia and Columbia graduate, she has taught at Sarah Lawrence, Williams, the College of William and Mary, the University of Hawaii, the University of Miami, the New School, St. Petersburg, Russia and is currently Writer-in-Residence at Fordham. She lives in New York City and will be teaching in Kenya this Christmas. Her opera WET premiered at L.A.'s Disney Hall in 2005.

Sarah Totton's short fiction has appeared in *Realms of Fantasy, Polyphony 5, The Nine Muses* (Wheatland Press), *Tesseracts 9 & 10*, and will shortly be appearing in *Fantasy: The Best of the Year, 2007* (Wildside Press). She is a Third Place winner in the L. Ron Hubbard's Writers of the Future Contest.

Tamar Yellin's stories have appeared in *Leviathan 3, The Nine Muses, Nemonymous* and numerous other publications. Her novel, *The Genizah at the House of Shepher* (Toby Press) was awarded the 2006 Ribalow Prize, and her collection *Kafka in Bronteland and other stories*, also from Toby, was longlisted for the Frank O'Connor International Short Story Award and received the Reform Judaism Prize 2006. *Tales of the Ten Lost Tribes* will appear in 2007.

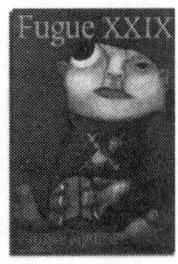